An Imperfect Lens

AN IMPERFECT LENS

A Novel

ANNE ROIPHE

SHAYE AREHEART BOOKS
NEW YORK

Copyright © 2006 by Anne Roiphe

Published in the United States by Shaye Areheart Books, an imprint of the Crown Publishing Group, a division of Random House, Inc., New York.
www.crownpublishing.com

SHAYE AREHEART BOOKS and colophon are trademarks of Random House, Inc.

Library of Congress Cataloging-in-Publication Data

Roiphe, Anne Richardson, 1935–
An imperfect lens : a novel / Anne Roiphe.—1st ed.
1. Alexandria (Egypt)—Fiction. 2. French—Egypt—Fiction. 3. Scientists—Fiction. 4. Epidemics—Fiction. 5. Cholera—Fiction. I. Title.
PS3568.053147 2006
813'.54—dc22   2005011250

ISBN-13: 978-1-4000-8211-7
ISBN-10: 1-4000-8211-0

Printed in the United States of America

Design by Lauren Dong

10 9 8 7 6 5 4 3 2 1

First Edition

TO HERMAN ROIPHE, M.D.
a man who studied to be a chemist but became
a psychoanalyst—my life partner

1

AFTER A NIGHT at anchor, a local pilot at the wheel, the *Andromeda* made her way around the small lighthouse that stood at the end of a long jetty. The dhows, brigantines, barques, and sloops entering the new port navigated carefully through the rocky channel of Boghaz.

Once in the harbor the ship passed the black hulks of rusting ironclads, from the sterns of which trailed the red flag with the star and crescent. Seamen with red caps were everywhere. Steersmen in beards and tarbooshes rowed out among the ships, where, above their heads, flew the flag of the United States of America and the Union Jack. Steamers from French and English companies shot into and out of the harbor or rested, temporarily moored, in the inner briny waters. Some of the pasha's feluccas floated back and forth. They showed a Turkish flourish painted on the stern, and long-tailed Arabian characters were painted in gold on their paddle boxes. Steam whistles erupted in noisy calls as gray smudges from smokestacks marked the sky, and bells screamed out over the port.

The sun was burning down on the wooden railings of the ship. The captain stood on the forecastle and watched as his sailors made fast the ropes, swabbed the deck, and rolled the barrels containing the cloth up from the hold, down the planks, and onto the docks below. The ship bobbed up and down gently on the high tide. The journey had not been unduly harsh. They had encountered only one storm and had weathered it without damage and with only the expected loss of sleep as well as the loss of one cousin of one man who was himself a cousin of a third, whose head was knocked by a swinging boom in the midst of an abrupt turn. The man's death was noted by the captain in his log, although his name was left unrecorded and his body dropped with a few Christian words spoken into the waters of the sea, where it disappeared along with the shafts of light, the puffed buds of a stalk of seaweed, the shimmering scales of fish, the rank smell of human waste released from a recently used pail, all mingled with salt spray, as the traces of blood washed off the deck.

The ship was carrying large bolts of dyed cloth purchased from a trader in Calcutta, cloth pressed and cut and stretched out on wooden poles. Dozens of barefoot men had poured water into the waiting barrels, stacked the cargo hold, packed the grain and dried fruit in baskets. As they worked, they often slipped in the low river that ran from behind the company's storage shed down to the docks. The men's hands were stained dark by the mud in the water. The bolts of cloth, blues and reds, some stenciled with gold dye in shapes of birds and vines, were destined for the bodies of the women of Egypt, to wrap around curves, to accentuate breasts, to decorate with bangles and brooches. This would be done in the manner of the women of Paris, to please in the privacy of their rooms the tastes of men. This was not cheap cargo, a fact that contributed to the captain's satisfaction.

The heat of the day was stifling. The sailors wore no shirts, and their shoes, made of simple turns of rope, were often kicked aside so they could scramble, climb, and pull and push their cargo more efficiently. The reserves of fresh water had almost been exhausted.

There were two barrels left, one on the port side, one on the starboard side. The first was hauled up on deck and the boy, who served many purposes and who was passed at night from hammock to hammock, dipped the copper cup again and again into the barrel and carried the water, carefully, balancing against the rocking of the boat, the passing of the men, the hauling of the cloth, the rope ladders swung up and down along the sides of the ship, and he gave water to those who called to him. As he climbed over the chain that held the anchor that moored the boat in the harbor, a seagull flew close by the boy's head, spread wings brushing against his cheek. The boy ducked and, in doing so, slipped. The water he was carrying fell on his own foot, seeped between his dusty toes that were cracked with the dryness of the sun, with the beating of the wind that so often rose out of the sea. He refilled his pail from the barrel.

Unseen pulsing crescent moon shapes, safe in their invisible, rapid motion, moved like vastly shrunken versions of the Word of God on the walls of a recalcitrant kingdom. The boy carried them on his foot, in his cup, in his pail. No one rejected the water he offered. Without water a man could not work in this heat. Even with water, some of the men needed to pause, to squat down on the deck, and all could feel their tongues swollen and dry against the roofs of their mouths. The tissue in their throats plumped with the water as it flowed with the tilt of the head back toward their throats, bringing relief. The captain called the boy, and the boy brought the cup to the captain, who, before he drank, poured some of the water over his hands, covered as they were with the dust in the air, churned up by the wheels of the carriages on the docks, the carts pulling cargo, the men climbing up and descending. It took a few hours for the English customs inspectors, surrounded by fully armed British soldiers, to emerge from their quarters from which flew the British flag that had so recently replaced the French flag, a matter of complete indifference to the captain and his crew.

Great palaces lined the wide avenue that curved along the shore, while more modest homes stood at the center of the city. The mosques rose, domed and white, above the smaller alleys. The dome of the Orthodox church shone like a half lemon above the trees that lined the streets. In the bazaar, the olive pits and the splashes of wine and overripe fruit mingled on the cobblestones with the blood of slaughtered animals. The noise of the city, the clacking of wooden shoes, the ringing of bells, the yelling of merchants, the clap of donkeys' hooves on the stones, the running of the donkey boys as they called "ride, ride," in Italian, English, Arabic, French, the barking of dogs, the screeching of birds in cages, the heavy wet heat of the day, the dust in which all these things stirred and sighed, shifted and changed positions, made the boy weary. He took a piece of bread offered by one of the sailors and ate it, pulling at it slowly with his hands. The bread turned dark from the dust on his fingers.

Later the boy fell asleep on a bench in a tavern. He woke with a start. There was a pain in his stomach. He rushed to the street and, in the early hours, by the light of the million pale fading stars above, the contents of his bowels flowed over the mud of the stone curb. When the sun rose and the first stirrings of animal and man began and the arched open windows, windows without glass, let in the innocent rays of a new day, he stretched out in the gutter, covered with dirt, his own and more that he had found in the street, his limbs trembling.

A child in the street, a dirty child, was not rare. Before most of the men of Alexandria had woken in their beds, washed their faces in the basins, tasted the coffee brewed in their kitchens, the boy's body had shriveled, flattened, lost its copper color, turned gray like slate. His eyes open, he lay dead. No hand had come in the middle of the night to comfort him. No mother had brought him sips of water, or prayed for his soul's redemption.

Out of the water life climbed, and all life requires water still. Human beings are more water than flesh, afloat in their own bodies, and yet, out of water, necessary water, welcome water, can come death. And so it was that a sailor from the same ship woke in the bed he had paid to sleep in on the top floor above the tavern. He was warm with fever, cold with fever, bowels running, eyes slipping back into their sockets. His barmaid pulled the now odorous sheets out from under his limp body and sent her young daughter to fetch water so she could wash them in the tub in the backyard. Before dawn the sailor had died, the water in which the sheets had been washed had been thrown into the alleyway where barefoot girls were playing with a wooden doll and the wheels of carts splashed through, catching the water on their spokes and rims.

The captain took a week to load his ship with cargo going back to Calcutta. He would carry hemp and boxes of brilliant blue turquoise stone dug from the hills, and his chests would hold gold coins, money for the owners of the ship, and treasures, souvenirs that each man had purchased in the markets, a feather, a hat, a postcard, a button made of bark.

In the following days the very young woman, breasts still turned upward, hips not yet pleasingly wide, but slim like a boy's, who had welcomed a sailor to her bed, taking a few coins for her efforts to please, drinking with him a cup of wine, allowing his mouth to kiss a burn she had received from the rack in the oven, collapsed in a doorway, trying to flee the thing that was inside her. She died there.

Some life-forms are meant for the desert heat and some are meant for the cold of the arctic, like the tiny worm that eats the smaller bacteria that survive all through the long dark winter in near frozen states under the snow in the turquoise ice of glacial peaks. Some organisms make their happy homes on the warm, hairy skin of deer and squirrels and bats. Some survive in the darkness of the earth, sipping moisture from the droplets of rain that seep downward toward the earth's boiling center. Some survive in the bellies of mosquitoes and some in the warm blood-stream of human beings. People are so proud of their souls, vaunted capacity for distinguishing between good and evil, for devotion to God, for service to king or country and charity to beggars, but in fact souls are easily crushed, vaporized, eliminated by the tiny microbes that swirl about, indifferent to Michelangelo's *David* and the Ten Commandments and the grand pyramids, or the Gothic arch, as well as the petty tremors in their lustful or loving hearts.

The day the ship was set to sail back to Calcutta, the captain had visited the offices of the Pacific Company, which were on the wide street beyond where the library of Alexandria, the fabled burnt library, had once stood. The captain had carried his logs with him and, while receiving congratulations for a job well done from the short British gentleman who had almost disappeared behind the large desk, was offered by an Egyptian clerk a piece of fruit from a glass bowl. The captain picked up a round green apple and then saw a more appealing-looking pear. He put down the apple and took the pear, which he placed on the offered plate. The clerk took the bowl of fruit back into his own office and there bit into the apple, devouring it to its core. The clerk went home to his wife and that night conceived a child whom he would one day take to the beach, teaching him how to dive into the white froth of the waves.

The captain, back in his quarters on his ship, had a headache. It was more than just a result of the full day he had spent on land. His legs felt weak, and the muscles in his thighs began to tremble. Within hours he was lying on the deck, having ripped off his shirt in his fever, and his men gathered around him as he thrashed about and his eyes seemed to disappear back in his head and streaks of blue and purple appeared on his skin and the sailors washed him again and again as his bowels turned thin and bloody and his fever rose. Perhaps he was over the worst of it, perhaps he was one of the lucky ones who might have recovered, but when the tide was right and the ship's first mate pulled up the anchor and the ship sailed out of sight of the port of Alexandria, the men in their fear pushed the still-breathing captain overboard into the dark moving waves.

The year was 1883. Cholera had come to Alexandria.

2

It was late winter, in Paris.

The famous scientist Louis Pasteur received in his laboratory at the École Normale a package of papers from the Academy of Science. It contained, among the thick sheets now spread out on his desk, this report from October 1831 in the *Sunderland Herald*, based on the report of two English doctors, Barry and Russell, who had seen for themselves the ravages of the disease in St. Petersburg. He read:

Early symptoms are giddiness, sick stomach, slow pulse and cramp at the tops of fingers and toes. This is followed by vomiting or purging of a liquid like rice-water . . . the face becomes sharp and shrunken, the eyes sink and look wild, the lips, face, neck, hands and feet, and the whole surface of the body is a leaden blue, purple, black. The tongue is always moist, often white and loaded but flabby and chilled like a piece of dead flesh. The respiration is often quick but irregular. Urine is stopped. All means to restore the warmth of the body should be tried without delay. Poultices of mustard to the stomach. Twenty to forty drops of laudanum may be given. No remedy of this disease has been discovered, nor has any cure been sufficiently successful to recommend its use, but the greatest confidence may be expressed in the intelligence and enthusiasm of the doctors of this country, who will surely find a method of cure.

Cholera was bred in water, dirty water, water with feces, water with urine, water with sweat, water with tears, water with blood and mucus floating in it. Cholera was fond of sewage and clung to the lumps of obscure matter that floated and sank, that rose and bobbed with the flow of the thing, invisible to the human eye. Cholera was a water baby, a water flower. It hid in the water. It fed in the water. It bred in the water. Its brief days were wet and its purpose, to make more of itself, fulfilled in streams of water, in bubbles of water, in droplets of water, in foam and mud. It clung to moisture as naturally as man clings to air.

The Germans read the news in their papers. The doctors in Berlin and Hamburg are uneasy. They gather old journals published by the Academy of Science in London. At the university in Vienna they hold a conference. It is well attended. Prominent scientists from Brussels and Amsterdam give papers on the known treatment for afflicted patients. Methods are compared. Opiates such as laudanum, hot water, tonics, brandy, calomel, salines, and wrapping the body in blankets, all are found wanting. Theories are offered: it is the uncleanliness of the poor that brings the disease; it is the wrath of God against the sins of man; it is the result of foreign traders and their spices and silks. All over Europe, letters are written to relatives who live in the countryside, suggesting a possible visit by wives and children in the coming months. In the end there is nothing to do but wait. Dr. Robert Koch, the scientist who had been a country doctor until he had made his reputation by discovering the tuberculosis bacterium, was on his way to Alexandria to find the cause of cholera.

PASTEUR WAS SITTING in his worn patched green velvet chair, the one he preferred over all others. A piglet, the runt of the litter, was curled in his lap. Pasteur cradled the small animal in the crook of his arm and stroked the small snout with his good hand. The animal was making snuffling noises of contentment. The letter Pasteur was writing to the Minister of Health was open on the desk before him. He was requesting funds to send a mission to Alexandria. The cholera microbe would be found. The glory should belong to France. It should belong to France's premier scientist and his lab. Pasteur stared at his page.

Pasteur was old now. When he woke in the morning his knees were stiff and his eyes blurred. He was afraid of dying in Egypt, away from his wife and his daughters. He would send Emile Roux and Louis Thuillier. He had already written this to the minister. Thuillier was young, but he had proved that he would work hard, that he was loyal, that he had the imagination to do the unexpected, to look again at the obvious and see something else. He had worked at Pasteur's side as they injected cows with anthrax, bored into the brains of the resulting carcasses in Hungary, in Alsace. Emile was already making a name for himself in Paris. He was thorough, imaginative, and passionate about his work.

Pasteur intended to appoint Edmond Nocard as the third member of the mission. They would have to use animals, and Nocard knew how to do this with as little pain to the beasts as possible. He was a veterinarian. He was swift and accurate. Pasteur himself did not have the courage to cut into an animal's skull. It made him weep to watch it done. He would send Nocard to Alexandria, stout, near-sighted, loud Edmond, whose laugh came from deep in his throat and exploded out into the air. If he could raise the money he would send his laboratory boy, Marcus, along with the others. Marcus would be useful in making arrangements, providing food, and carrying things. The ministry did not want to provide funds for Nocard and Marcus. They informed Pasteur of this in a letter. He immediately sent off a fierce response and wrote to other members of the Academy of Science, including his old friend Duclaux, the head of the academy, asking help in explaining the necessity of a full team for this mission. He called on old friends in government. He urged the Chancellor of the Treasury to support the reputation of France in this matter. He mentioned the tragic consequences of German triumphs in the race for knowledge. The ministry gave in.

CHOLERA WAS BORN in India. Pasteur himself knew the names of India's gods, Krishna, Vishnu, the elephant god Ganesh. He knew it was hot in Bombay and there were beggars on the streets and the English stayed in their clubs and played croquet while native servants bowed before them and brought them tea on silver trays. Its major river was the Ganges. The Ganges merged with the Yamuna at the city of Allahabad, and naked Hindus at festival times bathed in the waters, large numbers of them pressing down to the shore.

While Pasteur was extremely curious about the chemistry of chlorides and acids, he was less curious about the customs of India.

The Ganges and the Yamuna, brown and muddy at the shallow shore, dark and swift at the center, flowed out of the snow-tipped Himalayas across the great plains of northern India and into the primal oceans. The gods lived in those mountains, reaching their long arms up to the sky and sliding into the crevices of the darkest, sharpest rocks. Long ago the gods and demons churned the waters, grabbing treasures from their depths, but there was a fight, a terrible booming clash between the demons, naked but for the red and green turbans that streamed after them through the air, a fight for the final bounty, the coveted *kumbh*, a pitcher holding the sweet-tasting liquid of a most-desired, ever-elusive immortality. In the chase toward the heights of the Himalayas, some of the elixer spilled into the Ganges, some onto nearby cities, marking them instantly as holy, holy places for pilgrimage, riverbanks from which ordinary men and women would plunge, following swamis, gurus, wise men and their disciples, all seeking renewal in a bath of sacred water, shocking the skin, leaving teeth chattering and heart uplifted. Dogs and cows and monkeys waded in the water. Also sewage of the towns and the villages seeped over the shores of the river bank—foul, lumpy, swirling down with the currents, turning blue water brown and brown water to the color of tar. So was Immortality forced to keep humble company.

In the running waters of the Ganges a small vibrio microbe swam, pulsing forward by contracting and expanding its spongy form, thrashing its long, always unseen thread of a tail. Another treasure whirled into existence by the gods at the beginning of time or at a time when no man had memory, before man, when the dark and crawling things, swimming and eating undisturbed by floating net or knifing boat keel, or by five-fingered hand, multiplied and divided and consumed what they needed to consume. These were crescent-shaped creatures, millions of new moons invisible to the naked human eye. In their time they would become travelers, hitchhikers on merchant ships carrying satins and silks, wood and spices, clay vessels, beads, seeds, slaves. They were stowaways on water barrels, on cracks in hands and feet, thriving in the dark planks of wood damp with river smell, breeding everywhere in droplets of water, bubbles of organic proteins, tiny sacks of floating scythes, so small a foot couldn't crush them, but carrying in their ooze neither eternal life nor holy peace, but quick death, bowels spilling, blood vessels leaking, cracking: Cholera.

Louis Pasteur took down a heavy book from his shelves. It was Macnamara's *History of Asiatic Cholera*, published some twelve years before in London and already a classic. He read:

The people of Lower Bengal had for a long time past worshiped the goddess of cholera, it appearing that a female while wandering alone in the woods met with a large stone, the symbol of the goddess of cholera. The worship of the deity through this stone was according to the prevailing ideas of the Hindoos the only means of preservation from the influence of this terrible disease. The fame of the goddess spread and people flocked from all parts of the country to come and pray at her shrine in Calcutta. There was in a temple at Gujurat in Western India a monolith dating back to the time of Alexander the Great, the inscription of which said, "the lips blue, the face haggard, the eyes hollow, the stomach sunk in, the limbs contracted and crumpled as if by fire, those are the signs of the great illness which is invoked by a malediction of the priests, that comes down to slay the brave." Hippocrates described the diarrhea death. He had seen it on the ships entering the Grecian ports. He had examined the liquid ooze that flowed from the bodies of the victims and seen flakes of mucus in their bowels. In the Sanskrit writings found on tablets in the buried city of Hemoltius by the upper branches of the Nile there was a description of the devastation caused by the same plague. In 1563 a Portuguese physician at Goa, Garcia del Huerto, wrote down his experiences throughout the epidemic which lasted half a year as it paralyzed the city, emptying the fruit stalls, closing the orphanages, leaving no one alive in the monastery on the hill until almost every household mourned and the dead were carted away and burned in large fires whose flames leapt up at the sky month after month and the smallest breeze brought in from the far edges of town the odor of the burning flesh.

Unnamed, unseen, this tiny life, a curved shape with a waving tail, floated in the rivers where the great gods had splashed, drifted by rocks on which the women were beating the sheets, cleaning them of the stains of love and reproduction, blood and saliva, mucus, pus, fecal trace, bronchial clots. The beings had no poetry of their own, no myths sustained them on their way, but still they thrived on the bellies of fish and hid in the crevices of crabs where legs bent and claws opened and there they multiplied in the algae bunched together swiftly drifting in the currents, down to the sea. What was the purpose of this vibrio, what was its place in the master plan, if there was a master plan? Did it serve Satan in its meanderings, or was it simply a thing in itself, striving to continue, containing no memory, but blessed with a ferocity greater than the great tiger's, greater than the force of a waterfall, greater than the thunder in the sky, a ferocity focused on its own journey? Was this vibrio simply another one of nature's temper tantrums against humanity?

In Bengal as well as in the poor farm villages, all unknowing, sometimes people would sicken and quickly die from the comma-shaped form that floated in their waters, traveled in afflicted intestines, stayed in their streets waiting for a cleansing rain, hid in the folds of cloth, survived in the excrement of children. From time to time, at their own pleasure—uninvited, unwelcome—the not-yet-seen, not-yet-imagined, not-yet-named, crescent-shaped, mindless but hardly helpless organisms traveled long distances and arrived at the door of Europe, the port of Venice, or cruised up the Nile on ships bringing bolts of cloth or pots of clay or baskets of cardamom, curry, cumin, and entered the stone patios of merchants, hiding in palm-tree-planted gardens as well as in shacks and drainage ditches and irrigation canals, surviving in the warm armpits of slaves chained to the beams of rocking ships, out of Africa and into Arabia, where pilgrims to Mecca took it back to their wives and children. They, multitudes, more than the stars, more than the grains of sand on the beach, crossed long heaving oceans to the docks of New Amsterdam, the streets of Moscow, the alleys of London, serving up carcasses for the cemeteries of Paris, while en route to the ports of Japan and China.

Everywhere the organism pushed, floated, drifted, gathered, it erased, eradicated, ignored a mother's love for her child or a man's desire for his wife, devoured memories fond and unfond, left church bells ringing, bodies piled on carts. Like lava rolling down from the erupting mountain, it made its own path, without regard for gardens, schools, houses of worship. It passed along on the padded feet of gophers, beavers, cats. It rested in the lumps of feces, solid or soft, that were found behind the houses, in the fields. It pushed on in the rivulets left by the rain, or remained in the ditches. The invisible invaders moved swiftly, riding into the belly of a child drinking water from a well, or of an adult putting his fingers in his mouth to remove a bit of tobacco stuck between the teeth, settling in the lower intestine, feeding and feeding without thought or regret, without memory of other places, without destiny or hope of redemption.

In his book Pasteur read: *There are records of its presence in ancient Sanskrit. In 1817 in Calcutta and Jessore it killed 5,000 British soldiers within two weeks. The troops of the Empire carried the disease to Nepal and Afghanistan, to Japan and Brazil.* Time and again cholera had its way, its dreaded way, and then, having run out its path, having fewer mouths to enter, reproducing less, dying itself for want of another warm watery place, it would stop. Until it would return.

LOUIS THUILLIER TOOK a few days to visit his mother and father, who were disturbed that their son was traveling they did not know where. The papers in Amiens were full of news of the cholera in Alexandria. Louis did not want to alarm his parents, so he kept his destination a secret. Louis's younger sister made him promise that he was not going to far-off Egypt. His mother understood that her son was an educated man, while she knew only what the nuns had taught her. She made no objections to his travel, but she stroked his sleeve, patted his hair, brought him clear water in a basin, cooked his favorite stew, brought him beer from the tavern, went into his room when he was sleeping and watched his chest move under the blanket. His older brother embraced him. His father embraced him. It was an awkward embrace, but Louis caught its meaning and felt an unmanly stirring in his chest. It was harder to leave than he had thought. But he did.

HE TOOK THE train to Marseille and a carriage to the nearby port, where he boarded the *Marie-Claire,* which was carrying bottles of wine from Alsace, bundles of embroidered linen from the north, olives from the Pyrenees, and cheeses from the farms of Provence.

It also carried Louis Thuillier, Emile Roux, Edmond Nocard, and their trunks, as well as their assistant, Marcus, who was sick to his stomach for the entire journey and was unable to provide the scientists with even a half hour's companionship. Louis spent the journey at the ship's rail staring at the rolling sea, watching the silver pathways of the sun's rays slip across the ocean. He considered the matter of sunlight and the prism of color that he had studied in school. He watched for signs of fish beneath the surface. He saw the clouds' shadow darken the sea as if it were held in the claws of a giant bird. He smoked a pipe. Roux's wife had given him one with a deep bowl as a parting gift. It burned his lips, but he did not put it aside. He smelled the tobacco, and the scent reassured him that land waited. He liked biting down on the stem of the pipe hard with his teeth. He liked the sucking of smoke and the sense of himself, a man with a pipe, a man who was worldly, not to be dismissed easily, a man with things on his mind. He liked the feel of the smooth stem in his hands. He would get used to the burning and he would learn to master the thing, which now seemed to be either too hot or too quickly turned cold in his hand as the embers in the small bowl faded and died. Hour after hour on the deck he smoked his pipe, filling and emptying it, pushing it and pulling at it, waiting for it to cool, heating it up with a match, as he watched one lone gull loop in and out among the sails. He felt the chill in the air, the wind coming up the Seine. He thought of his mother and father, his sister and his older brother, in their small house in Amiens, the cat on the empty chair, the lamp lit for the evening, its small flame beating like a moth against the glass. He thought of the roses now appearing like a lifeless bramble in the small garden, dormant, waiting for the earth's regular path to bring back the heat of day. A grown man did not long for the taste of his mother's soup or think of her arms pouring a pail of water into a bathtub so she could scrub her child. It was time—past time, he told himself—that he let all the pictures of his mother float down to the corner of his mind that stored such things.

Louis knew that failure of this mission was a real possibility. The microbe that caused cholera might be different from those he had already seen on his slides. It might not respond to any kind of coaxing. It might not appear in the waters or the fluids found in the city of Alexandria. It might not multiply when warm or cease to multiply when cold. It might, in fact, not be life at all, but rather dust or mucus or a chemical or a mineral whose name was unknown. He had no illusions. Intuitions, suggestions, belief itself could prove useless. All previous assumptions could be invalid. What was true of anthrax, what had caused the disease of beets, what kept the yeast alive or killed it, what plagued the sickly silkworm, may have nothing to do with what caused cholera. A scientist must be his own heretic.

"We're mad," said Edmond one evening as the three men finished their evening meal in the captain's quarters.

"What do you mean?" asked Louis. "I, for one, am very sane."

"Why, then," said Edmond, putting his spoon into the remains of Emile's bread pudding, "are you traveling on this ship toward a city in which cholera waits? Most normal men would travel in the other direction."

Roux laughed. "You're right," he said. "We should immediately go back to France."

"If I die," said Nocard, "my dogs will be inconsolable. Also my greedy brother will inherit my house and my land."

"In that case," said Roux, "take care not to die."

Nocard raised his glass. "To all of us, a long life, and to my brother, nothing, let him make his own way."

Roux said, "Don't worry, we'll live to be old men, wishing we still had our teeth."

In the silence that followed, Louis considered the possibility of death, his own. He could not imagine it. He could not believe in it. What he did feel was fear, a vague, nasty dryness in his mouth.

The expanse of water that lay between Marseille and Alexandria made him melancholy as he watched it for the five full days of the journey. He saw himself disappearing, leaving no trace, as the keel of the ship separated the waves, which instantly reunited behind the hull, leaving no sign in the sea that it had passed. It was hard for a man, perhaps especially a young man, to catch himself on the cusp of disappearance.

These were Pasteur's instructions to his team, in a letter dated August 5, 1883:

i. Stay in the best hotel until you are settled. Use wine and other canned foods from France upon arrival. Have an alcohol lamp on a table at all time to heat glasses, silverware, and plates.

ii. Find immediately a very adequate apartment with the help of the Consul. Get Marcus to cook for you, and follow all caution regarding food.

iii. Try to establish a workspace in a hospital where both gas and water are in profusion.

iv. Examine blood samples and their culture.

v. Try to transmit the disease to animals by mixing suspicious matter with food.

vi. Try microbe purification through inoculation of various animals until one species becomes sick without dying.

Emile Roux read the instructions aloud to Louis and Edmond. Edmond said, "You would think we hadn't worked with him. You would think we were schoolboys."

Emile said, "It's his way of worrying about us. Don't be insulted."

"I am not insulted," said Edmond. "But I would rather leave his voice in Paris. Here we have our own responsibilities. Don't read any more of his letters."

Emile smiled. He put away the letter. "You are sure you don't want to hear the other fourteen points?"

Edmond lay back on his bunk and closed his eyes. "I need a nap," he said, and that was the end of that.

3

A T LAST, SHORE, the carts piled with goods rattling along the narrow planks of the docks, the strange sound of the muezzin calling the faithful to prayer, the gold sandy color of the buildings, the customhouse with its soldiers in uniform, braids and buttons glistening in the heat, and the donkeys with their long ears flattened back against their heads and the children with their hands out, crouching in the doorways, flies stuck to their encrusted eyelids. The smell was strange: dung, saffron, ginger, banana, human sweat, fish packed in barrels, waiting to be carried to the market. They saw turbans and loincloths, and sandals made of paper and wood. Bells were ringing, men were calling out numbers in Arabic and French and English, and sailors were tying up sails. A barrel of nails had spilled on the ground before him. Louis felt dizzy. Marcus placed the large carton they had brought on a wagon, and Louis hopped up on the front seat, with Roux and Nocard behind.

Marcus rode standing on a rail in the back. They headed for the Hotel Khedivial at the corner of rue Cherif Pasha and rue Rosette, where they had taken a week's lodgings.

The wind was blowing from the east, and with it came sand from the desert, whole grains of sand that stuck in Louis's hair and nestled in the sleeve of his jacket and blocked his nostrils and made him cough. He put his handkerchief to his face. "Is it always like this?" he asked the driver, who unfortunately did not speak French. The hotel clerk explained as he took the papers Roux offered. "The east wind brings the sand. The west wind will make the air clear and cool. You will get used to it, messieurs," he said, "if you stay among us awhile." When Louis closed his mouth, he felt the granules of sand that had come to rest on his molars. "I need water," he said to the clerk, who directed him across the lobby to a door with a beaded curtain, an arched opening. The three of them walked into the café. Marcus followed them, his eyes glazed. If he were a dog, someone would have patted him on the head; as it was, he sat at a table in the darkened room, repeating his uncle's words as he departed Paris: "Travel is broadening for a young man. Shakes you up, it does." He did feel shaken, but was he broadened? His stomach still heaved and he barely sipped at the absinthe drink that Louis had ordered for him. It sat on the table in a long thin glass, pale green, cloudy; the taste of licorice pleased him, but the burning in his esophagus did not. A boy who is not quite a man is not eager to know the outlines of his esophagus, the details of the act of eating, the route the food takes to his stomach. He prefers to think of himself as not so much a body with parts as a blossoming landscape, springtime in the pastures. He stared at his drink and grew sleepy. The men ignored him when he put his head on the cushion behind him and closed his eyes. The boy was with them to perform necessary labors, not to amuse them at the table. There were no other customers in the café. The lobby of the hotel had lacked the usual merchants with their bags of wares; also missing were the English ladies who traveled to exotic places when all else had failed them. The boy who sat on his heels behind a potted palm, waiting to bring a guest some cigarettes, a cigar, a towel to wipe the sweat off his forehead, was simply playing a game with a pebble he threw into a circle he had drawn with his fingers in the dust on the floor. A girl with an ostrich-feather fan was standing by the upholstered chair near the stairs, ready to make any guest of the hotel more comfortable. No one needed her attention.

To a town with cholera, to a town where cholera waits, few but the most intrepid travelers come. All who could had postponed or canceled their visit. This meant that the kitchen help had lost their jobs and the owner of the hotel went to the bank for a loan to see him through and the repairs on the marble counter of the bar, which had chipped over time, were not made and the rooms were not as free of sand as they might have been had the staff been more than minimal. Cholera did not simply attack the intestines of its victim, it ravaged the pocketbooks of the entire town, spreading hunger and despair and sending thousands to pray and thousands of others to shutter themselves up in their rooms.

The concierge of the hotel, a tall, thin Egyptian with a mustache, whose languages included Arabic, French, Russian, English, German, and Italian, with a reasonable grasp of Turkish, bowed his head slightly and offered Roux, who was clearly the senior member of the party, a large white envelope with an embossed gold seal on the cover. Roux, who was engaged in writing down his expenses since docking, handed the envelope to Louis. When Louis opened it, casually, as if he had often received letters in foreign countries, as if he were an experienced man of the world, he found an invitation to dinner with all their names at the top in fine calligraphy, at the home of the French consul, General M. Girard, that evening. The adventure had begun.

When they arrived in their suite and the bellboy brought up their bags and the carton of bottles and chemicals were safely stored in the Khedivial's basement, Louis immediately brought out his good suit, the one he had purchased for the trip with the money that Pasteur had pressed into his hand with express instructions as to tailoring and cut. The suit was placed by the window, where the wrinkles might hang out and the fine cloth breathe in the slight wind that blew in clouds of mosquitoes, allowing them to swarm over the bowl of dates and figs placed on the dresser by the maid. Marcus withdrew to his own small dark room at the back of the building, near the cook's quarters, and again fell asleep, successfully shutting out all the sounds of the alley below, the shouts in Arabic, the scent of cat urine, the pile of oranges rotting in a barrel, the wail of a woman who had some terrible complaint against a child whose loud weeping brought no forgiveness.

Nocard went off to meet an Italian veterinarian who ran a small animal clinic. Roux went out to find a French-speaking barber. Louis went for a walk. He turned the corner of the rue Cherif Pasha and found himself on rue Rosette. He was determined to keep the railroad station across the street in sight. He did not want to lose himself in the winding streets.

Roux was directed to the barber just down a few doors from the hotel. The barber had once been the personal barber of the French general who had administered the protectorate. The less said about the general's last days, the better. A barefoot Arab boy brought a bowl of warm water to the counter, and the barber wet his brush and began to lather Roux's face. The Arab boy brought a second bowl of water for the rinsing. There was a loud scream in the street. The barber cut Roux, a small cut, but a little blood ran down his cheek. The barber rushed to the door of his shop. The Arab boy stopped his sweeping. A woman carrying a sack of bread had been knocked down by some soldiers in a carriage. The English soldiers were gathered anxiously around her, picking up her bread, gesturing apologies. "It's nothing," said the barber, returning to his chair. But the water was no longer warm. "Bring me another bowl," he said to the boy, who took away the now too-cool water in which, invisible to the barber, his helper, or Roux, mortality had beckoned. If the water had fallen on his lips or dripped from his mustache onto his tongue in a moment when his mouth was open, what then? Roux closed his eyes while the barber trimmed the back of his hair. For a moment or two he fell into sleep.

As Louis walked and stared and wiped the dust from his face, the market stalls were gradually cleaned of the day's merchandise. The cafés on Place Muhammad Ali were empty. Soon only a few dogs prowled beneath the tables as rodents, bellies low to the ground, ventured out in the cover of the early-evening darkness. In the gutters lay rejected chicken parts, cores of fruit, shells of nuts with meat clinging to their brown-skinned sides, leaves from spice trees. A lamb's ear bled slowly into the puddles. A child's comb with broken teeth floated below the tea merchant's bench, along with a discarded packet of fine tobacco meant for chewing. The invading cholera bobbled along unseen among the day's refuse. Its desperate journey had already been long, and the hours were growing short for it to find its destination, a place to spawn, to fulfill its role, to be itself, amid the jiggling and rocking, the living and the dying, the chemical exchange, the impersonal but ever-so-personal assault that its own existence required. Louis had walked farther than he intended, and he hurried back to the hotel. He needed to change for dinner.

Dinner was served late in this country, long after the sun had gone down and the ceramic tiles on the floors had cooled in the evening air. A call to prayer floated over Alexandria. From the towers of the mosques came the sound, clear and demanding, harrowing in its claim. Thuillier smoothed his hair, put on his suit, which was perhaps of a heavier material than it ought to have been, and, looking in the mirror, found himself pleased. Roux had declared that tonight they would ask for space for their laboratory, perhaps in the French hospital. They would present their credentials to the consul, which included a note from Louis Pasteur himself, asking that all kindness be shown his assistants in their important task. Louis went down the hotel's winding staircase, running his hand along the banister, whose carved surface was made up of many loops of snakes, leaves, and berries, down to the lobby. In the lobby he remembered Pasteur's strict instructions on cautionary hand-washing. He went back up to the basin in his room and washed his hands in the water that had been boiled and sealed off some hours before. He went downstairs again without touching the banister, then out the door past a uniformed attendant wearing a red sash, with a sword at his side. The attendant bowed. Louis returned the bow, not certain whether this was correct form. He fairly leapt into the carriage that was waiting there. His colleagues, already seated, made room for him. Roux handed the driver a card with the consul's address as Louis leaned back on the purple velvet seat with long, gold-threaded tassels on the cushion, and tried to keep his left leg from bobbing up and down with unseemly excitement.

The hoofbeats of the horse on the stones below him, the rocking of the carriage, reminded him of his sea journey. Their carriage rode down the rue de Soeurs past the Café Ptolemy. In the warm night air, the sidewalk tables were filled. At one of them,

Dr. Robert Koch, a dour-looking German, his mostly bald head shining in the reflected gaslight, his long mustache groomed with care, his black Turkish coffee left untouched by his elbow, his thick glasses pinching his nose, was sitting alone. He was writing notes on a pad of paper that he would soon stuff into his pocket. A telegram from the Health Office in Berlin had informed him that the Frenchmen were coming. What did that matter to him? The year before, he had announced the discovery of the minute organism that caused tuberculosis. One out of every nine deaths on the continent was caused by tuberculosis. All Europe was talking about him, his genius. He had proved Germany the equal of France, a political matter that was not of much interest to the scientist himself.

The French consulate was in a white stone building on rue Nebi Daniel; the French flag hung at the entrance. A circular driveway for carriages provided ample space to view the narrow arched windows, glimpse the courtyard just beyond the entrance, see the orange trees that were planted like sentries before the door. It was as grand a building as the ministry where he had obtained his documents, and the opera where he and his friends from the École Normale had seats in the highest balcony, where he could almost put his hands on the gold carvings of nymphs and dolphins that decorated the ceiling above, and perhaps it was as grand as the hospital where he had visited his chemistry professor, who had been run over by a cart carrying bits of stone masonry down a narrow alley and had suffered brain damage from which he never recovered. That visit had much impressed Louis, who could recall the smell of carbolic acid and the hush in the halls, but the structure of the building itself had gone unnoticed due to his more pressing anxieties that day. Now he noted the iron grillework on the windows decorated with fleurs-de-lis, now he noticed the parapets with their tiny domes rising from the sloped roof. The lamps were lit within, so that the building itself seemed to glow with a man's brightest hopes.

Louis was inexperienced in the ways of society. He was not certain whether his gloves should be given to the servant or not. It was hot, he hadn't needed the gloves. He was not sure that his suit was exactly the style of those worn by other men of stature in Alexandria. He knew his speech still carried certain expressions from Amiens, a phrase or an emphasis here or there that marked him as something other than a Parisian and something other than a son of an educated man. It didn't matter, he knew. In his calling, as in the priesthood, it was mind that counted, rather than origins. It was loyalty that mattered, loyalty to the obligations of reason. He carried his faith in his breast as surely as any crusader moving east toward Jerusalem had ever done. Nevertheless he was awed by the footman and the consul general himself, who offered a warm hand and a glass of red wine. "Welcome, welcome," said the beribboned consul general, M. Girard, whose job it was to welcome his countrymen passing through.

"Here are our chemists from Paris," the consul said as he lifted his glass to them. "They have just arrived at our door in time to save us from the cholera. They have come directly from the laboratories of Louis Pasteur."

All heads in the room turned to stare at the three men, who stood at attention as if they were in a parade.

"No, no," said Dr. Roux, turning red. "We don't have the cure. We do not have the cause, we cannot save anyone until we have the cause."

"Then find the cause," said the consul with a hearty laugh. "We expect you to find it before the Germans do. France depends on you."

At dinner, Louis was seated next to the very round, rosy-colored wife of an Alexandrian doctor who had studied in Marseille and who served the consulate staff and the small French community with responsibility. His wife told Louis that her husband, Dr. Malina, had saved the child of the caliph of the city, who had been gasping for breath until her husband brewed herbs that cleared the child's lungs, steam had filled the room, and soon the little one was clamoring to be allowed in the garden. The first course seemed to be a thumb-sized fish lying on a bed of mushrooms. The concoction had a strange smell. Louis picked up his fork and mutilated the fish, mashing it into the mushrooms, without bringing the smallest piece to his mouth. Slowly he drank a glass of wine, after wiping the rim of the glass with his napkin. He was afraid the glass might not have been washed properly, with sufficiently hot water to kill any organisms that might have been clinging to its surface. While the wife of the doctor was talking about the tours he must take of the city's prominent ancient glories, he glanced down the table and saw a young woman with long dark hair tied back with a bright green ribbon. Her skin was coffee-colored, like that of the natives. Her eyes were dark and wide. Her neck was long and graceful. "Who is the young lady down the table?" he asked his companion.

"My daughter," replied the lady. "She is beautiful, is she not?"

"She is," he said.

"Beauty is an asset in a woman," said the wife of the doctor.

"Of course," said Louis. Not wanting to seem like a beast, he added, "Beauty is worthless without character."

"True," said the wife of the doctor, "but character is often worthless without beauty—in a woman, that is."

Louis fell silent. What should he say next? How could he approach the daughter? How soon? He fondled his pipe in his pocket. "I can see," said Louis, "that she gets her eyes from you."

The woman smiled, her full cheeks dimpling. "There are many beautiful young women in Alexandria," she said. "It's because of the sea air, which is so good for the skin."

"But your daughter is not yet married?" said Louis.

"No," her mother answered, "Este is not, not yet."

Louis had never in all his life been served by a butler. There seemed to be ten of them in the room. He had never before tasted the fowl with tiny bones that floated in a gravy on his gold-rimmed plate. He had never before eaten from such a plate. He had never put such a large silk napkin on his lap before. He had never tasted such fine wine. In fact he did not like it quite so well as the kind purchased by the glass at any corner café in Paris, but he knew enough to know that this was his failure, not his host's.

The table conversation turned on the possibility of a gold mine in the desert outside the city, which was being explored by some English company that had just hired forty day laborers and carted them off to begin work. With his napkin Louis rubbed his knife, spoon, and fork. He rubbed them hard. Pasteur had been very specific about silverware. Louis told his dinner companion that his mother, who lived in Amiens, made very fine soup out of lamb bones. Every time he looked down the table at the woman's daughter, he felt almost ill. A weakness in his muscles, a melancholy of enormous proportions, swept over him. It was here that he discovered that yearning was not entirely a pleasurable condition. He had discovered that the greatness of the mountain, the snowdrifts clinging to its side, the shadows of passing clouds, the rise and fall of green valley, the ridge of evergreens upright toward the sky—these things, because of their very immensity, the way they dwarf the human observer, seem to tear at the mind most unkindly, hinting at unattainable bliss, leaving trails of sadness behind like the lifting morning mist. This same sweet sadness Louis Thuillier experienced at the consulate's dinner table along with the taste of the meringue that crumbled in his plate, surrounded by raspberries soaked in cinnamon, pricked with cardamom. He left his dessert wine untouched. He could not wipe the rim without the risk of staining his napkin with wine.

"We need," said Roux, "gas and water, and an oven easily available. We need space for our animal subjects. We want to start immediately."

The consul smiled agreeably. Everyone wanted something from him. Everyone expected him to deal with the authorities, to explain, to arrange. This new group would be tiresome.

"We hear so much of your great Pasteur," said the consul.

Louis was pleased with this remark. Edmond ignored it. He was eating his second, or perhaps it was his third, dessert. There was a trace of crème fraiche on the edge of his mustache. Roux understood that the consul would help, but was not eager.

"I have seen too much of this cholera," said the doctor, who was a member of the Committee of Public Safety, a recently formed group of well connected Alexandrians.

"How many?" asked Louis.

"We don't count the dead, unless they are Europeans," said the doctor, "but among the natives, the dock workers, the sailors, the girls who amuse them, we have an uncomfortable number. The telegraph office at the west end of Boulevard Ramleh has lost two of its managers, the Banque Imperiale Ottomane has lost four vice presidents. The nuns at the Convent of St. Catherine have lost more than ten sisters. Our cook tells us that her cousins are leaving Alexandria and returning to the countryside. The hospital has devoted a floor to the patients who come in by the hour. However, many die within the hour, so we are not overcrowded. I have considered sending my wife and daughter to my wife's cousin in Germany, but they refuse to go. We are alarmed but not yet panicked."

"I understand," said Roux.

"And the dogs and the cats?" said Nocard. "Are they suffering as well? Are there many strays? Are they kept as pets? Have they had many rabies cases? Are the puppies well formed at birth?" The doctor was himself uninterested in animals. The wife of the consul general, Madame Cecile Girard, leaned forward to look more closely at Nocard. She liked a man who understood that animals are God's creatures, too. "Monsieur Nocard," she said, "my dog is well and my cat is planning on having kittens any minute now."

"That's good, Madame," said Nocard.

"Personally," said the consul general, "I don't like the cat. She leaves hair on the cushions."

"I myself," said the doctor to Emile, "believe that the air is foul in this city. The air is the most likely source of the cholera."

"How would that be, sir?" asked Louis.

"It just is," said the doctor.

"Pasteur——" Louis began.

"Yes, I know Pasteur thinks that invisible little organisms cause our troubles. Perhaps he is right. We wait for proof," said the doctor, slapping the young man on the back in a friendly manner.

Nocard supplied seeds for a parrot that flew free about his garden and would come when called. The bird spent the cold winter months on the shelf above the stove. Nocard felt a kinship with animals of all kinds, guinea pigs, hamsters, rodents, squirrels, and, above all, cats and dogs. When he put his big hands around their rib cages, and listened to their beating hearts, allowing wet noses and moist tongues to touch his face, he felt true love, accompanied by a desire to serve the beasts in all matters. If his passion was not tempered by scientific curiosity and a willingness to do anything to pursue the truth, he would have been an unpleasantly sentimental man. He was, however, able to cut, tear, nip, and cause great pain to the very creatures he nestled against his chest. The only sign of strain was an occasional tic in his eye.

Este had noticed the young man who was seated next to her mother. She had admired his long, slender fingers. She had liked the way he inclined his head toward whoever was speaking. She liked the way he pulled at the lip of his pipe, seriously, carefully, as if the pipe itself deserved a certain courtesy. His eyes were dark and his face intense. A few gentle curls rested on the back of his collar and bounced about with each step he took. He stared hard at everything, as if he had never been to a dinner before. She was sure he was a poet as well as a scientist.

When the men rejoined the women, Madame Girard brought her Persian cat, named Apple, into the room and placed him on Nocard's lap. Nocard appreciated the cat's spectacular fur and her fine sharp teeth and he felt the fetuses within. "All's well," he said, "six of them I think, the birth should be without complication."

Madame Girard then told him the name of the most distinguished veterinarian in Alexandria, as well as the name of the stable in town where the consul kept his horse and carriage.

"We must talk more. You should have dinner at my home," the doctor said to the three scientists.

"We would like that," said Louis. He would. He pulled at the stem of his pipe. A certain nervousness had come over him. He had trouble keeping the fire going. He hoped none of the other men noticed his difficulty.

Louis wandered over to the bookcase, where Este was talking with the consul's wife about Lord Cromer, the new British governor, whose not-so-private affair with the Egyptian wife of a prominent member of the shooting club was a subject at every gathering, at least among the women. The consul's wife crossed to the other side of the room. It was time to leave the young people alone. Este turned to Louis and said in perfect French, "Monsieur, what do you see in the sky when you wake up in the morning?"

What kind of question was this? Louis considered his answer carefully. "I see if it is likely to rain or not."

"I meant," said Este, with a hint of impatience in her voice, "the colors. What do you see above your head?"

"I see," said Louis, "whatever is above my head, blue, gray, the atmosphere. It doesn't arrive in surprising shades."

Este tried again. "When you look at the stars, what do you see?"

Whatever did she want him to say? Louis tried to give her the answer she was looking for. "The stars are far away. We see them in different parts of the sky as the earth moves around the sun."

"I know that," said Este. "The stars, when I look at them, make me afraid. They seem so cold and indifferent."

"They probably are," said Louis, "indifferent. I'm not sure about cold. They could be hot like our sun."

Este gave up.

Well, he wasn't a poet. She had always wanted to meet a real poet, or at least a man with poetry in his heart. That was not the man before her. She turned away from him and joined her mother, who was extolling the virtues of her seamstress to the wife of the owner of a steamship company. For his part, Louis found her peculiar. He had no further interest in her.

Two flights below the drawing room, the undersized Arab boy who was a relative of the cooks was washing the dishes as they arrived from the dining room. He was standing on a stool so he could reach the sink. The water came from a pail he had to fill and refill from a large jar. Carefully he placed the wine goblets with their gold-leafed rims into the water. Suddenly his hands shook as he reached for the next glass. He leaned against the edge of the sink and cried out in pain. He fell to the floor, staining himself, writhing in brown fluid and calling to God to save him. He was carried down to the servants' quarters, where he was left alone to face his maker. Another Arab boy mopped the floor, not as thoroughly as he might have.

WHILE LOUIS WAS dining at the consul's table, Marcus was making friends with the few remaining maids in the hotel. Young girls plucked from their village homes, still full of memories of wading in the Nile, walking through the high grass behind the goat, listening at night to the rain on the thatched roof, wearing little, carrying baby brothers and sisters on their backs. The maids, now far from home, uniformed, clung to each other at night, stroking hair, petting, leaning one female body against another. Marcus had found them in the laundry. He followed them back to their dormitory room, where there were so many cots that each girl had to walk over the beds of the others to lie down. They had startled eyes and rough hands from the washing they did every day, but a swinging of their hips revealed that they had not abandoned all hope for pleasures. Marcus spoke no Arabic. Their French was confined to *merci* and *oui*. This was sufficient for the encounter Marcus enjoyed on the top floor in a tiny room in which brooms and rags had been stored. It was sufficient to restore Marcus's full confidence in his good fortune, and to allow him to find his land legs.

When Louis knocked on his door, intending to remind him to wake early, Marcus was not in his room. Marcus in fact had fallen asleep in the bed of one of the maids, who had caught him in her arms and pulled down his trousers and played with him as if he were a toy.

IN THE EARLY morning, as the sun was pushing itself up over the waters of the Mediterranean, while waiting for Roux and Nocard to join him, while a sharp ray of light lingered on the rooftop of the loading shed at the end of the wharf, Louis Thuillier enjoyed a very pleasant breakfast on the terrace of the hotel, watching the carts of the merchants, piled high with fruits and chickens and almonds and baskets of figs, pass by on their way to the bazaar. His equilibrium had returned.

Nocard went off to the stable, wanting to check the condition of the horses and perhaps obtain some saliva samples to culture. He stopped at the market on his way to purchase some carrots for the beasts. He kept his gloves on while he held the carrots, even though they were wrapped in brown paper. The carrots looked innocent, orange and plump, with the normal bumps along the tips, but Nocard knew that a raw carrot might be as dangerous as a sharp knife.

Roux went to the Bank of Egypt on rue Tewfik Pasha with their letters of introduction, and so the task of finding the space in a hospital was left to Louis.

Dr. Abraham Malina had his offices in the rear of his own home. The tiles in the courtyard were green and blue. In the center of each tile was a figure of a bird with a tuft on its yellow head. Its wings were open, flight eternally suspended and repeated. There, underfoot, was a bird, or rather the outline of a bird, gone was its quiver, its tremble, its appetite and its fear. There remained a form only, imprisoned by bands of geometric lines. At the center of the courtyard was a pedestal and a bowl in which rainwater had gathered. There was a crack running up the side of the pedestal. A string of black beetles crawled along the crack. As he crossed in front of the pedestal, Louis saw a tiny salamander lying on its side, its stomach gone, its head mostly consumed. Ah, said Louis to himself, that's what the beetles have found. He had no sentimental feelings as a child might for the salamander, and none for the beetles.

Louis crossed the inner courtyard, brought the servant to his feet with a pantomime of knocking on the door. The servant opened the clinic's outer door with its small window at the top. Louis found himself in a room filled with cushions and couches. A Frenchwoman holding a small dog on her lap was waiting for the doctor, as were a German lady and her companion, who had strained her back when the sea turned rough on the voyage from Crete. The two held hands and pressed their bodies one against another in a manner that shocked the young scientist. Louis waited. The doctor did not call him.

The morning hours passed slowly. A man with a bloody nose was shown into the doctor's office immediately, but not before he had stained the stone floor, which was then mopped by another servant who appeared from behind a screen. Louis noticed that behind the screen lay the entranceway to the rest of the house, to the room where the daughter was sitting, reading perhaps, playing the piano. A small boy appeared at his elbow and offered to fan him with a big fan. Louis did not want someone to fan him. It seemed wrong. Wrong because the offer came from a child. Wrong because the comfort of one's body should not come at the discomfort of others, especially a stranger, especially a child. The child looked unhappy. The German ladies accepted the child's offer, and the overflow of the moving air cooled the room, which Louis couldn't help but enjoy.

At last he was sitting opposite Dr. Malina, sinking down in a blue velvet chair that forced him to look up at the doctor, who stood behind his desk. As Louis was about to speak, Dr. Malina interrupted him. "I am honored," he said, "to help you in any way I can." There was a loud knock on the door. A small boy stood there with a telegram in his hands. Dr. Malina jumped from behind his desk and, patting the boy on the head, ripped open the telegram. "My son, Jacob," Dr. Malina said. "He went to Palestine looking for commercial opportunity. I would have preferred him to go to medical school, in France."

"Friar Jules from my lycée went to Jerusalem on a pilgrimage and then decided to stay. He sent the entire form a letter from Bethlehem," said Louis.

"Monsieur Thuillier," said the doctor with a neutral tone, so neutral he could be reading the label of a prescription bottle or the timetable of the trains departing for Cairo. "Monsieur Thuillier, we are Jews, my family has been in Alexandria for three hundred years. We are Alexandrians and we are Jews."

"Indeed," said Louis. He felt himself pushing back in his chair and suppressed the impulse. The door to the office was off to the left behind him. He resisted turning his head to look at the door. He himself had not met any Jews, not in his village, not in his school in Paris. Though of course he had heard of them. He had read about them. Louis blushed and wished he hadn't. "I'm not a religious man," he said.

"Neither am I," said Dr. Malina. "We have that in common, then. But of course we disbelieve different things." With that, Dr. Malina smiled. It was a sad smile, a dignified smile, a smile that concealed as much as it revealed, but a smile nevertheless that intended to put the young man before him at ease but didn't quite.

And the subject matter changed to science and where beakers could be found, and a place in a hospital, but which hospital?

"When you have your lab," said Dr. Malina, "will you show me your invisible organisms?"

"I will. Dr. Malina," said Louis, happiness flushing his cheeks, "may I invite you to lunch with us at our hotel?"

Dr. Malina said, "I cannot have lunch. My clinic," and he waved toward the door. "But tomorrow night, come to dinner here, in the house. We would be honored by your company, and bring your colleagues." Louis took the pieces of paper on which the doctor had written the name of the chief administrator of the Hôpital de Europe as well as a hastily scrawled letter of introduction.

IN *A History of Medicine in English,* Dr. Malina read:

Celsus, who wrote about A.D. 30, had considered Cholera the most dangerous of all the diseases of the stomach and intestines. Lommius, a celebrated physician of Brussels, who wrote in the 1600s, speaks of Cholera as the most fearful atrocissium of stomach diseases. In September 1831 a physician of Birmingham, under the signature Alpha, wrote as follows: "I have been long quite familiar and know several others who are equally so, with Cholera in which a perfect similarity to the symptoms of the Indian Cholera has existed: the collapse, the deadly coldness with a clammy skin, the irritability and prodigious discharges from the bowels of an opaque serous fluid with a corresponding shrinking of the flesh and integuments, the pulselessness and livid extremities, the ghastly aspect of the countenance and sinking of the eyes, the restlessness, so great that the patient has not been able to remain for a moment in one position."

Enough, Dr. Malina thought, and closed the book.

Dr. Malina had a sudden need to wash his hands. He scrubbed at them as if they were recalcitrant children with the almond soap he kept by his sink.

UPSTAIRS, IN THE spacious apartment that the Malinas called home, Este Malina was holding her best tortoise shell brush with bristles made of porcupine quills and brought to Alexandria by a merchant who had ventured as far into the northern continent as Denmark. She was looking with satisfaction at herself in her mirror. Her hair was black and thick, and if she didn't tie it up with ribbons, it would turn wild in the slightest breeze and spring into a thicket of snarls, a large bush that suggested wilderness and wind and was hardly right for a woman who would live as other women lived with sheets and pillows, with dishes and goblets and tablecloths, with men who wanted to be near her and those who were afraid to be near her, so she brushed her hair, earnestly, energetically, and while she brushed she sang softly to herself, an Arabic song her nurse had taught her about a shepherd whose goat had wandered away. The song was sad, but it was the sort of sadness that brings pleasure, creates a mood of sorrow, affected sorrow, a very good sorrow actually. The curtains blew in the wind. The weather had changed and the fog was heavy in the streets and a storm, unusual for this time of year, was approaching.

4

THAT NIGHT, across the city, some miles still out of the Eastern Harbor, a steamer, the *Grey Falcon*, a British flag flying from its mast, was nearing land. There was heavy fog in the air, and the captain was staring ahead while holding his wheel with a tightness that revealed to his first mate that this approach to the harbor off the shore of Alexandria's eastern port might be more difficult than expected. The first mate promised himself that this would be his last crossing, his last staring at the sky, his last looking at the seabirds floating on the tops of gray and swirling waters. Enough, he said to himself. He had said that before. Because of the heavy fog, the high waves, the endless spray, the captain could not see the light that beamed from the lamp lit at the point of the harbor. The waves slapped at the hull, the ship rocked and clamored, and chains shook and the hooks that held the barrels to the sides of the ship let out a shriek as metal scraped against wood. There was a groaning sound, and then a howl from the port side, as the ship was pushed into the barrier. The furnace failed. The hull reared like an angry horse, the smokestacks belched black clouds, the ship's cat hissed at the wave that rose over its head, the sailors, kicking off shoes, dove into the ocean, praying each to his God for a deserved or undeserved rescue. Silver light from dead stars rained down on the sea, but was not seen by the men in the water because of the fog and the spray. The moon was at a lopsided lumpy stage. It, too, could not be seen because of the clouds, the wet air, the wind pulling darkness across the heavens.

So it was that the passenger Eric Fortman and the majority of the crew, grabbing barrels and planks and listening in the blindness for the sounds of land, saved themselves and appeared, wet and scraped, frightened and full of prayers, on the shore by the side of the old lighthouse. The men on the ship were saved except for two caught in the ropes and pulled out to sea, their shouts unheeded as the waves sucked them down and their souls did whatever souls do in the sea, most likely grow damp and sink into the green buds of algae looping together under the broken boards of the ship, or flake into the thousand unseen particles of scales that, like the dander of a cat, drift with no particular destination, no mind to steer them, just soul masquerading as protein and ammonia, just molecule and its mate, set in motion, until there is not enough matter left for any movement at all, and, like a held breath, the souls of drowned sailors are like the souls of dead men on shore: gone.

The captain and his crew and their passenger, who was a representative of Glen MacAlan Scotch, a company that had booked the cargo onto the ship in Liverpool, found their way to the piers of Alexandria. Word of the wreck went through the taverns. Men rushed down to the beach, boats were launched. What plunder could be salvaged was salvaged as hands reached again and again into the cold water to pull bundles and floating boards and a sailor's miniature portrait of his mother, and some perfectly intact bottles of Glen MacAlan Scotch, and as the survivors slept in boardinghouses while their clothes dried by the stove, others plundered and pulled, laughed and drank. The ship's two goats had been ripped from their pen and lay dead, flies and maggots already crawling over their carcasses. The mice and the rats had floated in the water; some had survived and dashed for cover in the brush at the edge of the shore. The dawn came and the mist lifted and what was left of the broken ship bobbed against the sharp rocks as Eric Fortman woke in the cheap inn with a hunger in his belly and feared for his future. Would he end as a beggar in his hometown, a drunk in the port, who had stories to tell that no one would listen to? Would his brother feed him, his old friends find a spot for him in the customs office, or would he be forever lost? He had lost all the money he had brought for the purpose of clearing the way for the whiskey into a country where it was forbidden by the local religious authorities. The British servants of the crown, the French shopkeepers, the French schoolteachers, the British lawyers, the members of foreign delegations, all needed their whiskey. A little money in the right places made this possible. That was why he had been on this ship, accompanying barrels of whiskey that were quite capable of making the journey on their own.

Of course, thought the Englishman, when the serving maid who brought him the breakfast he had no means of paying for, informed him that there was cholera in town. I'm such a lucky man.

WHILE LOUIS WENT off to join Nocard and Roux at the European Hospital, Marcus explored the city. He had cashed in some francs he had won in the kitchen of the hotel in a bet, and took a carriage. Riding in the carriage suited him. He resolved to do it often. He went down rue Nebi Daniel, where it was said that under the Mosque Alexander himself had been buried in a gold robe inside a glass coffin once upon a time, up to Râs el Tin, the Cape of Figs, where the fort had once protected the city, over to the shallow Lake Mariout, formed out of the sea, sealed into the land, like a sigh, unable to escape the lovesick breast. After a few hours, Marcus dismissed the carriage and set off on foot. He purchased an orange and peeled it slowly while walking. He sucked in the juice, letting some of it trickle down his chin. As he looked out over the port where their ship had docked only a few days earlier, he saw a crowd gathered and he wandered over. He watched the salvage operation as small boats rowed out in the still-turbulent sea and brought back seaweed-covered boxes of loose tea leaves dried on the docks of Burma. Marcus made his way to the front of the crowd and watched as a box carried by a black Arabian boy fell to the ground, spilling the tea on the damp planks of the pier. Marcus, so quickly that only an owl sitting on a cart a few feet away noticed, bent down and scooped up a handful of the tea leaves and stuffed them in his jacket pocket. They were damp and did not smell appealing, but they would dry again in the sun and perhaps offer some special pleasure at a moment when some special pleasure would be needed. Marcus saw a young girl with a rope of blue beads around her neck, carrying a basket of fish toward the market. He couldn't help the response of his body to the slow shifting of her thighs as she moved through the crowd. He followed her. Two British soldiers blocked his way. He moved into the street and made himself small, a child perhaps, an innocent child.

When they had passed, Marcus looked for the girl. He could see her back moving quickly down a narrow street. Marcus ran to catch up with her. A donkey cart appeared suddenly in his way. The man with the cart screamed at Marcus to move. The meaning was clear enough. Marcus pressed himself to the white stone wall. There was a cloth hanging over the open window. Marcus grabbed the cloth for balance. Cholera had gathered in the threads when the cloth was washed a few hours earlier in the stone basins in the back courtyard of the building where all the families brought their wash, including one that had lost a child the night before to the vomiting and bowel sickness. The cloth that hung across the doorposts was clean to the naked eye, but the microbes grouped about the red threads that served as a border for the fabric. They waited for someone's fingers, fingers to go to mouth, once in the mouth they would swim to the gut and there it would begin. Marcus clutched at the cloth for a few seconds, but his hand didn't go near the border, not near where the microbes waited. When the donkey cart passed, he could no longer see the girl and he returned to the main street and headed back to the hotel.

The chief of the hospital was eager to be associated with the French mission. He read Dr. Malina's letter and barked out orders to several sisters who were passing by. The sisters led the visitors to the back of the building, to an area that had been used for storage. The place was a jungle of discarded beds with their frames bent, and there were piles of sheets so ripped as to be worthless except for rags. There were basins that were dented, and rubber blankets with holes, and boxes of cotton squares that had turned green with mildew. There was, however, an oven that would serve for heating beakers, and there was a gas supply that could be used to bring water to a boil. It would be fine. Roux asked for some orderlies to clean the place. Nocard explained that animals would be kept in cages in the far back or outside in the dusty yard. There was a walled-off corner where Marcus could sleep.

Out the small side window, covered now in dust, Louis could see the café across the street, could hear the clicking of the back-gammon pieces on the boards, could smell the tobacco, heavy, as if a woolen blanket had been pulled across his mouth. This would be a lucky place. It would be a fateful place, perhaps one worthy of a plaque on the building one day, but that was as far as he was willing to let his imagination go. The men went to Café Fort to celebrate their new laboratory. Louis pulled at the stem of his pipe. They ordered Turkish coffee, which came in a large enameled pot with a long, skinny spout. Louis tasted it and made a face. Nocard slapped him on the back. "Adjust," he said.

"Are you ever going to get married?" Roux asked Nocard, who shrugged.

"My mother is always asking me that same question. But I have no need for a woman to tell me what to do, to take my money, to bring her many garments into my closet. A woman is not as good a companion as a dog."

Roux picked up his beer and said, "You're a fool. A man gets many more pleasures from a woman than he does from a spacious closet or a dumb beast."

Nocard said, "It simply has never interested me, all this fuss about women. I don't like their perfumes. I don't want to talk about the weather. What would I do with a woman?" he asked.

"Have a child," Emile answered.

"I'd rather take care of a litter of piglets than a child," Nocard said.

There was silence at the table.

"I'm an odd fellow," said Nocard.

"I know," Louis said. "We don't all have to live the same life."

"You'll be a lonely old man," said Emile.

"No, he won't," said Louis. "He'll have me as a friend."

Nocard smiled and, putting down his spoon, reached out to pat Louis on the back, enthusiastically.

"We should start to move our things," said Louis.

"Relax," said Roux. "Herr Koch has to eat also, and sleep, and pay attention to his bowels."

THE CHIEF OF the hospital, who had not been invited onto the Committee of Public Safety because he had been rather outspoken in favor of the nationalist leader General Arabi in the recent difficulties, was nevertheless determined to stand with his colleagues on the front line of defense of Alexandria. He found in the hospital library a copy of an old journal of medicine in which he read this account, supposedly translated from the Sanskrit, believed to have been written in Tibet during the reign of Ti-Song De-tsen, somewhere between A.D. 802 and 845.

When the strength of virtues and merits decreases on earth, there appear amongst the people, first among those living on the shores of the big rivers, various ailments which give no time for treatment, but prove fatal immediately after they appear. It suddenly destroys the vigor of life and changes the warmth of the body into cold, but sometimes this changes back into heat. The various vessels secrete water so that the body becomes empty. The disease kills invariably. Its first signs are dizziness, a numb feeling in the head, then most violent purging and vomiting.

The chief of the hospital, who had trained for some four years in Toulouse, did not pay much attention to the decrease in the world's virtues or merits. After all, he had never known an increase in virtue, and cholera seemed to come and go regardless of a man's merit on individual or national grounds. There had already been four major outbreaks of cholera in his own century. Here it was again, the fifth pandemic. How small it made a man of medicine feel to see the thing sweeping toward him, a tidal wave no human hand could stay.

ESTE MALINA WAS eighteen years old, and it was time she became engaged. She had studied piano with her aunt's cousin on

Memphis Street. She had gone to the Jewish school, in the Jewish quarter, with a girl named Phoebe, whose father, an architect and designer whose family came from Constantinople, had done the restoration on the synagogue. Phoebe had an older brother, Albert, who had just begun to work at the Bank Loewenwald, known to all in Alexandria as the Bank of the Jews and highly valued for its clear understanding of markets and its astute managing of funds. Over the years Albert had often watched his sister's friend playing under the orange tree that stood in the center of their courtyard, her voice rising and falling with the intensity of whatever game the girls were playing. One Sunday afternoon Albert was recovering from a late night and drinking lemonade on a balcony above the garden. This was after a summer rain that had dampened the yellow tiles on the courtyard patio. The sun came through the leaves of a potted orange tree and rested on Este's black hair, and her hands fluttered as they brushed away a cloud of approaching flies, and then she leaned back in her chair and clapped her hands as if ordering the insects to alter their route, and frowned at them as if they were naughty children. In that instant, Phoebe's brother Albert chose his wife.

It was a choice he knew would please his family and hers. Some men are drawn to politics. Albert was not one of them. He found excessive passion on the subject of government unseemly, grotesque, and possibly dangerous. Este's brother was a perfect example of the results of such foolish passions. Albert was not interested in poetry or music, although he liked a good song sung by a lady of the night. He was most certainly uninterested in architecture. His father's drawings bored him. His buildings, while admired by others, seemed ordinary to the son. He was not interested in antiquities, although he had been surrounded by them all his life. He was most certainly uninterested in debates about religion, although he did what was required for the reputation of his parents. He did not think that his own comfort and convenience were minor matters in the universe. He did not think that every little Arab boy that begged alms from him deserved his generosity. He was certainly not an unkind man. Rather, he had seen at an early age that the blind and the deaf, the lame and the poor, the thousands of poor, the dreary girls and dirty boys of other quarters, other places, were a fact of life, like the jellyfish in the sea that could sting a swimming boy, or the insects in the air that left welts on your arms. He had looked up at the constellations and had for only the briefest instant marveled at the distance of stars and the brilliance of moon. He had simply seen the earth for what it was, a temporary abode for his temporary existence, and he intended to make the most of his time.

He disliked it when his shirts were placed in his drawer without attention to their colors. He did not want his servants sleeping or smoking, or pilfering from the family kitchen. He believed in history as entertainment, something one enjoys as a schoolchild, but not as a force in one's own life, which he expected would be as comfortable as the accounts rendered in his office. He was fond of his sister, Phoebe, who would put her soft hands around his forehead and rub gently if he had a headache. He believed in his family, mother, uncles and aunts, cousins and their children as a factual good in the world, worthy of feasts and good wines and entertainments of song, and he was obligated to them as he assumed they were obligated to him. He believed that all men wanted money to preserve what they had and to gain more of the sweet goods of the world. He loved a good brandy, a fine cigar. In other words, he was a happy man, and there can be no doubt that happy men make good husbands. They do not drink themselves to death or challenge the authorities and end up in prison or run away with maidservants or take any steps that would upset the order of things. This is preferable to a revolutionary or an artist dreaming in his garret and losing his teeth to malnutrition and his lungs to the foul air in the alleyway.

Despite the fact that Albert had made up his mind, one morning he followed Este and her mother to the market and, lurking behind a pile of barrels that contained dried fruits from the farmlands outside of town, he watched as Este ran her hands over a red fabric. He observed her while her attention was focused on the juice stand at the end of the street, where the Italian vendor was calling out to potential customers, "Cold, cold, refresh your tongue, cold, cold, on your parched lips. Cherry and chocolate, raspberry and lemon." She would do, he decided. He appreciated her white blouse and the dark blue ribbon that tied her hair back from her face and the heat of the day causing drops of perspiration to appear on her forehead. He also told himself a mate for life should not be picked by appearance alone, character was important, family mattered and good health mattered and good teeth counted, and he considered the question of fertility.

How could one know if a woman would bear children? "Most of them do," said his father. "What a question," said his cousin Martin. "It is bad luck to think up problems you do not have." Albert went off to dinner, a cigar in his pocket, money enough for the ladies of the night who invited visitors to board their houseboat anchored by the shores of Lake Mariout, where musicians played all night long, one could smoke anything, and strange brews were offered that burned the throat and caused the heart to rush about in the chest. Also the ladies themselves, Arab but speaking French, or French but speaking Arabic, or Greek, or Italian, a breast or a thigh exposed, who laughed at anything said, and danced in ways that were stirring. Albert was particularly fond of Bennu, who had a bright red scar that ran down her back, which she claimed came from a guard at Tewfik Pasha's palace who had grown angry with her when she refused to marry him. In the houseboat there were private rooms, closed off by thick curtains, in the back and down some little steps, small rooms where you couldn't stand tall, your head would crack against a beam, rooms in which the beds rocked with the tide, rooms that let a slice of brittle moonlight in through tiny windows, rooms in which the ladies of the houseboat allowed, for a price, almost anything. Not that the young man was imaginative or capable of endless play or needed to extend his time. He flung himself at the women and fell back drunk and exhausted, and went home flapping his arms as if he could fly back to his childhood bed, where a serving girl might bring him a cup of mint tea and some clean pillows on which to lay his head.

Albert drank many beers that night and fell into a sound sleep on the cushions of the lounge while the houseboat rocked with the slight motion of the harbor waves and the more ferocious rhythms of the human body in natural, if not proper, agitation. As the dawn came up over the Pharos and the light on the water turned silver, Albert struggled to his feet and pressed his hair flat to his head. There were red lines in his eyes. He considered that all the animals went two by two into the Ark. He considered that a banker needed a wife to bring the blanket of civilization up over his injudicious nakedness and present him to society in a flattering light, and that a man was not a man until he had his own household and that it was time for him, never mind the uncertainties, to proceed. The houseboat would always be here. He would not be banned because of a wedding ring.

It was time to get his father to ask Dr. Malina for his daughter's hand. His step, as he went home that morning, watching the early-morning moisture on the hibiscus in the doorways, watching the terns that had steered into the city looking for garbage on the port streets, watching the windows open and the curtains blowing forward, meaning the wind was from the east. A China wind like this was good luck. His step was not as direct as it might be, but his body was alive with anticipation, satisfaction with his decision.

As he pulled the bell on his door, signaling the sleeping servant to rise, a man in a dark hat, better suited to the cold winters of Germany than to the warm nights of Alexandria, a man with glasses and a small, well-groomed beard, passed behind him. It was Dr. Koch, hurrying to his laboratory. He wanted to see the slide he had prepared the night before, and he could not wait for the sun to rise. He had cut tissue from a cholera victim's bowel. He had examined it carefully next to the tissue of a woman who had died in childbirth. He had obtained his samples by insistence, by bribery, by sending his assistant, Gaffkey, into the funeral home at the corner. He would compare the two tissue samples. If he found anything of interest in the tissue from the cholera victim, he would draw it in his notebook. He would save it to see if it could be seen again. If something appeared under his lens that was not in the bowel of the dead woman, that might *be* something. On the other hand, it might not. Women in childbirth might have different fluids in their bodies than men do. He would leap to no conclusions. He would simply record what he saw. He had confidence in his eye. He had confidence in his drawing hand. He had confidence in his brain. He also loved the opera. Unfortunately the Alhambra, an open-air theater where opera was performed, was closed for the season. At the opera he would have relaxed, allowing his brain to float with the music. If there had been an opera in this strange city where he must stay for a while, he would have felt more at home. He hummed the melodies he remembered as he walked along. This soothed him.

The sand was blowing again in the streets. It caught in his mustache and his sideburns. He brushed it away. Thank God, Berlin had a decent climate, not overheated like this Alexandria. It was planted with evergreens and maples along the avenues, and was only a short distance from mountains and lakes. Berlin did not stink of animals and yesterday's oranges, the air held no grains of ever-blowing sand, and a person could find an opera company in full performance almost at any time of year.

Of course, Albert's father approved, despite the unpleasant trouble that Jacob Malina had brought down on himself. He met with Dr. Malina that very afternoon. Dr. Malina had to talk to his daughter and his wife. But he shook the architect's hand cordially and offered him a drink of his best port. Dr. Malina half expected Este to swoon in horror, to shriek that she loved the cook, or that big-eared Arab boy from the corner house, whose kite kept falling—not so accidentally, he had thought—into their courtyard. He expected Este to complain, she was too young, she was not in love. His reasons for this expectation were based solely on experience. Nothing ever went as one wished, graciously, simply, well. He sighed and prepared himself for the worst as his wife and daughter came down to dinner. However, Este smiled a small, sweet smile and shyly asked his opinion. What was this?

What he didn't know was that Phoebe and Este had long planned this match. It would be a way of altering their friendship into a sisterhood. Phoebe had sung the praises of her brother. Este had been thinking about him long before her body changed, long before she understood what she was thinking and that certain images that intruded on her thoughts had best be kept from her mother, and some even from her friend. "I am ready, Papa," she said, "whenever you wish."

"Six months at least," said her mother. "I need to prepare. She's still so young, perhaps we could wait a year?"

"Eight months," said Dr. Malina. "I will talk to the rabbi."

That night, as she prepared for bed, Este became sad. It was surprising to be sad at such a moment. But there it was. She felt sorry for herself. Her story, her life's story, the only one she would ever have, was reaching its climax. The plot was coming to a narrative peak. She would marry Albert and abandon childish games and turn to her husband for advice rather than to her mother or father, and she would do as her husband wished and serve the food he liked and do her best to please him, as was her obligation, and all this was fine, just as it should be. He did not seem to be a reader of poetry, but Phoebe said he had a poet's soul, thinking deep thoughts and feeling everything with a full heart. Phoebe had said that Albert was the kindest boy in the world. Perhaps Albert had a poet's soul that had not yet found a way to express itself. Perhaps he had an imagination that she would discover as they became closer. But perhaps not. It did make her sad, wasn't it too soon for her to be married? Did it need to be right now? A deep anxiety touched her, one that was only evaded by sleep—dull, dreamless sleep.

Through her open window the voice of the muezzin echoed. This call to prayer was not for her. The moon hung misshapen above the harbor, the ships docked there rocked gently back and forth, the tides moved as tides move, small black insects flew about Este's sheets, a lost dog howled down the street, and at the club over by the lake, men still played their card games, still called for servants to bring them whiskey and tobacco for their pipes. As the dawn approached, the German scientist, Dr. Koch, sat at his desk, going over again his day's notes. Down by the docks the sewage leaked into the gutters and someone cried out in pain as a stomach spasm returned, and then was silent and in the silence a life ended. A man vomited near a palm tree, and a blind man walked barefoot in the bile, leaving footsteps in the dust. The heat hung in the air.

Where the great library of Alexandria had once stood, where the Temple of Apollo had once received worshipers, homes and businesses, courtyards and stables now rested, inside tiled entrances, up stone staircases, rugs lay across marble floors, maids swept, the smells of food rose toward the sky. The fires set by the Muslims so long ago no longer mattered. The burned books no longer mattered. Even last year's long night of riots that came after the British shelled the city had left little trace behind. Este woke in the morning restored. Her mood had shifted. All she had needed was a good night's sleep.

WHICH IS WHY Este Malina was on the edge of being engaged when Louis Thuillier met her at dinner at the French consul's home. She had not liked the French scientist particularly, and he had found her foolish. Which was fortunate because there could never be anything between them. It wasn't just Este's imminent engagement that stood between them, nor was it his own poverty. It was the matter of religion that barred his way. To Dr. Malina, to Dr. Malina's wife, to the assembled relatives of the Malinas, the Jewish faith was more than a faith, more than a question of traveling to the Jewish quarter and entering the old synagogue at the right times of the year, more than a sentimental affection for the lost city of Jerusalem, where the Malina son was trying to make his way at the moment, more than a matter of solidarity against the viciousness of others. There was a cord that bound them, that nourished them, that kept them with their fellow Jews when they suffered and when they prospered. It was a matter so central to the heart that it could hardly be explained, but was *felt*. Like the noon heat it entered every organ, every orifice, colored what the eyes saw, pounded in the ears, was taken for granted and yet never taken for granted. Dr. Malina, whose patients came from all quarters of the city, who was a man with few prejudices, was not open on this subject.

5

ERIC FORTMAN NEEDED a berth on a steamer sailing for England. He needed funds to book his space, for food and drink and lodging, and he needed to send a telegram to the owners of the bottles full of whiskey he had been bringing to Alexandria, hoping to guide them through the customs office before the Muslim customs officers could confiscate them. He needed to send his company a telegram reporting the loss of their shipment. It was a mournful prospect. He would not be hailed as a hero in Liverpool, although the ship's misfortune was none of his doing. What could he do? He could do accounts. He was a good salesman. He was a sturdy traveler. He enjoyed making a profit for his company. He could slip money into the right hands at the right time. It might be months before the company would wire him funds for a return passage, and in fact they might simply ignore him. He had heard that a man of even higher rank in the office had been taken by pirates and the ransom was never paid and the man's left ear was sent to the office in a small wooden box, where it was immediately discarded with the rubbish.

Walking through the market near Babel Gedid Station, Eric caught sight of himself in a shop window. He needed a shave, and his mustache was ragged, but his height was impressive. He could count on his face to win him friends, at least among women, and his teeth were still perfect and his body strong. His eyes were black. He smiled at his reflection in the window and it smiled back. He had a dimple in his chin. Women always exclaimed over his dimple. He was, in fact, very acceptable, although what good that would do him in this city at the end of the earth was hard to see. He was young, not so young as to be spindly or awkward, but young enough to expect large things from his single life. Now he was lost in thought, desperate thoughts that could make a man impervious to those in front of him, which was how he collided with Este Malina's mother, Lydia, who, with her servant trailing behind, was selecting the ripest fruits, the softest dates, the fish most recently caught, for her dinner table. Her servant picked up a large bass caught that morning in Lake Mariout. "No," said Lydia. "I'd rather have two smaller ones." The large fish was thrown back on the pile. Alien microbes clung to drops of water under its left gill. Eric Fortman apologized and apologized again to the woman he had nearly knocked off her feet. He explained his absentmindedness, his rumpled appearance, his entire predicament to the most sympathetic lady he had ever seen, whose dark eyes were both maternal and alluring and seemed to him like a pair of lighthouses, directing the ship to its proper berth.

"What a tragedy, what a catastrophe," said Mrs. Malina, allowing her slight smile to show that she believed that all could be put right. Which was how Eric Fortman found himself walking along rue Memphis with the servant a few steps behind and telling his new friend all about the wonders of birds seen at sea who seem never to alight but always to float on drafts of air. "Ah," said Mrs. Malina, "I wouldn't mind being such a bird myself." It was not surprising, then, that he found himself in a room in the Malina house, changing into borrowed clothes (a son departed for other parts) that did not quite fit, feeling, if not at ease, at least comforted. He was distressed that he did not have even one bottle of Glen MacAlan scotch to offer in return for his dinner.

LOUIS THUILLIER WALKED down the street and nearly stepped on a small boy with flies stuck to his eyes, which seemed to be oozing a yellow pus. The child held out his hand and mumbled. Louis did not understand his words, but what was the need of that? He would have given the child a coin, but he didn't want to step closer. Instead he hurried off, eager to forget the lines of dirt in the small extended hand. In the alley he saw the coconut shells and fish heads of a discarded meal and a brown fluid that smelled of human waste running like a slow stream across the cobblestones. He saw a woman with no teeth and a bent back moving toward the corner, carrying a bundle of sticks. He saw a woman with a naked baby in her arms, with a scar across her cheek and a soiled apron. He had seen the men in Paris living beneath the bridges. He had seen the old crone in his hometown who hissed at the children and seemed to have a beard. He had seen misfortune and calamity, but never before had he been in a place where the air smelled so unclean and the dark looks and hollow eyes and scabby skins seemed so open, so insistent, so common. Someone, he thought, should be taking care of these people. Where were the street sweepers, the lamplighters, the Sisters of Mercy, the signs of compassion that keep most of the starving out of sight. Where were the hospitals and the doctors to aid the poor. Here was a city by the sea in which all was washed clean, from which Darwin had claimed life itself began, and here everything was soiled, things left where they were dropped. He stepped across a mound of feces left by a horse or a donkey. Wash yourself, he wanted to yell at a little girl who was sucking on her fingers. *Ya, ya,* came the call of a donkey boy urging his beast to move faster.

When he returned to the hotel, he joined Roux and Nocard at a table in the garden. Roux was holding his beard tightly, a sign of trouble. Nocard was trying to coax a starling from a nearby bush to come a little closer. Roux handed a telegram to Thuillier.

KOCH HAS SENT WORD TO THE SCIENCE ACADEMY IN BERLIN THAT HE IS MAKING PROGRESS. ARE YOU ALSO? SPEED ESSENTIAL. PASTEUR.

Louis read the telegram. He bit his lip. He refilled his pipe and cradled the bowl in his hands.

Even under the central fan in the hotel lobby, he felt the Alexandrian summer heat. It was in his ears and made his mouth dry and his fingers stiff and his palms wet. His eyes were rimmed with dust, and his black hair was damp across his forehead. "This stupid country," he said. "It's filthy."

Nocard took one of his big hands and patted Louis on the shoulder. "There are worse," he said.

Louis puffed at his pipe. "I will never again leave France."

In the kitchen of the hotel, the fourth assistant to the cook was pouring scalding water over the silverware. She splashed a spoonful on her arm and put down her bucket to look at the small burn mark that appeared on her skin. Then she removed a knife and fork from the sink, thinking they had been washed along with the plate that accompanied them. In fact they had simply been cleaned almost to perfection by the person who had eaten his breakfast sausage hours earlier. The silverware was placed in a large drawer. The plate was stacked in a wire crib.

ALBERT HAD NOT been invited, although this made no difference to Louis, who did not know that Albert existed and would not have cared that Albert hovered over the table, the way the future always inserts itself into the present, invisibly but insistently. Louis was seated next to Dr. Malina. The chairman of the committee, a Dr. Fochere, wanted reports of all deaths as soon as possible. But there was a certain lack of interest in the paperwork this involved, and sometimes the family of the deceased claimed the death was due to other causes, and the funeral homes could be persuaded, for a very small gratuity, to keep a secret. Therefore no accurate account of cholera in Alexandria was possible. Nevertheless, a chart that hung on the wall of the committee's meeting room, which was at the rear of the Finance Ministry building, clearly showed a line moving upward on a graph, upward like a rearing snake.

The doctor wanted to know what Louis thought about burning all the clothing and bedding of the infected. Would that perhaps confine the cholera, starve the cholera, send it out of Alexandria? They had tried this method of controlling the epidemic in New York, but no one was certain whether it had been effective. Louis had no idea, but didn't want to say exactly that. "First," he said, "we need to find the cholera. Then we will understand it better, learn its habits."

"Your method?" asked Dr. Malina.

"We will inject substances of infected matter into our animals until one of them sickens with the disease."

"That will take a long time," said Dr. Malina.

Louis looked at Este, across the table. He noticed a mark on her left shoulder. It was a scar from a childhood fall off her brother's shoulders. He noticed that her nose was not entirely straight, but that a slight rise in the bone gave it a very distinct slope.

"Have you seen anyone die of cholera?" Dr. Malina asked.

"No," said Louis. "In Paris we have no cholera, and even so, I am rarely away from my workbench."

"Ah, then," said Dr. Malina, "here you will see it without doubt."

"I would like to see the soul leave the body," Este said. "Do you believe in the soul? Papa, have you seen the soul?"

"That's a large question," he said. He had not seen the soul, but he had seen the body foul with disease, crippled with pain, bald where hair should be, hair where skin should be clean, with rashes and odors and bruises and blisters, gashed and gnawed, genitals mutilated, breasts erupting in stinking sores. He had long ago abandoned any interest in the soul, the thing that might float away, slide out of the throat, slip between the dry lips and emerge to dance in the clouds, or haunt the living, or find its just reward. He himself was uninterested in the soul, and thought it a woman's invention.

Este asked the same question of Louis.

He shook his head. "I've never seen the soul," he said.

Este considered his words. The man is boring, she decided. Her first impression had been correct. He only believes in what he sees. How unlucky that such a dullard as this should arrive at her table from Paris, a city she imagined as burning brightly with wit as well as the latest fashion and the best theater, a city where great poets were sending loops of wondrous language across the tables of aristocrats. How disappointing it was to have Monsieur Thuillier as a dinner guest. She made one more try. "I am very fond of the poems of Monsieur Baudelaire. What do you think of them?"

"I do not know them," Louis said.

"Pity," said Este.

A foolish young girl, Louis thought, pleasant enough to look at, but not intelligent.

"What instruments will you use in your search?" Dr. Malina asked the young scientist by his side, as the fish was passed to him on a platter decorated with nuts and currants and smelling finely of cumin and coriander. Louis began to describe the autoclave and the filter Pasteur had especially designed. This did not interest Este.

"Were you safe away in the countryside when the British shelled Alexandria?" Emile asked his host.

"No," said Dr. Malina. "We hid in our houses. We shuttered the windows."

Mrs. Malina added, "We put our hands over our ears. It was not happy, believe me. The riot afterward was worse."

Este said, "My brother went on a ship to Palestine before the British fleet appeared in the harbor. We were all very worried until we heard from him."

Eric Fortman said, "I hear Palestine is a swamp. In Amsterdam once I shared a table at dinner with a fellow whose ship was carrying dates from Palestine to Portugal. He said the place was hot as hell, the desert was ugly, the trees were scrawny, and the people, like their donkeys, were covered with dust."

Este laughed. "That's probably true enough," she said. "My brother wants us all to come and live there, and says that the land is the most beautiful in all the world, which in fact he has seen practically none of."

"Enough, Este," said Mrs. Malina. No one understands how a mother feels when a son departs and and no longer sits at the table with his parents and no longer sings in the hallway, or teases the bird in his cage or calls for the servants to bring him a particular shirt. The way one misses a child cannot be spoken of, not whispered to the father in the night, not told to the cook in the kitchen, because the words fall so short of the feeling, the feeling of *missing*. Lydia Malina consoled herself with the thought that if she became a widow she would pack all her possessions and follow her son to Jerusalem, and would he want her then? It didn't matter. She would go.

Roux turned the subject back to the reason for the French mission's presence in Alexandria. "Are you seeing more cholera in one part of the city than in others?" he asked Dr. Malina. There was a sudden silence at the table. Everyone wanted to hear the answer.

"The deaths are concentrated in the area down by the docks, and there are many in the Arab town, but there are also cases in our section here, and in all the neighborhoods by the lake and down by the old fort."

"In other words," said Lydia Malina, "we are not safe anywhere in this city." She was startled by her own voice. A wave of fear washed over her.

The same wave soaked all at the table. No one stirred. No one said anything. Everyone wanted to jump up from the table, to avoid the place where the fear had settled on them. Lydia Malina considered her own funeral. She heard her daughter sobbing above her coffin. She hoped she was wearing her purple gown. She hoped her daughter was sensible enough not to bury her with her ruby brooch. She saw her husband's grieving face in her mind's eye. It was hard, a very hard moment, although it occurred only in her imagination. Everyone sat perfectly still.

"Papa," said Este, "what can we do so we won't get the sickness?"

Another man might have said, *Pray.* Still another might have said, *Take the boat to Istanbul.* A third might have said that her fears were exaggerated, most everyone would be fine, but Dr. Malina said calmly, "This is the world we live in. We share it with cholera."

"That's intolerable," said Lydia.

"Yes, it is," said Dr. Malina. "But, my dear, don't we have a dessert to serve with this meal?"

Lydia signaled the maid. The dessert, a pastry of honey and cream, was served and the conversation turned to a performance of *Hamlet* by a touring German company at the Zizinia Theater, which was said by the reviewer in the *Express* to be more remarkable than last year's *Comedy of Errors* by the same troupe.

After dinner, coffee was served in small cups with gold handles.

"My son," said Dr. Malina to Louis, "would have enjoyed meeting you. I am sorry he is not here."

Envy of the absent son sprang unwanted into Louis's brain. He pushed it away, but in its trail a longing came for his own father who had never left Amiens, who had taken his Sunday meal at his sister's for over thirty-five years, and who believed that doctors were charlatans, only after a man's purse.

"My son," Dr. Malina said, "is looking for business opportunities. He plans to make a fortune. He is a romantic, my son, in a world that little tolerates romantics. You, on the other hand, I can tell, you are not a romantic."

"I leave the dreaming to others," Louis said. That was not completely true, although it was the answer that pleased Dr. Malina.

In fact Jacob had not gone to Palestine entirely of his own free will. He had been a student at the university, studying the law. Ismail Pasha, the Khedive of Egypt, had spent his money so foolishly, on so many massive palaces and grand gestures, that the treasury was bankrupt and Ismail had to sell the Egyptian shares in the Suez Canal for a fraction of their worth. The great powers of Europe feared that Egypt would fall into financial ruin and political chaos. Due to political and military defeats, debts were owed each year to the Turkish sultan. Debts were owed to other European banks. Pressure was put on Ismail Pasha and he agreed— bitterly, one imagines—to leave Egypt and transfer the power to his son, Tewfik Pasha, who would do whatever the foreign powers expected of him. In June of 1879, Ismail went by carriage from Cairo to Alexandria and then out onto the quay. He stepped into his yacht, the *Mahroussa,* and sailed away. The *Mahroussa* was furnished with large Goebelin tapestries, depicting bloody battles in delicate embroidery, Italian marble tables, mirrors with gold frames, mosaics with rubies and emeralds, and mother-of-pearl decorations. The problem was that many who were on the quay, many who saw the ship being loaded, many who did the loading, many who in the darkness of the night walked across the ship's decks before it sailed, knew that the pasha had, in addition to the ornaments already in the yacht, stripped Egypt of many bars of gold, of gilt mirrors, of jewels of great value, of rare antiquities, of gold candelabra, of vases made of mother-of-pearl, of a fortune's worth of Egyptian treasure. Rumors abounded, and Jacob published a signed piece in the university's student paper about the theft of the heritage of Egypt, accompanied by the looting of the treasury of cash, bonds, and stocks by the former pasha. It was a bold piece, full of a young man's righteousness. It contained a call for restitution and a plea for a government unburdened by corrupt officials, royalty or not. It was seen by some as a support of Arab nationalism, and by others as treason. It would have been wiser not to write or publish such a piece.

The Malina family was visited two days after its publication by the Egyptian police, who were prepared to take Jacob away. Lydia had cried, and Este had stood by her brother's side, holding his hand. Abraham Malina promised to bring his son into court the following morning. He also went to his vault and withdrew a bundle of banknotes, which he gave to his suddenly very polite visitors. In the night he visited the chief of police, and it was arranged that Jacob was to leave Alexandria within days and never return. Never, as Abraham Malina, explained to his son, doesn't mean never, it means until political events turn again. A week later, Jacob sailed. Abraham Malina said to his son, "If you have opinions of any sort, write to us, not to the papers." Father and son embraced. It had been a sad parting.

Este leaned toward Eric Fortman. She had noticed his straight back, his dark and somewhat bloodshot eyes that spoke of rum and gambling and late nights. What good stories he would have to tell, if she could get them out of him. "Come to the concert with us tomorrow night," she said. "It will be Mozart and it will be lovely, and they serve tea and cakes afterward."

How could he do that, he thought to himself, his pockets were empty. He could not let these people pay for him, even at a concert. These Jews were not very practical people, he thought to himself. But he was wrong. Mrs. Malina had already figured out what to do with Eric Fortman.

It was a hot night, the shutters were open to the street. The light that had been in the Pharos had been extinguished over a year ago by the British shells, but the lamps were lit on the balconies of the yellow stone houses, and on the floors made of timber brought by ship from the forests of Lebanon lay carpets of orange and blue and crimson, swirls and diamonds, vines and berries, carried from Asia in long, slow caravans. The fountains in the courtyards below sent streams of water into the basins made of stone quarried from the banks of the upper Nile. Inside the Malina apartment, Louis heard sounds of carriages going by, wheels turning on the stones. He heard a group of boys heading out to a café, their harsh laughter rising to the terrace above, a vendor of orange drinks called out to his customers as he pushed his cart along. The clip-clop of donkey hooves receded down the street.

The moon had risen, a simple sliver in the still-pale sky above Lake Mariout. Louis went out on the terrace. Along rue Sultan Hussein the street lamps were lit. At the Café Noir, beneath a large poster of the pasha, men sat at little tables that spilled out along the sidewalk, under the arches that led to more cafés, more mosaics on the floor, more coffee urns, more water pipes with their long stems, smoke billowing up in the draft reaching the terrace across the street. Louis could, if he leaned off the balcony far enough, see the round window of the Orthodox synagogue. He could not see its great red door. The sound of backgammon chips, or was it crickets in the marshes by the lake, floated up toward the starlit sky. In the back of the café the men were playing billiards. Louis smelled the salt of the sea, only a quarter of a mile away, lapping against the barriers of the Eastern Harbor, gently rolling the ships that waited in port. The drinks on the tables down the street were pale ambers and greens, and the glasses were shaped like tulips. There was music from the end of the street, a strange instrument wailed on and on. Louis didn't like the music. He couldn't find the melody. It sounded to him as if someone was moaning.

Beneath the balcony on rue Sultan Hussein a man walked slowly, slowed by the Alexandrian heat, slowed by his own thoughts. It was Dr. Robert Koch, who was this evening concerned about exercising his muscles, keeping fit, keeping his notes in order. He was taking a stroll.

Over by the opposite side of the room, Este stood by Eric Fortman's side. Smoothing down the satin ribbon at her waist, she said, "What a good night for a drive. We should go to the beach and see if the little insects with their lights in their behinds are crawling in the sand." Eric had never heard of little insects with such lights. He nodded his head. Este moved closer to him. "See the moon," she said. "I used to watch it out my window when I was a little girl, and thought it disappeared when I could no longer see it. How stupid of me."

Mrs. Malina saw her daughter's back, and she saw the muscles in the man's neck tighten and she saw her daughter's hand on his sleeve. She moved quickly. "Este," she called, "come away from the draft."

Este replied, "There is no draft, Mama, the air is still," and did not move.

"Mr. Fortman," said Mrs. Malina, "I call on you to bring my daughter to my side." He did so immediately. "Has Este mentioned to you," said Mrs. Malina, offering Eric a tray with toffee candy wrapped in gold paper, "that her fiancé, Albert, was sorry not to be able to meet you this evening. He had work to do at his bank."

When her mother turned to Emile to describe to him the joys of swimming at the Alexandria seaside, Este whispered in Eric's ear, "I am not married yet, so you may talk to me all you like."

6

M ARCUS WAS HAVING a far less pleasant evening. He had taken Masika out for a stroll on the promenade down by the sea. All had begun well enough, with Masika licking her ice with her bright pink tongue and letting some of the sugar water drip down her small and very pointed chin. She was wearing a yellow dress she had made from some curtains the hotel had thrown in the waste bins, and the threads of the dress glittered in the light. The ocean smelled of salt and dead fish washed on the shore and shellfish and orange peels and date pits tossed by Alexandrians off the promenade onto the sand below, and the light of the moon on the water made Marcus dizzy with joy. Perhaps it would be days more before he had to spend real hours in the laboratory, boiling and stirring and stoking the brick oven, feeding the animals and cleaning their filth. Tonight he was as free as a bird, and holding on to his hand was a girl who did not speak French but who laughed at everything he said. Thank God, thanks for the mercy of God, he thought, for unlike his employers he was a believer.

Marcus did not take an ice from the vendor. He was worried that the sweet water would drip on his chin and on his shirt and make him look foolish. He needed one hand to hold Masika by the waist. He needed another hand to wave at the wonders of the boardwalk, the musicians by the café, the old man feeding the birds. So the pair spent the evening in the cool air by the sea, and the moonlight and the lamps from the shops were like invitations to pleasure. Later, when the moon was in the middle of the sky,

Marcus found a spot on the sand under the boardwalk. Above them the pair could hear the steps of passersby, their voices rising and falling. He moved slowly. He didn't want to frighten her away. He slipped his hand over the top of her dress. He felt the smooth skin of her breasts and he reached farther down and found the rising nipples, full and erect. He lay down on the sand with her. She was not without experience. She had liked her experiences. There must be some reward for hours of drudgery in the backrooms of the hotel. She was not afraid of the baby that might come of such things. It would or it would not happen. The hotel would fire her or they would not. She would return to her village or she would not. Her mother would raise the child or she would not. The future was too far away, too shadowy for concern. At the moment she could only pay attention to the French boy with his curly hair and his big eyes and his hands doing all the right things to make her willing, although she had always been willing.

Her dress did not have many buttons, but they were small. They were cheap and seemed to break in his fingers as he pulled at them. He was concentrating hard on extracting the girl from the folds of material when she cried out in pain. Had he hurt her? He stopped. She had a pain. She pointed to her stomach. She had a cramp, she demonstrated by opening and closing her fist. She smiled at Marcus and he pulled off the dress, picking it up by the hem and gently moving it over her shoulders and then her head. There she was. She had no slip. She had only a cloth wrapped around her important parts. She herself took off the cloth and the two lay next to each other. She shivered, although the air was warm.

Before Marcus could remove his own clothes, she screamed again. She moaned and waved at him to move away. She scrambled to her feet and moved farther back under the boardwalk. Marcus heard a sound, and smelled a foul smell. When Masika came back to him, her thighs were soiled and her eyes were wild and her lips, just a few moments ago so full and succulent, seemed now to be dry and thin. She sat on the sand and panted. "I need to go back to the hotel," she said. But Marcus, of course, did not understand. He stood there, uncertain. The smell was not an aphrodisiac. She looked at her belly, which was now swollen, and whispered, to no one in particular, the name of the grass used in her village when the stomach turned sour. Marcus didn't know the word, or the grass. What should I do? He ran sand through his fingers as if he were still a small child.

As he stood there, the illness invaded her intestines. It was sending out its poisons, against which the lining of her stomach was helpless. They entered the stomach wall and served as pumps, pulling fluid from her body, turning everything solid into liquid, creating a flood of liquid that pressed against the walls of her intestines and forced itself out. The illness took over her body like the army of a colonial power, spread out, killed whatever was in its way, and settled itself in groups, in clumps, in prime territory and began rapaciously to mine the area, to claim the reward for its troubles. It reproduced itself a million times. It sucked out minerals. It dried up everything around it. Masika's heart beat irregularly. Her lips turned blue. The blood could not reach her hands, which curled in pain. Little white flakes of tissue were washed away in its rush downward. Pools of fecal liquid gathered by her hips. He suggested she go wash in the sea. He showed her with gestures and walked himself to the water's edge and back again to illustrate his point. She understood him but seemed unable to stand. She tried to crawl forward. She was hit again by another spasm. This time she did not move away.

Marcus did not know what to do. He could get help from someone on the boardwalk, but then he would have to explain what he was doing with a naked Alexandrian girl. Was it a crime in this country to make love to a girl on a beach under the boardwalk? What would his employers say? Would they send him back to Paris, and then what would become of him? All these thoughts kept him in one place as the girl vomited and sweated and seemed to be running a fever. He would have held her hand, but he was afraid of her now. He didn't want to touch her.

An hour passed, and Marcus had retreated up to the boardwalk. It was now well past midnight, and there were few people in sight. A man and woman in fashionable clothes that might be seen in Paris. A man with a cigar, brooding at the water's edge, a group of small boys pulling something they had just taken from somewhere, laughing to each other, smoking cigarettes whose ends glowed in the dark as the group passed Marcus. The shops had closed. The stars were moving in the sky in their orderly manner, constellation by constellation, Milky Way spilling down over the dome of heaven and underneath the boardwalk. Masika had lost more water than a body can lose, she had emptied her bowels and then again and again until only thin water emerged and she sobbed to herself, and prayed to her God, and asked for her mother. She knew she had done wrong, terrible wrong, and was being punished. What had she done? She had no idea. The odor around her rose, although she no longer cared. The smell was of bad eggs, old garbage, dead creatures stuck in the corners of the hotel floorboards, a spoiled-fish smell, and something else, worse than all those put together, a smell that would make a passerby choke. Above her, Marcus, watching the iridescent insects spring through the sand, appear and disappear with the blink of his eyes, grew faint as he attempted to breathe only through his mouth. She was alone and grew weaker, and then, while Marcus leaned on the railing above, a lone figure on the deserted, late-night boardwalk, she died, covered in her own body liquids. There was sand in her hair and under her fingernails and grains of sand stuck to the sweat of her skin. With the first sign of dawn in the sky, Marcus went back to the hotel. He didn't look under the boardwalk. He knew what he would find. He felt ill himself, tired and frightened and wanting forgiveness, but for what exactly he wasn't sure.

AFTER THEY HAD returned to their hotel room, Roux wrote a long letter to his wife. All was well, the laboratory space had been arranged at the European Hospital. The next day they were moving into an apartment nearby that had been given to them by the French consulate. Madame Cecile Girard herself had arranged for the comforts of home, sent her maid to stock the kitchen and air out the bedrooms. Emile and Edmond would share the larger one; Louis would take the smaller. Alexandria was hot and dirty. On every corner, at the doorposts, there were beautiful clay pots filled with huge red flowers whose name he did not know. He would have the concierge mail his letter in the morning. Roux lit the gas under the copper plate on which he had placed a small amount of mercury. He didn't want to fill the room with toxic fumes, but a small amount would protect them, might protect them, was better than no protection at all, probably. The small flame glowed in the dark. Nocard, who had accepted all offers of wine and brandy, fell into his bed with his clothes on and wheezed so loudly that Roux shook him awake several times, but then, exhausted himself, he let the man snore and ignored all but his own night visions.

Louis had checked Marcus's room again when he returned to the hotel and had knocked with all his might on the door, loud enough to wake the dead, he thought. No Marcus. He went to his room and fell on his bed. He wanted a glass of water, but was too tired to light the lamp and heat the glass that rested on the lip of the basin, so he ignored his thirst.

Nevertheless, sleep did not come. It wasn't the heat. The night had cooled the temperature in his room. It wasn't Nocard's heavy breathing that kept him awake. The wine he had drunk had been more than he was accustomed to. He had never liked the poetry they had read in school. It seemed to him without use or valuable information. Was it perhaps a sign of ignorance on his part? Should he have read Baudelaire? Did he care if Este thought he was ignorant? He did not. With that thought, he fell asleep. In the early morning he awoke to the calls to prayer from the mosque at the square. He listened to the strange words with their mournful reminder that man is not in control of his fate, and he bolted upright with hunger. Yes, he needed breakfast, a good breakfast, and then he would be ready for work.

THE CHILDREN OF the cabana cleaner, three of them, who lived with their father in the hut behind the rows of cabanas that led to the boardwalk above the sea, rose early in the morning and went down to the sand to see if anyone had dropped some coins, some treasure, a handkerchief, a piece of candy still wrapped in colored paper, a letter, a pin. They raced across the sand and then stopped as they smelled something foul. They followed the smell beneath the gray wooden boards, a little away from the steps, and saw a girl, a naked girl, lying with her lips blue, her arms spread, her body limp, and over her thighs and in pools beside her was the watery substance that had belonged to her when she lived. The oldest child had a good heart and stepped near the girl and took off her own small shawl and draped it over the girl's exposed parts. In doing so she stepped in the mud beside the body and she brushed at it with her hand. The children all ran to tell their father, who came running down the steps. He reported the body to the local police. When the police did come and found no identification on the girl, only a dress some yards away, now stained and torn and wet from the dampness of the sea, they put her into a cart and took her off to the burial grounds for paupers and indigents, where her remains were thrown in a pit without ceremony or pause.

The cabana keeper's daughter had her breakfast, which, as always, consisted of a piece of round bread with a quarter of an apple, and she ate the bread with her hands, and a piece of the apple's peel got stuck between her teeth and she put her fingers in her mouth to release it.

Her small body held on longer than one might think possible.

Masika's mother had walked with her daughter down to the road that led to Akubir and from there to Alexandria. Word had come back to the village that girls could work in hotels and make more money in a week than their families could gather in a year. It wasn't quite true, this rumor, but it led many girls who were not yet married, who had fed the cow and petted the dog and carried baby brothers and sisters on their hips, to imagine other things.

Masika's mother had a story she told herself each night. It was about her daughter, who one morning serves coffee in his room to a widowed merchant from Cairo who finds her shy smile the solution for his heartsickness and buys her a ring and gold bracelets and promises her servants and riches if she will marry him, and Masika, with joy in her heart, embraces the merchant. The Goddess Isis, who is perhaps one of Muhammad's wives, has arranged all this in return for Masika's mother's constant devotion. When Masika's mother had seen her daughter walk until her back disappeared in the rising dust made by her footprints, when she could no longer make out the small pack of belongings her child carried on her shoulder, she had wept. It is not true that because you are poor and have more mouths to feed than food to feed them, each child is not inked into your story, indelible ink, ink that stains, writing on and on in the most illiterate of mothers' minds. Human beings are not cats, to let their litter range out into the world without another thought. For Masika's mother there was a grieving for her child that would never go away, a grieving that had nothing to do with Masika's death, which the mother could not know of, because who would tell her, who there in the large city of Alexandria would know that Masika lay in the pit? The hotel manager assumed she'd run away. Because of the lack of tourists, he did not hire another girl in her place. When one of the other girls, the one who spoke French, asked Marcus if he knew where Masika was, he told her to mind her own business. Masika vanished from Alexandria with the same fanfare that had accompanied her arrival.

THE CHOLERA WAS in Alexandria, but where was it in Alexandria, how were they to find it? Pasteur had given them written instructions—unnecessary because the three men had worked with Pasteur for many years. Roux had been his first assistant in the discovery of the two silkworm diseases, flacherie and pébrine, and Nocard and Thuillier had been with him in the anthrax studies on sheep. But Pasteur double-checked everything. He left nothing to chance.

i. Examine under the microscope the stools of cholera-infected individuals at various stages of the disease.
ii. Examine blood samples and their culture.
iii. Try microbe purification through inoculation of various animals until one species becomes sick without dying.

    iv. Find out if, in areas affected by the disease, animals have gotten sick or died from any disease.

    v. When trying to transmit the disease, focus on individuals from this species, but not exclusively.

    vi. Try to transmit this disease to animals by mixing suspicious matter with food.

    vii. Use the organ parts as well as bodily humors and excrement in your experiments.

    viii. Gather all information regarding the current epidemic.

MARCUS HAD SHOWED up early at the laboratory. He had circles under his eyes. His long lashes seemed crusted. His lips were dry. He swept the floor with great energy. He wiped the beakers so they would be sparkling clean. He carried out the one oversized green notebook that Louis used to record his experiments and dusted off its cover and then placed it in the center of the table. He filled the inkwell. He scrubbed the one window in the back of the small room so that the glass shone. He was in fact worried. His hands had been all over Masika. Did cholera leap off a girl? Was it in the air between them as they walked on the boardwalk? Why had it selected her and not him? Did he not have impure thoughts, all the time? Was that a pain in his stomach, or just a small pull of a muscle when he lifted the last barrel that had been shipped from Paris? He breathed deeply. But then he breathed shallowly. What was the safer way to breathe, how to avoid the air as much as possible? Avoid women at all times. He resolved to do this, but knew, even as he made his silent resolution, that he would not be able to keep it for very long. It was natural to lust after women, and it was natural to die. Should he have become a priest as his sisters urged him, ready as they were to sacrifice his pleasure for their own glory?

When Louis and Emile and Nocard arrived at the laboratory, Marcus begged for a chore, any chore. Louis was surprised at his assistant's sudden dutifulness. "Are you all right, Marcus?" he asked.

"Have you had breakfast?" Emile asked.

"Did you drink too much last night?" Nocard asked, in a manner that implied that drinking too much was hardly a crime and could be understood between friends as a necessity of life.

Marcus shook his head. "Let's go to work," the boy said. "Now I am ready."

THUILLIER, ROUX, AND NOCARD opened the heavy metal door that led to their new storage room. The barrels had arrived and were piled in the middle of the floor. Nocard, who had been carrying a basketful of rabbits he had bought in the market, put them in the cages in the back of the laboratory. Emile ran his hands over the workbench. "Marcus," he called, "this should be washed down." It was crucial that everything be clean. At the very least, they needed to rid the space of the visible crawling things that might contaminate experiments. Roux leaned into the large open oven and declared it ready for use.

Thuillier and Roux and Marcus worked together, barely talking, until noon, the beakers here, the bowls there, the little dishes in which they might grow the cholera cultures piled up over by the oven, the fire started, the long shovel hung on a hook, the gas tube linked up to the autoclave, the filter standing tall on the table, the shovel to reach into the oven placed by the brick wall, two soft chairs, a small ottoman purchased by Marcus for considerably less than he told Roux it cost, were hauled into a corner of the room by two native boys, barefoot and with scabs of unknown origin on their arms. Marcus went down the stairs to talk to the girl who sold tobacco in the corner shop. He learned at least ten Arab phrases in the course of his encounter.

Louis and Emile went to the hospital administrator's office to report their arrival. Nocard brought in two small, whimpering puppies, and a half-dozen chickens. He placed them in cages near the rabbits. He avoided looking the animals in the eye. He would need a sheep. Later he went to the café across the street and, sitting at a small table in the shade, he ordered a beer, and then another. He took two bottles back upstairs for Emile and Louis.

The café owner was in high hopes that the need for beer from his café for the French scientists would become a permanent condition. Perhaps his beer was addictive like the white powders sold on the docks, and passed on by the ladies of the night who sometimes came to his café after midnight.

For lunch, Louis ate figs that had been washed in boiled water, and a sausage that Marcus brought him from the same café. He examined drops from a carafe of tap water through his lens. He saw nothing unusual. Some dust, perhaps, a tiny mite that had fallen from somewhere into the drops. He filled the bowl of his pipe and it lit quickly as he puffed hard on the stem. The pipe comforted him. He felt its warmth in his hand, and the smoke tickled his throat. The smell of tobacco was good. He decided to examine his fig leavings under the lens. What he saw was fig: its brown flesh, its watery texture, its fiber, its seed. A fig in Alexandria is the same as a fig in Paris.

Sinking into the soft cushion of his armchair in their new laboratory in the rear wing of the European Hospital, he reassured himself, he forced himself to stop the anxious knocking of his foot against the chair leg. All would be well. Koch was more experienced. Koch was famous. But Koch was older, and an aging brain in a scientist is not an advantage.

Louis knew that studies had been done on the blood of cholera victims. They had shown that the proportion of serum to solid was reduced in those who were sick with the disease. What this meant, no one knew for sure. They had tried injecting some saline solution into the victims' veins, but that didn't seem to help. But if the blood fluids were affected by the disease, it must be that the disease could be found in the blood.

Roux asked Marcus, whose contrition had disappeared by mid-morning, to go to the infectious-disease floor of the hospital to obtain blood and excrement from cholera victims. Roux had equipped him with several vials and a large canvas bag to carry them in, as well as a syringe and a funnel and a pair of thick leather gloves. Marcus was not pleased with this assignment. "You do it," he said to Roux, who then threatened to send Marcus home on the next boat. Voices were raised. Marcus had tears in his eyes. "I don't want to die," he whimpered.

"If you die," said Roux, "I will write to Pasteur and he will ask the government to award you a medal."

"Just what I need when I'm dead," Marcus said.

"What we need is bowel, bladder, vomit. Go find the cholera ward," said Louis. "Get me some cloth, a piece of linen from the pillow the victim lay on, or a piece of the cotton used to wipe down their sweat or a blanket that covered them."

It was true that the sick would not welcome the taking of their blood, no matter how delicately it was explained. It was also true that most people with severe stomach cramps were not interested in science or saving anyone else, or anything at all beyond their own release from pain. Marcus did not move. Louis said, "I'll go."

Roux said to Louis, "Wear those gloves, don't touch anything, afterward wash your hands." It wasn't necessary to tell him that; Louis didn't answer.

Louis had spoken to the mother of a small boy who had not let go of her child's hand although the child had let go of his life. He spoke to her gently. He said he hoped to be able to save other children. The mother was not interested in other children. She closed her eyes. In a flash, Louis took the child's drinking cup. He slipped his prize into his shirt. In the corridor, under an empty cot, he found a basin filled with the brown fluids of a victim. No one had yet come to clear it away. The body was down in the basement, awaiting a carriage to bring it to the funeral home. The bowl was not small, and it was filled up to the rim with foul-smelling liquid. He put the child's cup under the cot for later retrieval. He carried the bowl in his arms away from his chest. He walked slowly, although he wanted to run. Back at the laboratory door, he called out for help. Roux opened the door. Louis covered the contents with a towel. He went back to the cholera ward to collect the cup. He also retrieved some bed linens that were stuffed into a bag in the hall.

In the hospital corridors he spoke in whispers with the sisters, whose gray robes with white aprons over them made them seem like moths hovering at dusk. He made his request for samples. He promised to show them the microbe when it was found. They helped him gather blood, stool, and a scrape from an open wound in a knee. After he had placed his harvest on the proper shelves and alerted Emile and Nocard to their new material, he went out in the street for some fresh air. But the air was not so fresh, it was hot and humid and damp and there were flies buzzing around his face when he tried to puff on his pipe, when he tried to wipe his forehead with his handkerchief. A fly lit on his eyelid. He shook it off. Never in his life had he seen so many flies. Was it the garbage in the streets, was it the smell of the dung from the donkeys and the horses? Why were there so many more flies in Alexandria than in Paris? As he walked toward the harbor he saw many children with bare feet, with encrusted eyes, closed with a pus that seemed to ooze down their cheeks. The children paid no attention to their eyes. They climbed and ran, chasing each other, and some begged with a small bowl by their side. Now that he was looking, he saw blindness, blindness everywhere. The man at the tobacco shop, the seller of limes and lemons at the bazaar, the rug dealer in the far stall, all blind. He had not seen so many blind people before. He had not seen so many eye infections before. When he reached the harbor he leaned over a rail on the walkway and closed his eyes. He let himself stay in the darkness for a while, the way children will play at blindness. Inside the gray wall that sealed off his sight, he felt a new rage. He would ask Pasteur, after they had found the cholera microbe, to consider the human eye. What was in the pus that flowed down the children's faces? What was in the air of Alexandria, the sand from the desert, the salt from the sea, that made so many in the city blind? Was it something that fell into the eye from the birds above? He opened his eyes. Could it happen to him, there on the walkway by the harbor? He shuddered. He brushed the thought away. He wouldn't accept the fear that accompanied it. He had work to do. He hurried back to the European Hospital. On the way he dropped a coin into the hand of a mother who was holding an infant whose face was covered with flies that she didn't attempt to brush away.

LYDIA MALINA SAT with Eric Fortman at her breakfast table. A young girl with a white apron brought in a bowl of grapes, and there was strawberry jam to have with his pastry. Lydia had eaten earlier with her husband, who had called the carriage at first light to make a visit to an elderly patient who lived at the far edge of town, and had sent word to him of some new suffering through his manservant. Two donkey boys were arguing loudly, and their insults rose through the open window. A fat dove with a crooked beak sat on a palm frond outside the balcony and opened its wings to take flight and then changed its mind again and again. The sun was already warming the white stones of the building and fading the colors from the wash that hung in the back of the house from a lemon tree and an improvised pole.

"Have you been to the Orient?" Lydia asked. Eric had not, but he had been to Spain and Portugal, and he knew the ports of Morocco. He had been working as an officer of one import firm or another ever since he was eighteen. He had started as an office boy and made his way to the ships, and there he had stayed, making new contacts in port after port and cementing friendships, his own and the firms'. He told Lydia he had been orphaned at the age of five and raised by his mother's elderly aunt, who had died before his twelfth birthday. To be so alone in the world at such an age seemed unthinkable to Lydia. Her face darkened. "How proud your mother would be if she could see you now," she said. "We will go this morning to my cousin Rudolph. His parents lived a while in Freiburg with others in my family. He has a company on the wharf where he holds the shipments of cargo that are coming and going, and perhaps he can find a place for you."

Eric expressed his gratitude. This was a good woman. This was a good place for his misfortune to have occurred. The end of his world had not come. He would begin a new chapter.

Lydia was eager to tell her sister about her new friend, an Englishman, a world traveler. Her sister would pretend not to be interested, but she would be. Lydia put the story into her next letter to her son. It was hard to think up things to write about when the person you were writing to seemed so far away and you couldn't imagine his life, what he ate, where he slept, who he spoke to, and in what language, and what dangers he faced and how long it would be before you saw him again. She kept by her bedside the last letter she had received. He had described a camel hitched to a post and the stones of the old temple wall where a few old men were praying. It annoys Dr. Malina when she bends over and kisses this letter. "What are you," he says, "some idiot girl from a village on the Nile? It is not your son, that piece of paper," he mutters. But she pays him no attention.

7

I N THE CROWDED STREETS down by the piers near the Eastern Harbor, more deaths were reported every day. And there were other deaths that were not reported, where family members simply took a body and left it on the promenade or in an alley, and the smells of the city became even more putrid than usual. There was talk in these crowded streets, talk in the cafés and in the bazaar at the stalls that sold rice and barley and goat meat, that the rich of

Alexandria were poisoning the poor, that it was a plan to get rid of them, a way of ridding the city of an unwanted population. People who made it to the hospitals, died in the corridors, died in their beds, died waiting for admission. Despite the storm that had wrecked Eric Fortman's ship, this was not the rainy season and the gutters went unwashed as human waste gathered in the streets and people crossed over it when they walked, horses tracked it from neighborhood to neighborhood. In the grand homes along rue Memphis, along the road to Ramleh where the British had built houses to remind them of Hampstead and Bath, the occupants considered the matter of cholera and agreed that the drinking and the lack of morality in certain parts of the city caused the disease to spread. Some thought that the police should cordon off certain streets and not let the occupants out until the disease had left the city. Some thought that the government should burn the bodies of the dead or send them out to sea on barges that would sink once they were far enough away from shore.

The authorities were considering issuing an order that the sick be removed by force, if necessary, from their homes and taken to an old edifice once used to store stones brought from distant quarries. Mothers and fathers, sisters and brothers, grandparents would be pulled by policemen and soldiers out of their beds, denied the comforts of their religion. The idea was not popular among the people.

Papers were made available to the members of the Committee of Public Safety. Keeping his patients waiting, Dr. Malina sat in his office and read:

In 1832, as Cholera spread across Europe, in Spain you could face the death penalty for leaving a town infected by Cholera. In Paris a rumor circulated that the rich had poisoned the wells and fountains to get rid of the poor. In the Philippines a group of biologists and naturalists were killed when their cases of reptiles and insects were found. The natives thought that they were sorcerers spreading the disease. In Prussia, beggars turned up at rich people's houses saying that they had just left infected areas and that they would go away if paid. In St. Petersburg a rumor spread that the sick were being lured into hospitals to be quietly butchered. In July 1831 a mob in St. Petersburg attacked hospitals and rescued the patients. In Budapest a rumor spread that the rich had poisoned the wells. Some rich people were captured and tortured by mobs until they confessed that this was true. In Austria soldiers were posted on the border with orders to forbid entry to cholera victims. In 1823 in Persia, guns and muskets were fired in the streets to frighten the Cholera away.

Dr. Malina said to his colleagues on the committee, "We have to think of the cholera as if it were a mad dog running through our streets. We are the dogcatchers. We must do our job." Everyone at the table nodded. No one at the table knew what to do.

LOUIS KNEW THAT they wouldn't see the microbe instantly. How could they distinguish it from all the other living organisms that would squirm across their slides? But they could begin. Emile's long face and sad eyes seemed less long and less sad. The basin was placed on the workbench between them. They put on gloves. They put more water up to boil. They dipped their lenses into the water. The hot plates with mercury on them warmed the air around the table.

They were preparing slides dipped into the bowel fluid. They placed some fecal material in a syringe that Louis brought to Nocard to inject in a few rabbits. Perhaps the rabbits would fall sick with cholera, and then when they examined the rabbit blood they might see the microbe. There was a deep quiet in the laboratory. The two puppies had exhausted themselves in a chasing game around the edges of their cage. The only sound came from a windowsill on which a starling sat and croaked his song into the day. There was a hum of insects on the high fronds of the palms that lined the street.

Marcus, coerced by Roux, made several trips into the main wards of the hospital. He brought a sack filled with clothes, a towel, a piece of sheet, a child's rag doll, a baby blanket. Louis had seen nothing remarkable on his slide. Emile had noticed strands of unrecognizable matter in the bowels, but he wasn't certain they were alive. The men took careful notes on what they saw. They drew pictures in their notebooks. They numbered their slides. Nocard injected four rabbits in the soft tissue under their right shoulders with the fluid found in the bowel that Marcus had retrieved. Would it sicken them? He wrote down the amount he had used, the color and number of the particular rabbit he had injected. He listed the colors and numbers of the rabbits he had not injected. He waited. The rabbits moved their whiskers up and down. One ate the bits of bread that Nocard had placed in a dish in their cage. Little pellets of rabbit waste were on the bottom of the cage. They looked normal. Nocard waited. In a box on one of the tables was his anesthetic, his cutting tools. He would examine the brains of the rabbits. He had anesthetized animals, cut open their skulls, and taken tissue from their brains before. He had trephined sheep, pigs, and dogs more than two dozen times in Pasteur's laboratory. It was never pleasant. It gave him nightmares. He had become a veterinarian to ease animals' pain, not to cause them suffering. But he had good hands, a clear eye when he had his glasses on, and he did not believe that animals had souls. He wasn't certain people did, either, but he was quite clear on his duty to his own species.

Louis paused. His eyes were growing tired. He was mixing bowel samples with water to create a substance that could be injected into the puppies. He wrote down the exact amounts of water and bowel he used in his notebook. He numbered the experiment and recorded the day and the time.

ALBERT SAT IN the Café Loup with his best friend, Achmed, who was the son of an importer of bicycles from England, china from France and Holland, clocks from Switzerland, silver from Belgium, diamonds from the mines in Africa, fine diamonds that he sold to the men of Alexandria to decorate their women in a suitable manner. His importing firm was called the House of Horus, after the falcon-headed god of ancient Egypt. The firm had its offices on the large wharf in the Eastern Harbor with the old lighthouse in view from its second floor. The young men had met at the university, where Achmed had been a sportsman, a discus thrower, and Albert had been a fan. They had learned that despite the difference in religion of which Albert's mother made much, they had everything in common. They enjoyed jumping off the dunes at the far end of the boardwalk, they enjoyed a good smoke, and they both believed that the British were joyless and the French were cowards and they liked to go to dog fights together and bet all that they had brought in their purses. They spent evenings together, allowing their brains to go soft with the liquids offered, the smoke swirling around, the moon rising and setting. They both liked large-breasted women with big hips and were happy to pay for them as often as they could.

"I need," said Albert, "a diamond ring for my fiancée. Can you get it for me at a special price?"

Achmed grinned. "Of course," he said.

"I don't understand," Albert said, "why women need such expensive stones. What is it, really, just a piece of glass with a nice shine to it? I wouldn't want it if it were free."

Achmed did not like to hear his business, or the one that would be his when his father finally died, mocked. "You have the sensibility of a pig," he said.

"I dare you to eat one," said Albert, knowing that neither of them would cross that line, no matter how high the wager. He poked his friend in the arm.

Achmed laughed. "Diamonds," he said, "are the most beautiful of the earth's fruits. Think how they sit deep in the dark earth underground, embedded in dull gray rock, until a man with a pick descends into darkness and chips away at the rock and pulls out the small treasure and brings it up to the sun, where, with the right treatment, it will let out rays that compete with the light of the sky." He had heard his father make that speech a thousand times. "Without diamonds, no woman would marry us, and then where would we be?"

Albert said, "Better off, I suspect. But I will marry and you know it, and so will you, and Este Malina is mine all but for the diamond. But I am short of ready funds, and you know why."

Albert had, just the week before, lost a considerable sum at a card game at which Achmed had been among the winners. Albert said, "I need a diamond I can afford."

Achmed calculated quickly. A friend at the bank was an asset, not one you marked in your books, but an asset nevertheless. Friends who owed you a favor and who were sure to rise at the bank were not to be found like lemons on a tree. A small flaw in the diamond would not be noticed or suspected by either his friend or his friend's bride. Business, after all, was business. He clasped Albert's arm. "I will find for you the best diamond in my safe, and we will have it set in a beautiful gold circle, and your family will be proud of you, and your betrothed's family will be pleased at their wisdom in allowing their daughter to marry you, and in the Belgian Congo one of my representatives will open his velvet case and fill it with more diamonds for more women in Alexandria, so all is well, all is fine, don't you think?"

Achmed and Albert drank to their friendship, to the diamonds that traveled long distances to grace the fingers and necks and ears of women in Egypt, and to the stars that watched the boats as they sailed, and to the House of Horus that should prosper forever, and to all the objects, tables and chairs, rugs and teacups, that moved from country to country as if the material world were itself restless and in search of adventure.

A boy with bare feet and a smudge of dust on his cheek, a pretty boy who was so young he seemed like a girl, appeared from around the café's corner. He was carrying a tray with pineapple slices. They were cut fine and rested in the shape of a heart on a wooden tray. The knife used to cut the slices had been sharpened by the boy's father, who had dipped the whetstone in water in a shallow pail, a pail that had been used to wash the boy's sister's sandals. The tray was heavy for the boy to carry even with both hands, and he walked slowly, calling out to those sitting at little tables at the café. "Do you want one?" said Achmed. "Let me buy you a dozen," he laughed.

"No, thanks," said Albert, who did not like pineapple. The two young men waved away the pineapple seller, who then crossed the road to offer his wares to those on the other side.

IT WAS THE hour of the day when the sun was nearly unbearable and sensible people went indoors and lay down on their beds and closed their shutters against the light. It was the time of day when women put damp cloths on their heads and allowed their servants to fan them with palm leaves bound together with strips of leather. It was a time when the bank was nearly empty and the bankers took coffee in the courtyard of the nearby hotel or walked to the beach and, taking off their shoes and socks, waded in the cool water that lapped against their ankles. It was a time when the train from Cairo pulled into the station, letting a puff of white smoke rise into the Alexandrian air.

Este and her mother had taken off their dresses and in their slips lay on the couches of their dressing room and Este asked her mother a question. "If you had not married Papa, if you had not married at all, what would you have done?"

Mrs. Malina looked at her daughter. She understood the question perfectly. "I would have run off to Paris and become a dancing girl," she said.

"You're teasing me," said Este.

"Perhaps," Mrs. Malina added, "I could have become the wife of an African chief and worn necklaces of zebra teeth." She felt a pressure in her chest, as if there was not enough air in the room. She breathed deeply.

"Mama," said Este, "this is not a time for jokes."

Mrs. Malina turned her back to her daughter. She did not want to look at her. "I did," she said, "what I did, and have lived the life I expected to lead, and it has been a good life. You will do the same."

Now it was Este's turn to look away. Her eyes might have betrayed her thoughts, which ran backward toward her childhood.

Saturday morning, mother and daughter set out by foot for the synagogue on rue Sultan Hussein. Este's hat had a bird made of real feathers stuck in the brim. Mrs. Malina's was gray, with a large ribbon of yellow tied to look like a rose. They held each other by the arm as they made their way past the chestnut vendor, the fish cart, the café on rue Rosette that had placed its tables far into the walk so it was necessary to go into the gutter to go forward. As they turned the corner of rue Nebi Daniel, a man staggered toward them, perhaps a porter at the docks. His face was pale, his hands were trembling. He reached out for Lydia. She caught his arm and steadied him. She did not understand the language he was speaking. She led him to the side of a building and helped him to sit down on a step. His hands left smudges on her blouse. Lydia patted his shoulder with her gloved hand. She wiped the perspiration from his brow with a handkerchief she drew from her pocket. She ordered Este to get him some water from a nearby café. Este hurried back with the glass. Before she could offer it to the man, she spilled some of the water on her own fingers. The water soaked through her glove. Lydia offered the man the water and then called over a small boy who appeared in a doorway. She gave him some coins to bring the man to the hospital. He said he would. He didn't.

Lydia and Este went on. Este took off her wet glove and threw it away. It was ruined. When they arrived at the synagogue, they went downstairs to the women's area, where mothers could stay with children during the services. On a large table, a basin with warm water and soap waited. Este washed her hands well, and then the two women made their way up to the balcony. The service had started. When Este peered down over the railing, she could see a crowd of men covered in white prayer shawls. She could hear the chanting of the words she did not understand. She could see the ark, which was open, and the light from the far window glinting on the silver handles of the Torah. Her father was not among the men downstairs. He was meeting with city officials about the current health emergency. Albert was not there because he never came except on the High Holidays, when it would have been scandalous if he were not there at his father's elbow.

Este tried to catch Phoebe's eye. She was sitting two rows behind, and the effort was noticed by all the other women along the bench, one of whom eventually whispered in Phoebe's ear, who then looked over at her friend and smiled. They all rose and sat down again. They rose up again. They sat down again. The ark was opened. The ark was closed. The ark was opened. The Torah was walked through the congregation, and the men touched it with their shawls and kissed it with their lips. The women watched. Mrs. Malina sighed. Time passed slowly. She apologized to God for her boredom. Este let her mind wander. When she married Albert, she would at last know what other women knew. The mystery would be over. Soon she would have her own children. What would Albert talk about with her at dinner? She hated being bored. Would he be boring?

Lydia insisted that her daughter accompany her to visit a cousin. They spent the whole afternoon discussing wedding dresses, linens from Austria, and the bleak prospects of the cousin's sons, who were both at the university and not applying themselves to their work. They had nibbled at sweets that the cousin's cook made in the large kitchen in the back of the building, honey and raisins baked in a crescent shape. Este had tea with mint. Lydia did not like mint, and so skipped the tea. Just as they were about to enter their carriage to return home, they saw Louis and Edmond, who had been to the French consul asking for funds to make additional purchases of chemicals. Their supplies were quickly depleted. Este waved. Lydia grabbed her daughter by the wrist. "You have no interest in these strangers," she said. Her voice was not sweet as she said these words. Este did not receive them well. She would have interest in whomever she pleased. But this she did not say. There were no further words between them, and the silence in the carriage was not amiable.

ROUX WENT TO the Committee of Public Safety to present the credentials of the French mission to the officials there. Also at the meeting that morning was Dr. Robert Koch. Roux shook his hand and expressed his admiration for the German's work on anthrax. He relayed Pasteur's respects. They were rivals, yes, but they were also colleagues. Both Roux and Koch agreed that, based on John Snow's work in the 1857 cholera outbreak in London, it would be a good idea to keep the city water clean. "And how should we do that?" the president of the council had asked Koch, and Koch had replied, in a weak attempt at a joke, "I am a scientist, not a specialist in aqueducts. For that," he added, "you need a Roman."

Roux and Koch agreed. They did not think that burning the clothes of the victims was the answer. They did not think that quarantine would work in a city like Alexandria, where the public was always in motion on bicycles or carriages or moving carts or loading and unloading packages. They didn't think prostitutes were spreading cholera, but then, neither had any evidence that they were not. Koch invited Roux for a glass of beer after the meeting.

Later that week Koch and his assistant, Gaffkey, had dinner with Emile Roux and Nocard and Louis Thuillier. Louis was prepared not to like the German, but in fact he found that once they started talking about their slides, their cultures, their favorite lenses, their methods of boiling water quickly, the borders that marked off the nations fell, the pride that had separated the two countries so bloodily ten years before seemed trivial. They spoke in French and English. Koch's French was heavily accented, as was his English. Things had to be repeated several times, nevertheless the men at the table understood each other perfectly. Except that Koch was still determined to find the microbe before his new friends, and the French team was certain that despite the German's thorough and even engaging ways, the prize would be theirs. What Koch didn't tell them was that his plan to catch the microbe differed from Pasteur's in certain important ways. They did discover that he did not have a veterinarian working in his laboratory. "He must handle the animals himself," said Louis.

"That's foolish," said Emile. "He wastes time that way."

Albert went to his father. He said, "I need five thousand francs for the ring." Achmed had asked for thirty-five hundred, but Albert saw an opportunity and took it. "You don't want me to show up poorly before the Malinas," he added.

Albert's father sighed. He was not convinced that his son was interested enough in hard work, that he would be a success in this cutthroat world. But then the path had already been smoothed for the boy, and he was able to speak many languages and made a very good appearance at the table. "Son," said the father, "you are a fortunate man, this girl is charming and a dear friend of your sister's. We have known her most of her life, her character is beyond reproach. Can I say the same for you?" The father smiled to let his son know this was not a criticism, just an idle thought.

"I will honor her," said Albert, "as you have honored my mother."

This made the father rise from his seat and go to the window and pull at the curtains. "It is hard," he said to his son, "with so many females pulling one about to stay loyal. I think it is unnatural, against a man's nature, to wed for an entire life and pour all his capacities onto one lady's frail bosom. Our father Abraham," he said, "had his serving girl, and Jacob had Rachel and Leah and Bilhah and Zilpah, and you, you will not be the first to pay respect to the mother of your children while bringing presents to your friends of the night."

Albert patted his father on the shoulder. "I've learned from you," he said, "not to be so solemn. Nine commandments are more than enough."

Albert pocketed the funds and stored them in his shaving kit, where he assumed they would rest peacefully until needed.

"YOU MUST COME downstairs to your father's office right now," said the Arab boy as he raced into the drawing room. "Your father wants you now."

Este was sitting at a small desk, about to write a letter to her brother, telling him of her engagement. She had never before been summoned to her father's office. She followed the Arab boy down the stairs and through the back door to her father's surgery. He led her into one of the small rooms. Dr. Malina was there, standing over a table on which lay a woman, an older Arab woman, the woman who had been Este's nurse until just a few years ago. The woman was hardly recognizable, her features had sunk back in her head, her legs were stained with brown matter. Her gray hair was matted. Her eyes were bloodshot. Her hands were shaking. It was Noona. Este cried out.

"Be calm." Dr. Malina took his daughter's hand in his own. "She asked for you. She wanted to see you. You must be brave."

He would have liked to protect his daughter from this grief, from the sight and the smell in the room. But he knew that the woman who had held his daughter in the night, who had been the first to teach her to say yes and no and thank you and please, this woman had a right to see the child who was no longer a child, who wasn't her child but was her child. He had no choice but to call for Este. Noona had come to his office a few hours before. She had waited patiently in the waiting room, but then she had been in great pain and screamed, and the boy had taken her into this room and it was clear there was nothing he could do.

"Papa," said Este, in a voice so small that she might have been a tiny child again.

"Nothing," he said. He could see in her eyes her disappointment in him.

"Noona," said Este, "you'll be all right, Papa will help."

Noona did not believe her. She stroked Este's arm. "My darling," she said. "My darling."

Este said, "Papa, call the boy, let's clean the floor."

"Not yet," said her father. "We will have more to clean before it's over."

"Stay," whispered Noona.

Este had not thought of leaving. She thought of waiting at night in the dark for Noona's footsteps to approach her bed. She thought of Noona tying her hair ribbon in the morning. She thought of Noona telling her stories from the village where she herself had grown up. Stories about cats that changed into girls, and fish that learned to talk. "Noona," she said, "don't die."

Dr. Malina put his hand on his daughter's shoulder. He had to go back to his other patients. After he left, Este let her tears come. Also, she was angry.

Later, when two boys came and took away the empty shell that had been Noona, and Este had recovered from her first shock, she opened the door to her father's office. "What is it, what brought it, how is this possible?"

"I don't know," he said.

She ran into the street without her hat, although the sun was high in the sky. She went to the European Hospital, to the laboratory of the French scientists. She went alone, without a companion. She didn't care if anyone saw her.

In the laboratory, Nocard was mixing bowel matter with grain for dog food. Emile was boiling water he brought back in a jug from the café so they could safely drink. The heat in the room was oppressive. There was no point in starting a fire in the oven until it was needed. Louis bit down on his pipe stem. He tried to imagine his foe. It was tiny, of course, not visible to the naked eye, but it surely had a form, a mite's form, an insect's form, means of digesting something, means to divide itself, or mate with others of its kind. He stopped himself. He should not imagine his foe too closely or he would be looking for the wrong thing and miss it altogether. Nothing must be assumed until it was demonstrated. He knew that. If only the lens of his instrument were better, could enlarge one thousand times further, then no secrets could be kept from his peering eye. *If only* was not the way a scientist should think.

Louis Thuillier knew that the space he walked in, the food he ate, the gums of his teeth, the bruise in the peach he had left in the bowl three days before, all were teeming with creatures that gnawed and consumed parts of things, other things, made yellow what was red, made pus where clear skin had been. What Louis knew was that no matter how benign the morning, sun shining on green leaves and blue water sparkling at the landscape's edge, something unseen was killing something else unseen and using its body for fuel. It wasn't just human beings that needed to eat, but all living creatures, those you saw and those you didn't. A sailboat riding the ocean's waves, a branch of a tree floating down a river, all looked peaceful to the poor, inept human eye, but underneath the water, on the ridge of the leaf, on the blade of grass, something was dying in the mouth of something else and all creation was consumed in a continual munching and destroying, eating and eliminating and eating again, and the eating was not harmless or sweet or ceremonial or symbolic, neither wholesome nor sanctified, but simply constant. One thing lived because another thing died. No wonder Pasteur rarely smiled.

Microbes don't think, have souls, fear death, or regret their past, so their fate doesn't matter, shouldn't concern the superior human mind at all. But as Louis considered the matter, he wondered if perhaps all living things didn't have some pleasure in sliding along, in lifting wings, in guzzling dirt, in moving filaments, in letting rain and sun touch their skins. Was their death, the death of even invisible creatures, of no matter at all? These were thoughts no man should ever tell another man, for fear of ridicule. Louis ridiculed himself.

These peculiar thoughts were taking him away from action, and what he needed to do was act. Emile was boiling beakers, pincers, slides, cups. Louis left the laboratory, walking down hospital corridors in which visitors leaned against walls, an Arab child was mopping the floor, and a small lizard hung from the doorframe of the stairwell entrance. Louis found his way out and went for a walk. Perhaps if his legs moved, his mind would clear.

He walked from the promontory of Silsileh, where Cleopatra had killed herself in her barge when Antony returned after his defeat at sea. He walked past the docks where Pompey had disembarked, hoping for the friendship of the Ptolemy children, whose agent plunged a knife in his back as he stepped ashore. Louis walked past the corner where, in the time of the Ptolemies, the Mouseion had stood. Once, behind its walls, there had been a park and a zoo. All the knowledge of the ancient world had been stored inside its great library. In its study rooms were philosophers and scientists and astronomers and poets, albeit mostly bad poets, and it was there, in the third century B.C., that the scientist Eratosthenes had dissected a small desert rat. It was there that he'd almost uncovered the way blood circulates through the veins. He had measured the earth at the Mouseion observatory. He'd drawn almost accurate maps of the world. The scientists at the Mouseion knew that the world was round a thousand years before Columbus set sail. It was there that Euclid's works were collected and preserved. There were the scrolls of Theocritus, Callimachus, Plotinus, and Hypatia. It was there that magic and superstition were held at bay by human minds eager to understand the curious circumstances of their earthbound lives.

This did not help Louis at all. The spirit of Eratosthenes did not tap him on the shoulder and whisper in his ear. He was on his own.

He saw an archway down at the end of a narrow street, so narrow the sun barely entered and the air was cooler. The street reminded him of the rue St.-Denis in Amiens, behind his lycée, where the boys would go to smoke before the bell. He turned into that street. Above his head a woman leaned out a window and threw the contents of her pail down below. The foul-smelling water splashed up at Louis but did not touch him. He went on.

His step was fast. The warm wind from the ocean stroked his face and blew his hair about. He walked quickly past the mosque at the corner and noticed the intricate iron vines that looped around the now-closed gate. How long it must have taken for someone to have made that gate. How many days or perhaps years it must have taken, and it was worth it, look at it. He almost paused but did not.

Back in the laboratory he tapped his foot, he bit his lip. He waited for more ideas to come to him.

There was a knocking at the metal door. Louis opened the door to find Este standing there, her shawl pulled over her shoulders as if she suffered from a chill. Her pale face looked up at him. "May I come in?" she asked in a small voice. He nodded. She walked over to the laboratory table. "Tell me about the cholera. How are you looking for it?" Her manner was neither polite nor rude, she was simply intent on answers. She had many questions. Why is the cholera in Alexandria? How did it get here? Why are you sure it is some living creature that is causing this? Can you prevent it? Can you cure it? When you find the small thing, will you know how to kill it?

Louis answered her questions one after another. He was ashamed at how often he had no answer.

"What is this?" she asked, pointing to the autoclave, and he explained it to her. "What is this, what are these?" she asked, and he explained the plates set out in a row, where he would try to grow something from the matter of cholera victims. "May I look?" she asked when he explained about the lens and the small size of the enemy and the need to distinguish its shape from all the other living shapes that moved across the lens. He brought over a high stool so that she could peer down and see the glass he prepared for her, just water with something swimming in it, moving back and forth across the surface. He had placed his hands on her waist, naturally, to help her climb on the stool, so intent was he in helping her to see. But then an instant later he was embarrassed.

This was not right. He felt her ribs through the material of her dress. He blushed. She was not thinking about his hands. Este had trouble with the microscope. She saw her own eyelashes, dark and long, flickering in the reflection. Louis leaned over her shoulder, inhaled a smell of coconut and sesame oil, and adjusted the lens for her. He slipped another slide under the lens. At last she saw the living thing crawling across the lens. She turned toward him, amazed. "How wonderful, Monsieur Thuillier!" she said. Este put her hand on his shoulder. "You are a real adventurer," she said. Louis blushed to the tips of his ears. Este saw his blush and knew exactly what it meant.

Roux took Este to the back of the laboratory and showed her the animals in their cages. "Oh, the poor puppies," said Este.

"We must defend our species," he said.

Este was not entirely convinced. Louis had little patience with people who shed tears over the lives of beasts. Este heard his unspoken criticism.

"You have to sacrifice them, I understand," said Este. "I want to see more," she said to Louis. "Please, I want to see more."

"I have to work," he said. The words were short, but his voice was kind.

"Let me stay and help," she said.

"There is nothing you can do," he said.

"I'll watch you," she said. "I'll learn."

Louis hesitated.

"Of course she can stay," Roux called out from across the room. "Just don't touch anything without asking, and stop talking so we can think."

Este nodded. Louis looked at her across the table. He sighed. Would she interrupt his train of thought? Would she make ignorant comments and drive him mad with constant questions? Why had Roux been so agreeable? Louis looked at her black hair, a strand now loose and falling over her eyes, eyes still red-rimmed from tears. "I thought," said Louis, "you were interested in poetry, not chemistry."

That was then, this is now, Este thought. She said nothing.

Nocard staggered through the small door holding two large cages, in one of which ten rats had been placed. It had cost something to pay the little boys down on the docks to capture the rats alive, as Nocard had insisted. He had to go first to the consul, wait for two hours for the secretary to see him, and then wait while an allowance of funds was produced from the account that the ministry had set up for its scientists. In the other cage was a kitten curled in a ball, barely alive.

"You remember Este Malina," said Roux. "She wants to watch us awhile."

Nocard nodded, put out his hand to shake Este's, decided that might not be right, patted her on the shoulder instead, grinned at her. He hoped he hadn't made a fool of himself. He assumed Roux had agreed to the girl's presence to enhance the mission's friendship with necessary and useful friends. Nocard left.

An hour later, there was a banging of metal against the wall, a low howling, and Nocard reappeared in the doorway pulling a wooden cart with wheels. On the cart was a large cage in which a brown dog was snarling and whining and drooling. The dog was frightened, as well he might have been. Nocard was pleased with his find. "A stray down by the lake, some boys were throwing stones at him. He was hungry. I gave him some of my bread. I caught him with a rope. Look at him," he said. "Strong muscles, good coat, not sick. He will serve us well." Emile came over to look at him. Louis turned his head away. He did not like to see the panting and the heaving of the chest. He did not like to see the dog's eyes searching the room with terror. He did not like the smell of the dog, which had soiled its cage. But he accepted the dog as a necessity. They would, as soon as they were able, give the animal cholera, and when the dog sickened they would have material to work with.

Emile bent down to the cage. "What is this lump behind his ear?" he asked Nocard.

Nocard bent over too. "It could be a healed bite, from another stray," said Nocard. "It could be an additional bone in the skull."

"Is it a wound?" asked Emile. "I think I see some blood beneath the fur. Is it infected? We need to know."

"I'm not sure," said Edmond.

The animal was pacing back and forth. He was whining a low, terrified whine and occasionally opened his mouth and cried. He barked and snarled and backed away as far as he could when Edmond tried to put his hand into the cage to feel the lump. "We have to take him out," he said.

Emile opened the door of the cage, and Nocard was putting the rope on the dog's neck when he leapt forward, knocking Nocard down. His glasses fell on the cement and broke into three pieces. The rope lay on the floor, useless. Este backed up against the wall. She did not scream or call out. The dog was larger than he had seemed in the cage. He snarled. He stood there. Edmond, blinded without his glasses, started to rise from the floor. The dog stood over him, growling a long, low growl. Emile rushed to the oven to get the iron shovel. The dog lunged at Edmond, who threw his hands up to protect his face. Louis bent over and forcefully pushed Nocard out of the way. Louis stood before the dog, which now rushed at him, sinking his teeth into his knee. Nocard stumbled to his feet. Louis knocked the brass gas lamp off the table and it fell in front of the dog, which, startled, paused a second, releasing Louis's flesh. In that second Louis moved behind the table. Edmond recovered his rope. The dog, confused, stood still and Emile had no need to use his shovel. Este saw that Louis was a brave man. She said nothing. She had not uttered a sound, for which all the men were grateful.

Back in the cage, the dog settled down. He drank some water and curled up in a far corner and went to sleep. "This is not a rabid dog," said Edmond, who had left his spare glasses in his bedroom, but couldn't remember exactly where. "The dog," he said, "was just alarmed."

"Reasonably so," said Louis.

"Let's pour some alcohol on that wound," said Emile. Louis boiled some water and, although it was still hot, swabbed his wound.

Nocard put alcohol on the bite marks, which were not very deep, hardly a scratch. He said, "This will heal quickly."

"Thank you," said Edmond to Louis. "You saved my handsome face." Despite the sharp stinging in his knee from the antiseptic, Louis smiled.

Edmond went to the back of the laboratory to see his other animals. Este went with him, and was asked to tilt the small cage of a rat downward. The rat clawed at the bottom of its cage and slipped and slid into the bars while Edmond poured the urine that then collected in the corner into a container.

8

ERIC FORTMAN CLIMBED down the carriage steps, paid the driver, and decided to walk the rest of the way to the Malinas' home, where he was headed.

He had just been employed by the Marbourg & Sons importing firm, run by Lydia's cousin Rudolph. There was no question he would be an asset to the firm. He was on his way to report the good news to Lydia Malina and thank her for her kindness in making it possible for a stranger to begin a new life in a foreign land. He had taken lodgings near his place of work, and now he was certain good fortune was smiling on him once more. He was hoping that when he was ushered into Lydia's drawing room, her lovely daughter would be there. He had almost taken a wife in Liverpool, but then had decided against the lady in question, who had acne scars across her cheeks that were visible in bright sunlight, and he had thought that in time he might do better and anyway his ship was soon due to embark. This Malina girl was perfectly complexioned. He understood she was almost engaged. But engagements could be broken.

DR. MALINA TRIED to finish with his last patient a little early. In fact he finished rather late. Albert was coming to dinner, along with his father and his sister Phoebe. Albert's father had sent Dr. Malina a note informing him that Albert had purchased a ring and wished to give it to his intended as soon as possible. The news had made Lydia's head swim. She had to lie down immediately. This was pleasant news, of course, but it brought home the reality of her daughter's fate, and actually she had preferred her daydreams to any reality at all. There was no hiding from the passage of time and its necessities, but she was certain that when her daughter left her house she would be doubly bereft.

IT WAS IMPORTANT to find out if any particular animals had gotten sick in the areas where cholera had killed. Animals sickened all the time, but it was possible that dogs or cats or birds in cages, or sheep kept in pens or chickens in the yard, were more likely to harbor the cholera virus than other animals. If many of one kind had died recently, then perhaps the microbe could be found in their remains, perhaps their tissue could be used to give other animals cholera. Louis was given the task of exploring the neighborhood down by the wharf to see what he could learn. Marcus was to go with him.

Behind the café, they passed a dark stream running down an alley. In the foul-smelling water, human waste and dog waste combined. A glass jar floated by, and a woman's stained cloth disappeared far ahead. The water washed over the cobblestones and the stream ran past a door, which opened and an arm reached out and dumped a few cooked potatoes from a pot, around which tiny flies swarmed into the dark stream. The waiter at the café had taken his break in the back alley, where he urinated against the wall. His water joined the stream. As he stepped back, his heel sank into the dirty water. He walked back into the café, and his footprint stained the floor. He wiped up the mark with his hand, a swift motion, one bend and it was gone.

"I'm hungry," said Marcus. "We need to stop and have some sausage. I can't go on without food."

Louis glared at him. "Not yet."

Marcus sat down on the curb. "I can't go on without at least something to quench my thirst."

Louis noticed that his own throat, too, was dry. "No," he said, "we have work to do."

At the Grand Square, Louis asked about the health of the cat that slept on the rug in the back of the tobacco shop. The cat rolled over on its back to let the sun's rays fall on its stomach. It was fine. No cats had been found dead in the streets of the neighborhood. Marcus asked a group of little boys headed off to the lake to fish if they had seen any dead cats or dogs. The boys shook their heads. Had they understood the question? Louis wasn't sure. They asked in the back room of the bar at the wharf where sailors were smoking and a strange sweet smell filled the room. Rats, dead rats, but there are always dead rats, one sailor told Louis.

Perhaps in the countryside, Louis thought, perhaps the cholera has attacked the sheep and the pigs in the villages. Marcus and Louis took a carriage to the Office of Agriculture, which was in the large white government building behind the Exchange. It was guarded by two English soldiers playing cards at a small table near the entrance. No unusual reports of animal deaths. Nothing of interest, said the clerk. Except that the third assistant who did the filing in the office had died of cholera just the week before. That explained why papers were piled on every surface of the small office.

THE MEAL WAS over. The serving girl had carried the dishes out to the kitchen, where Abbas was waiting with heated water to scour the pots and pans. Dr. Malina had moved into the drawing room and was smoking his last cigarette of the evening, and his wife was writing a letter to her son, telling him about her day, how she had picked out a peach-colored satin fabric to be made into a dress and the leftover yardage to be used as a shawl. She wrote to him about the crow she had seen on the balcony whose angry eyes had warned her that danger was everywhere. She wrote to him about his Uncle Tomas, who had been walking in the rue Nebi Daniel when a workman carrying a long board had knocked him down and he had lost consciousness and hadn't regained it until his wife produced a steaming apricot pudding by his bedside. He had always been very fond of apricot pudding, and he immediately opened his eyes and asked for a spoon. She didn't want to bore him with her letters about nothing at all, but she wanted him to know that her days were continuing, to remind him that she breathed the same air that he did and was close by even if she was not in fact close by.

Albert's father had excused himself after dinner and walked home. Albert asked Este if she would like to walk down to the sea. She would. She put a shawl around her shoulders and ran her hands through her hair to make sure her curls were at their fullest and most appealing.

The couple, and they were almost certainly now a couple, walked, not holding hands but with shoulders almost touching, down the wide avenue. They were followed at a discreet distance by Anippe, Este's maid. They heard the wind rustling in the long leaves of the palm trees and they heard the rattle of carriage wheels, and they saw the lights in the windows of homes and they passed the hibiscus that guarded the path to the boardwalk. When they came to the beach, where their families had cabanas, they walked out onto the sand. The moon was no more than a sliver, but its light cracked open the heavens, the Milky Way spread across the dome.

Este said, "I used to hate going to bed on a night like this. Perhaps when we are married I will never go to bed."

Albert put a hand gently on her shoulder. "I have this for you," he said. He took a box from his pocket and handed it to her.

She knew, of course, what was inside. She opened the box and saw the diamond ring, clear and large, set in gold prongs, lovely, the moonlight glancing off its sides. "Yes," she said, "it's perfect," and slipped it on her finger.

Albert wanted to tell her how he had gotten it at a bargain price, but thought perhaps that wasn't the most tactful thing to say. "I will get you more jewels," he said instead. "You will have enough diamonds to open your own jewelry store."

"Thank you," she said. "I always wanted to be a shopkeeper."

He laughed. She was not stupid, his bride-to-be, and that was something.

"Have you met the French scientists?" she asked him.

"No, I haven't. Are they very boring?" he asked.

"No," she said, "not boring at all." She started to describe to him what they were doing in their laboratory.

"Enough," he said. She stopped.

As he led her back to her house, he slipped his pocket watch out and glanced at the hour. His night was not yet over.

When Este returned, she found her father at his desk. "Look at my ring," she said.

He looked. His saw that the ring was of substantial size. "Fine ring," he said, and kissed his daughter on the cheek. He saw the round curves in her face in the orange light of his lamp and the small scar on her chin that came from a fall from a chair before she had gone to school. He would have said something to her, something about the passage of the years, the pleasures that he hoped she would have, the way it would be when her own time came to bring a child into the world. He wanted to say that he would allow no pain to reach her, but that would be bravado, a lie. A man did not tell lies to his daughter. His jaws ached with something he could not name but that had everything to do with his child and his desire to keep her as she was, in the lamplight, her eyes reflecting the glow, her hair a little damp, down on her forehead, and her smile, the one he believed she saved for him but probably gave indiscriminately to all. "Good night," he said abruptly. His voice sounded curt, even rude, in his own ears. Este left the room.

He considered the cholera. Should his wife and child move elsewhere for the time being where they would be safe? It might cause panic if he, a physician on the Committee of Public Safety, sent his family out of town. Cholera would leave Alexandria in time, it left everyplace it visited in time. How soon would it go? When would it be satiated? He turned to read in the sheaf of papers on his desk.

It traveled in caravans across Syria, where it reached Aleppo in November 1822. It appeared in 1821 at Basra in the Persian Gulf, and killed, in less than three weeks, between fifteen thousand and eighteen thousand human beings. The Persian army which had defeated the Turks near Erivan and had pursued the enemy westward fell prey to cholera. The soldiers retreated to Khoi in Iran, where they dispersed, disseminating the infection throughout the country. Cholera appeared in 1819 in Port Louis, Mauritius, where it had arrived with a ship from Trincomalee, Ceylon. The disease had broken out mid-ocean. It killed six thousand on the island within weeks. In 1829 cholera crossed the Chinese Wall, swept through Mongolia, and eventually traveled to Moscow. It sailed on the Arabian dhows that traded all along the shores of Arabia toward the East African coast. Cholera broke out among the troops of Said-bin-Sultan while they were attacking Bahrein. It broke out in Mecca in 1831 and killed some twelve thousand pilgrims. It appeared in Nicaragua and Guatemala and in New Orleans and Charleston, South Carolina. Cholera progressed along the trade route from Canton to Burma and branched south along the Irrawaddy River toward Rangoon in 1842. Cholera appeared in 1851 in Cuba and in the Grand Canary Island, where it caused nine thousand deaths in a few days.

Statistics, graphs, numbers of the dead disturb the mind but do not panic it. Piles of bodies lack conviction. It doesn't matter that we know the body stinks in death or that it bloats with gas as the hours pass. It doesn't matter that we know that each number on the chart, whether from a town or a city, a farm or a jungle, represents a single person who was necessary to himself, to a mate, to a child, to a friend, to a fiancé, to a mother. When the numbers grow so large, we can no longer imagine faces, arms and legs, necklaces and moles, haircuts and earlobes. When the numbers jump far out beyond our capacity to feel, they produce a numbness that is not so much protective as genuinely bored. This is natural. Even when the numbers of those lost to tidal wave, volcano, hurricane, train wreck, fire, flood, or war change their numerical account, are revised downward or upward, we are not shaken into a new conviction. Fear for ourselves comes slowly. The numbers may have been exaggerated or undercounted, but they always crash into the smallness of our imagination, our inability to hold reality in both hands at once. We mime horror at what we have heard, but our souls do not shake or tremble. Large numbers of bodies are in many ways far less upsetting than a single corpse. Anyone who could grasp the statistics, hold in their minds the fingers and toes, the lift of the bridge of the nose, the short finger of the left hand, of the three-billionth victim, would go mad. We are capable of mourning only one by one, and a mass grave leaves as light a touch on our hearts as none at all.

For now all was well in his family, all was as it should be. This made Dr. Malina uneasy. Something would shift, something in the fortunes of the family would change. He had no evidence for this premonition except his experience, or perhaps it was Alexandrian history that made him gloomy. He thought of the Macedonian who had taken the spit of land that was once an island empty of civilization. He thought of Antony, who died because Octavius defeated him, of Cleopatra, who died because she had backed the wrong general, and of the Ptolemys replaced by the Roman emperors, and of the Roman emperors replaced by the followers of Muhammad, and the Christian martyrs, a hundred thousand of them, slaughtered like chickens for a feast, and of the Jews beaten and mutilated by the angry Greeks, and of the Copts and the Catholics assassinating each other, and of the French chased by the British and the warships in the harbor with their loud guns and flags flying high or flags drawn down, and the wounded in the hospital and the bin of limbs that gathered in the basement awaiting disposal. He thought of General Arabi and his followers defeated in distant sandy battles. He thought of Alexander himself, lying under the streets, wrapped in gold cloth, resting in his glass coffin, bones now and dark air surrounding the sightless sockets where his eyes had been. He thought that something evil would come to his family, something that all his skills could not avoid.

With that he went to bed.

Lydia threw her arms around her daughter when, at the breakfast table, her daughter thrust out her hand. "Look, Mama, what Albert gave me last night." There was the diamond. It was raining hard, and water leaked in through the closed doors of the terrace.

"How lovely," said Lydia. It was of substantial size, but size, when it came to diamonds, was not the most important factor. But of course Albert would only have given his bride-to-be a diamond of the finest quality. He was in fact giving it to himself, since his wife's assets would become his, and his wife's financial security would be tied to his, and his father, a man of excellent reputation, would only allow his son to give his future daughter-in-law a ring worthy of the family name.

Mrs. Malina admired her daughter's ring. In its shiny surface she saw, like a fortune-teller reading the tea leaves, the best china plates, large silver candlesticks, a linen cabinet of silk sheets, a lifetime of choice cuts of lamb, servants folding laundry in the rear quarters, a courtyard with an orange tree and a lemon tree, and children with shining hair and dresses made from patterns sent from Paris and woven with fabrics brought over the seas from the Far East. As Lydia ate her breakfast she looked out her window and saw a yellow bird shielding itself against the rain between the ironwork on the balustrade and a potted plant whose long leaves shivered from the blows of so many drops of water descending.

An absurd impulse overcame her. She stood up, threw open the doors, and stepped out onto her terrace, letting the heavy rain soak her hair, stain dark her dress, run down her face in streams. The yellow bird flew off in terror as she stepped forward. She hung on to the balcony rail as though she were in a ship caught in a storm. Her shoes were damp and seemed to cling to her feet. Her hair came unglued from the pins that had held it up, and it floated down her back, dark and heavy, a few gray streaks at the temples. There is a looseness, a permission granted by the rain, that a woman of middle years needs now and then, a woman whose daughter is about to leave the house and furnish a home of her own. Such a woman knows more about the passage of time, the passion of love for those who no longer need you, the way you stare at the backs of departing children and memorize the slope of their bones, the length of their eyelashes, the way the love of the mother for her child is destined one way or the other to become a bruised love, a wounded love, an almost unrequited love, an unbalanced love, a suffering love. It was this that Lydia Malina was for a moment putting aside as she turned her face into the rain and allowed it to drench her very bones.

"Mama, what are you doing?" Este shouted out to her mother. "Come inside, close the doors, are you mad?" Lydia reentered the room, leaving a puddle on the very fine carpet that had come on a ship to Alexandria from Kashmir, imported by the Marbourg firm where she had placed Eric Fortman, who was such a gentleman, he had immediately sent her a huge bouquet of red roses to express his gratitude.

"What were you doing out there?" Este scolded her mother. Lydia had no words for it, the joy of standing in the pouring rain.

WITH AN ADVANCE on his salary Eric Fortman bought himself two new pairs of trousers, a jacket, and several shirts. He purchased socks and garters and boots. He told his landlady that he had been at sea, a representative of the Glen MacAlan Scotch Company for many years, but was starting a new life as an importer, a business-man, a person who remained in one place for years at a time. "Roots is it you want?" said his landlady.

"I just want to be dry," he said, because a man didn't admit to a woman that he was ready to be given his tea and wrapped in a pair of arms, ready to see the same yard year in and year out and maybe even to plant some seeds of his own.

Eric Fortman intended to become a merchant prince in no time at all. He had seen other men do it, one good purchase, a few good gambles and a man with nothing to his name, a man such as himself, a shipwreck of a man, could find himself on top of the heap, his bank account stuffed and his future assured. As it was, he now had an office at Marbourg & Sons on the quay in the Eastern Harbor.

He was ready now for his future. He walked about among the barrels of cumin and saffron and pickled herring and stepped carefully in his new boots as he made his way through the drying fishnets. He looked out at the harbor and saw the gulls that rested on the masts of ships gathering on the jetty's edge, and on the railings of steamships lolling in the water. He felt no regret. Home, he thought, was where England ruled, and England ruled in Alexandria, even if everyone spoke French. Cats may have nine lives, he considered, so he himself could certainly have two without disturbing the universe or calling forth the wrath of the gods.

His first assignment at Marbourg & Sons was to inspect the *Lorraine,* a ship that had pulled into port that morning and was now unloading its cargo on the left dock. The ship was to sail for Lisbon in a week with fifty barrels of Marbourg-owned powders that were meant to cure arthritis and stomach ailments and were made from the pits of pears from orchards in the valley of the upper Nile. Marbourg & Sons did not want to send this cargo on a ship that might go down, whose hull had rotted away, or whose crew was rebellious or stupid and might endanger the barrels through their actions. They wanted a ship whose furnace fired up without trouble and whose promise to deliver was not subject to revision or apology. Marbourg & Sons had had their share of disasters at sea and had learned to inspect ships before they set sail. They assumed that their new employee, Eric Fortman, having survived a disaster, would be able to distinguish between a good vessel and a weakened one. He was dispatched to check that all would be well with the expensive powders. A simple task, a simple matter, a beautiful day on the harbor, the lighthouse rose tall at the edge of the limestone ridge, the stones in the shallow water shimmered in the refracted rays of the sun.

Eric went on board, introduced himself to the captain of the ship, an Indian with a strange turban on his head who spoke a thick and heavily accented English. Despite his many years of travel with the barrels of whiskey sloshing in the hold below, he was not certain where the flaws in the ship would be found if they were there, but he knew how to chat up the men and ask a few key questions. He was perfectly able to pick up the mood of the sailors, angry or sad or hungry or undisciplined. He spent the morning looking at the condition of the pots in the scullery and the oars on the lifeboats, and he pulled on the ropes and checked knots and looked at the polish on the table. All was in order, he hoped. As he said his good-byes to the captain, the Indian placed a fat brown leather pouch in his hand. What was this?

"A thank-you for a good report," said the captain.

"Everything is fine," said Eric Fortman.

"I know, I know," said the Indian, "but it is our custom to thank you for your help in speeding us on our way."

Did he say speeding or spending, it was hard to be sure because of the Indian lilt to the sentence. Had his examination of the boat and its cargo been sufficiently rigorous?

Once on shore, Eric opened the pouch. It was filled with piastres, as well as some pounds. Was this money for Marbourg & Sons, he considered. It could not be. He had not been instructed to pick up any payments. It was for him. The tables had turned.

A FEW DAYS passed, and then one morning Este reappeared at the laboratory. Her maid, Anippe, waited outside the metal door. Her mother believed that she was spending the morning at the dressmakers. Este offered to wash and boil the glass beakers. Roux looked around for Marcus, who should have already completed this work, but who was late as usual. "Thank you," said Roux to Este.

Louis reported that there were no extraordinary deaths among the animals in Alexandria. The three men walked over to the rabbit cage. Este followed. The rabbits were nuzzling each other, scratching at the papers at the bottom of the cage. Drinking water from the small cups Edmund had placed there. These were not sick rabbits. They wrote down the condition of the rabbits in their notebooks. The rabbits had not contracted cholera yet.

Emile prepared more syringes filled with small drops of the victims' fluids pressed from tissue. They would inject the rats this time. It might be possible to grow the cholera on a dish prepared with beef broth and gelatin. Louis dropped some bowel matter into a beaker and added a small amount of water. With heated pincers he sealed off the neck of the glass container so no air could enter. He repeated this procedure until he had six beakers sitting on a shelf. Perhaps when they opened the beaker in a few days the cholera would be visible in the water.

Marcus burst into the laboratory. He wanted to go for a swim down at the shore. He talked about the cool water, the smooth sand, the long jetty, the red algae floating near, the red and blue panels of the cabana drapes, the turtles he had been told slept on the rocks.

"Go," said Roux.

"Please go," said Louis.

"Bring back a turtle," said Edmond. He was curious. The turtles of Egypt were said to be of a particularly large genus and were said to live five hundred years. Marcus went.

Roux wanted to talk to the family or lover or friend of a victim of cholera. The waiter at the café where he had gone for his cigarettes had told him that during the night the carts had come and taken off four more bodies right from the quarter in which he lived, as well as two children and a man who worked as a beekeeper at a big house at the end of rue de France. Roux needed to find out what they had eaten last. The cholera, like the fly on his pastry, might have been in the meat, the lettuce, the flour, some ingredient of their last meal. He needed to find out what they had eaten before they got sick. Emile was not as discouraged as one might think. He had a new idea. There was more cholera in Alexandria than when they had come.

AFTER THE EVENING meal, when her father was reading his paper, Este came to him and said, "Papa, I would like to be of service to the French scientists."

"I'm sure they would appreciate it," said her father. "Are you going to give them a party?"

"No," said Este. "I meant I would like to go to the laboratory and do whatever I can do to speed their work."

Dr. Malina put down his paper. "But you know nothing of science," he said. "I thought you liked poetry. You wanted that Keats book for your birthday. You said you were more interested in poetry than anything else in the world."

"I did say that," said Este, "but I was younger."

Dr. Malina smiled. "And now," he said, "you want to help the scientists. What do they say?"

"They say they would like my assistance. They will explain things to me. I am a quick learner."

"It is dangerous work," he said.

"Your work is dangerous," she answered. "I will be careful."

"Tell your mother I gave my permission," he said, "but you must take Anippe with you. It will not look right otherwise."

Lydia Malina was not disturbed by this plan. Soon enough her daughter would be married and have other things to think about besides the French scientists and their laboratory. Most likely she would be bored in a few days and this new interest would pass. It was agreed that she would continue to do those things required for her wedding as well as continue her German lessons, a language for which she seemed to have a gift.

"I think," said Louis to Este, who had been waiting at the laboratory door when he arrived as the light was filling the sky, "I will examine the droppings of the birds on our roof this afternoon." He had discovered that above the slanting roof of the lab a flock of starlings had settled. If he listened carefully he could hear their shrill whistle, their two-toned call as they landed or took off. He could see the droppings on the side of the building, a white stain with a brownish center. Just this morning he had found a dead member of the bird community in the alley. It had already been torn apart by a rat or some other sharp-toothed creature that lived in the holes in the stones that formed the gutter of the street. A thousand insects were crawling across the bird's now-mangled chest. One wing had broken off from the rest of the body, and its bone had been eaten bare. An eye was torn from its head, and its feathers were flattened, as if a cart wheel had rolled over them. The droppings might hold the cholera, if the bird had died of cholera, but perhaps the bird had died of old age, or had eaten a poisonous plant. He intended to examine the droppings. He might be able to grow the microbe from the droppings in a pure culture. He could warm up his glass, he could sprinkle lye on the concoction. He could try.

Este was holding a pail and standing in the narrow alley. The plan was for Louis to throw down anything he wanted to keep and she would place it in the pail. On the roof, the birds rose on their wings and flew off to look for food in the alleys where the garbage lay, sometimes in sacks but most often just jumbled together and tossed, waiting for time and the rays of sun that managed to seep into the narrow lanes, and the flush of rain that would come now and then, especially in the rainy season, to carry off the bones, the leaves, the roots, the shells, the meats of nuts, the lumps of gruel, the ends of bread, the unwanted food. The starlings returned to the roof and shared their pickings with their young, and sometimes they fought over a fragment of rice, a grain of wheat, a fish head, a bony tail. They squawked and fluffed out their chests in efforts to intimidate one another. If they were ill with cholera they did not seem to stop, lie down, change their tune. All they did was pause in their activities and release their droppings onto the roof or the side of the building or the dirt below. There would be ample intestinal syrup to study with the microscope, and they did have the dead starling that had fallen so providentially right outside the laboratory.

Roux prepared the slides with ooze from the small bird. He mashed its brains. He picked up tissue from under its wings, carefully marking left and right. He examined the tiny beak and looked at the multiple small bones. Nocard prepared the dishes in which they would put the retrieved substances. Would anything grow? Was there cholera in the smashed bird? They injected some bird flesh into the dog. He growled as they approached. Some days went by. Nothing grew in the dishes. The dog was not affected. He had begun to yelp in pleasure now as Marcus, half awake after a night in which for the first time he smoked a soothing brew in a water pipe, brought him his lunch.

All three Frenchmen had grown used to Este's questions. When had the cholera first appeared in Alexandria? They told her what they had been told by Pasteur. Cholera had appeared in Egypt in April. It appeared first at a fair in Damietta, which was situated at one of the mouths of the Nile not far from Port Said, or perhaps it came on the ships that stopped at Amsterdam. Or were the pilgrims returning from Mecca once again responsible?

How did it travel? Louis could not give Este a firm answer. Cholera had been carried to Alexandria by some means. It was not on these shores a year ago, or five years ago. He needed to consider its means of transportation. It could have come by ship, of course. Could it have come from the desert on the sand on a man's sandals? It could also have been carried in the clouds and spilled on the city by rain. Was that possible? Had anyone considered that possibility? He doubted it. He would check the rainwater. "Emile," he asked, "could it be in the rain?"

Emile did not have an immediate response. He was silent for a few minutes. The idea did not seem right to him, but he had learned that a careful demonstration was better than his instincts, which had their limitations. "Why not?" he said.

Louis went into the alley outside the hospital's surgical ward and followed the line of gutter pipe. He climbed on the windowsill and from there pulled himself up on the slanting rooftop. In the pipe he saw some leaves, with bird droppings and rainwater clinging to them. He scooped up the debris and attempted to climb down. It was slippery on the roof. He had only one hand to grasp the red tiles. He moved very carefully and slowly. A seagull circled above, perhaps curious or perhaps sighting something edible below.

Back in their laboratory, his coattails soaked with dirt and his hands covered with slime, he put his prize down on the lab table and proceeded to take drops of the water and place them on glass and peer at them through the microscope. He saw a small mite with wings. He recognized the mite. It was not cholera. He saw nothing move, nothing swim, but it was hard to make out the forms on his glass because the water was dark and viscous from the disintegrating membranes of the leaves. It might be in there, his prize. He took drop after drop and examined it. He used Pasteur's filter, removing the larger forms like twig and leaf and worm remains. Hours went by. Este went out and returned with some cheese and a pastry. Emile was placing a culture of rabbit feces and boiled water in a jar. What might grow? Louis didn't want to stop to eat. He saw nothing. How was he to get the water clear of the leaves? He must find the microbe alive. He put the water through the filter, which served as a sieve, and pressed out the thickest part of the leafy substance, but the water was still not clear. He threw his gutter water into a barrel and rushed out into the street, calling to Marcus to search the garden of the hotel or to look in the park over by Lake Mariout. He had to find clear rainwater. It had to have gathered somewhere where it was protected from leaves. He walked through the alley. He saw an abandoned chamber pot filled with fluid. Some rainwater had mixed in there, but it was not clear. He walked to the café. He looked out back; perhaps they had discarded a bottle that had filled with rainwater. They had not. He walked toward the wharf, where a fisherman's bucket that he used for storing fish bones or heads might have been out in the boat and picked up the rain and kept it clear. It would have been easy to find clear rainwater if he hadn't been looking, wanting it in the way that he did.

On her way home Este came upon a boot, a single boot that was sitting behind a bench. How had the boot been left by its mate? Had a one-legged man decided to go barefoot? Had the leather chafed or pinched the single foot of its owner? This she couldn't determine, but she took the boot and carefully carried it into her house and into the kitchen, where the maid gave her a glass jar. She took her prize to her room and poured the water in the boot into the jar.

Hours later, as darkness set in and the gas lamps of the cafés at the edge of Lake Mariout flickered and the dancing girls were painting their faces and the women of the city were stirring things on a stove, and smells came from windows of almonds and dates and lamb soaked in thyme, while the feathers of plucked chickens drifted down the gutters of alleyways along with the unwanted parts, necks and feet, livers and spleens, Louis and Roux and Nocard went to the French Café. Louis said to Nocard, "There are no women in this café."

"There are many woman in this café," said Nocard.

"I mean no one special."

The two older men looked at their younger colleague in surprise. Defiantly he looked back. "I mean," he said, "no one as special as Este Malina."

There was silence at the table.

LOUIS TOOK DROPS of water from Este's boot. Would he find the cholera? The water was almost clear; under the glass he saw a few flat shapes that did not move. He looked again and again. He tried different drops. He mixed a blue acid with the water in the hope that the tiny cholera would absorb the dye and stand out clearly. Nothing. He was discouraged. He could not test every drop of rainwater that fell from the sky. The fact that it was not in this shoe did not mean it was not in the rain somewhere, in some part of the city.

How else might it have come to Alexandria? Birds did not fly across oceans. It would not be in birds. But then he considered. Birds drank rainwater. Perhaps cholera did not make them sick but remained in their tissue nevertheless. If the cholera were in the rainwater, perhaps it was also in a bird. "Marcus," he called, "we are going to look for more dead birds. Perhaps we will shoot some."

Marcus sighed. He was not happy. "You don't have a gun," he said. "You don't know how to shoot." Louis's father had not admired men with guns. He was a man of the town, not the woods.

Louis said, "I don't think you can just shoot birds in the park. I will get Dr. Malina to go with us. He will know how we can capture a bird."

"You want to buy a chicken in the market?" Marcus asked.

"No," said Louis, "I want a wild bird, one that has been drinking from hollows in tree trunks or puddles formed by stones or swallowing water in the lake with his fish." Suddenly Louis felt certain that he would find cholera in the wild birds. He would see the tiny microbe move across his slide. How would it move? Would it float? Would it have legs? Would it divide itself in two? He would send a telegram to Pasteur announcing his victory.

"Find out," he said to Marcus, "where we send a telegram. Is there a telegraph office near?"

"You want me to do that now?" asked Marcus.

"Don't bother me," said Louis, "I'm thinking." He was thinking about Este. When she arrived at the laboratory he would tell her about his new hope.

So it was that Dr. Malina, leaving his house before dawn, accompanied Louis and Marcus along the road to Aboukir. Nocard did not shoot. He had rejected the invitation to join them. Emile

wanted to work with his bowl of feces. They crossed the Mahmoudian Canal and took the road alongside the railway tracks,
past the grand villas and castle of a former pasha, into the sand and
swamps that marked the route to Cairo. They had with them two
guns that had belonged to Dr. Malina's father. These were kept at
the shooting club of which Dr. Malina was a member in good
standing, even though he had not had time to visit the club for
more than half a dozen occasions a year. These not very modern
weapons had been handed to two servants to defend the women of
the house at the time of the rioting a year before, when the British
ships had sent thundering canon balls into the town, blasting
the walls of the dike and smashing down the castle that stood on the
ground of the great lighthouse, the Pharos that had once been the
pride of all Alexandrians.

"The British," said Dr. Malina, "have no respect for other people's homes." Louis easily agreed. "The stones are still crumbling
from their clumsy diplomacy," said Dr. Malina.

Never sorry to hear the British scorned, Louis asked what had
happened. Dr. Malina told him, "It was the fault of the followers
of General Arabi. They thought they could yell the foreigners
out of the land. Arabi inspired them, a false prophet. In the days
following the British assault they turned into savages, wild animals. The shopkeepers, the carriage drivers, the cobblers and
tobacco salesmen, the porters on the docks, the makers of rope
and the spinners of cloth, the servants in the houses, the clerks in
the businesses that lined the wharves, all went berserk. Not just
the Arabs, but the Italians, and Greeks, and Germans, too, went
wild. They took what they wanted in the fires that followed the
shelling. Look at the Grand Square, it is hardly itself. The great
consulates were reduced to bare walls, and the shops were emptied of goods. They screamed and howled at the sky and they ran

through the streets smashing windows. No one was in charge, no one could stop the screaming and the stealing. It was as if the city were trying to eat itself up, to devour its own avenues. There were fires everywhere. I went to the hospital to keep the looters away from our patients and our supplies, but they pushed me over and raided our pantries and carried off blankets and sheets and jars of jelly and pounds of eggs. I looked one of those thieves in the eye and I called him a coward and he hit me in the jaw. Nothing serious, of course."

"How many were there?" asked Louis.

"Enough," said Dr. Malina, whose lips were drawn tight in memory. "They tried to burn down our house of worship, but they were stopped."

The British didn't come on shore. For many hours they stayed in their boats and watched through their spyglasses. Dr. Malina was not fond of the British. Neither was Louis. This they had in common.

They found a marsh that seemed to stretch out miles in the distance. Long grasses grew by its shore. No sign of human life. A string of birds flew low over the muddy water. "Shoot," called Marcus. Louis lifted his rifle. He missed. He hesitated. The line of birds went past. They drove a little way farther and the road grew narrow and almost impassable. Dr. Malina got out of the carriage and the three of them sat down on a rock. Two large geese alighted in front of them, unaware of danger, trusting to the breeze in the air, the smell of small fish gathering in pools underneath their feet. Dr. Malina picked up one of the guns and aimed at the birds. The largest one fell first. The second opened its wings in panic and rose on its spindly legs, but it, too, was shot and tipped over into the water, sinking down into the mud.

Marcus was dispatched to get the birds and put them in a

pouch. "How did you learn to shoot?" said Louis, who did not think most doctors hunted.

"I am not a trusting man," said Dr. Malina. "We have had our troubles here. But I trust you to make good use of these fowl. Let me know what you find."

"I will," promised Louis.

On the ride back to town, Louis asked Dr. Malina, "Is it better here now that the British have taken over the city?"

"As many people as ever need my services," said Dr. Malina. He sat back in his seat and closed his eyes. The two men were silent. The wheels turned on the road, a donkey brayed in the grass by the railroad tracks. A train came by and released black puffs of smoke into the sky. Louis said something, but the train whistle sounded and Dr. Malina did not hear or respond to his words.

With high expectations, Louis took the geese to the laboratory and watched as Marcus plucked the feathers, reserving a handful for examination, and placed them in a sack, which he later dumped into a large box of hospital waste—bandages, syringes, and empty ointment tubes—which he had found in one of the corridors of the basement.

"Should we cook the birds for dinner?" asked Marcus. "After you're done with them, of course."

Louis shook his head. He did not want science confused with cooking, although there were many similarities in the practice of each.

He had to begin by cutting into the bird on the table. He pulled out its intestines, and scraped a little of its spleen onto his glass. Would it be there? What small creatures were moving still in his goose? The bird's body was not yet rigid, and the tiny creatures that always eat the dead had not yet arrived. Maybe he would find his cholera.

Hours later the two geese had been finely chopped, their inards examined on slides. Dye had been placed on the slides. Este had helped him prepare the slides. He had shown her how to carefully boil the glass, holding the tongs as far from her body as possible. There were microbes in the tissues, all right, but when they were cultured in the gelatine-filled glass, they seemed to die almost immediately. When placed inside the rabbit Nocard had selected for this purpose, nothing happened to the rabbit, whose pink nose wrinkled, whose ears pricked up at the sound of his footsteps, who seemed to greet him affectionately even though he had injected into the creature something that should have caused cholera. Five days passed and the rabbit nibbled on grass and the geese rotted inside a box and nothing happened, no cholera.

This was a dead end. It had not been a bad idea, but it had led nowhere. He needed a new idea. Where did ideas come from? Would he get another idea, or was he dry like a well in a time of drought? He tried to force an idea to come into his mind. He opened his notebook and wrote down again everything that he had tried and that had not worked. Failure should teach him something; this he had learned from Dr. Pasteur. No failure was wasted. Cholera seemed not to jump from one person to another because of simple proximity. The wives and husbands of cholera victims did not necessarily fall ill with the disease. Those taking care of the ill sometimes became ill, but often did not. This meant that air itself was not the carrier of the disease, breath of the victim was not dangerous. But what was and why? He threw himself down in his chair, and a snatch of music came to him, a childhood song his mother used to sing, something about a baby squirrel eating a nut his mother brought to him. He hummed the tune. He had forgotten the words. He thought about his favorite soup. He fell into a light sleep. He could almost hear himself breathing in his sleep. He woke with a start. A black fly was sitting on his eyelid.

ESTE WOKE IN the morning and looked at herself in the mirror. She was satisfied by what she saw. She was eager to get to the laboratory. Everything there was interesting. It was all strange and new. She was useful. She knew she was useful. But of course she couldn't stay there all the time. She put her hand up to the mirror and saw her diamond reflected in the glass. She was to be a married woman, a person whose word must be taken seriously. She would give orders in her own house. She would invite Phoebe over to afternoon tea. She would sleep in the biggest bed in the house. She would have her favorite desserts every night. What a shame she could not show her ring to her brother. She would be the first to make a success of herself, although everyone always thought so much of him and now he was far away and possibly would never return and she would be the only child the family had. These, she understood, were not exactly proper thoughts. She erased them as soon as she thought them. She dressed herself and went downstairs. "Mama," she said on seeing her mother at the breakfast table, "we must get started on my wedding dress."

The next day she and her mother were looking at sketches of wedding dresses that had been sent by boat from Paris to Lydia's sister's stepdaughter last season, when an unexpected visitor was announced. It was Eric Fortman, who wanted to express again his gratitude to Lydia for having found him a place in the Marbourg firm, giving him a second chance, opening the door for his happiness, and so on. The man was so grateful he not only kissed Lydia's hand but placed in her lap a box of the toffee that was sold at exorbitant prices on the rue Rosette, saying the roses he had sent were not enough. Lydia blushed. Este told Eric to sit down and tell them a story he had heard in his travels. Este rang the bell, and from the kitchen the maid brought another setting for the table and offered Eric a hot roll and some jam. He told them of an island where the natives had coal black skin and none wore clothes except for necklaces made of large pink and white seashells, where giant tortoises crawled along the beach, and where the children hung from slings made of palm leaves in their mother's arm. Monkeys lived in the huts with the people, and small green and yellow birds sat on the shoulders of the children. They had no marriage on this island, no priests to tell people what to do.

The women were appalled. "Did you make this up, just to shock us?" Lydia asked.

"Of course not," he said.

"Did you see this yourself?" asked Este.

"No, ma'am," said Eric, "but I heard about it in Toulouse when I was introducing some café owners to the virtues of Glen MacAlan scotch." He helped himself to another roll and some more butter.

"Savages," said Lydia, in a voice fierce enough to make Eric move his chair back a few inches.

Este said to her mother, "They probably wouldn't think too much of you, either."

Eric laughed. The girl had spirit. The girl was glowing. Virginal juices running, of course. He would have to make a fortune for a girl like that. He had spent his life among salesmen and their customers. He did not know much about the ways of women in the parlors, with drapes at the window and chairs with little monkey paws for legs, and he knew nothing of Jews, who he had never before realized had wives and mothers and daughters, too, just like everyone else. He had thought of them as peddlers who had sprung full grown from some dark place in ruined cities ready to take advantage of decent men who had fallen on bad times. He had been mistaken.

In his laboratory, Louis waited for Este to arrive. He was disappointed as the hours passed and it became clear she was not coming. "Perhaps she has fallen ill," said Louis to Nocard.

"She has other things to do, my friend. She does not belong to us." Nocard said this kindly. "We're a temporary amusement for her, that's all."

"Too bad," said Roux, "she has a good way with her hands. She works well. Perhaps she'll be back tomorrow."

Louis said nothing.

9

I T WAS FORTUNATE, perhaps, that most cholera victims never made it to the hospital. It was fortunate that most of the poor in Alexandria did not think of the hospital when they fell ill. They returned to their beds and died there, leaving the problem of the bodies and the sheets and the foul smells to those they loved and left behind. Nevertheless, the hospital was full.

A child had died no longer than fifteen minutes ago on Ward B. The chief administrator wrote a quick note to the Sister of Charity who sat in a chair at the ward's door, and stamped it with his seal. She showed the Frenchman to the bed on which a little boy lay, his hand still in his mother's, although she could no longer offer him comfort.

How were they to get this child away from his mother? Emile

and Louis had no reason to be embarrassed. No harm could come to the child now. Louis, however, *was* embarrassed. He pulled on the stem of his unlit pipe and coughed a small anxious cough. Emile put his hand gently on the mother's shoulder. "Madame," he began, "I am Emile Roux, and this is my colleague, Louis Thuillier. We are scientists from Paris, from the École Normale, the laboratory of the famous Dr. Pasteur. We are searching for the cause of the cholera that has just taken your little boy. If you let us have him, we would appreciate it. He will help us in our cause. He will be a hero." The woman said nothing. She threw herself on the body of her child. She grasped the side of the cot. She would not look at them or speak to them.

"She won't," said Roux. The two men went back to the lab.

An hour later there was a knock on the door. It was the sister from Ward B. "We have another child," she said, "without a mother or a father, found on the quay an hour ago. He was alive when brought in, but no longer. You could have him." The sister peered around Louis and stared at the oven and the glasses and the autoclave and the gas lamps. She heard the dog barking in his cage at the new intruder. She saw the rabbits. She let out a long sigh. "Hurry," she said. They followed her.

Louis picked up the child, whose hair was matted and whose sunken eyes revealed the small shape of his skull as if the grave had already done its work.

Once back in the laboratory, they cut some tissue from the child's arm. As they began, there was a knock on the door. Este was there. She turned pale when she saw the child on the table, but did not hesitate to steady the small chest as Roux cut out some bowel. It was not easy to do. Roux had never done this to a human being before. He pushed away a wave of nausea. He pulled out some bowel and put it in a bowl.

"We should take the brain and the heart and the lung," said Louis.

"Yes," said Roux.

The two men worked for three hours, very carefully. Este brought them bowls and jars and recorded carefully the part and the date, with a large *I* on each note. The *I* stood for Italian, because the child seemed to her to have come from the Italian community.

Nocard joined them. He drilled a hole in the side of the head and, with a syringe, pulled out tissue that might be valuable. Este, no longer pale, labeled the brain tissue.

For Louis, there was transgression in this act. No matter how he reassured himself that his purpose was noble and the child would have a finer destiny under his knife than he ever had enjoyed in his living days, he could not entirely repress his fear of the ghosts that lingered around the graveyard of Amiens and his reverence for the holiness of the human soul and his fear of retribution by some watching fate that might not approve of his disrespect of the child's body. He saw the boy's small male genitals and averted his eyes.

Nocard took a small knife and pulled out the child's left eye and placed it in a jar Este offered him. Este shook the jar so she could see the eye from every angle. Edmond was very interested in diseases of the eye. He had puzzled over them often in the collies that accompanied shepherds to the fields.

Later they closed up the skin as best they could, covering the many places where they had entered the body. They pulled a blanket over what remained of the child's face. Este washed down the table and boiled the cloth that she used to do it. Roux said to her, "Thank you for your work."

She was pleased. Louis had said nothing, but he looked at her with fondness in his dark eyes. She left. It was time she went home. Her mother would begin to worry. Anippe, who always accompanied her, was leaning against Marcus in the alley. The two of them smelled of sweat. "Hurry up," Este said to the maid. When they reached the square, they found a carriage.

Este washed her hands again and again before changing into her dress for dinner. She did not feel sad, which was curious. She did not feel tired, which was also a surprise. Perhaps it was silly of her, a conceit that was bred of exaggeration, but she was convinced that she was changed, altered, improved. She was a new person who only seemed to be the old one. She had seen the human body as it really was, a tangle of blood and tissue, purple matted bulges that ran from leg to heart, from brain to finger. She had not been useless. She wanted to tell her mother about her day, but thought better of it. She would not even tell her father.

The men were tired. What were they going to do with the remains of the body? Nocard went back to the apartment and brought his own smoking robe. The three men wrapped the body in it. It was easy for Louis to carry the body out the back entrance without being noticed. It was late at night, and the shops on the street were closed. A few carriages went down the main avenue, but none came in the side street.

Emile took the wrapped body from Louis when they reached the Eastern Harbor. He pulled off the robe and waded out into the softly breaking waves. Louis and Nocard took off their shoes and joined him. Together they pushed the small body far enough into the waves so that it didn't return to shore on the next lip of foam. There were no carriages on the street. They walked along like three friends out for a night's frolic. Finally they arrived at the hospital and made their way back to their laboratory through the silent corridors. After cutting off a small piece of the robe's inner fabric for later examination, they burned the cloth in their oven. Smoke billowed out across the room. With it came a smell of scorched cotton. They washed their hands in freshly boiled water. Emile fell asleep in his chair. Nocard went back to the apartment to sleep. Louis couldn't sleep and he couldn't sit in his chair by his lab bench. He was too tired to work, too tired to think, but still unable to close his eyes. He wanted to say some words, a prayer. But what words, what prayer? He had wanted to tell Este that she had been a help, that he was glad she had been at the laboratory, but the words had not come. Why, he wondered was it easy for some men to say the right thing and hard for others? Was something wrong with him that he was most quiet when he most wanted to make an impression?

He was a logical man, and there was no logical reason for the anxious way he paced the room. But there was an illogical reason. He had behaved like a grave robber. He had behaved like an insane criminal. There had been such a case in a village not so far from Amiens, it was in the papers, a lunatic who chopped up his victims either to hide his crime or to achieve some unholy pleasure. Louis defended himself against the accusation of sacrilege, but of course it was he himself who made the accusation. A scientist should not fear God's judgment; that was for priests and mothers.

In the morning the three men washed and shaved, changed their clothes, and ate breakfast at their regular café. They were all suddenly full of high spirits, hope had returned. Surely they had harvested the cholera microbe. It was waiting for them.

ON SUNDAY, ESTE did not go to the laboratory. She and her mother went to a birthday luncheon for Madame Clotilde Auguste, who had been the headmistress at Este's school, a school for Jewish girls in Alexandria, with an emphasis on French culture and the domestic arts. The luncheon was held at the home of one of the graduates of the school who had married a lawyer who now worked for the Crown, representing their interests in issues of maritime law. The women were dressed in pinks and beige, in lace blouses and silk skirts. It was a great pleasure for Este and Lydia to see what everyone else was wearing. The table was set with crystal glasses and Limoges plates. The silverware was monogrammed, and Este admired the tiny silver saltcellars that were in the shape of swans with silver wings that actually moved. The windows were open and the wind blew hard and occasionally a shutter would slam, startling everyone. Nevertheless, the summer heat was heavy. The women drank orange juice with slices of lemon floating at the top of each glass. Este showed off her ring to her former classmates. They were impressed. Este was the first among them to be engaged.

"Are you so happy you can't breathe?" asked one.

Este said, "I can breathe."

"Do you dream of him every night?" asked another.

Este paused. She did not dream of Albert. "I never remember my dreams," she said.

The young women talked of linens and glassware. The older women talked about their children. They boasted without seeming to boast, this one is giving me such headaches because he can't decide whether to take his exams in philosophy or architecture.

"I have had such wonderful letters from Jacob," Lydia said. The hours of the afternoon passed swollen with heat, eased with conversation.

Madame Clotilde kissed Este on both cheeks. "You are beautiful," she said.

"As are you, madame," Este replied.

"I've heard," said Ruth, who had been in the class behind Este, "the Arabs are savages in Jerusalem and there are no conveniences and the hotels are dirty and Jerusalem belongs to thieves and kidnappers. They don't even receive the papers from Paris or Moscow until six months after they're published, can you imagine?"

Another young woman interrupted, "Your brother had to leave Alexandria. He must be lonely without his family."

"He's well," said Este, "very well." Her eyelids felt heavy. She was bored. She wished she had gone to the laboratory. She was never bored there. She thought of Louis bending down to pick up a beaker, his fingers gently placed around the glass neck, his head turning to look at her looking at him. She was no longer lethargic. A strange new sensation seized her body. It was not unpleasant, but it was alarming.

A pastry with almonds and honey was passed around by the maid. "Delicious," said Lydia.

"Wonderful," said Este.

"If only it would rain," said Madame Auguste.

"The fish from the lake are dying on the shore. The lake is so shallow," said Este's friend Margarette, whose family came to Alexandria from Amsterdam.

"It always is, this time of year," said Lydia.

Sunday afternoon, while his wife and daughter were out, Dr. Malina read in his Macnamara about the history of the 1817 outbreak of cholera in India.

According to a conclusion arrived at in 1819 by the Bengal Medical Board, "the proximate cause of the disease consisted in a pestilential virus, which acted primarily upon the stomach and the small intestines and the depressed state of the circulatory powers and diminished action of the heart were consequent on the severe shock which the system had received in one of its principal organs."

Dr. Malina put down the heavy book and picked up to read again the paper sent to him by the Committee of Public Safety. It was written in 1849 by John Snow, the English naturalist.

The morbid matter of cholera having the property of reproducing its own kind must necessarily have some sort of structure, most likely that of a cell. It is no objection to this view that the structure of the cholera poison cannot be recognized by the microscope for the matter of smallpox and chancre can only be recognized by their effects and not by their properties. The most important means of preventing the progress of cholera is that the poison which continues to be generated in the bodies of infected persons should be destroyed by mixing the discharges with some chemical compound such as sulfate of iron or chloride of lime, known to be fatal to beings of the fungus tribe.

If only all this scientific exchange would have resulted in finding the cause and the cure. Perhaps there were limits to what man could do. Perhaps cholera would evade the lens, evade Pasteur and Koch, hide from them all and never reveal its shape, its secret. He was not a pessimist by nature. He quickly shook off that thought. What use was it?

MARCUS WAS DOWN on the docks, inquiring about signing on as cabin boy, kitchen boy, waterboy, whatever, on a ship headed for Toulouse or Normandy. He had had enough of this strange country, and he didn't want to be a member of the French mission anymore. He wanted to go home. He wanted to go away from the strange smells and the corpses of creatures that he was obliged to carry off to some remote spot, staining himself with their blood. No matter how often he washed his hands, he never felt clean. He had had enough of this city in which cholera could take a person's girl in the middle of the act, spoiling everything, terrifying him even in his sleep, where he kept seeing the stained yellow cloth of her dress appearing at the corner of his vision and waving to him as if it were greeting him. There must be a port somewhere without cholera and without the shadow of Pasteur following him—and no Thuillier, no Nocard, no Roux—where no one had ever heard of a microscope. He was headed there.

LYDIA MALINA SAT down at her dressing table and reached into a back drawer that was hidden by the drapes of cloth that formed a skirt around the table. She pulled out a purple case. In it were her pearls, the same pearls she had received when she became engaged to the young doctor Abraham Malina. These were not her mother's pearls. Those had actually been stolen when the family was crossing the Mediterranean when a wave of anti-Semitism had erupted in Ulm, where her grandfather had sold furniture bought at auction, very fine furniture, out of a barn set up to resemble a nobleman's home. It had, Lydia's mother had told her, a six-foot-wide crest on the door, with two blue herons curling their claws around golden spears. These pearls had been fastened about Lydia's neck the evening before her own wedding to Abraham Malina by an uncle who had been in the jewelry business in Amsterdam and had come to the wedding in Alexandria because of his interest in antiquities as well as to set up some business possibilities.

Lydia Malina had decided to give the pearls to her daughter. Este watched her mother pull out the purple case. She threw her arms around her mother when she saw the contents. But when she tried them on, both women saw instantly that Este, who was taller than her mother, was also broader, and the pearls seemed unimpressive and almost choked her. "We have to add to them," said Lydia.

So, one morning, despite the fact that Este wanted to go to the laboratory and had tried to postpone the errand, the two women, with the best and most innocent of intentions, sat at the counter at Goldstein and Brothers, Jewelers, on rue Rosette. "These are for my daughter's marriage. We need to enlarge, add to the string, match them up exactly," Lydia explained.

The co-owner of the store, one Robert Kremetz, noticed the ring on Este's finger. "You are to be congratulated," he said.

Este smiled her most brilliant smile. "Thank you," she said, and modestly looked away from his staring eyes.

"What a large and extraordinary ring," he said. "May I look at it closely?" He wanted an excuse to hold her hand.

"Of course," she said.

He brought her hand up to his eye. Something did not seem exactly right. Tactfully he said, "Dearest lady, I need to look at your ring with my jeweler's glass."

"Why?" said Lydia. "Is something wrong?"

"Most likely not," he said, "but I think I should look nevertheless."

Este smiled at him again. She did not doubt for a moment that her ring was perfect.

"Will you have a glass of lemonade while you wait?" he asked.

The servant he summoned appeared with a silver tray and two glasses of lemonade, each with a slice of lemon floating on the top.

"Thank you," said Lydia. "That's very thoughtful." But she was too worried about what Robert Kremetz might find when he examined the ring to drink. Este did not like lemonade. She left her glass sitting on the tray. She ignored the small piece of chocolate imported from Sienna that rested beside the glass. She was looking at herself in the mirror.

In a blink of an eye she would be an old woman, older than her mother, in her grave. It seemed wrong that time could not be stopped in its tracks. Her finger felt bare, even though she had only worn her ring for a few days. "I think," she said to her mother, "your Eric likes you more than he should."

Lydia turned her head away. "It's you he likes," she said.

"Don't be ridiculous," Este answered. "I'm far too young for him, and besides, I'm engaged to be married."

"So much the worse for him," said Lydia. And she added, "He is not one of us."

Este saw Robert coming through the curtain that separated the back room from the front of the store. He was looking puzzled. It was his duty, his honor, to tell the women the bad news, but he knew that their anger might fall on his head.

"Ladies," he said, "it is my solemn duty—"

Este interrupted him with a small laugh. "Oh, please, don't be so solemn." But then she looked at his face and saw that he really was serious, very serious.

"This ring"—he handed it back to Este—"is a very flawed diamond. In fact, it is worth no more than the setting, which itself is actually brass."

"I don't believe it," said Este.

"There's been a mistake, I'm sure," said Lydia, who wasn't so sure. "Look again," she insisted. "Perhaps there is something wrong with your glass."

Robert brought out his glass and a blue velvet cushion. Este placed the ring on the cushion and he bent over it with the jeweler's loupe in his eye. "There you can see it," he said.

"I hardly see anything," said Este, when he offered his glass to her.

"Look," he said, and he took out a gold key and opened a cabinet door and removed a tray of glistening diamonds of many sizes. He picked one of a similar size to the one they were examining. He placed it on a red cushion and pinned it down with a curved pin just in case he should turn his back and the ladies should think to make a switch. He trusted them, of course, but he trusted no one absolutely, which was a mark of the professionalism on which he prided himself.

Este looked. Lydia looked. "I'm sorry," said Robert Kremetz. He asked if they would like to look at pearls. But the mother and daughter both shook their heads. This was no time for pearls. Perhaps I shouldn't have told them, the jeweler thought to himself as he watched their straight backs walk out of his store, each of the women pretending that nothing of importance had happened.

They would be back. He sat in synagogue two rows in front of Dr. Malina. He had served as president of the synagogue and was honored every year because of his contributions to the building fund—the endless building fund. They would not go to another jeweler. But they would rely on his discretion, and discreet he would be. In certain ways a jeweler had to be like a priest, a keeper of secrets.

A LETTER WITH foreign stamps arrived in the post. It was from Jacob. Lydia took it upstairs to her bedroom to read. She sat down at her dressing table and then, with quick fingers, tore open the envelope. Jacob had had a fever, but it seemed to have passed. "Don't worry, Mother," he said. "Many people have fevers here."

He had used quinine, which had helped. He had obtained a small warehouse in Jaffa where he would store the olives he would purchase and begin the process of making oil. He had ordered a press from Istanbul, which should arrive soon. He would send her a sample as soon as his firm was operating. He had found a partner who had given the Czar's army the slip and was a man of great energy. All would be well. "Hope you and father are content, and tell Este I miss her. There was an article in the English paper about cholera in Alexandria. I couldn't tell from the report if the outbreak is serious. As you can imagine, my finances are low with all the starting expenses. If you would replenish my account, it would be helpful at this critical moment. Affectionately, your son, Jacob."

Lydia imagined Jacob's warehouse. She saw his name over the door on a large red sign. She thought of him lying on his bed, the sheets wet with his fever. She wanted to go to Palestine. That was where she belonged. But that was not where she belonged. Jacob would have to return to Alexandria for Este's wedding. But he might be too busy. He might not come. She had a headache. She sent the servant to Dr. Malina's clinic. She needed to see him immediately. By the time he came to her bedside an hour and a half later her headache had gone. All that remained was an irritable feeling, having as much to do with Este's worthless ring as her distant son.

THE BRITISH OFFICER in charge of the customhouse had heard from one of his informants that several thousand pounds of hashish were to be brought ashore in the late evening. He dressed his men as Greek fishermen and spaced them far apart on the empty beach. Around midnight, clearly seen under the bright moon, a small skiff appeared and men covered in scarves pulled their boat up on the shore and began unloading barrels. The British officer did not tell his men to move in for the arrest. He waited until all the barrels were loaded on the donkey carts that appeared as if by magic out of the darkness. He and his men followed the carts at a safe distance to a glass factory down one of the many narrow alleys in the Arab quarter. There they arrested everyone they saw, including Marcus, who had agreed to aid the smugglers because he would be paid. He had been offered the work by a new friend from the Arab quarter whom he had met on the beach and with whom he had shared a bottle of cheap wine. The British arrested the woman who was leaving the brothel two doors down, and the glassblower, who had no business at his place of work at that time of night. Among their catch was the Arab boy who worked for Dr. Malina. In fact the boy kept insisting that Dr. Malina would post his bail if someone just notified him. The name rang a bell with the arresting officer, who had chased a thief to the doctor's surgery some months before. The doctor had given up his patient reluctantly, insisting that medical attention be supplied him, pushing a clean bandage into a soldier's hand. The Malina name was recognized by the higher officers, who remembered the son's hasty departure. The name had a sour taste in the mouth of the arresting officer, who had always assumed that wherever you found Jews, you found crime. But as the officers were about to get their prisoners to reveal the name of their boss, who they were certain must be Dr. Malina, the head of the customs office himself came to police headquarters and insisted on the release of all their captives. This particular group of smugglers had relatives in high places in the Khedive's government, a shadow government to be sure, but it would be unwise for the British to offend them, to put a hole in the curtain that covered British control of Egypt all the way to the Sudan. The police officers were furious that their night's work was for nothing. The Arab boy said nothing to Dr. Malina about his near imprisonment, but fell asleep at his post at the door and could hardly be aroused, not even when the cook kicked him. Marcus did not appear in the laboratory the next day but this was no longer unusual, and the French scientists did not find out that they almost had lost him forever.

ERIC FORTMAN WALKED along the sea side of the bazaar and looked at a table set up with odd objects. There he saw a small elephant statue, an elephant from India with red and blue flowers painted on its gray back, and real—or at least they looked real— ivory tusks, and he saw that it was a Ganesh. His cabinmate on the *Grey Falcon* had been a student from India who had spent three years at university in England and had been on his way home. He was to board a steamer for Bombay in Alexandria. Eric wondered if he had survived the wreck. The student had told him that images of Ganesh were good luck. The young man had pulled from his pocket his own small Ganesh, which he claimed had kept the ship afloat across the dangerous waters and through the heavy winds. Here on the table was an identical Ganesh. Of course it hadn't been so effective off the shores of Alexandria, but it was a pretty little thing. It was placed beside a great tortoise-shell bowl and near a gold necklace with a jade piece in the center. Eric stared. A man appeared from behind a hanging curtain, smiling. "Are you looking at something in particular?" he asked in French.

"*Oui,*" said Eric Fortman.

Recognizing his mistake, the shopkeeper shifted into English. "What do you like? What caught your eye?"

"The Ganesh."

"Ah," said the shopkeeper, "a very valuable Ganesh, good fortune accompanies him, some think. Even some Christians and many Muslims think this is so," he added.

"Superstitious nonsense," said Eric, who didn't want the price to go above his willingness to pay. He was offered a beer, a good English beer. As he sipped it, the merchant talked on and on.

The Ganesh had been brought to him by a child who had made a voyage from a small village outside of New Delhi, and was headed up to Cairo with his master, who had bought the figure from the boy's parents for a few pence. The boy had stolen it from his master because he had been badly beaten and intended to run away. The peddler himself had seen the welts. The master had been a collector of fine art. This was a very valuable Ganesh.

"Hadn't helped the child, had it?" Eric said first in English, then in French.

"Did you know," asked the man, "that Muhammad Ali himself had a Ganesh that he kept with him at all times?"

The statue of Muhammad Ali in the Grand Square depicted a man accustomed to command.

"I have no doubt," said Eric who was a salesman himself.

Eric Fortman held the small elephant statue in his hand and did not put it back on the table. He wanted it not for himself but as a gift for a young woman, to show that he had nothing but good intentions toward her, to bring her luck, to bring himself luck with her. He bought the Ganesh, and it was wrapped in purple paper and placed in a small white box. The minute he had the box in his hands, he knew that his luck, the luck that had kept him from drowning at sea, that had brought him to jostle a kind lady with a connection to Marbourg & Sons, the luck that kept his black hair full and bushy and kept the earache he had as a child from doing away with him, that good fortune would hold. Even though he did not for a moment believe that little elephant statues could actually sway the fates, he did believe that he himself was blessed and it could do no harm to purchase a Ganesh for a person whose affections he sought.

After the merchant was certain his customer had turned the corner, he put the bills he had received in a locked box, and from a bag under the table he took out another Ganesh, one of about a hundred he had purchased for a song from a wharf rat who, on a false tip, had taken a barrel from a ship in port in the middle of the night when the watch was sound asleep, thinking the barrel contained gold bars, only to find in the excelsior packing enough tiny elephants to populate a miniature African country. The new Ganesh was placed in the center of the table to wait for the next customer.

LYDIA BROODED. What to do about the ring that was less than it should be? That was another discovery made by a magnifying glass, proving only that seeing more was not always desirable. On the other hand, she thought it was better to know what was there than to be fooled. Albert might be a good-looking young man, but he might have a character that was as flawed as the diamond he had given her daughter. She intended to proceed cautiously, to test out the situation, to be rational in her approach. This she owed her child.

THE OVEN WAS hot and the coals glowed. On the rack, just removed from the heat, several glass beakers were resting. Louis filled them with his prepared solutions and then, using his gas torch, he heated the necks of the beakers and bent them until they looked like swan necks. Louis explained to Este that this way they could keep dust and the invisible life-forms that floated in the air out of their concoctions. Louis and Este were standing next to each other at the laboratory table when a bat from under the eaves of the building entered the open window and flew over their heads, flapping its black wings. It startled Este, and she let out a small cry of alarm.

"It's nothing," Louis said, "they live here, too." His dark eyes looked into her face as if he could see through the bones.

Este said, "There are some creatures that are unnecessary, just mistakes, don't you think? They serve no purpose at all."

"I doubt that," said Louis.

"Before I die," Este said, "I would like to see every animal there is on earth. Do you think that's possible?"

Louis shook his head. "You would have to travel all around the world to do that," he said.

"Well, maybe I will," said Este. "There is no law that says a woman can't sail to places far from home."

Louis himself had no desire to travel. He wanted simply to uncover the workings of fluids and microbes and chemicals, and there was enough to discover in one room for a man to satisfy his curiosity for a lifetime, maybe several lifetimes. "Travel can be dangerous," he said.

"Oh, I know," said Este. "But staying home can be dangerous, too."

She was thinking of cholera. He knew she was thinking of cholera. Louis said to her, surprising himself with the force of his words, which seemed to come out without his permission, "You will be all right."

He looked down. He was afraid he had made her angry by asserting something he could not possibly know for certain.

He had not, but she changed the subject quickly. "Tell me how the swine fever kills pigs."

"I will," he said, and went over to the table and opened the small doors to the autoclave's lower level, revealing the gas tubes that heated the shelves. She waited for him to return to her side.

Another bat flew down above their heads. It spread its black wings, supported by their tiny bones, and moved its almost square head, with its yellow, flat eyes, from side to side. What role did bats play in the spread of cholera? They didn't seem to sicken themselves, but perhaps they brought the disease to the streets in their droppings. Louis sent Marcus out to get a net. He wanted to catch a bat and open its brain. He wanted to find its droppings and put them under his microscope. Este had a sudden strong desire to see how the bat's tongue was connected to the back of its throat. She was not thinking of Albert, his ring, or her wedding.

THAT NIGHT MRS. Malina was undressing in the privacy of their bedroom. With the shuttered windows open and the stars outside sliding across the sky in orderly procession, the moonlight settling across the waters of Lake Mariout, and the sound of the sea pounding against the jetty on the Western Harbor, she said to her husband, "I think it would be wise to find out if Albert has any debts that might be dragging him down. I think you should make an effort to find out if the young man is a gambler or perhaps was already keeping a woman. It would be a tragedy for your daughter if he turned out to be less than we had hoped."

Dr. Malina was barely listening. He was thinking that it would be a good idea to send his wife and daughter out of Alexandria until the cholera had departed. He was thinking about asking his aunt to house them at the country place, away from the ports and the smells of the city. He was thinking about a woman he had seen in his service that very morning with a cyst in her breast that had broken through the skin and would surely kill her before the month was out, and he had nothing to give her that might save her life. He was thinking that if his own wife should die, he would mourn her so profoundly that he himself would die, which would be a relief, only of course he wouldn't feel the relief because he would be dead.

His wife went on talking about Albert and a possible connection to some theft or some disgrace or other. His mind was on his son. He would send more banknotes to Jerusalem as soon as he could arrange the funds. He had no sentimental attachment to Jerusalem. He was concerned about hostile natives. He was uneasy with the distance that separated him from his child. He had heard of the malaria that had appeared in the spring in the hills beyond Mount Scopus. He wanted his son to come home. But this was not yet possible. Lydia Malina was still talking about Albert when he returned his attention to the present. "Come to bed," he said. He wanted to hold her, to feel her body press against his. What would happen after that was also a good thing.

"What is the matter with you?" he said to his wife. "Why are you suddenly alarmed about Albert? We have known this family all our lives. The boy is hardworking, energetic, intelligent. We attended his mother's funeral. We should be sending money to the poor in gratitude that our daughter has accepted his proposal. What if she were sullen or difficult or had in mind a penniless poet or, worse, a Muslim or a Greek? Why are you looking for trouble?"

Lydia Malina began to weep. At first these were silent tears, but then they changed into little gasps, and the tears became sobs and the sobs racked her body.

"For God's sake," said Dr. Malina, "what is the matter?"

She hadn't meant to tell him, wanting to be sure, wanting to think the matter through by herself before his voice reached into every corner of her mind. But she told him. "The ring Albert gave Este, that ring is not a good ring. It's very flawed. He gave her a ring fit for the daughter of a furniture polisher, not for the daughter of the Malina household, not for your daughter."

What a fuss about nothing, thought Dr. Malina. "It's just a ring," he said. "It's not a sign of his character or a sign that their life together will be impoverished. How can it be impoverished? He is a banker. His father is an architect. The family gives to the synagogue and to the hospital and every year to the fund for crippled children, and they support the burial society. Phoebe is our daughter's best friend. What difference does the quality of the ring make?" Women, he thought, and not for the first time, were trapped in the surface of things, in the appearance of beauty and the appearance of morality. They reasoned like cats. One minute brushing against your thigh, the next preening in the sun, and after that running away. Women were unbearable burdens on a man's existence. He turned his back and opened the doors to the terrace and went out. Lydia wept on. She followed him out on the terrace.

"It's a deceit," she managed to say. "It's a dishonesty. It's a very bad sign."

From her bedroom, Este heard her mother's voice. She knew that her mother was sobbing, even if she could not make out each sob. She heard the anger in her father's voice, but was unable to make out the exact words. She rushed to her mirror and reassured herself that nothing had changed in her features. She was still herself. The room felt larger and she felt afraid, afraid in her own room. Afraid of what? Nothing, she told herself.

In the early morning she had a dream that she forgot the instant her eyes opened. In her dream she roamed an empty laboratory, running her fingers over the tables, peering in the lens at small forms swimming in cultures. She heard the sound of a dog barking and the scuffling sounds of rabbits in their cages. She was calm.

NOCARD WAS STILL asleep in his bed, Roux was writing a letter that he wanted to post early to Paris, informing Pasteur of their efforts, so far unsuccessful, when, at the breakfast table, Este noticed that her mother's eyes were all swollen and her face looked bloated, the result of tears. But she also noticed that the argument was over. No one was angry. All was well. This was because Dr. Malina had agreed to discuss the matter with Albert's father. He had agreed despite his fear that he would be seen as grasping for a higher-quality engagement ring for his daughter for his own mercenary purposes, but he knew that the matter had to be settled. If it was a mistake of some sort, it could be resolved easily. Women, he thought to himself as he looked at his wife and daughter. They needed his protection. Unreasonably, this thought gave him considerable pleasure, and he ran it through his mind again and again as he walked down the stairs and across the courtyard to his surgery.

There an envelope awaited him, delivered by a messenger from the Committee of Public Safety, reporting an upswing in cholera deaths in the two preceding days. The numbers for the entire country were alarming. In all of Egypt there were now 58,000 dead from cholera since the beginning of the epidemic. Most of the deaths had been in Damietta and Cairo, but the weekly numbers in Alexandria were rising. The outbreak seemed most severe in the Râs el Tin neighborhood, where, centuries ago, the small village of Rakoutis had stood, its inhabitants living off the fruits of the sea and weaving grass for the roof of their huts. But some of the cholera deaths were in the Jewish neighborhood and some were in the houses along the lake where the British government officials themselves lived. The envelope was marked *Private,* and the instructions on the inner page included burning the message. The government did not want to cause panic, although it wasn't the government causing alarm but rather the disease itself, a distinction governments never grasp.

Louis was walking about in the first light of morning as the shops were pulling back their curtains and the newspaper was being delivered by bicycle to the cafés and the pale light of the day had not yet become heavy. The stones of the buildings were yellowed and their edges still soft, and the sounds of the muezzin echoed through all of Alexandria from the large mosque on Nebi Daniel, and the women of the city were throwing basins of dirty water in the streets, and the dogs were stirring themselves to begin their wanderings, and the destroyed Pharos, nothing left of its grandeur, was suffering the indignity of weeds springing to life among its fallen bricks. Three British soldiers were sitting at a table of a still unopened café. They had the morning papers in front of them. The wheels of the donkey carts began to roll over the stones and the drivers called out to their beasts and the fishmongers were down at the docks making their choices from among the day's catch. The barrels of cotton waited on the dock for the porters to haul them aboard waiting ships. The schoolchildren in their uniforms walked down the stairs and out the doors of their houses and the bells of the churches rang and the seagulls cawed into the air and sat turning their heads from side to side along the jetty waiting for the sun to rise higher in the sky. Louis quickened his step. Had he seen Este rounding the corner? When he turned in to the next street, he could see that he had been mistaken. It was another young woman, pulling by the hand a child he hadn't noticed. He was disappointed.

Later that morning, Este was turning the microscope's eyepiece around, trying to get a clearer view of the glass beneath.

There was something moving there. As the focus came clear, she recognized the moving thing. It was not cholera. It was of no interest at all. She now knew the names of the living creatures that were harmless but nevertheless crawled about in the cultures they made, the brews they mixed.

"Do you miss Paris?" she asked Louis as he filled his pipe, standing by the shelf on which the bottles of dye rested. She believed that Paris was the center of the universe, where everything worthwhile was born and flourished. "Here in Alexandria," she said, "we're so out of date."

"The Paris of fashionable people, I don't live there," Louis said, his voice curt, almost unfriendly.

"Do you have a family in your country?" Este asked.

Louis nodded.

"Ah, families," said Este, "they do have their opinions, opinions that quite limit what a person can do."

"On my last visit home, I didn't tell my mother where I was going," Louis said. "She would have been afraid for me."

"Naturally," said Este. "I would be afraid for my son, too, if I had one who left for a far place to find a terrible disease that was waiting for him there."

"And if you were a scientist, what would you do?" asked Louis.

Este didn't pause. "Go, whatever anyone said," she answered. "I would go to the very ends of the earth." She laughed at herself. "Maybe I am not so brave as all that. But I would have gone with my brother to Palestine if they had let me. But they wouldn't let me and I didn't go, at least not yet."

"I'm not brave," he said. "I have obligations that have nothing to do with bravery. Don't think I am something I'm not."

"I hardly know you," Este said, "but your work is important."

There was a silence between them. Anippe had fallen asleep in the far corner of the laboratory. She moaned without waking. Louis and Este walked to the window and spoke in low tones.

"I wish I knew what you know," Este said.

"There are so many things I don't understand yet, might not discover in my lifetime," Louis answered. He said this so seriously that Este had to laugh.

"It doesn't matter," she said. "I can breathe and eat and sleep and dress and go for a walk, all without knowing everything."

Louis knew he was being teased, and he liked it. What he wanted was right before him, but was not his. He wanted her. He did not have words for this wish. He had not expected it. He had never before experienced it. It was simultaneously awful and riveting. She was right in front of him, looking at him, but he still was racked by need, the need to look at her, the need to say the right thing, the need to keep her there. He took a pull on his pipe, too strong, and coughed.

"Are you all right?" she asked as he struggled to breathe normally.

"Yes," he said finally.

"Perhaps you should put down the pipe," she said gently.

"Yes," he said, but he didn't.

"Shall I bring you the chloride now?" she asked.

"Yes," he said, but he didn't want her to move away. Este did move. She went to the shelf and pulled down the bottle they needed for the morning's work. She could feel him staring at her back. Of course it was impossible. She knew what her father would say: he was not one of them. She knew her mother would begin to weep. She wondered if she was a bad person, an untrustworthy person.

Louis said, "Come, we'll see what our oven has produced." He forced his limbs to move. His steps were stiff. He came close to the open fire. He stared at the flames for a long moment. She wanted to follow him, but she didn't. His face was flushed from the heat. A bead of sweat appeared on his forehead. Outside the window, a flock of small black birds had settled on the ledge. They ruffled their wings, they hopped about on their bent legs, legs that seemed too thin to support their bodies. They let out sharp cries, plaintive, unlovely. Louis went to the window and banged on the glass. Alarmed, the birds took flight. Este told Louis that she must go out for a walk. She woke Anippe and they left the laboratory.

Why did she leave so suddenly? Louis was confused. She would return. She said she would return.

But she didn't come back. Sitting in her own drawing room hours later, she was thinking about the flawed diamond, and she knew she would not marry a man, the brother of her best friend or not, the object of her imaginings for years or not, if he was less than honorable, less than fine. She wanted, in fact a man, an unsuitable man, from a different place.

That evening, Abraham Malina sat in his favorite chair reading a paper from the English Academy of Science.

Whether it was 1865 or 1866 when cholera appeared in America is uncertain. Some say it came to America on the German steamer England. *It is certain that cholera was rampant in New York during the summer of that year. The railways that had been extended from the coast into the interior carried the disease all the way to the frontier. A military camp in Newport, Kentucky, became a breeding ground from which the disease spread to the surrounding area, and New Orleans lost about 1,200 lives from the disease, which disembarked from returning troop ships. The entire number of deaths in America in this outbreak are estimated to be about 50,000, which is not so very many considering other waves of the epidemic worldwide, but on the other hand, consider the unbearable sorrow that followed when the young soldiers who had escaped the perils of the battlefield returned home to die of cholera.*

10

THEN THEY FOUND IT. It was Louis who saw it first, a round form, a new form that his eye had never seen before. He called Roux to come and look. It took Roux a long time to locate it, but then he too saw it, pressed between the two pieces of glass, floating in a drop of blood from the stool of the child who had died of cholera. Nocard left the rabbit whose brain he was examining and came to the table. He jiggled the microscope with his large hand and then apologized again and again in case he had dislodged the microbe or ruined the slide. He hadn't. When they took turns and looked again, there it was. When Este arrived, they were laughing and slapping each other on the back. "Be cautious," Roux said, "we haven't proved it, we haven't tested it." They knew that work would have to be done, hard work, experiments repeated over and over in order to demonstrate its existence without a doubt, to convince those who would challenge them. Este looked through the microscope. She saw it, too, a round little ball that seemed to move purposefully in the blood fluid.

Roux did send a telegram to Pasteur that they had found something promising, a strong possibility that it was the cholera microbe. They would test it carefully. *Be of good cheer,* the telegram said. Dr. Koch was waiting in the telegram office to send a request for more funds to the Berlin Institute. Roux said to him, "I think we've found it."

The German's heart sank to his heels. He had worked in this hot, foreign place for nothing, if the French had found the object of their search. They would ridicule him in Berlin. They would forget his other accomplishments. They would remove him from his position. He would have to go back to being a country doctor, treating babies with rashes and women with boils. He offered his congratulations to Roux and asked if he might come visit the Frenchmen's laboratory and see their discovery for himself. "Of course," said Roux graciously. "We would welcome your advice on the next steps to take." Roux was very pleased with himself, but remembered to be both polite and cautious.

Este was excited. This would be the first really important thing that had happened in her life. She was flushed with excitement. She couldn't wait to tell her father. He would be so pleased. An hour later Dr. Koch knocked on the door. He was brought in and given the stool by the microscope. He adjusted the lens. He stared at the round ball. He tried not to smile. He tried not to let his delight show. He did not want to be considered a man without morals or decency, but he was relieved, very relieved. The round ball the Frenchmen had found was only a blood platelet, necessary for clotting to take place. This he had discovered for himself a long time ago, when he was working in his makeshift laboratory in the back of his doctor's office in Wollstein. He told Roux and Nocard and Thuillier what they had actually uncovered. He demonstrated to them that these round balls existed in everyone's blood. He took a drop from Este's finger, and there they were.

Dr. Robert Koch went back to his own laboratory feeling quite content, but still sorry for the French, who had thought they had grasped the grand prize. As for the French mission, along with Este, they were too disappointed to do anything else that day. It was a hard day. Roux sent a telegram to Pasteur. *Ignore previous telegram. Error found.*

INSIDE A LARGE, nondescript, white stone government office building, now inhabited by the English, guarded by a few British soldiers, the heat was heavy. The open windows carried the dust from the street into the rooms, where it settled on heavy wooden desks, on deep Oriental carpets, on brass ornaments and gas lamps. Outside, a few camels were tied to a post, their owner trying to get a travel visa through Egypt to the Sudan. The British had trouble with the Sudanese. Uprisings were put down, only to rise again. There had been the decisive but costly battle against Arabi just a few years before. This man who was trying to obtain a pass had some ordinary commerce in mind, unless he was a spy for the nationalists who wanted the British to leave Egypt. In these offices, no one was trusted, no one was assumed to be a friend. The natives were still speaking French, reading French newspapers, despite the fact that it had been months since the French essentially granted the town to Lord Cromer. The English soldiers and the English diplomats tried to go everywhere in threes. They wore their pistols at their sides. They shook their heads and frowned at passersby as if daring anyone to assault them, and yet they were assaulted. Sometimes they were merely pelted with soft melons and peaches, or sometimes a woman poured some slop down on them from above. Sometimes they were jumped from behind by someone with a knife, or a rope was pulled around an English neck. Sometimes they were found in an out-of-the-way alley, their boots taken, their jackets gone, their throats cut.

Which is why three English lieutenants were trying to compile a file on Dr. Malina. He might be spying against the British for the French, or reporting on troop movements for the Turks, perhaps for money or perhaps out of pure Jewish hatred for decent Christians.

The intelligence office had discovered that his son had written an article for the university paper that embarrassed the Egyptian royal family. The son was gone now, out of the country, but the father might be in communication with him. The British believed that they should at the very least learn more about this Dr. Malina. Never mind that he was a respected doctor and a member of the Committee of Public Safety. That very position might give this Jew cover to report on the Alexandrian situation to enemies of the crown.

A young officer, his mustache not yet respectably thick, said that he had noticed an Englishman coming from the Malina house the other day. He had engaged him in conversation. He was a former employee of the Glen MacAlan Scotch Company and was planning on staying in Alexandria for a while. He seemed like a decent enough fellow. He had befriended Dr. Malina. He had explained the circumstances and they sounded reasonable. He might be a source of information. The officers agreed he was just the sort of man who might serve his country well enough if asked. One of the lieutenants stood up, preparing to leave. He said, "We have had instructions from London to avoid those parts of town where the cholera has visited. Tell your men to stay away from the wharves and their usual pleasure pursuits for the time being."

One of the lieutenants shook his head. "What are the odds of my men obeying that order?" The others laughed.

THE FOLLOWING DAY, Este's mother had a headache. She took to her bed and closed the curtains so the light of the sun would not bother her eyes. Este's friend Phoebe, sister-in-law-to-be, had invited Este for lunch. She walked the few blocks to Phoebe's house, stopping at the glove store to order a replacement for the white glove with pearl buttons that she had ruined. The salesman at the

glove store bowed when he saw her. He bowed to all his customers. He, too, was a member of the synagogue. He tried to de-
tain her with an offer to show her the long suede gloves that had
just arrived off the boat from Lyons the other day. He offered a
plate of strawberries that she could dip in the saucer of sugar that
he kept on the counter. She declined, afraid strawberry juice might
drip on her dress. The store owner had a pharaoh hound, whose
long neck and pointed ears were signs of his good breeding. Este
petted the dog on his head and allowed him to lick her face. "Ah,
sweetness," she said to him.

Outside in the street, the heat made her gasp. She drew in the
air but it didn't seem like enough air. It was moist and humid. A
donkey cart moved quickly down the street, splashing dust and
water and the remains of a persimmon on the bottom of her dress.
She hurried on, brushing by Dr. Koch, who was only now on his
way to his own laboratory, having slept longer than usual because
he had been up into the early hours of the morning considering
the cholera's elusive ways.

Este wrapped her arms around Phoebe, smelling the fresh orange water her friend had used to wash in the morning. How
good it was to have a friend, even if you can't share your confusion or confide the trouble that you could see ahead. "We can
now call ourselves sisters and it will be true," said Phoebe squeez-
ing Este's arm.

"Let's wait until after the wedding," said Este.

"But why?" said Phoebe.

"Because," said Este, "I don't want to tempt fate to harm us."

"That's stupid," said Phoebe. "You're my sister now, really.
All of our lives we'll share our troubles, when a child is sick, when
one is born, when we get fat and ugly and when we have swollen
ankles and loose teeth, we will know each other, and there will be

no secrets between us, ever. Isn't it lovely?" she asked, feeding a small yellow bird in a cage a little of her cake. Este agreed it was lovely. There was, however, something a little false in her smile, a little diffident in her hug. Her own childhood, she thought, had vanished quite suddenly while Phoebe's remained.

While the two young women visited with each other, promising a fidelity more serious, perhaps, than that of man and wife, the shop owner, as he was putting away a tray of leather gloves, felt a cramp in his stomach, a cold in his fingers. He shuttered his store, left his merchandise on their shelves, sorted by color and size, some in boxes and others in fine paper, and went home to his wife and lay on the bed and, despite the cold compresses, the warm tea, the blanket his wife wrapped around his feet, he died just as Este returned home and hurried up the stairs to see if her mother's headache had improved. It had.

Later she found Louis in the drawing room. He was waiting for her father to come in. He had promised to tell the doctor of any progress in the laboratory. Dr. Malina was too busy to come and see for himself. "Louis," Este said, "do you think God created cholera, and if he did, why?"

"I suppose," said Louis, "the cholera, if it had a brain, could ask the same question about us—what are we here for except as a food source, and surely, if we disappeared, another equally felicitous meal would become apparent, one that was not attempting to discover its hiding places."

Este laughed. This was good conversation. She so rarely had good conversations.

EMILE HAD PURCHASED in the market three wooden camels in graduated sizes, for his children. They had miniature reins and red carpets on their backs. Carved by some villagers in the swamp area near Aboukir, they smelled of cedar and palm oil. He packed them carefully in a towel and put them in his suitcase. He had bought a silver beaded shawl for his wife. Would it seem strange in Paris, this object that was so common in the stalls of Alexandria? He hoped it would seem exotic but not peculiar. He had been working with chicken blood. Chickens had their own cholera, perhaps different from the kind that affected human beings. He wanted to see if he could transmit the chicken cholera to a rabbit. The problem was that his particular chickens did not seem to have the disease. They pecked eagerly at their grain, they hopped about and fluffed their feathers as if life would go on forever. They left waste all over the papers Edmond had placed in their cage. Perhaps the chickens in Alexandria were not susceptible to cholera. He mixed a little of the feces they had saved from the cholera victim with some water, and injected the substance into the chickens. If they became ill, that would provide a valuable clue. They didn't. Emile had gone to the Exchange and sent a telegram to his wife. It was an expense, but he felt he needed to reach her as soon as possible. He felt this with an urgency that startled him. *Working well, am fine, nothing to report as of now. Miss you and children.* He knew that when his wife received his words, she would read not only the actual message but all the things left unsaid, the non-telegram things. It would all be clear to her. This thought steadied his hand as he pulled a chicken up toward him by the throat.

Nocard's dog had developed a large tumor on its left hindquarter. It made him limp as he moved around his cage. His eyes had become bleary. His fur was matted. The dog was sick. This was interesting news. But the dog did not exhibit any of the signs of cholera. When Roux and Thuillier examined its blood under the microscope, they found nothing unusual. "The dog seems to have a cancerous tumor," said Nocard. "An unfortunate coincidence. In a place of cholera, under our very eyes the beast has become cancerous." The dog licked Nocard's hand when he put it through the bars and fed him a sugar lump, then he lay down in a corner of the cage and whined in his sleep. Nocard said, "I will put him out of his misery. He is no longer any use to us."

Louis said, "Let us at least look at the tumor. Perhaps there is a kind of cholera tumor that grows only in dogs."

"Do you imagine," said Nocard, "that just because there is cholera in Alexandria, there is nothing else that eats at us?"

When Emile and Louis went out to the café at the corner for their coffee and baguette, Nocard carried the weakened animal, which offered no resistance, to a table and there injected him with a solution that soon caused his heart to stop. "Damn," Nocard said. "Damn everything." He kicked at the leg of a table on which Louis had prepared a culture in a dish of raspberries and oil to study under the microscope. The table vibrated, the dish crashed to the floor. The microscope threatened to follow, but wobbled on its base and remained upright. Nocard went out to find a new dog.

Louis said to Emile while they were drinking coffee at the Café Noir in the Grand Square, "When you met your wife, did you love her immediately?"

"No," said Emile, "she was several years younger, a second cousin whom I met at a Christmas party one year. I thought she was a pretty child, that's all. But then, two years later, she came with her mother to my sister's wedding and I had some thoughts about her. Pleasant enough to encourage a visit to her family where they lived in the country, and then to take a few walks with her in our uncle's vineyard, and there was no doubt in my mind that she regarded me with warmth and would look favorably on a proposal, and that is how it happened that I am the father of three."

"My God," said Louis, "was it really so easy?"

"Not exactly," said Emile. "Her father had someone else in mind, but he was soon dissuaded. I did, after all, live in Paris and had my degrees, which impressed them with my importance."

Louis nodded and smoked his pipe. Emile stared at the donkey at the corner, which seemed to be in a particularly bad temper. Emile got up from the table and walked over to the donkey. "Hey, hey," he said to the animal, and stroked it behind the ears. The donkey brought his head forward toward Emile and calmly let him rub the soft gray spot over his nostrils. The donkey opened his mouth and drooled on Emile's hand. Back at his table, Emile wiped his hand with his napkin and put the napkin in his pocket. "We might just as well see what's in that donkey's mouth," he said to Louis.

Robert Koch was out for his noonday stroll. He was absolutely regular in his habits, and exercise was one of his habits. He passed by the café where the two French scientists sat. "Gentlemen," he said, "good morning."

Emile jumped to his feet. Louis followed.

"All is progressing well with you?" asked Dr. Koch.

"Very well," said Emile.

"Excellent," said Dr. Koch.

"Are you enjoying Alexandria, Herr Doctor?" said Louis.

"Fine city, and such history everywhere," he said, and then went on his way with a wave of his hand.

ESTE HAD INTENDED not to return to the laboratory. She suspected that it was improper to be there, even with her maid. She considered it was dangerous, not because of the cholera but because of the very excitement she felt in the room and the reasons she felt it. However, a day later she found herself in the very last place she had expected her walk to lead her. Was it the science or the scientist that had pulled her there? How could she separate one from the other? Louis did not waste time wondering why she had stayed away. He was simply happy to have her back.

Nocard was attempting to brew a concoction of horse dung and cholera-infected bowel. He rubbed at them furiously. Este came and stood behind Louis. Louis thought of Madame Pasteur, who did indeed prepare slides, watch over animals in their cages, serve as her husband's assistant when his other assistants were elsewhere. He could teach Este how to be his assistant. He thought of them together in a laboratory, his own laboratory. Louis told Este about the living yeast that died in the great vats of beets, thereby spoiling them, if the enemy organisms were not killed through heat. Louis was wanting to redo his tie, the high collar around his neck seemed loose. He thought perhaps the knot in his tie had pulled apart. There was no mirror in the laboratory where he might catch his image. Suddenly, Este reached up and pulled at the strings. "Your tie is askew," she said, and as she came toward him he smelled her lilac soap. He scolded himself for being surprised. If the purpose of all life is to sustain its species, then he, too, would be led to reproduce. It was natural. It was normal. It was fine, the feeling he had when Este put her hands around his neck and fixed his tie. Este was embarrassed. She should not have been so forward. She should not have touched him. Was this shameful? Este walked away to the other side of the laboratory. She asked Roux what Koch was doing in his laboratory. Roux said he imagined that Koch was also injecting animals and waiting for something to develop. Este did not look at Louis again for the rest of the day. She was, however, determined to learn the name of every chemical in the jars on the shelf that very day. She had them all memorized within an hour.

Marcus had taken Anippe out back. He had found out that the servant was in need of a dentist. She had a swelling in her cheek and a throbbing in her jaw. He had given her a lemonade he had been saving for his own lunch. The two of them went into the hospital and found an empty bed in a dark corner of a long corridor. They took advantage of the moment their brief meeting provided. The girl forgot about her tooth. Marcus felt the strength in his arms and legs. "Look at my muscle," he said to the girl as they walked back toward the lab.

"Very big," she said in Arabic, and then translated the words into French. Her accent was terrible. It grated on Marcus. People should not speak French if they can't do it right.

THE BRITISH OFFICERS decided to find out exactly what Dr. Malina was doing. Was it treason or drug smuggling? Like father, like son. Like son, like father. They sent off a dispatch to Jerusalem. *Find out what you can. What is Jacob Malina doing in Palestine?*

NEXT TO HER own wedding night, what could be a more wonderful moment for a mother than the marriage of her daughter? Was this not how the seasons were intended to move? One was married oneself, and showered with candies by one's friends, and lifted on high by the men of the community, and everyone admired you and then real life began and you had a daughter and the daughter grew and you went with her to purchase the dress for the most important event in her life. Was this not the way it had always been, generation after generation, *l'dor v'dor,* as they said in Hebrew. What did it matter if the diamond that had been given to her daughter was less than perfect? Lydia tried to banish the gray mood that had invaded her mind. She could find no good reason for it. What was wrong with her? Was she afraid of becoming an old crone whose juices had dried up and who was left with sagging bones and thinning hair to watch others touch and flirt, smile and dance? She would become that old crone whether or not Este married Albert, or even if she never married at all. How could a simple woman hope to stop time?

What she wanted most was that her daughter should not be sad. She had never been able to bear the child's tears, over a top that had rolled under a couch or a doll that had become stained in the rain, or the loss of their cat which had been most miserably defeated by a neighbor's mongrel. She could not bear it, ever, the things that her child suffered, even this child who had hardly suffered at all.

She was not a particularly superstitious woman, nevertheless she kept turning the matter of the flawed diamond over and over again in her mind. Was it a sign of some imperfection in the character of her future son-in-law, or was it a sign that something tragic that would split the family forever was already written in God's book? Was it a sign that Este herself was in danger? Lydia called for Anippe to bring her some coffee. Was the flawed diamond simply a chipped stone, or was it a premonition of catastrophe awaiting them all?

IN JERUSALEM, IN a small room in the back of what seemed to be a hotel, Lydia's son, Jacob, sat with his head in his hands. He was hungry and thirsty and exhausted. He had not been able to shave or comb or wash. The evening before, he had been stopped by several large and unfriendly Turkish men wearing no official uniform, but carrying pistols. Around their waists they wore belts with sheathed knives. He thought he was being robbed, but he was mistaken. The men had pushed him against a wall as he was leaving the small office he had just built for himself in the back of the rickety building he intended to turn into Malina & Co., World Suppliers of Olives and Olive Oil Ready for Your Table. He had inked out the sign on a piece of wood himself and was waiting for the men he had hired to bring a ladder to help him hang it above the door. The sign repeated itself four times, in Arabic, in Italian, in English, in German. He had wanted to add Greek but there was no space on the board.

There were as yet no olives in the building, but he had ordered a press to make oil. It should be arriving at the quay in Jaffa within a few weeks or perhaps months. Nothing was so certain in Palestine as that everything would be delayed, everything would cost more money than expected, primarily because the pasha, whichever pasha was in the neighborhood, would take a cut, and his top man would need a cut, and a simple merchant would bleed and bleed. He had planted three small lemon trees in the hard dirt around the building, which had once belonged to a farmer who had kept his tools and his animals under this roof. Certain odors persisted that did not stimulate the appetite, but Jacob assumed that he could air the place out, that time would make it his. He was eager to begin, to build his business, and now this misunderstanding would probably cost him many shekels, many of his father's piastres. He knew that he had come to his ancient homeland and should feel at home, but he also knew he was an unwanted stranger here. He didn't belong with the long-bearded ones who walked in groups in black coats and seemed not to notice that their clothes were too heavy for the warm climate. These were men, unlike himself, who had turned their back on progress. Although they were familiar to him from Alexandria, he did not belong with the Armenian priests who walked through the streets in robes and swung gold censers. He did not belong with the Arab camel dealers, or the sheepherders or the farmers of oranges and apples who loaded the carts pulled by donkeys. He had noticed the British, who were keeping an eye on everyone. They appeared in the cafés at night and asked questions about everyone's activities. Some of them wore their red uniforms and marched about as if they owned the place, which they didn't. The Arabs laughed at them, hated them, killed them on occasion.

He had lived in Jerusalem as an entirely private person. He had promised his father that he would not write anymore, never again publish his thoughts in any newspaper or periodical. He had seen that words on a page could have serious consequences, could threaten a man's life and send him miles from home. He intended, many, many years in the future, to write his memoirs, a document that might be of interest to a few members of his family. Writing, he had decided, was a profession for those who cannot *do*, and he wanted now to make a success of his business, to bring pride to his family and wealth, wealth enough for a Jew to provide protection from those who would harm him. He had decided he would rather be the object of criticism in the press than the critic.

Jacob waited for someone to come to the room. He was thirsty but unafraid. He had done nothing to annoy the Turkish pasha or the British, nothing at all.

A YOUNG MAN, the son of Monsieur Jean Vernon, a patient of Dr. Malina's, a student in the last year of his study of law at the university, was lying on the floor of the hospital's entryway. The porter at the École des Jesuits had brought him there in a blanket and then left him on the floor. He had not had the strength to get up on a chair. The sister bent down, her sense of smell the only diagnostic tool she needed. The pool of feces that had collected around the boy's hips, that had seeped through his trousers, told her all. The young man's lips were blue. His eyes had sunk back in his skull. His teeth were chattering. His hand trembled as if he had had a stroke, but this wasn't a stroke. The sister knew exactly what it was. What she didn't know was what to do about it. What good had it done the young man to make his way to the hospital clinic? The boy gave his name. A note was sent to his father. She gave him some laudanum, which seemed to calm him. She put another blanket on his legs.

The sister knocked on the laboratory door. Emile and Louis hurried to the room where the boy lay tossing on a cot. The sister would have stayed with the young man in his last hours, but there were others in need of her attention. The fact that there was cholera in Alexandria did not mean other threats to the human body retreated or moved on to Cairo or Damascus. Louis and Emile discreetly took some of the boy's feces and some of the fluid that gathered at the edge of his lips. They wiped him with a towel, which they kept. Louis could just grab his arm and cut in several places and take what he wanted. But he could not do that. The boy was trying to pull himself to a sitting position but was unable. He looked like a new calf, out of proportion, not yet fully firm. What an age to lose your life! Louis felt a sudden rage. He brought out his small tube with its cork stopper and a stick for stirring, which he had brought in his bag. The boy kicked at him. The kick had no force but its intention was clear. Louis waited a moment and then he again approached the boy and wiped his stick against the vomit on his chin and placed his prize in his glass tube and put in the cork and left the room just as the boy's father could be heard calling his son's name in the corridor.

They were returning to their laboratory when they saw Dr. Koch, immediately followed by his assistant carrying a large bowl. "Good morning, Dr. Koch," said Emile. The doctor barely nodded in return. He was in a hurry to take the intestines of a dead woman in whose body he had seen all the signs of cholera back to his laboratory.

ERIC FORTMAN HAD been announced by the serving girl, or at least Lydia and Este were able to make his name out of the garbled words she spoke. "Ladies," he said, in his large English voice, "how happy I am to find you at home. The *Cassandra* and the *Olympia,* one flying the British flag and the other from Istanbul, have debarked without unloading. They were told about the cholera and simply pulled out to sea. Cowards, I think," he added. What of their responsibilities to the firms that stocked their cargo, entrusted the goods and expected service? "What kind of behavior is that?" he asked, without actually expecting a reply. But he got one.

"You can't seriously expect the captains of these ships to put their men at risk, simply for the sake of the cargo. A human life is worth far more than any bolt of cloth, any piece of timber, anything under the sun that doesn't imagine its own death." As Este spoke, her face flushed. Unfortunately, he could not mention the considerable dent in his financial plans that accompanied these ships' unseemly retreat.

"I don't fight with women," he said. "I bring them gifts. Look what I brought you." And from the pocket of his jacket he pulled the Ganesh, its small painted flowers gleaming in the morning light that drifted in as the curtains blew apart. "Look, it's an elephant," he said. "You have heard, I'm sure, that the brown people on the Indian continent believe in an elephant god called Ganesh, and this is him." The women stared. "Well, not him, but a representation of him."

"An idol," said Lydia.

"You don't worship him," laughed Eric, smoothing down the edge of his black mustache, "you put him on your desk to look pretty, and he is pretty, isn't he?"

"Yes," said Este. She took the Ganesh and ran her fingers over its smooth glazed back. She held it in the palm of one hand and ran a finger down the slope of its small trunk. "Thank you," she said, and in fact, for some reason she hardly understood, she was enormously pleased with the gift.

"It will bring you luck, I'm sure," said Eric.

"Nonsense," said Este, but she smiled again. "I've never had a Ganesh before," she added.

Lydia felt she had to say, "Jews do not believe in elephant gods."

"Neither do Christians," said Eric.

"Tell me about India," said Este. "I want to go there myself someday."

"I haven't actually been to India," said Eric. "Glen MacAlan Scotch had no business there. I've been to Portugal, though."

"Tell me about Portugal, then," said Este. "I wish I could go there, too."

Lydia looked at her daughter. She wanted to shield her from disappointment, Portugal, India, wishes that would never come true. The world might be round and vast, but what any one woman would know of it was limited to the classroom, the library, and the newspapers. "Este, my darling," she said, "we must go out on our errands. Perhaps Eric will accompany us as far as the Muslim cemetery." She wasn't entirely displeased when he explained that he had to return to the docks in case any new ships were arriving.

"I'm sure I would get seasick on a boat," said Lydia.

"I'm sure I wouldn't," said Este.

"The sea is very boring," said Lydia.

"Not at all," said Este. "It has a million colors, a thousand birds, and the wind blows hard and soft and the whitecaps rise and fall. I'm sure I should love it."

"I doubt that," said Lydia, and the subject was dropped.

DR. KOCH HAD a far larger laboratory than the Frenchmen's. He and Gregor Gaffkey had several assistants, and he worked night and day. He had no other distractions. He recorded every attempt they made in a black notebook, the fifth in the series that he had begun when he arrived in Alexandria. He, too, was having trouble. The cholera that was surely in the city, killing more and more each day, evaded his glass, his experiments, melded with his dye, or dissolved on contact with the air or in some way that frustrated the doctor as nothing else ever had, hid in plain sight. Dr. Koch knew that after he discovered its shape, it would seem obvious. Other generations of scientists might wonder why it took him so long. They would admire his hard work, but speak of him and his accomplishments condescendingly. After all, it was right in front of his Germanic nose all the time.

A LETTER WAS waiting on the hall table. It was from Jacob. Lydia read:

Dearest parents, don't be alarmed, but I have been interviewed by several British intelligence officers in Jerusalem. It seems they are concerned that I am part of a Jewish conspiracy against the Crown. I believe I have convinced them that I am now a simple businessman dealing in olives and my foolish publication when I was a student is long behind me. I told them I no longer write or have any ambitions to write. They let me go but said they will keep watching me. They have spoken to the pasha here and may ask him to remove my papers. The political situation is treacherous. The Grand Rabbi, who claims he is a descendant of Rabbi Hillel (who could prove him wrong?), is anxious to avoid any incident with the authorities. He, too, suspects that I am an agent of foreign interests. On what grounds I cannot tell you. He will not speak up in my favor. I am on my own. The British officers asked me many questions about Father's medical practice and his position in the community. They implied he was smuggling in hashish. Needless to say, I have suffered many sleepless nights. Hope this means nothing, but I did think you ought to know. With affection always, Jacob.

Don't be alarmed, don't be alarmed. Lydia repeated the words over and over. How could she not be alarmed? Why shouldn't she be alarmed? She waited until Este had gone to feed the birds in the courtyard and her husband had finished his dinner to show him the letter. He put his hand on hers. "Listen to your son, don't be alarmed," he said. "It's most likely that the interest of the English Crown in the Malinas will fade quickly since in fact we do nothing to harm it."

"Well, then," said Lydia, "I won't be alarmed."

THE COMMITTEE OF Public Safety held a luncheon meeting. They invited Roux, Nocard, and Thuillier along with Dr. Robert Koch. But Louis did not attend the meeting. He had returned to the hospital to see the young man who had denied him tissue samples some hours before. Dr. Koch reported some progress in his laboratory, some significant leads, some hope that he had perhaps sighted the microbe, but it was too soon to present his work, the proof was not yet there. He would keep the committee informed of his progress. They were all invited to his laboratory to see his experiments if they wished. "But don't expect to see the microbe," he said, "not yet."

Emile reported on the French mission's work, not admitting that they had not made any progress besides the progress of elimination.

"The water has been boiled?" Nocard asked the servant who was pouring from a pitcher.

"No, sir," said the servant.

"Well, boil it, then," said Nocard, who did not touch the fish or greens that had been brought to him.

Emile pushed the food from one side of his plate to the other. "I'll have some beer," he said.

The Belgian doctors, the Arab surgeon, the Italian anatomist, the Turkish throat specialist, all members of the Alexandrian academy along with Dr. Malina, ate with full appetite.

AT NOON, NOCARD was sitting in a chair by the cage of a lamb recently injected with some tissue from the brain of their cholera victim, waiting for it to show signs of illness. Este announced she was leaving the laboratory. She was on her way home. Her mother had insisted she return in time for lunch. Her mother was lonely for her company.

"Walk with me," she said to Louis. Her face was relaxed, as if she expected nothing of importance to occur.

"Let's take the long way," Louis said.

Este said, "No, my mother expects me at home."

"All right," Louis said, "let's walk slowly."

Anippe was trailing them. Marcus was teasing the maid by trying to undo the ribbons of her apron. Este wanted a drink of cream and ice from a vendor at the corner. Louis explained that it was not safe to eat food from the carts. The vendors did not boil their pots, they did not keep their hands clean.

"When will it end?" she asked.

Louis said, "No one knows."

"I've heard from the cook that some in the Arab quarter were setting fires on the banks of the Nile to scare the cholera away," Este said.

"It won't work," said Louis. He became quiet. A shyness fell over him. Este saw it.

"Tell me about your home," she asked, and the shyness lifted. He told her about his mother and the park in Amiens where he had played as a child, and how here in Alexandria he sometimes dreamed that he was still a boy at home. He told her the name of the priest who had buried his friend Bernard, and he described for her the bank where his father worked, with its high brass rails and a great mahogany clock on the wall. She listened carefully. They walked past the bazaar, but did not stop to look at the wares spread before them. Louis told Este about Pasteur, about his useless arm and about his fierce eyes and the way he sat for hours unmoving in his chair in the corner of the lab. He told her that the world was changing, soon there would be no more unreasonable prattle about miracles and magic, and everyone would understand that things needed to be proved, evidence given, so that human life could be saved, disease defeated.

"But that will take a long time," said Este.

"It will," said Louis. "But it will happen. No more fairy tales."

"I like fairy tales," said Este.

"Enjoy them," said Louis, "but don't believe them."

Este told Louis about her friend Phoebe's brother Albert whom she had always thought she would marry but now wasn't so sure. It was not fair, she said, that her brother took a boat to Palestine and she had to stay here, where day after day everything was just the same. They talked to each other with that whispered frenzy which does not imply clarity, but does reveal a magnetic pull, one sex to the other.

ALBERT'S FATHER CALLED him into his study after dinner. The younger man was ready to go out for the evening. He was playing cards at the club Au Quatre Deuce, placed discreetly off a side street of rue Bab Sidra, with some friends. He was already late because the servant had been slow in bringing the dessert to the table. His father, who had been unusually quiet during the meal, turned his head away from his son: a bad sign.

"I have had a visit," he said, "from Dr. Malina. It seems, and I can hardly believe this to be true, that the ring you gave his daughter is a fake. The man was embarrassed to bring this to my attention, but thought I ought to know. I ought to know. What happened? Did you buy the girl a cheap ring? What's the matter with you?"

Albert was stunned into silence. He had not paid the normal price for the ring, but he had been told he was purchasing a fine jewel. He cursed Achmed. He had been cheated. He pulled at the edges of his small, sharp beard and screamed at his father. "The ring was intended to be of the first order. I was promised that it was. I have been robbed."

Albert's father had known his son to shade the truth, to evade punishment, to make himself appear better than he was, but now he believed him. His obvious fury seemed entirely genuine.

"It's about the honor of our family," he said in a gentler tone.

"And what about them, the Malinas?" said Albert. "What did

they do, take the ring for an evaluation, what kind of in-laws will they be, grasping and distrustful. For God's sake, we have known these people all our lives. How dare they think I would cheat their daughter?"

"But it seems you did," said the father. He reached into his desk and pulled out the velvet box. "Dr. Malina returned the ring in case you would like to replace it."

"I will immediately," Albert assured his father, but then he added, "perhaps you could help me with the purchase."

The father stared at his son. "You don't have it?"

"I don't have it," Albert answered. "A few gambling debts," he mumbled.

The father sighed. He did not want the engagement called off, the embarrassing reason running through the lips of gossips, reaching the ears of potential clients, whispered in the balcony of the synagogue. He pulled out a ring of keys and, finding the correct one, pushed aside a beautiful Persian rug that hung on the wall, revealing a metal box set into the wood paneling. There was a harsh scraping noise as the door to the box swung slowly open.

ACHMED WAS HAVING his hair and beard trimmed by his personal barber when Albert announced himself to the servant who opened the front door. "My friend, have a seat," said Achmed. "This won't take much longer." He flashed his very white teeth at the barber and motioned to Albert to come closer. Albert did not take a seat. He stood silently.

"What's the matter," said Achmed. "Bad news? Are you hung over and mean, like a camel with a bad tooth?"

Albert didn't say a word. Achmed finished his haircut in silence, then waved the barber away, and when both young men could hear his steps on the stairs, he turned to Albert. "What, what is it?"

"This is what it is," said Albert, and thrust out the box with the ring in it. "My fiancée and her mother went to a jeweler. The ring is no good, the ring is not what it should be, and I trusted you. I gave you my good money for this ring." Albert was shouting.

"But," said Achmed, "you wanted a bargain. I gave you a bargain. So it was a little less than perfect. Who would have expected the girl to discover that? What kind of people take an engagement ring to be checked? I would break the engagement if I were you." He turned to the mirror to smooth his hair. "You want some coffee?" He pointed to the small turquoise enamel tray with cups and a long-necked coffeepot, that rested on a nearby table.

"I don't want your coffee," said Albert. "I want you to make good on your word. I want a perfect ring, larger even than this one, compensation for my grief."

Achmed laughed. "Business is business, my friend," he said. "You bought the ring. Buy her another if you don't like it. I could sell you another, but the price will be higher, much higher."

Albert was not a man who found humor in a situation such as this. He grabbed his friend by the back of his shirt and pulled him up. He glared into his eyes.

"Poor boy," said Achmed, and tried to shake himself free. The way he said "poor boy" was unfortunate. Albert flew for his throat. Achmed, who was the larger if the flabbier of the two, pushed back, and they both fell into the mirror, which had green and yellow geometric tiles embedded at its border. The mirror slipped from the wall, the glass cracked, and shards spread out across the floor. One of them flew into Achmed's right eye. "You fool," screamed Achmed in a mixture of pain and anger. Albert saw the blood run down his friend's face. "Jew, dirty Jew!" screamed Achmed. And there it was.

This is how Achmed appeared at Dr. Malina's office with a piece of glass, not a small piece, in his eye and was shown immediately into a room where the doctor examined him and extracted the glass after giving the patient a pint of brandy and tying down his hands so his work would not be interfered with. "How did this happen, young man?" asked Dr. Malina as he was wrapping a bandage around Achmed's head, covering his right eye, which, in his professional opinion that he kept to himself, would never prove useful again and might have to be removed in its entirety if infection set in.

"I was set upon," said Achmed, "by your future son-in-law, a man of foul temper, a former friend. I'm calling the police and issuing a complaint. I did nothing to him, nothing to provoke such a vicious attack."

11

ERIC FORTMAN HAD inspected a ship carrying rope from Burma that morning. The captain of the ship was a large black African whose vessel had seen better days. Marbourg & Sons should not send a return shipment on this particular vessel. Eric wrote up his report. The captain of the ship had a scimitar strapped to his waist. He was far taller and broader a man than Eric. His wide bare chest was alarming. "You give good word on ship," the African said. Eric nodded. "Let me see what you have written," he demanded. Eric opened his hand and let the notebook in which he was writing fly into the water. The captain opened his own hand, in which he held a small knife with a beautiful pearl handle, carved in the Orient but with a very sharp point.

"Wonderful ship," said Eric. "I will tell the office. Wonderful ship," he repeated. The two men shook hands. Back in the captain's shabby quarters, the captain opened a bottle of whiskey and poured some in an unwashed glass, stained with some brown tobacco spots. The African took a drink himself and offered the glass to the inspector from Marbourg & Sons, who wished to decline but didn't.

Back in his office, with its window overlooking the port, Eric wrote an accurate report on the Burmese ship, not leaving out the peculiar smell that permeated the hold, some kind of spoiled food. He was not in the business of offering favors for free. He did not like having knives flashed in his face. In the afternoon he went to the Marbourg & Sons warehouse and assisted in a count of sacks filled with feathers that were set to sail for Marseille. It was difficult work because the sacks were piled in an irregular manner and it was hard not to lose count, since one sack looked exactly like another. By the time the sun was sinking and the birds were cawing loudly and the harbor was settling in for the night and the donkeys had been taken back to the sheds behind their owners' rooms, Eric was eager for some diversion and joined two young men who had also been counting sacks of feathers. The three of them took a carriage out to the edge of town to watch the dancing around a huge explosive bonfire by a group of very dark villagers who had come to the city, turning into performance a ritual that had once lured fish into the nets, and caused the sun to rise, and the flat, dry land to yield some fruit. A cherry-tasting drink was passed from hand to hand as the audience cheered the dancers on and the fire lit up their faces, which seemed absent, as if they were ghosts, not men.

He woke the next morning on the beach under a palm tree with a large frond covering his body. The heat of the day was beginning. His head was heavy. The moist, hot air settled unpleasantly in his lungs. There was stubble on his face. He felt in his pocket. His money was still in his purse. His tie was gone. His jacket seemed to have been torn in several places, but otherwise he was fine. He brought himself to the main road, where an Englishman, an official of some kind, offered him a ride home. He asked him if he had enjoyed his evening. The Englishman had some position in the consulate. He invited Eric to dine with him and handed him his card. He did not tell him that he had followed him to the dancers, would in the future observe all his movements in Alexandria, that this was his assignment, without excitement or obvious purpose as it may have been. Eric dozed in the carriage quite peacefully. Although he remembered little of his evening, he regretted nothing.

One of his companions from Marbourg & Sons had become ill on the tram back to the center of the city. He had been tossed out by the other riders, who were offended and frightened by his odor. He did not arrive home.

IN THE EUROPEAN Hospital, the boy who had refused to let Louis take samples of his skin stirred. He felt weak. His legs trembled. His mouth was dry. But he opened his eyes. He smelled himself. He was embarrassed. It was not his fault, he knew. He was sick. It was cholera. He knew it was cholera. He would die. But then perhaps not. He did not believe in his own death, the way young men do not, not with any conviction, not with their whole minds. He would not give in. He was as pale as the porcelain bowl that had been placed by his body. He needed to get up. He moved his legs. He moved his arms. He was thirsty. Are dying men thirsty? "I need water," he called out. His voice was weak, but it was his voice. He recognized it. So did his father, who was hurrying down the hall, Dr. Malina at his side. When the two men entered the room, the father grabbed the wall to steady himself. But the doctor walked to the patient's side and looked into his eyes, opened his mouth with his fingers, and said, "He may be one of the lucky ones. It seems to be passing. The worst might be over." The father heard the *may* and the *might*.

"Water," begged the son. It was brought to him in a bowl and he drank and he drank. He vomited up some of the water, but not all of it. He lay there on the hospital bed. He was breathing. His heart was beating. If he picked up his head, he could see his chest moving. He saw his father's face. "I'm all right," he said. His father was silent. He was promising many things to God in return for his son's recovery. He promised more than he would ever be able to deliver, but that didn't matter at the moment. The deal could be renegotiated later.

The father had understood from the days right after his child's birth that he was less of a man than Abraham. He had three sons and he would never sacrifice any of them to God. He would have run. He would have hidden his child. He would have begged God to bless some other seed, to leave him and his son watching the sheep, seeing the sun rise over the mountaintop, watching the river shrink in drought and fill in fullness when the rains came. Therefore he was an ordinary man, not a leader, not a hero whose name would be remembered for millennia. The father wanted his son to recover from cholera far more than he wanted his name in books, holy or otherwise. "Do animals love their children this much?" he asked Dr. Malina, who was listening to the boy's stomach as it rumbled on.

"Quiet," said Dr. Malina. He had no time for this sort of conversation. He was feeling the muscle tone in the boy's legs. His lips were not as blue as they had been.

Later, many hours later, when the boy sat up and worried if he had dropped his schoolbag on the way to the hospital and the father called for a carriage and, wrapping his son in a blanket, carried him away, thanking Dr. Malina and the sisters again and again, no matter how the doctor protested that he had done nothing, deserved no praise, would charge no fee, had simply stood by. Monsieur Vernon, whose family had exported wool from Egypt to the Continent for a hundred years, swore eternal friendship to Dr. Malina, which thoroughly embarrassed the doctor, who knew well enough how little he had done. Later Dr. Malina wondered why the boy, that particular boy, had chased the cholera out of his system when others, no stronger, no better, no wiser, no more or less healthy, had succumbed. Could the French assistants of Pasteur ever answer that question? Was it in fact God who made the choice? That idea offended the doctor, reduced him to helplessness, an ant before the Lord on Judgment Day. He shook off the thought.

In the future, everything would be explained. What a comfort that idea was to a man still in the dark about who lives and who dies, a man whose lifework it is to ensure that fewer die and more live. What had happened just now in the hospital? Would he ever know? The boy had survived and the sheets were being washed by the hospital laundry in great vats of hot water, and science would not be served any more specimens that afternoon.

Discouraged is what the news of the boy's recovery made

Louis feel. The microbe must be there, but had not revealed itself. None of the animals in the cages at the back of the laboratory had sickened when injected with any suspicious mixture. What was Koch doing? Was he working the same way that they were? Had he an inspiration, an innovation that would show the microbe, round, skinny, long, short, on his slide? He had exhausted himself trying to force an inspiration to come into his mind.

ESTE ARRIVED AT the laboratory. Her cheeks were flushed with excitement. In the evening, just as she was falling asleep, a thought had come to her. Perhaps a good soak in seawater, saltwater, would produce the cholera, since heat had failed. She wanted to try it. She came up behind Roux, who was busy peering at the cultures he had made several days before. Nothing. He saw nothing. She could tell from the set of his shoulders, from the fact that he did not turn around to look at her, although he must have heard her approach, that this was not the right time to present her idea to him. She went over to the table where Louis was carefully taking some bowel matter and mixing it in a jar with some sugar. He turned toward her. The shadows in the laboratory made it impossible for him to see every angle of her body, but he already knew them. He listened carefully to her idea. He gently explained to her why it was useless. He told her about Darwin. It took millions of years to produce life from the sea. She was disappointed. He told her that he had many ideas that were useless, several a day. He smiled at her. This restored her spirits. She stood next to him at the table. His hand brushed against hers. He was embarrassed by the touch. He had not meant to be so forward. It was an accident. She felt the warmth of his fingers for a barely a second. It is strange, she thought, how such a brief moment, such a little matter, could make her so eager to live forever. He was distracted by his longing for Este, and his fear that nothing would end happily for him.

In the late afternoon, after Este went home, Louis curled up on the couch in his lab and, pulling the cloth at the base of the couch over his legs, fell quickly into sleep. When Marcus entered, he found Louis deep in dream and didn't disturb him. He went outside and in the alley smoked his cigarette and told his own fortune with the tarot cards he had obtained from the bazaar. He cheated, but only a little. After a while he checked back on Louis, who was still sleeping, although dusk was falling over the harbor and the lamps were lit in the café at the corner. He walked off to the Corniche and smelled the sea air of the Eastern Harbor and watched the waves, the dumb waves, repeat and repeat their only trick, to curl and unwind, to go forward and then back. He saw Venus in the sky, the evening star. He saw a fat man sitting on the sand on a small stool. He walked down to him. The man smiled, a fat man's smile. "What has the sea washed up?" said the man. He said this in Greek, he said it in Arabic, he said it in English, he said it finally in French. Marcus understood. He put his hand on Marcus's knee. Marcus moved away, but not far away.

"Come home with me," said the man, "and I will reward you well."

Here, so far from home, from anyone who knew him, who cared for him, Marcus paused. Why not? he thought to himself. One day I'll be old and I will remember when I was on the sand in Alexandria and an old man bought me for the evening.

"I want the money on the table before," said Marcus.

The fat man laughed. "I won't cheat you," he said. "Why should I? Cheating is wrong." When the man laughed, his chins shook. His teeth were small for his big face.

⌒⧓⌒

ESTE ARRIVED AT the laboratory early one morning with her maid and found the animals wailing with hunger. Marcus had not appeared. She began to feed them, talking to them as she moved down the line of cages. Nocard came in and asked her if she wanted to help him operate on the skull of a pig, extracting some brain matter so they could examine the tissue.

"Yes," said Este.

"Will this upset you, Mademoiselle?" asked Edmond. "It is difficult. It makes some people sick to watch this, and you are, after all, a woman. I mean no insult by this."

Este was not insulted. "That's all right," she said. "I can do it."

"This afternoon, then," he said. She agreed.

Louis came into the laboratory, and she told him of the plan. "That will be unpleasant," he said.

"I know," said Este.

"It took me a long time to get used to watching Nocard drilling into the skull, and then an even longer time until I could do it myself," Louis said.

"I'll get used to it quickly," Este said.

Louis led her to the far side of the room. Nocard could still hear them if he listened, but he had no interest in listening.

"Papa says he met Dr. Koch at the ministry, and the German says he has made no final progress. He is not ready to present his findings," Este said.

"Neither are we," said Louis.

"It'll be good when you find the cholera," said Este, "but then what will I do? You will go back to Paris. I will have no laboratory to visit, no slides to prepare. I will sit in my room and go mad."

"You will get married," said Louis. The words came out of his mouth as if they were stones.

"I don't know," said Este, "maybe not. What about you? Will you marry someone in Paris?"

"Never," said Louis.

"Why not?" said Este.

"Because," he said, "I would never marry if I did not want the woman to be by my side in everything I did ever after."

"You'll find such a woman," said Este.

"I have found such a woman," said Louis.

Este gasped. He turned away. He was afraid he had said more than he should. She said nothing, but she felt many things, among them triumph.

ERIC FORTMAN SAT at the table in the British offices in a back room of the consulate. He had not been escorted there voluntarily. "It seems," said one of the uniformed officers, "that your bank account is growing very well in Alexandria."

"That is true," said Eric. "I am employed by Marbourg & Sons."

"We know," said the officer. "We have been talking to certain captains of ships you have inspected."

Eric felt his lip tremble. "Everyone takes a little on the side," he said meekly.

"We are interested in you," said the officer. "We are concerned that you will lose your position."

Eric pulled at the edge of his mustache. He was trapped. Adrenaline raced through his system. But he wasn't trapped after all. The officer went on, "We would, however, overlook this unseemly matter if you would perform a small service for the Crown."

"Anything, anything at all." Relief rushed through his body, his arteries pumped eagerly, his brain cells trilled and shook. All would be well.

"You know Dr. Abraham Malina."

"Yes," said Eric.

"We need information on his political activities."

"I'm not quite certain," said Eric, "that he has political activities."

"That is not for you to decide," said a junior officer, picking up the thick file before him, which had Eric's name in bold print across its face. "The man is a Jew," said the junior officer.

"There are many Jews in Alexandria," said Eric.

"And they are all untrustworthy," said the junior officer.

"He has a lovely daughter," Eric offered.

"We are not interested in his daughter," said the officer.

"I am," Eric muttered as he rose to his feet, but then he came to his senses. What could one man do to right the injustices of the world? Was it his fault if the Crown decided it had an enemy in a man of medicine in a distant port? His responsibility was to himself. He had no one else to rescue him from difficulties, no family, no connections in the foreign office, the home office, or the palace. He had only himself, and while he would never, without reason, have harmed the family that had been so hospitable to him, he now had more than a reason, he had necessity, a cold wind on his back. He promised the officer he would do his best for England because he was a true patriot. This is all nonsense, he reassured himself. Nothing will be asked of me. It will blow over, and the little agents of the Crown will find someone else to scare.

"A TERRIBLE THING has happened," said Dr. Malina to his wife. She held her breath. "Albert has attacked his friend Achmed. It seems Achmed supplied Este's ring to Albert from his stock. Achmed claims he gave his friend exactly what his money would buy, but Albert expected to be given a higher quality ring. At least that is what Achmed says. Achmed will likely lose his eye."

Lydia felt relieved. Whatever she had imagined the terrible thing to be, it was far worse than the words she heard. "Achmed can see with his other eye," she said. "A man can go through his entire life with one eye without ever missing a sunset."

Dr. Malina stared at her as if he had never seen her before. "That's not the point," he said. "Albert attacked his friend. What might he do to our daughter if he gets angry with her?" Dr. Malina glared at Lydia as if she herself had harmed their child. "What kind of a man is he?"

"A young man," said Lydia. "A hotheaded young man who felt insulted by the crack in the ring he had given his fiancée. He was embarrassed. He was ashamed. Perhaps his behavior was not the best, but it is over now."

"No," said Dr. Malina, "I don't think it's over. Achmed's father will not think the matter closed. There will be more trouble."

Lydia put a light hand on her husband's shoulder. "No," she said, "the families are friends. The boys have known each other all their lives."

"I heard at the Medical Society meeting on Tuesday last that some of families of the dead are blaming the Jews for the epidemic."

"Jews again," said Lydia. At last she allowed some worry to enter her voice. "We poisoned the wells in Zurich with the Black

Plague, and we brought the pox to Hamburg, and we're dropping cholera into the streets so the Christians will die, is that it? What monsters we must be."

"None, not a single one, of the doctors at the meeting thought the Jews were at fault," her husband assured her. "Dr. Loudine said that superstition and ignorance should be ignored."

"That's a comfort," said Lydia. "But this has nothing to do with Albert."

"Only that Achmed is Muslim and Albert is Jewish and the argument between them might force the communities to take sides, adding fuel to the small fire already started," said Dr. Malina.

"This is just a private quarrel. If anyone is injured, it's Este, who was given a poor ring by a man she has entrusted with her life," Lydia said. "We are at home here."

"At the very least, this engagement must be broken and broken now. I do not want our family involved in this dispute," said Dr. Malina.

"Your daughter needs to be married," said Lydia.

"Not to Albert, she doesn't," said Dr. Malina. "That matter is finished."

ESTE LAY ON her bed, the moonlight came in through the window. Almost a full moon, it cast its white glow over her sheets, over her nightgown, and made her pale skin seem even paler, ghostlike. She had unpinned her hair, which lay on the pillow around her, dark and curling. She was not sad that Papa had broken her engagement. She did want to be a married woman and have children of her own. But she was not sorry that her father had insisted that Albert was now an unsuitable mate. She had wanted to be Albert's bride for such a long time. But that was a while ago. Other things mattered to her now. Perhaps she could join her brother in Palestine and take care of orphans or lepers. Perhaps Louis Thuillier would take her to Paris and introduce her to the great Pasteur himself. The thought of Louis Thuillier sent a small shiver down her spine. This made her happy and unhappy. It did not seem possible, a future with Louis, but it did seem right, right in some profound way that defied her sense. She knew that Louis did not have enough money to take care of her and the children she would bear him. But she continued to think of herself in Paris with Louis, his hand on her arm, his shoulder leaning against hers in a train, his eyes on her back as she walked away from him, his eyes on her face as she walked toward him. It did not displease her that her destiny was not yet known, that the book of life was still open for her, that she was now safe in her own bed and all lay ahead.

She considered Louis Thuillier. The thing she felt for him she gave no name, but she recognized that there was nothing commonplace about it. What if he became a famous scientist and she was his wife accompanying him to Paris and Berlin, to London and Istanbul and Geneva, where other scientists would praise him and place ribbons around his neck, which he would give to her and she would keep in a velvet-covered box on her dresser? What if she helped in the laboratory? What if she herself made a contribution to her husband's work? She imagined herself in his laboratory in Paris, preparing the small dishes to receive the drops of diseased matter, recording the day's activities, labeling bottles and maybe more. She would learn more. She would learn everything he knew. Would it matter to her if she couldn't see her mother and father every Friday night? It was only natural for children to move away from the family. If her brother could do it, she could do it, too. Of course the thought was also worrying. Papa would never allow it. Louis was not one of them. It was unthinkable. She couldn't stop thinking about it. She got out of bed, turned on the gas lamp, reached for her often neglected diary, and wrote, *I am an eagle and must fly away from my nest.* She filled the page with question marks that grew smaller and smaller and stretched out line after line. On the next page she wrote, *Poor Achmed. I hope nothing happens to his remaining eye. It would be so terrible to be blind.*

ON HIS OWN bed, in his own shirt, having left his socks on because he didn't want to see that they needed both washing and mending, Louis, too, was unable to sleep. He was working. His notebook was on his lap. His lamp was burning dully by his side. He had written, *All living things eat to survive. The cholera eats what?* He thought of his enemy like a swarm of ants, though far smaller, of course, swarming over the water, like water bugs looking for something to eat. He thought of the cholera like an army of raindrops falling on sheep and cattle and chickens, looking for something to eat. If he knew what it was that they ate, he could coax them out of hiding.

He thought of all the munching and crunching, chewing and swallowing, the gulping and sipping and grinding and clawing and pulling that was required to live. We are nothing more than digesting machines, thought Louis, and the thought was comforting. The mountain lion and the yeast are different in size but not in behavior. They both devour, open their mouths and absorb and send out waste and live on because they do so and would die if they did not. Man, too. Why was it this way? Louis did not know. Perhaps it was God who had created all living things, who had designed them to consume each other in an unending round of mastication. Even human beings were no more than a food source for maggots and even smaller things. That was certainly so. Louis held his pencil in his hand and nibbled on his own lip. Were there unseen creatures on his pencil, climbing the spine of his notebook? Were they all killing something smaller and weaker than themselves? He felt like weeping. But why?

The sisters in his school had taught him that there were two main branches of life, plants and animals, and insects rested somewhere in between. Could the cholera be an animal without an enemy? If so, it would be unique. Everything else that lived suffered and died at the hands of something else. What would eat the cholera? He thought of the tigers in India. He had seen pictures of them. They had eyes that blinked when the light changed. They had noses that smelled prey. They had cubs that climbed rocks after them. He thought of his dog, who leaped about and barked with joy when he returned from school. What thrived, what nourished itself on the cholera? But what of the cholera? It wouldn't be drowned. It wouldn't die in a fire. Was cholera the only immortal creature on earth?

His mind slipped to Este. What was she doing? Was she, too, in her bed? He thought of her there, and the muscles deep within his body were pulled tighter. He was ashamed. Edmond was writing a letter to his mother while eating a honey pastry, his fifth for the day. Emile was sound asleep in his bed. Marcus had not returned to the laboratory for several days. The mattress on the floor was unoccupied. Where was Marcus? Louis wondered if he was in a café, listening to the songs of a woman wrapped in silk, with the flesh of her arms appearing and disappearing under the gyrations of her body.

There is more to life than eating, he said to himself. There is also reproduction. Without reproduction there is no history, no story, no breathing, no copulating, nothing but rock and mineral and death. How did the cholera reproduce itself? The answer to that question had to wait until he could see the cholera. But still in his mind he heard the sucking sounds of creatures smaller than ear mites consuming flakes of things that had themselves once lived. God help me, he said to himself, and tried to sleep. The very trying kept him awake.

Dr. Malina was also having trouble sleeping. He was hoping that Achmed's eye would begin to heal. Had he been right to cancel his daughter's engagement? He was not a man given to self-doubt, but banishing Albert from his daughter's future would have consequences that he could not imagine, good or bad. He rose from his bed, entered his study, and read in Macnamara's book an entry for 1817.

Within three months from its appearance the disease has been generated throughout the province of Bengal, including some 195,915 square miles and within this vast area the inhabitants of hardly a single village or town has escaped its deadly influence. The army of the Marquis of Hastings camping in Vindhay Pradesh was devastated. The march was terrible for the number of poor creatures falling under the sudden attacks of this dreadful affliction and from the quantities of bodies of those who died in wagons and were necessarily put out to make room for such as might be saved by conveyance. It is ascertained that above 500 have died since sunset yesterday.

Achmed was recovering at home. His mother had made a bed for him in the downstairs library. She had placed her best sheets on the bed and brought pillows from all the other beds in the house to prop behind her wounded son. Every hour, she sent the servant in to ask him if he needed anything, and she herself stayed outside his room all through the night, sitting on a small stool and praying that his sight would be restored. When Dr. Malina arrived in the late afternoon of the fourth day after the attack, he removed the bandage. He looked at his patient's eye, from which a pale green pus was flowing, and felt his patient's sweating forehead. He shook his head. The eye would have to be removed. Dr. Malina sent his assistant for his surgical tools. He told the man to bring from his chemical closet enough anesthetic to blur the pain. Achmed's mother wept. His father cursed the Jew who had done this. Dr. Malina ignored the curses. It was natural that the man would be upset. A Jew does not pay attention to every insult to his tribe. If he did, he couldn't live with his neighbors or do business in the marketplace or move about his city without fear. Dr. Malina assumed that the insults were signs of the pain in the other man, not the shadings of his own portrait. It was not entirely clear to Dr. Malina why the eye had become infected. Was there something he should have done to prevent it? What? The young man screamed in pain despite the anesthetic that was poured through a tube into his mouth. It had not been enough. It often was not enough, although too much was sometimes mortal.

ALBERT HAD TROUBLE concentrating on the report on his desk. It had something to do with a request for investment in a business that would import knives from Damascus to Alexandria and from there send them in small gilded sheaths all over the Mediterranean. The figures before him jumped around. Was it a good investment opportunity or a bad one? Albert was not concentrating. His father was furious with him. The marriage would have been good for the family, not so much in terms of actual funds coming in, but in family prestige, honor. He had botched it with his cheapness about the ring. His father insisted he fix his mistake. The girl would have to be convinced of his undying affection and her family persuaded by their daughter's tears. It was the only thing he could do. At lunch Albert had a cramp in his leg, which he massaged with his hand under the table. His fish in lemon oil was barely touched. Why was it so damned hard just to get a woman in a house with servants around her, her mother nearby, and all her needs taken care of ever after. Resentment rose in his breast. All he had done, after all, was give her a ring with a small flaw in it. He was entitled to a little pleasure himself. This was such a primitive business, this getting a bride. It was as if he were a fisherman on the Nile, counting out the nets he would give to the bride's father. It was a wonder, he thought, that more men didn't just go it alone. He was not feeling friendly when he came to the Malinas' door and begged most humbly to see Este. "Just a few moments of her time," he said to the girl who opened the door.

When he entered the drawing room, Este was standing by the window. She was very pale and stood very straight, as if a medal were about to be pinned on her chest.

Albert's black hair was combed down over his forehead on one side. His shoes were shining. His suit was formal, his tie subdued. His smile was tenuous, eager, sweet. "This is all my fault," he said. "I asked my friend, my good friend, Achmed, to find a ring for me that was worthy of my bride. He betrayed me, but I should have suspected as much. I should have taken the ring to be examined before I gave it to you. I have been careless, but not because I thought you should not have the finest jewels in the universe." He stared into Este's eyes.

He was earnest. He was sincere. He was handsome, as always. He was her best friend's brother. But her affections did not burst forth. She was surprised at her own reserve. Perhaps he seemed *too* sincere; a sincerity this intense was suspect. After all, no great harm had been done. She didn't mind, not really. She hadn't seen any flaw herself. She would have preferred him to laugh at all this parental concern about a mere ring. She would have liked him to tell her she was the only woman he would ever marry, even if she were poor, even if her father were not so well known in Alexandria, even if she were a tailor's daughter. This he did not even think to say. When she was silent, he pressed on, "I will make it up to you. I will buy you an even more wonderful ring and deliver it into your hands as soon as you say that you still want to be my bride." Here, unfortunately, his hiccups began and interrupted his speech.

"You need water," said Este, who rang for the servant. "Sit down, perhaps that will help," she said. "Hold your breath." Her nanny had taught her that secret cure for hiccups. Albert sputtered and choked and tried to hold his breath, but whatever he did, his chest heaved and a small squeaky sound came from his mouth. "I'll open the curtains," said Este. "Perhaps more air." Este looked at Albert, who was now turning red from the effort of holding his breath.

"Perhaps we could continue this later, when your hiccups are gone," she said. "I am beginning to think," she added, her own heart throbbing in her chest, "that maybe I am too young to get married. I think a wife should be wise as well as beautiful, and I am not yet wise. Don't you agree with me that too many girls marry before they've thought the matter through?"

Albert nodded his head, but he had never before considered the matter. "You are wise," he said, but he hiccuped between "are" and "wise."

Este wanted to laugh but knew that would be very rude. She turned her head away to hide the smile that came to her face.

"Don't turn away from me," Albert moaned, but he hiccuped three times between "from" and "me."

"Oh, do go," said Este, who had lost patience with the man, which she knew was very wrong of her, but there it was. Besides, Papa had said no, and she would never go against his wishes. Or would she? Perhaps, she admitted to herself, she would.

ACHMED'S FATHER HAD called the police. He wanted to press charges. "An eye for an eye," he roared, "that's what those people understand." Achmed refused to call the police. "I'll get this settled myself," he said. Achmed's mother wept. Her son's face was swollen. His socket would not be ready for a false eye for some months, and there was terror, some shame, some disgrace in her son's disfigured image. When she thought of the bones of his eye, naked to the air, leading back into his skull, she cursed the day that Albert had been born. She cursed Albert's bride-to-be, and she flung her arms around her wounded son, who pushed her away in irritation and vowed to move out of the family home as soon as possible.

Achmed called on two of his friends from the university. He told them he had been attacked by a greedy Jew. A Jew? Yes, a Jew, and Achmed said the word from deep within his chest, as if it were a word he never used, a word that implied a curse, carried a curse, was itself dangerous, sent a foul odor up into the air.

WHICH IS HOW Albert found himself in his bed, bruised in his legs where he had been hit with a metal tube, and suffering from a painful bruise on his cheek from a punch one of the boys had thrown. Someone had cut his finger so that it dangled uselessly on his hand. His ribs hurt. His hair had been pulled in patches out of his head. He had been punched into unconsciousness, found by a passing donkey boy, and delivered to his house in a folded heap. The donkey boy was well rewarded for his consideration.

Albert's father had wanted to call the police to arrest Achmed, but first he called his lawyer. A prominent member of the synagogue, a Monsieur Florent, who had studied in Paris, who wore a monocle, who smoked thin cigarettes imported from Italy that stayed clasped between his lips unless he needed to eat or to speak. Monsieur Florent said, "We must offer a settlement to the family so that they do not press charges about the eye. We will not be able to prove that Achmed was responsible for the beating. Albert cannot clearly identify his attackers. If it comes to the courts, there will be no sympathy for your son. The other boy will show his face with its lost eye, and your son will have little defense. This will not be good for our faith. It will be in the newspapers. It will confirm certain prejudices. Your son did, after all, purchase the diamond for less money than every gentleman knows a diamond of that size should cost." Monsieur Florent sat down in a Louis XVI chair covered in a strawberry and vine pattern. He leaned forward. "Do not think I am critical," he said, "but I am certain that others in our community will find it peculiar that your family was stingy with their offering to the bride. We tend to judge the worth of the groom's family by their generosity to the family of the bride. People will think that you have fallen upon hard times. People will think that perhaps your skills have deserted you. Of course I know better, but we don't want too much of a scandal here."

Albert's father was furious, although he did not reveal it to his lawyer. He simply said, "I thought it was your role to fight for our rights in this matter."

Monsieur Florent sighed. "I am protecting you, I promise."

Albert's father puffed on a cigar. He stared out the window. He was not a fool, only a fool goes deaf in the presence of his lawyer.

Albert's father agreed that Monsieur Florent should negotiate a settlement, although the sum proposed made his heart sink.

Achmed's father still wanted to put the Jew in jail. He listened to Monsieur Florent. He called his wife into the room, who wouldn't hear of a settlement. It wasn't money she wanted. It was revenge. Achmed himself was interested in the offer, but he said nothing. His father would not have allowed it. After four cups of dark coffee, after several hours in which Monsieur Florent explained again and again how embarrassing the matter would be for Achmed and the family—doubts cast on their honesty, the integrity of their merchandise, and so on—a settlement was agreed upon at three times the amount that Monsieur Florent had proposed to Albert's father. Albert's mother's jewels would have to be sold. The cabana at the beach would have to be given up. The household would, at least for a while, be on a tight budget. Phoebe would have to wait for her own marriage until some funds were recouped, unless a wealthy boy would have her with a very reduced dowry. It was not a small matter.

Albert spent three nights and three days in his bed. When he rose at last, he was not greeted as a hero, as the victim of injustice that he felt himself to be. He could feel the chill in his father's voice as he called him into his study. He saw that his sister had been crying, and his mother turned her face away from him when he bent to kiss her.

AT THE BREAKFAST table, Lydia Malina read about the affair in the paper, which reported that Achmed had a huge bandage over his eye and contained a statement from Monsieur Florent that the unfortunate matter had been amicably concluded by the two families, who understood that young men had high tempers and no harm had been intended and the loss of Achmed's eye was a terrible accident. Lydia said to her husband, "We will go to the Sonnenscheins' for dinner next week, they have a cousin who I hear is most eligible."

"I hear he is a cripple with a hunched back, that cousin," said Este.

"You heard no such thing," said her mother, and the two women laughed.

Dr. Malina got up from the table and went to his surgery, where he knew a woman was waiting whose baby had a bulge in his small belly that boded ill. He would hint at its nature to the mother while not quite telling her all that he suspected.

LOUIS AND EMILE and Edmond decided to increase their hours in the lab. They would work until sleep overtook them. Louis vowed not to think about Este. He would concentrate all his mind on his work. Emile would abandon his wife and children and turn all his attention to the elusive microbe. "There are too damned many people in this filthy city," said Edmond. "You can't get a coffee without mud in it. I tell you, I've just about had enough. I'm ready to go home."

Louis said, "Don't worry, my friend, we'll have years to walk on our clean streets and eat our own food at our own table, and read *Le Figaro* on the day it's published. This is just a small interruption."

He smiled at Edmond, whose bad humor disappeared as quickly as it had arrived, and who smiled back. "Is that a promise?" he asked.

"It's a promise," Louis said. "Courage," he added.

"Courage it is," said Edmond, who went off to the tents pitched outside of town, where the camels grazed near the river and their owners seemed to doze perpetually on carpets spread on the sand. Camel dung was what he needed.

If a man concentrates, there is nothing he cannot do, or so one of Louis's favorite professors had said. Of course the professor, despite a very amiable manner, had himself published nothing of note and had, while Louis was still in school, been passed over for a senior administrative position. Nevertheless, Louis stared at the mouse guts that had been gathered in a bowl by his elbow. Was the germ perhaps in the mouth of the mouse, or did it have nothing to do with the mouse? Did mice have a way of avoiding cholera, of spitting it out, or pushing it out with their waste products? Did their tiny ears flick it out with fine hairs, did their eyes close when the germ came near? There were dead mice around, but they did not seem to have cholera in them, not even when he took his syringe and pressed the blood of the cholera victim he had taken from the hospital into the mouse, not even then did they get sick. Lucky mouse, what spared you? asked Louis.

Eric Fortman responded immediately to the note delivered to his office by an attaché at the British consulate. As he was walking up the steps at the entrance to the building, Lord Cromer himself, flanked by several officers of the Royal Navy, brushed past him. It was as if an avalanche had gone by, leaving him untouched but breathless. The Union Jack hung limply above his head. He was well aware of the fact that Britannia had her foot on his neck, as well as on all of Alexandria and most of the known world. He was escorted up a grand staircase, in a rather firm manner, by the attaché, and ushered into a back room. He was offered a glass of water. The water was poured from a pitcher that had been brought from the officers' quarters in the rear of the building. He refused the water. This was no moment for congeniality. The room was as hot as a steam bath from the sun beating down on the roof above. Eric was sweating. He took out his handkerchief and wiped his brow. "We need some information from you," said the large man in a fine suit who stood above him.

"There is nothing to report," said Eric. "I have had dinner with Dr. Malina and his family. I have heard nothing about plots against the British, here or in Palestine. Their son seems to be dealing in olives, and the father is concerned about the epidemic in Alexandria, and the mother and the daughter are going to teas and lunches and buying clothes, things like that." Eric was embarrassed. This was ridiculous.

"We can have you on a ship back to England in a matter of hours," said the other man in the room. His jacket was tight across his stomach. His posting in Alexandria had not brought hardship, unlike his five years in India, where he had lost his wife and child to malaria. "We can have you in a jail in Cyprus as quickly as you boil your morning egg. You can be deported on an English ship and never reach England. Is that clear?" said the man.

It was clear, but what was he to do?

"We are not asking you to lie," said the fatter one, in a far gentler voice. "We are asking you to observe the Malinas with a clear eye. You understand."

He understood.

"And we haven't years to wait," the one with the good suit added. "This matter needs to be concluded. These people are dangerous wherever they live, camouflaged among the citizens, holding a seat on the Committee of Public Safety, this man may do us grave harm."

"But," said Eric, "I don't think the Malina family——" He was interrupted and sent on his way.

Eric Fortman was not a stupid man. His position in England had not enabled him to rise very far from his origins, which were humble without being disastrous. He had a perfectly decent moral code and a conscience that, while obviously not unduly harsh, still worked efficiently. He believed that when he accepted funds from captains of ships doing business with Marbourg & Sons, he was acting as any sophisticated man would in a less-than-perfect commercial world. He admired the Malina family and felt gratitude toward them for their kindness to him. He was genuinely fond of dogs, and he quite seriously believed that birds should be free and not kept in cages. He most definitely did not want to be kept in a cage himself. He would gladly have married Este and settled down among the Malinas for the rest of his life. She was a good girl, with a high spirit. He liked that. He knew that Lydia Malina had a kind heart and had extended her hand to him, a stranger. He was, however, no dreamer. The threats from members of the British Foreign Service, here so far from England, seemed real enough. Who would notice or care if he fell off a ship as it was crossing the Mediterranean? Who would protest if he was found in an alley with his throat cut, another victim of robbery in a quarter known for its predatory inhabitants? He went immediately to the café at the docks where he had established himself as a regular. He ordered a beer and followed it with a harsh local whiskey, the kind that burns holes in your intestines. It was unlikely that the Malinas were plotting against the Crown, but the fools in the Foreign Service would not change their minds, that was clear. His choice was to leave Alexandria on the next boat (a city he was finding most pleasant) or implicate Dr. Malina and his son in some dubious activity, some political nonsense. There was something comic about these British gentlemen. What were they? he asked himself. Just well-dressed bullies with good positions in the service. Lucky them. As he drank, he found them more and more amusing. But as he staggered back to his rooms he remembered that he had no friend in high places to protect him. He hoped Dr. Malina did.

AFTER MANY NIGHTS in Alexandria's darkest and most secret places, Marcus returned. He made a vegetable soup and poured it into a bowl in the center of the table that the French mission used both for dining and writing letters.

"What's the matter with you?" asked Nocard, turning to Louis, who had not said a word for hours.

"I believe," said Roux, "he has a woman on his mind."

Louis said nothing.

"I think that must be it," said Nocard. "I have noticed he has the pallor of a man who has lost his heart."

Louis said nothing.

"There's no shame in it," said Roux. "She's a good-looking woman."

Louis said nothing.

"Ah," said Emile, "have you told her how you feel?"

Louis reached for his spoon and then put it down. His hand was shaking. "You know who it is?" said Louis, turning quite pale.

"I know," said Emile.

"I know, too," said Nocard.

"I've known for weeks," said Marcus.

"I've said nothing," said Louis.

"Not necessary," said Emile.

Nocard said, "She's good with the animals, that's in her favor."

Turning to Marcus, Nocard said, "This soup tastes like soap."

Marcus defended himself. "You want everything scrubbed and boiled, the flavor goes, what can I do?"

Louis said, "It's all right, we'll eat it."

But the three of them left their soup and went back to the laboratory. When they arrived, they found Dr. Robert Koch at the door, waiting for them.

"Any progress, Messieurs?" he asked.

"None," they assured him. "And you?" asked Emile, first in French, then in German. *"Und sie,* Nothing definitive," he said.

"He looks pleased with himself. He might have something," said Nocard to Roux as the metal door closed behind the small German's back. This was not comforting, but not as discomforting as a report of a demonstrable finding would have been.

12

THE MOON WAS high over the Western Harbor and lit up the upper windows of the Râs el Tin Palace, casting its reflection down on the muddy shores of Lake Mariout. You could observe it peering over the rooftop of the Babel Gedid train station. The hot wind was whipping over the Corniche, bringing with it clouds of sand, sand that seemed like fog, that stuck in the throat and burned the eyes. Louis was so weary and hungry that he had to leave his laboratory. Marcus had long ago left for whatever his evening promised. Emile was sleeping at his table. Nocard had returned to his bed in their apartment. Louis walked over to Emile and gently placed a towel used for drying beakers and tubes over his shoulders.

A sleeping man needed a cover. He pushed Emile's notebook out of the accidental reach of his arms, should he stir in his sleep. He had an impulse to touch Emile's head. He stopped himself.

Alone, Louis walked out in the warm night. He crossed the intersection where Alexander the Great had been laid to rest. Now he was just dust like any other mortal, not so great at all. Walking toward the center of town without conscious intention, he found himself in front of Dr. Malina's house. He stood across the street and wondered if anyone was sleepless in the house, or if they were all like the dead, immobile. He saw only darkness, pulled curtains. He heard the footsteps of a passerby, a drunk singing of love in Italian. He heard the grinding sound of carriage wheels on cobblestones as it pulled past him. A man veered near him, a sweet smell trailing him, a smile on his face. The smell hung in the air for a few seconds. The wind pulled at the palms on the street and their fronds bent low and made a whistling sound as they snapped back toward their trunks.

He seemed impaled on the building wall. He could not cross the street. He could not move on. In that house a woman lived who would change his life, who would inspire him to find the answer he was looking for. If only she would come to a window and wave to him. He willed her to come to the window. He willed her to pull back the curtains and look into the street, just in case someone was there, waiting for her. He imagined her surprise on seeing him. She would open the window and call to him. He waited. He would find the right words if she would just come to the window. He heard the muezzin's call to prayer. He heard a clap of thunder from afar. His jacket lifted and fell in the wind that blew the storm out to sea without ever reaching the shores of Alexandria. He stood there until he was almost asleep on his feet, his head drooping to one side in an attempt to find rest on his shoulder.

She was, however, asleep under her covers. She was holding her Ganesh, her good-luck elephant, in her hand. She had picked it up from her bedside and examined it carefully as she settled her head into the pillow. She had meant to put it back on the table before falling asleep. But she had missed the moment to act, and the elephant spent the shank of the night in her hand, and then as dawn was draining the sky of its ferocity and the stars were no longer visible, she opened her hand and the Ganesh fell out onto the carpet woven in the hills of Uzbekistan and carried on the back of a donkey across the mountains and placed on a ship and sold in the covered bazaar of Alexandria, where, before she was born, her mother had admired the bunches of grapes and the pink-petaled flowers that moved across the weave. The Ganesh was on the floor in the morning when she woke and put her feet out of bed and felt the hard wood of the elephant under her heel. She picked him up, ran her finger down his trunk, and replaced him on her table. How kind it was of Eric Fortman to have brought her this elephant.

She did not believe he was a lucky elephant. She was the daughter of a man of medicine, a reasoning man after all. But she did believe that there was little harm in pretending that the elephant had certain powers over fate. She did not believe in idols, but she did believe in games, and her Ganesh had his role to play in her life.

As she bathed before breakfast in the tub of warm water brought to her by the houseboy, she looked at her body, her private body, that no one saw but someday someone would see.

Louis had gone back to his apartment long before dawn, and so he didn't see her in the breakfast room when she opened the curtains and looked out on the street just to see who was coming and going, what might be approaching this new morning. "The coffee is perfect," she said to the serving girl. She dressed in a hurry and, after kissing her mother good-bye, rushed off to the laboratory.

"Are you sure," said Lydia Malina to her husband, "that it is all right to allow Este to visit this laboratory so often? My sister thinks—"

She was interrupted. "I don't care what your sister thinks. Este has Anippe to accompany her. She is never alone with the men. She is interested in their work, which is much better than her brooding over a lost marriage."

"She's not brooding," said Lydia.

"Good," said Dr. Malina, and that was the end of the subject.

THEY NEEDED MORE material infected with cholera. Este redeemed from the sisters a shirt of one victim and a diary of another with some unpleasant fluids spilled over the pages.

They went down to the sea so that Louis could think. Anippe followed discreetly behind. Louis said that he needed to change his view. His eyes were tired from peering through the lens, and his head hurt. There were terns rushing in and out of the foam. Este took off her shoes and stockings. Behind them the palm trees stood still, their craggy trunks peeling in the heat. Este waded up to her ankles in the cool water. The gently rippling waves went on as far as the eye could see. The horizon met the sky in a gray blur out there, far away. Louis took off his shoes and stockings and placed them neatly one next to the other. Then he, too, went into the water, his trousers rolled up. Louis took Este's hand and pulled her back when a larger wave threatened to splash up on her dress. He quickly let go of her hand. He hoped he had not been disrespectful. She seemed not to notice. She threw a pebble out into the waves. "Look how far it went," she said.

"We'd better get back," he said.

∽

AT THE MEETING of the Committee of Public Safety in the back
room of the Ministry of Health, the usual members had been joined
by the administrator of the ports and the representatives of the
Greek Orthodox church and the imam of the mosque and the chief
rabbi of Alexandria. The mood was bleak. The banking establish-
ments were working on skeleton staffs because the senior bankers
and investors, the importers and the more affluent tradesmen with
any reserves behind them, had removed themselves and their families from Alexandria. They had gone to country homes or to relatives in Cairo or Rome, or even to Istanbul or the small islands off
Greece. This meant that the shopkeepers and small café owners and
suppliers of linens and figs and meats and fruits were suffering from
a sharp loss of clients. The bars and cafés were thinly occupied.
People somehow thought that an evening's enjoyment might make
them sick. There had been few tourists at the hotels. Pyramids and
palaces, tombs and obelisks lacked visitors, which meant that guides
and donkey boys, postcard vendors and beggars, were all without
income. The churches were full of prayers. Candles burned night
and day. Funerals were almost constant. "How long will this last?"
the head of the company that ran the train that connected Alexandria to Aboukir, Rosetta, and Cairo asked Dr. Malina.

"All we know," said Dr. Malina, "is that at some point the epidemic will recede."

"Why will it retreat?" asked the railroad man, who was a German from Düsseldorf.

"We don't know," said Dr. Malina.

"You know very little," said a Coptic priest.

Dr. Malina said nothing.

"Mama," said Este, "would you miss me if I went abroad?"

"You're not going abroad," came the answer.

"I want to do something great with my life," Este said.

"Do you have something in mind?" asked her mother.

"I could marry a great scientist and help him in his work," said Este.

"Rubbish," said the mother, "girlish rubbish. You like your petticoats ironed. You like orange juice in the morning. You like soft sheets and you like to ride in comfort when you go to the beach and you want the servants to bring your biscuit at night and wash your clothes. You keep asking your father to purchase a private carriage for your comfort."

"I don't care about the carriage," said Este. But she did care, just a little.

Late that afternoon, Eric Fortman came to call. He found himself alone in the drawing room with Este. Her mother was visiting her old aunt in the Jewish Home for the Aging, where Este had refused to accompany her.

"Your brother," he asked her, "does he dislike the British?"

"You mean all the British?" asked Este.

"No, I mean the British soldiers."

"I don't know," said Este, who didn't. "Now he is just thinking about olives."

Eric asked, "Is there a secret passageway in this house?"

"Don't be silly," said Este. "Whatever for?"

"I was wondering if your father sent many letters to Palestine?"

"Yes, of course," said Este. "He writes to my brother often."

"In the Great Event," asked Eric, "did your father support the British?"

"Of course," said Este, "we're of the European community. We're not Arabs. Stop being so tedious. I hate politics myself. I'm really interested in science." This interest, though recent, was sincere.

"I think," said Eric, "that if I were of your people, I might have an interest in politics."

"Why?" said Este. "Whatever for?"

Eric shrugged. He wasn't sure what he meant himself.

"Have you taken the train to Aboukir yet?" asked Este.

"I haven't had the time," said Eric. "Come with me one Sunday," he suggested. She smiled.

She was a lovely woman, he thought. If he married her, then the British consulate might be satisfied. He would be right in the middle of the family, and if any plans were laid, he would be sure to hear of them. He could use a wife. He was of the right age. His future would be assured at Marbourg & Sons, and who knew what place he might find if Dr. Malina wished the best for him, his only son-in-law.

"Este," he said, "I must confess something to you."

"Really?" she said. She knew it was coming, the way you can tell when it will rain, by the turning of the leaves and the darkening of the sky and the wind rustling through the bushes. She sighed.

"I do not have a fortune," he said, "but I am a hard worker and clever, and my future here in Alexandria is bright, and I have feelings for you, deep feelings." (Was this the way it should be done? He hoped so.)

"I feel friendship for you, too," said Este, moving to a chair a little farther away from him.

"I am perhaps a little mature for you," he said, "but that makes me wise and able to protect you. If you encourage me, I would talk to your father. I have no doubt he would approve of our union."

Este, who had many doubts, said, "I think this conversation is too serious for such a lovely afternoon." She rang quickly for the servant, who was on her knees washing the entrance floor, which Dr. Malina had recently insisted be cleaned three times a day.

Eric decided to move quickly, decisively, women liked it when you moved with certainty. "I want to marry you," he said.

Este said, "You've startled me."

"I didn't mean to be so sudden," Eric said.

"That's very kind of you, but my father would not approve. It's not you," she added quickly. "He likes you very much. But we marry within our people," she said, thankful for the excuse. "But I'm sure you will find the right bride. So many women would be happy to have the honor of your company."

"But not you," said Eric.

"It's not that," said Este, although it was exactly that. "I am really too young to marry, don't you see?" She did not want to hurt him. She did not want to see the hurt in his eyes.

"Please," she said, "don't be angry with me, we must be friends." She had wanted to say, *I am already taken,* although that would not have been true, at least not outside the confines of her own mind.

She did want to tell Phoebe that she had received another proposal, but of course, with the matter of Albert between them, she thought better of the idea. She did want to tell her mother, at least, about Eric's offer. Este wanted Eric out of the drawing room, but he showed no signs of leaving.

He changed the subject. "I am very interested in stamps," he said to her.

"I didn't know that," said Este. "You've never mentioned an interest in stamps before."

"Haven't I?" he said. "I thought I had. I would be interested in seeing the stamps on your brother's letters from Palestine."

Relieved that the conversation had turned, Este promised to show him the letters from Jacob one day.

"I'd like to see them now," he said. She hesitated.

"As a special favor?" He looked at her sadly.

She left the room to fetch them. He changed chairs. He paced about on the rug. He saw nothing of interest to report. There were medical books on the shelf. There were books in Arabic whose titles he could not read. There were books in German and Italian that seemed to be about myths, judging from the embossing on the leather covers. There was nothing about a plot against the Crown. The furniture was excellent, but hardly revealed designs against public order. The painting on the wall was a portrait of Lydia as a young woman. He lifted the painting up. Some dust rose from the disturbed frame. Behind it might be a safe that held the secrets he had been told to find. Behind it was the wall, faded to a lighter shade of rose than the rest of the room.

Este returned with the packet of letters she had taken from her mother's drawer. They were wrapped in a violet ribbon. She opened the ribbon and handed him a letter. The stamp was blurry, blue, and nothing more than a stamp. Just then Lydia returned.

"My dear," she said to Eric, "how very nice to find you here."

"I was just admiring the stamps from Palestine," he explained to her.

She took the letter that was in his hand and wrapped up the pile with the ribbon and left the packet on the small table near her elbow. The conversation went on. No one wanted refreshment. Este excused herself, claiming exhaustion. Lydia explained to Eric that she needed to retire to change for dinner. Her husband would be coming in at any moment. She stood up. Eric went to the door, thinking he had no hope of obtaining the letters, when there was a loud sound in the hall. Lydia rushed out the door to see her maid standing in a jumble of broken dishes and glasses that were intended for the dinner table. The maid was weeping. Lydia had to console her, picking her way carefully through the broken glass. Eric swiftly took a few of the letters out of the packet, placed them in his jacket pocket, called out a farewell, and made his escape down the stairs.

The Malinas had been kind to him, of course, a shipwrecked stranger, an accidental meeting. They were not people deserving of an unfortunate fate, but then the decision was not his. He was only a spear-carrier in some larger drama that he barely grasped. A man does what he has to when it comes to his own skin. So Eric Fortman believed. As for the pretty young lady who had no intention of marrying him, she was not his concern. He thought of her with contempt. She had wounded his pride. That galled him. A burning sensation rose in his chest. She would regret her haughty manner. It was probably true, he decided, that these people did not mean England well. He would do what was necessary.

Back in his room he read the letters. They could be coded, hidden meanings underlying the innocent sentences. He read them again and again. Finally, toward midnight, he grew tired and lay back on his pillow. It was then that his tooth began to throb. A deep, aching pain in the jaw that grew worse as the constellations drifted across the sky and the moon, shining its light into the harbors of Alexandria, slid across the dark dome of the universe and shooting stars fell through the air, their brief light flickering high above the waves. Eric heard the call to prayer, the hooves of a horse on the stones, and the cry of a child who had woken hungry. He tried a warm washcloth on his face. He tried a glass of the whiskey that he kept in a cabinet by his bed. He tried to think of pleasant scenes from the days of his boyhood. Nothing brought sleep. His tooth throbbed on.

In the morning he obtained the name of a dentist from his land-lady and, sitting in the chair staring at the curtain pulled in front of him, he waited for the dentist to put the big metal instruments in his mouth, to pull at his tooth, to pour alcohol on the bleeding gum, to torture him with the pain of it all, and he took comfort in the thought that pain could be passed on, given to someone else. He felt misused by fate. He felt justified in his actions. He was afraid of the approaching footsteps of the dentist. Later his jaw was swollen, his mustache stretched oddly across his puffed-out upper lip. He bought a pipeful of soothing hashish from the boy behind the bar of the café on the corner. He went home and slept like an innocent child. He woke with a plan in his head, a way to serve the interests of his country.

PASTEUR HAD WAITED for a wire to arrive. He rushed to gather his mail from his front hall every afternoon, hoping that a long letter from his mission in Alexandria would bring good news, some progress, some hint of a direction, perhaps one that he, in Paris, could propel forward with some insight gained of experience, washed in his own genius. He had some concerns. It was taking a long time. He was a patient man—any scientist is by definition the very soul of patience—but this after all was a race and in a race if you are standing still you are falling back. Emile had sent progress reports. They were working, no doubt, but everything tried so far had proved useless. How long would the epidemic last? This was the time to find the microbe, while the disease was sweeping through the city. Later it would be more difficult.

MARCUS HAD A purse now in which he kept his private money. It was fat. This money was earned in the late-night hours by the shore. It was easy. During the daylight hours he ran his errands for the French mission, boiled their plates as he had been instructed. Boiled their water as he had been told, washed their sheets. In the early evening he cooked the dinner for the men and cleaned up after them. But he had filled out some since his arrival in Alexandria. He was no longer a mere boy. He was looking for investment opportunities. He had learned that he had assets, cards in his hand to play. He enjoyed his evening walk along the promenade. He enjoyed the ladies in their silk petticoats and the men smoothing down their hair, tousled by the wind from the sea. He enjoyed the smell of peanuts and palm oil and beer and perfumes. He had learned a good deal of Arabic in the marketplace. He had made a few friends among the boys who drove their donkeys through the streets back and forth on errands for the owner of the dance palace by the dried-up stream behind the railroad tracks at the far end of the lake.

Everyone in Alexandria was always moving. They did a good business, Marcus saw. He had spent an evening with several Alexandrians who dressed in women's shawls and painted their faces and listened to a violinist play Mozart on a terrace concealed with muslin curtains from the peering neighbors. He had seen the dawn arrive in Alexandria with his young arms around someone whose name he would forget by noon, but whose smell would stay with him until dinner. He had learned enough Arabic to persuade a respectable shop girl to come with him for the sake of pleasure alone. He had learned enough to converse with the little boys who played in the alley behind the hospital. He had picked up some

English and could wish the officers at the port a good morning, and wave at them in a manner that elicited a return wave. He had tasted absinthe and had smoked hashish. He was expanding his mind. He believed in his fortune, his good fortune. This was a perfect city for a boy with ambition, and he had become a boy with ambition. Which was why he now resented the fact that his name was omitted from the invitation that had come from the Academy of Science to a reception for the visiting scientists from France and Germany, their names in large script.

Dr. Malina received a packet from the Committee of Public Safety. It contained the week's count of cholera victims. It was the same as the week before. Dr. Malina checked the numbers twice. It was good news, or possibly so. Epidemics grow in intensity. When they stop claiming more and more victims, they ebb quickly. One week of stability was not cause for rejoicing. The count could be wrong, the stability an illusion. Or it could be an accurate count but simply reflect a pause in the epidemic, a moment for the cholera to rest before surging forward again.

Dr. Robert Koch had worked as he always worked, whether at home or away, with steady concentration, a cool head, and a critical eye, especially on himself. He looked for organisms that were invading the tissues around and in the intestinal lesions, and isolated them. Koch had examined slide after slide, culture after culture, and could not make out a specific organism that might be responsible for cholera, and then, late in the afternoon of a day that had begun shortly after dawn, he saw something that he had seen repeatedly in the tissues of the cholera-infected patients. It was possible that this was the organism. He wasn't sure. He needed more tissue, he needed to test it more carefully. He thought he was on the right track. He drew pictures of what he had seen. He searched through all his slides to see if this particular creature appeared in all of them. It was work that required a steady hand and a good eye. He prepared slide after slide with the suspected organism pressed down between two thin pieces of glass. He put blue dye on the slides, hoping it would make the organism stand out clearly. It wasn't always possible to make out the shape of the creature he thought might be responsible. He drew pictures, wrote in his notebooks, checked and rechecked what he had seen through the lens. He took the sample in which he had seen the organism and tried to grow it in cultures. It grew, but so did many other organisms. When he injected his brew into his mice, they did not sicken, but this did not prove that the small, wiggling form he had seen was not the source of the disease. Every few hours Koch washed his hands again in bichloride of mercury, a solution that would kill organisms on his fingers, keep peril and contamination at bay. Koch was hopeful. He was not ready to announce to the scientific community that he had seen the cholera and had drawn its picture. He was almost certain, but almost was not good enough. He did not want to be embarrassed before his colleagues, made a laughingstock in the academies.

His was not a temperament to exult, to dance in his bedroom. He was a solitary, sober man, but he did allow a small trail of happiness to follow in his footsteps as he went about his usual day.

ESTE WAS HURRYING to get to the laboratory. She was hastily pulling on her clothes, trying to button faster, to smooth down quickly, to get Anippe to tie the ribbons with more speed. In a dish warming near the oven was a culture that she was particularly hopeful might be of use. She pulled a comb through her curly hair. It stuck in a tangle for which she had no patience this morning. Anippe was extracting the comb carefully so as not to hurt her mistress when Este, exasperated, found herself in tears. She wanted to see Louis. She wanted to be by his side. She needed to be by his side. Her haste was not just a concern for the growth in the dish, but also for the man who was telling her everything important she needed to know, who had made interesting the most ordinary of matters. Her haste was to see him. He is the man I am meant to marry, she thought, and the certainty of that, the firmness of the fact that fate had so intended it, dried her tears. And soon sent her on her way.

Eric Fortman was sitting in his office at Marbourg & Sons. He considered his finances. The salary paid him was sufficient to keep a single man in good order. The additional monies that fell his way were, if managed well, not spent extravagantly, enough to provide a man with the option of starting his own business, a matter that Eric Fortman had always considered beyond his capacity, his place in life. But here in Alexandria, all things were possible.

That afternoon he made his way to the tent at the bazaar where a man, sitting on a small stool above a wooden box with a bottle of ink resting in one corner, would write a letter in French or German or Italian or Arabic for a few pennies, for those who were unable to do it themselves. He was an Arab scribe and he made decorations on each of his letters, little drawings of flowers or insects. His customers, who might not be able to read the words he had transcribed, appreciated the drawings. They always smiled. They thanked him. Therefore the scribe was in high demand, and the line for his attention was long. The blind used his services, and this was a city where the eyes roamed about in the heads of many, unfocused, veiled, useless. Those who had come to Alexandria to save themselves from local droughts or from arrest sought his services. The smells of the bazaar nearly overwhelmed Eric as he stood in line. Juice from betel nuts stained the streets where it had been spat by a thousand passersby. Peels of oranges lay on the ground along with pieces of fig and ends of cigarettes, and a muddy puddle had gathered in which small, dark insects were moving over the surface. Eric Fortman did not like this slow line. He was an Englishman, entitled to faster service. He did not want to stand like this. But he knew that should he shoulder his way to the front there would be an outcry from the others, a screeching in Arabic that would bring a policeman or a soldier. This, at the moment, he did not want. So he stood there, outwardly patient, inwardly cursing the slow-moving hand of the scribe.

When at last it was his turn, he presented a letter to the scribe. It was Jacob's letter to his parents.

"I want," he said, "a letter that I dictate to you, in similar handwriting as this, as close as you can come."

The scribe looked at him. He shook his head. "I don't do that," he said in English, and repeated it in French and Italian and Arabic.

Eric was prepared for that response. He took out his purse and pulled out some bills. The scribe's eyes opened and closed. He considered for a moment, and then pulled out a piece of paper. Placing Jacob's letter on one side, he wrote what he was told. Eric Fortman kept it simple and short. The less of the letter there was, the less likely anyone would contest its authorship. The letter spoke of plans to start a fire in the English barracks in Alexandria. It spoke of friends in Jerusalem who were willing to supply money to aid the cause of driving the British from Egyptian shores. It spoke of plans to cause chaos in Alexandria that might spread to Cairo. The handwriting was almost that of the letter he had presented the scribe. It was not exact. Eric could see certain errors, but it was close enough that at a glance it would appear to be from one Jacob Malina writing from Jerusalem. He took his letter back to his office and placed it in the envelope of the original. He paced back and forth. Had anyone seen him at the bazaar? Would the validity of the letter be investigated? Would he end his days in a prison cell? It will be all right, he told himself. The British officers for whom he was working were not so particular. They would be pleased and would not inspect the handwriting, or doubt his good English word.

In this he was right. When he sat down in the small room, the same room in which they had previously met, and handed them the letter, claiming he had obtained it at the Malina home, where it had been sitting in a pile of letters he had taken when the opportunity arrived, they asked no questions. They passed the letter around. They thanked him for his service to the Crown. They told him that he was a true Englishman. They promised that if he had special needs, they would do whatever was possible in his favor. They offered him a beer. He drank with them. That's that, he said to himself, when he left their offices. He felt as light as a feather. He noticed the beautiful English girl who passed him on the street. He noticed the swallows on the rooftop. He appreciated the multicolored beaded curtains in the doorway of the café he passed. He went down to the docks to check on the expected arrival of a cargo ship from the Ivory Coast bearing valuable animal skins that would be made into coats for the ladies of London and Paris. The air was heavy and humid. He heard the shouts of the donkey boys. There was sweat on his forehead. But all in all, he thought, the climate of Alexandria offered many advantages over other ports.

JACOB WAS FOLLOWED wherever he went. Several Englishmen were at the corner when he emerged from his quarters in the morning. Several others stood outside his warehouse all through the day, leaning against the wall, reading their newspapers, smoking their cigarettes, wiping their brows in the heat, swatting at flies. When he went to dinner with his friend, they were there in the small restaurant at a nearby table. What had he done? What did they suspect him of, and how could he show them that he was a person of a law-abiding nature, that he had no opinion about politics? He did not care if England or France or Germany or the Ottomans or the Egyptians or the Indians took the taxes from the country in which he was living. He only wanted his small chance at finding a place of comfort for himself and the wife he would one day have and the children he intended to father. What were the British waiting for him to do? The fever he thought he had beaten back forever returned and he had to stay in bed for several days until it subsided again. He did not want to die in Jerusalem, so far from his family. He was not a young man given to self-pity, but under these circumstances, when there was no one to pity him, he sometimes succumbed. What an absurd thing to do, to write an article, to be proud of one's words in print, and to think you could change the real world by what you said about it.

LYDIA WAITED FOR the mail to arrive. Each day she was at home an hour before the time it usually appeared. She was concerned because it had been some time since she had heard from Jacob. It was time for another letter to arrive. Day after day, no letter arrived. She was also uneasy about her daughter. Perhaps Este was only enjoying her work in the laboratory. She seemed to be learning so much, but the child had a new secretiveness, a veiled glance, as if she were holding something back. She could hardly look at her mother, not directly. Lydia knew that her daughter had taken a step away from her, but she had no idea why. She looked through Este's dresser and vanity, and found nothing that would explain her remote manner. Perhaps she was imagining it. Perhaps everything was fine. She did not believe everything was fine. When she spoke to her husband, he ignored her. "Please," he said, not in his kindest voice, "you are merely having an attack of nerves." She felt it, however, the wrongness of things.

Albert's father had instructed him to visit the Malinas. There were matters of public gossip that needed to be put to rest, and if Abraham Malina could find his way to forgive Albert for his loss of temper and understand that the young man had changed his ways and regretted his impulsive act and was in fact the very person that Este should marry, as everyone had known all along, that indeed would be a very good thing.

Albert sent a long, apologetic note to Este. He explained that Achmed had cheated him, but said he should never have fought with him. He was ashamed of his actions. He was in mourning over the loss of her affections. He wanted only to repair the breach between them. He would do anything she asked, he would give her anything she wanted, if only she would see him and give him some reason to hope. She read the note carefully and then gave it to her mother. Este said, "I have other possibilities."

Lydia paid no attention to her daughter. She gave the note to her husband, who said, "I'm not in favor of this marriage, and a fawning note will not change my mind."

Albert's father came to Dr. Malina in his office and was greeted cordially but with reserve. He said that his son was truly penitent and had promised to behave himself in the future. He said that he had always admired Este and would wish their families to be united through marriage. Abraham was touched by the kind words. He saw that the man was sincere, but he also thought he knew human nature, and he would prefer a different husband for his child, one without a history of violence and whatever sleight of hand was involved in the business with the ring. "Let us give it a little time," he said. "Este needs to recover from her disappointment." He knew this was not true, even as he said it, but there was no sense in offending his visitor.

THE WAR, THE endless war between man and bacteria, is never won entirely, by one side or the other. Truces are declared, time and again. Truces are broken, time and again. When all the vulnerable have been infected, when the rains and the rivers rise to dilute the concentration of swarming infestation, when the majority of human beings who remain were always protected against this particular enemy and many of those who remain have survived an attack and their bodies are armed and now impenetrable, then the enemy dies instead of kills. Then the enemy becomes weaker and weaker, fewer and fewer in number, until it disappears for a while, beaten back to another shore. It needs a large enough pool of fresh bodies to infect. It must move rapidly from the human it killed an hour ago to the human it will kill within hours. When it waits in vain for another opportunity, it withers, it dries, it disappears into that swirl of matter, organic and inorganic, that has no pity and is unimpressed with former glories. The cholera microbe becomes like a toothless lion, hiding in the brush, awaiting the hunter. The community breathes a sigh of relief. The religious thank their God, the superstitious credit their copper bracelets, their amulets, their burning of incense. The scientists know that the enemy has overreached as it always does, like Napoleon in the snows of Russia.

The number of cases starts to decrease rapidly, as if, numerically speaking, graphically speaking, it had fallen off a high cliff. So it was that the reported deaths from cholera in Alexandria plunged downward and the Committee of Public Safety was enormously pleased. Some thought that their efforts at sanitation had defeated the enemy. Some thought it was their prayers that were at last being heard. Dr. Malina felt as if a burden had been lifted from his already burdened shoulders. Cholera was departing, back on the ships it arrived on, or back to the dust that had given it birth, back to the muddy rivers and the seas in which it bred. He had no illusions. This was not the last of it. It would not remain curled in sleep, innocent as a newborn suckling at its mother's breast, it would not be dormant ever after. But for now, in Alexandria, the tide had turned and the disease would disappear within weeks. Alexandria outlasted the invaders as it had other conquerors, Alexander himself, Brutus and Antony, Amr and Muhammad, pashas good and bad, the French and soon the British.

This dismayed Dr. Koch, who needed fresh cholera tissue to examine to confirm his suspicions. Meanwhile, he walked about like a woman in the early months of pregnancy, a great secret hidden within. He asked everywhere for bowel and bladder tissue of cholera victims. He obtained a small amount. Cholera still existed in Alexandria, but each day it retreated. There was now a paucity of cholera-contaminated tissue.

THAT CHOLERA WAS leaving Alexandria was clear also to the members of the French mission. They, too, had trouble finding fresh material. They, too, had exhausted the samples of cholera victims, guts, eyes, legs, bowels, stomachs, that a few weeks before had been so easy to obtain. "Marcus," Emile said, "take a carriage to the countryside. See if the villages have any new cases of cholera."

It took Marcus a day to reach a village along the Nile in which cholera had claimed a victim just the night before. And the family accepted his considerable offer of financial reward for their participation in modern science. It took him another day to return to the laboratory with the tissues already decaying and the smell from his box so odious that the carriage driver threatened to leave him on the road hours out of the city.

Several cases of cholera appeared around the train station among the vendors of nuts, and in a newspaper boy. All the victims died. When word came to the French mission of the newsboy's death, Nocard and Louis rushed to his home only to find that Dr. Koch had just left, having harvested all the critical organs.

Emile Roux sent a telegram to Pasteur, saying, *We will pack up and book passage back to France as soon as possible.* Robert Koch had in his hands a telegram from the Academy of Medicine in Berlin. There was a report of an outbreak of cholera in Calcutta. The numbers were still small, but each day they increased. There the disease was growing in strength even as it was fading in Alexandria. He sat at his favorite table in his favorite café on the Grand Square and made a list of his options. Return to Berlin and wait for the cholera to come closer to him so he could conclude his work, or persuade the Academy to finance his voyage to Calcutta. He could also stay in Alexandria and hope that in the waning days of the disease he could find enough tissue samples to test his observations. Days had gone by and he had not found it again, this *vibrio*, a swimming monster. When he closed his eyes he could see it racing across the darkness of his eyelid. He drank a beer. He brushed the crumbs from a cake off his pants. He made a decision. He would go to India. The cholera he was so sure he had seen must not be allowed to get away.

Emile and Paul and Louis sat at a sidewalk café in the early evening and decided to book their passage back to France. They agreed that they would use their remaining days in Alexandria to continue their work on swine fever. This had occupied Pasteur for the preceding year. Louis had himself gone to Hungary to vaccinate pigs at the Animal Institute there. Perhaps the pigs in Egypt would reveal some aspect of the disease that might be helpful. They had not said it aloud, but they each knew it and they each felt it deeply. They had failed to find the cholera microbe, and in failing they had disappointed Pasteur and in failing they had disappointed France and in addition had spent large sums of money to no purpose. They would not be hailed in Paris as heroes. They were not heroes. Was there something else that they should have tried, was there some other path they should have taken? Emile had dark circles under his eyes. He was not sleeping. The three men shared a common shame.

Nevertheless, the following evening they arrived promptly at the Academy's reception. Emile wore his red tie and his striped waistcoat. Louis had on a blue jacket that Marcus had insisted he have made for him by one of Alexandria's more famous tailors. Edmond was wearing a somewhat wrinkled green jacket he had saved for just such an occasion, but that did not button over his vest. He did not like dressing up, or so he said, and repeated all the way to the large, white-columned building in which the academy had its home.

"Don't drink the water," Emile reminded Louis as they walked up the stairs. "It's still dangerous to drink the water," he added as Louis looked at him irritated. Louis knew as well as he did to continue to be cautious. There were butlers serving champagne. There was a table of fresh meats and fruits and little plates at the side. The room was lit with gas lamps with golden tassels attached to their bases. The women were dressed in their best laces and silks. The curtains were pulled back and the warm Alexandrian air entered the room. In the corner a violinist and a cellist played, although no one was listening. The president of the Alexandrian Academy of Scientists embraced each of the three members of the French mission in turn. Dr. Koch entered, accompanied by his assistant Gaffkey. Several young men from the university pressed around him, asking questions about anthrax. Word of his success on anthrax had electrified the community the year before. Dr. Koch peered around his admirers and signaled greetings to Nocard and Roux. Emile was captured by the wife of a diplomat who was hoping to be stationed soon in Paris. "We want to return to our home," said the wife. "Perhaps if you meet someone in the Foreign Ministry, you will speak for us, I will give you our card." Emile made a promise he did not expect to keep. He did not dine with members of the Foreign Ministry. The mirrors on the walls of the room reflected the red threads woven into the carpets, the shine of the men's buttons, the ribbons and the gold and silver medals on the chests of many of the men. Only the servants brought in the native air with their tunics and their slippers and their dark skins.

The French consul general was there and greeted Edmond warmly. He said nothing about government funds wasted. His wife immediately pulled Edmond aside to talk about the stomach problems of her cat, with whom Nocard was acquainted. This was a good conversation. The kittens had been born. Madame Cecile described each, the color, the disposition, the size of their paws. The smallest one had died. Edmond explained to her why this was not as sad as it seemed. She put her arm on his sleeve and thanked him for putting an end to her not insignificant grief for this unfortunate newborn. The two stayed close together, discussing the habits of cats and the ways to increase their life span.

Louis hung back along the far side of the room, against the wall, until he saw Este arrive with her parents. He waited a few moments as she spoke with an older man and kissed him on the cheek. She accepted the offer of a glass of champagne. She left her mother's side to talk with a young woman who whispered something in her ear. Louis walked over to her. "I hoped you'd be here," she said, softly. Her friend drifted off after a brief introduction. "Papa hates these affairs and didn't want to come, but Mother convinced him it is good for me to be seen in company."

"I would have been disappointed if you had not come," said Louis, then was embarrassed by his words. He was afraid to look at her face. But she was smiling at him. The crowd grew. He walked with her to one side of the large room, catching Emile's eye as he moved behind a pillar. He missed Emile's encouraging wave, so intent was he on Este's shoulders moving under her lace mantel, her black hair, his beating heart. Louis was not a man who easily found his tongue. But now he knew he had to speak.

"Este," he said, "I have grown accustomed to your presence in our laboratory." She smiled at him and waited. "I am not a man of words," he said.

"I know that," she said, and there was silence between them.

"I wish," he suddenly managed to say, "to be with you when I am an old man with white hair and no teeth."

The musicians changed, and now it was three Arabic men with strange, sad tunes, playing songs of love and loss. Louis did not want to hear any songs of loss. He did not need any songs of love. Just then the president of the Academy called for silence, and the guests at the reception moved toward the small podium to listen to the speech that followed, a long and dull one that spoke of the triumph of man through the victories of science. The words seemed hollow under the circumstances. Defeat was in the air. Emile was talking with Madame Cecile about his daughter's education. Lydia Malina approached her daughter, catching a glance between the two young people that shocked her. Could that be it? Was that her daughter's secret? She said nothing. Este also said nothing, but was feeling many things, mostly joyous. Her secret kept threatening to burst out of her mouth. *I love, I am loved.* The words brought color to her face, light to her eyes. She looked, that evening, more extraordinary than she had ever looked before.

THE FOLLOWING DAY a sandstorm blew in from the desert. The fronds of the palm trees turned gray in the dust. Este put her shawl up over her face as she left her house. Her eyes stung. As she rounded the corner she saw Louis hurrying toward her, his head down. He saw her. They sought shelter in the archway of the building that belonged to the Ratousa Steamship Company. "Este," he said, "we will have to go back to France. With the cholera leaving the city, we will not be able to work here now. I had hoped we could stay another few months, but passage has been booked in ten days."

Este turned very pale. Louis said to her the first thing that came into his mind: "I am very fond of Alexandrian coffee."

"I imagine the coffee in Paris is better," said Este.

There was a pause. An Arab man selling rags from the back of a cart called out for customers, passersby hurried on, there was a stifling heat in the air. It muffled the sound of their voices. "Do you know," said Louis, "that the frog, the simple frog, has to get rid of the poisons in his system exactly the same as we do?"

Este smiled. "There are many frogs out in the bog by Lake Mariout, at night you can hear them calling to each other."

Louis said, "Frogs have teeth, small, conelike teeth on their upper jaw, and some of them have a row of teeth on the roofs of their mouths. They also shed their skins and eat them."

"It's not their fault, I suppose," said Este, looking disgusted. "But why are you thinking of frogs?"

"Because there are so many different kinds," Louis said. "Red frogs that are poisonous, green and brown, toads, river and lake frogs, and they can all breathe through their skin."

"Yes," said Este, "but why are you telling me about frogs?"

Louis stopped. Why *was* he telling her about frogs? Perhaps because he was trying not to beg her to come to France with him. He shrugged. "I am interested in frogs," he said.

She touched her hair and smoothed back a strand that escaped her comb. "I can't stay here talking to you. My mother is expecting me at her sister's."

Louis did not look at her but stared at his shoes, which Marcus had polished for him just hours before. "At least give me permission to return to Alexandria after we have taken our research notes to Paris. I will take the next boat back. Would that be pleasing to you?" He didn't have the savings to do that. Would his father lend him the money, would he ask his father for such a favor? How could he return? Why had he said he would, when it was probable that he couldn't? Had he frightened her with his words? He had spoken very softly.

She held herself very straight, as if posing for a photograph at the studio in front of a curtain. "You must understand," she said, "my father would not wish me to talk with you this way. But I would be very sorry if you sailed away and never returned. I would think of you often. Did you know that when Ismail Pasha dug the Mahmoudian Canal to reconnect us to the Nile, they found a Greek sarcophagus, and when they opened it, inside was the skeleton of a monkey?"

"I want," said Louis, "to marry you. I am proposing to you." He suddenly realized that he had no ring. "I have no ring," he said, abashed. "I should have a ring."

"That's all right," said Este. "I don't need a ring."

"I want," said Louis, "to go back to Paris with you as my wife."

Este felt a wave of relief flow through her body. This was what she had planned, although a moment ago she might not have been able to say it so simply, so clearly. "I want," she said to Louis, not daring to touch him, "to be your wife, and go with you to Paris."

"Then," said Louis, feeling dizzy with the rush of her words, "we will go to Amiens and you will meet my mother and father and brother and sister."

The mention of parents caused Este to take a small step back away from him. "I have to talk to my father. He must be convinced. You are not . . ." and her voice became very soft, her head bent downward. "You are not one of us."

"I will be," he said. "I'll be anything he likes."

She smiled at him, but there was worry in her eyes. "It's not so easy," she said.

"I'll try," he promised.

"I'll talk to my father tonight," she said.

"I will come tomorrow morning and talk to him myself," Louis said, then, as he turned to leave, he added, "Este, I feel as if we were already man and wife. You have possession of me, as of now."

"And you of me," she said.

13

EARLY ONE EVENING, Marcus was down at the docks waiting for a ship's mate who had hired him for an evening of pleasure. An American gentleman paced up and down, waiting for his purchases to arrive and be loaded on board the ship he was taking to Venice. From there he would sail home, his precious objects following him to Philadelphia. Five large wagons pulled up to the quay, their wheels rattling and knocking against the wooden boards. The objects within were wrapped in muslin, some were in crates.

"What's he got?" Marcus asked of the man standing next to him, who happened to be Eric Fortman, who had just inspected the ship in the next berth.

"Damned if I know," said Eric.

Just at that moment, one of the Arab boys dropped one of the crates and it crashed on the ground. It split open and a stone obelisk appeared. Not a large one, but a real one. The American yelled, "You idiot, you bastard, you ass." He started to strike the boy. The boy ran. The American stood there. "I'll kill the next one of you who drops anything," he howled and pulled his pistol out, waving it at the young men now cowering behind a wagon. The boys fled up the quay.

"Some God damned boys help me get these to the ship," shouted the American. Marcus appeared at his elbow.

"What's this thing worth?" he asked.

"A few thousand American dollars," the American answered.

"And in the crates, what have you got in the crates?" asked Marcus.

"Vases, vessels, small statues, a mural I chipped out of a wall, a few things from the tombs for my home. These are genuine antiquities." He was pleased with himself, this American.

Eric said to him, "I'll get some men for you. Your packages should be on board in a half hour."

The American thanked Eric.

"I'll help you, too," said Marcus.

"Lots of Americans like this stuff?" asked Eric.

"You bet," said the American.

"What about the English?" Marcus asked.

"They take what they want," said the American, "but sometimes they buy it, the small things, the necklaces, the earrings."

"Where's it come from?" asked Marcus.

"Pyramids," said the American. He waved his hand up toward Cairo. "It's just sitting there for the taking," said the American. "When I get back to Philadelphia, I'm going to have a big bash and show everyone my own obelisk and I'll be in the papers. Philadelphia's own Pharaoh, I can tell you that."

"How did you get it?" Eric asked.

"Paid some fellows to bring it here," the American said.

"I wouldn't mind selling you some," said Eric.

"Have you got anything?" asked the American.

"Not yet," said Eric.

Together, Eric and Marcus brought a few men they found in the bar to help load the American onto his ship. He put some bills in Eric's hands. Eric counted the money and gave half of it to Marcus.

"Hey," said Eric. "I like the idea of selling things that you just pick up from the ground." He laughed.

Marcus decided to abandon his evening date. The two men, one older and one younger, went off for a beer together. They chose the closest bar where the noise was louder than a roaring sea, the smell of salt and half-eaten mollusks drifted in and mingled with the sweat of the loaders and the donkey boys. They found a small table among the ones on the right side of the law and the ones that were not, and the policeman who was dressed as an old lady and who was fooling no one, and the ship's carpenter who was carrying a bag of hashish around his neck and protecting it with the regular slash of his knife through the air. There they talked. Eric had some money he might spend and, amazingly enough, Marcus, who seemed so childish, so pretty still, he had money too. One was French and one was English, and that made little difference in this port. One was seasoned in trade and one had just begun, but together they would make a good team. The older one wanted to be chief, and he declared the younger one to be his assistant. The younger one balked. He was not ready to be told what to do again. He had served long enough. "My money buys in equal," he said, "or I go by myself."

The older one laughed at the younger one. Well, what difference did a title make? They would share the billing. The firm would not be in either of their names. They named their company Pharaoh's Treasures. This would attract the tourists as well as please the natives who could afford their merchandise. Pharaoh's

Treasures: they would bloody the waters with their competitors, if they had any.

"Perhaps," said Marcus, "it will be impossible to get permission from the authorities to sell these stones."

Eric clapped his new partner on the back. "Don't worry," he said. "I can get anything I want in Alexandria. The highest office in the customs department is as good as in my pocket."

Marcus hoped this was so. If it was, there were many lucrative possibilities that leapt into his mind. When he trusted his new partner more, he would make some interesting suggestions.

By the time three hours had passed, Eric had told his new friend about his long employment at Glen MacAlan Scotch, about his first time at sea, when he had been robbed by a cook with one arm. Eric had put his arm around Marcus and rocked him tenderly, an emotion born of liquor but founded in the high hopes of profit from the Pharaoh's Treasures Company, and from the intuition he had that this Anglo-French alliance had a brilliant future. Marcus, for his part, promised to inform the French mission that he had no intention of sailing back to Marseille, that his life from here on out would be upward and forward, as he would be his own master.

"WHERE IS MARCUS?" Emile asked. For weeks now, their cook, their housekeeper, their attendant had drifted in and out of the apartment, in and out of the laboratory, paying no attention to their needs. They had to eat at restaurants, and piles of laundry had accumulated on the rug. There were long black bugs in the pantry.

"Damn him," said Nocard. "We should leave him behind when we return."

☙

DR. MALINA WAS in his clinic. Ten patients were waiting in the outer room. A woman with a child who was sleeping in her arms was crying softly to herself. A man with a sore on his arm was pacing up and down. The air was hot, but outside in the courtyard a yellow-tailed finch was singing his heart out, calling to a drab female bird, enticing her closer and closer. He was opening his beak as far as he could, singing from as deep in his small throat as he was able and letting the sound fly into the palm leaves, bounce up against the air, and float toward the object of his affections.

The door to the Malina house was opened by the maid. The two officers of the British Army and the two Englishmen in civilian clothes although they were not civilians pushed right past her into the courtyard. They moved like a wave bearing down on the sand toward the clinic door. They were not deterred by the Arab boy on the step outside, and shoved him out of the way. One of the men in suits announced to the waiting room at large, "Go, the doctor will not be able to see you." He made this announcement in clumsy Arabic, in accented French, and in perfect Yorkshire English. Everyone understood, and the room was emptied within moments. The sleeping child woke and cried. His mother put a hand over his mouth as she moved. The men walked into the small office where the doctor was examining the thin and bony chest of the owner of a furniture factory, who, on seeing the British officers, grabbed his shirt and fled. There were many reasons he did not want to stop and talk with the officers.

Dr. Malina understood instantly that the matter was serious. It was the two men not in uniform who most alarmed him. "I must talk to my wife," he said, "before I leave with you." He sent the Arab boy to find Lydia and come back with her as quickly as possible. The men agreed to wait. They were not in a particular hurry.

"Come into my office," he suggested. "It will be more comfortable there."

"My leg," said one of the uniformed officers, "it keeps cramping up on me. Is that a symptom of illness?"

"I'll take a look at it, if you like," Dr. Malina offered.

The man started to roll up his trousers, but one of the non-uniformed men put a hand on his shoulder and said, "No, this man is our prisoner, not our doctor."

"What is the charge?" said Dr. Malina. The fact that he was innocent of any wrongdoing was not as reassuring to him as it might be to another man. He understood that guilt and innocence in the eyes of the authorities were not moral issues as much as tactical ones.

"We will have a chance to talk, I assure you," said one of the men.

Lydia burst into the room, alarm in her eyes, her arms waving as if she could chase the offending men out of her home the way one might an infestation of insects. "Go to the chief rabbi, and to the lawyer Florent," her husband said. "Let everyone know that I have been taken." Lydia nodded. "Be ready, my darling," he said, "for anything."

She wanted to throw her arms around him, but not in front of the invaders, to whom she would not give the victory of her distress. She said calmly, "I will go immediately."

He tried to tell her with his eyes to take their money out of the bank, to hide her jewelry in her clothes. She did not need to be told these things.

THE COMMITTEE OF Public Safety met again, but Dr. Malina did not appear at the appointed time. The assembled men waited for him for more than fifteen minutes and then began the meeting. They were all pleased at the figures before them. But, as one astute businessman pointed out, cholera would not disappear from their streets overnight. It would take some weeks or more before the last case would be reported. There could be no rejoicing until there had not been a death from the disease for at least a month. "Can cholera return in a second wave?" asked the Coptic bishop, whose success in church politics had depended on his pessimistic vision. The assembled group was not sure of the answer. They had no idea why the scourge was weakening, and they had no idea if it could regain its strength.

The day was humid, there were no clouds in the sky. The ocean lapped against the jetty without force. Out in the harbor a steamboat left in its wake the straw hat of one of its lady passengers who had leaned too far over the rail to catch a last glimpse of Alexandria as the boat moved off for the open seas. The mollusks that clung to the rock and coral buried in the depths of the waters swayed with the vibrations of the steamship that passed far above their small but resilient shells. A long, extended rope of brown matter floated in the tidal pull toward Africa. Inside its mucus strands, cholera, unmindful of its certain dissolution, drifted without mind or despair or anger at its approaching end. It would last a long time in the moist waters, weeks, maybe months, but it would find no nourishment, and without nourishment no life continues. It did not need oxygen, it did not need sunlight, it did not need affection from another of its kind. It needed a human host, and it would find no such host in the sea.

IN THE MORNING, as the British officers approached the Malina home, Louis Thuillier set out for the same destination. Emile and

Edmond had offered to accompany him, but he had declined their kind support. As he walked he rehearsed over and over again his words to the father of the woman he wanted to make his bride. He practiced them again and again. He knew he did not have the funds to keep her as comfortable as she was in Alexandria. He knew that he was not yet a famous scientist, a man of high repute. On the other hand, he had expectations. Pasteur thought highly of him, had selected him for this very mission. He had a reputation among his colleagues as a hardworking man. Would his good prospects sway the doctor? Would the matter of religious difference be overcome by his promise to take on any religion that Dr. Malina preferred, although he himself would prefer none? He intended to explain that the French mission was leaving in a few weeks and he planned to take Este back to Paris with him. They would have to be married quickly. He wanted them to travel as man and wife. Over and over he rehearsed his speech in his head, correcting this word or that. He didn't want to mumble. He didn't want to be searching for the phrase he needed. He wanted to seem confident of a positive answer. He knew that if Dr. Malina just promised to ask his daughter what she wanted, all would be well. He had announced to his friends that he would not return without at least this promise. His colleagues had applauded his resolve, although Edmond kept repeating that if the father should refuse him, although regrettable, this disappointment would not be anything like the tragedy that Louis would make of it. "Hearts are like earthworms," he told Louis. "If you cut them in half, they grow new parts."

"Not mine," said Louis. But he understood his friend was merely protecting him from an excess of optimism.

When the carriage arrived at the Malina house, he knew immediately that something was wrong. The front door had been left wide open. The servant who answered the bell was weeping. There were suitcases in the hall. When he ran upstairs and entered the drawing room, he saw that the curtains had been pulled down, the shutters were open to the street, and papers were strewn everywhere. The contents of the drawers in the main chest had been thrown on the floor. Este was not in sight. Neither was her mother or her father. Had they been robbed? Louis tried to find out from the girl who was holding a bucket of dirty water and scrubbing the same spot over and over again. She did not seem to speak any language other than Arabic and screamed in fear as Louis approached her. He went to Dr. Malina's clinic on the other side of the courtyard. There, too, the door was open. In Dr. Malina's office the desk had been overturned. The medicine cabinet had been opened and the bottles thrown on the floor, and the glass of the cabinet had been smashed into many small pieces. As he walked about the deserted clinic, Louis could hear the crunch of splintered glass beneath his feet. Running back to the house, he found the cook was in the kitchen putting the silver spoons into a large carpetbag she had open on the floor. The jewelry, unfortunately, for her, was locked in a safe. She was startled when she saw him. "They will not need these now," she said in perfect French. "No use in giving good silver to the rats."

"Where is the doctor, his wife, his daughter?" Louis asked.

The cook shrugged. "It is not for me to say," she replied.

Louis said, "I'll have you arrested for theft if you don't tell me what has happened."

The cook looked at him. She calculated how long she had to get to the rail station. The train to Aboukir did not leave for several hours.

She said to Louis, "Sit down, are you hungry? I can fix you a good dinner if you like."

"I'm not hungry," said Louis. "Where are they?"

"Do I have your word as a gentleman that you will not bother me any more if I tell you? After all, what do you care, a few spoons here and there, what difference will that make in the end, when we all answer to God?"

"Yes, you have my word," Louis shouted.

"It's not necessary to yell," said the cook. "I'm not deaf." She told him that the doctor had been taken by the British authorities. It was a matter of spying, one of the British soldiers had told her. Mrs. Malina had gone to the synagogue and Este had simply disappeared into the streets. Louis hardly let her finish before he rushed out to find a carriage. Outside the house, he now saw Egyptian police guarding the door and a dozen more idly standing across the street. The neighbors were staring down from their terraces. A small crowd had gathered across the street. The Arab boy who guarded the doctor's surgery was lying in a heap on the street. One of the police had twisted his arm until it snapped like a twig. "Why did he do that?" Louis asked.

"Monsieur," said the boy between wails, "I do not know." But he did, and he decided he had better get away from the house as soon as possible, and so he rose and ran, holding his wounded arm with his other hand.

Louis looked for a carriage. There were none. He looked for a donkey. There were always donkeys around. He found none. He began to run. He would go back to the laboratory at the hospital and enlist Emile and Paul and Marcus to help him find Este. This must be a mistake. Dr. Malina could not have been spying. On whom, for whom? It made no sense.

He ran down the hospital corridors, turning corners without slowing his step. He ran past the cholera ward, which was now empty except for an old man who was lying very still, perhaps already dead. Louis pulled open the door to the laboratory and saw Este sitting on a chair. Her shawl was on the floor. Her hair was falling out of its clip. Her eyes were red from crying, but she was smiling at Nocard, who had brought her a piglet that was sitting in her lap, licking her fingers, smelling the sleeve of her dress, small snorts coming from his nostrils, making his white whiskers move up and down.

ESTE LEANED FORWARD in her chair and wiped her eyes and straightened her hair. She described to Louis the entrance of the soldiers, the removal of her father, the searching of their rooms, even her room, the taking of her diary, the overturning of her small white bureau, the flight of her mother. She smiled at Louis bravely. She did not want him to think that she was without courage, or that she could so easily be reduced to helplessness.

"I will go out now," she said, offering the piglet back to Nocard, "and find my mother."

"Wait," said Louis. "Let's think first. Where might she be? We cannot search all of Alexandria."

Este heard him say "we," and she was grateful. Louis heard her say "I," and was afraid he might lose her in this turmoil.

"It will turn out to be a mistake," he said. "They will apologize to your father and send him home."

"That's what I told her," said Nocard.

Emile nodded in agreement, but he was not so sure. She placed the pig back in Nocard's hands. "This one," she said to Nocard, "his ears seem to be infected."

"I will look carefully," Nocard said.

"He is number thirty-two in my notebook," Este said. "He has such sweet eyes," she added.

"They all do, Mademoiselle," said Nocard.

Louis said, "We haven't time for this. We should go find your mother. She will be worried about you."

Este gave in. There was a small tremble of her lower lip. She washed her hands carefully in the bichloride of mercury solution. She moved toward the laboratory door. "Thank you," she said to the two men standing by the long table. "Thank you for your kindness."

Louis opened the door and they quickly walked into the hall. Nocard followed. He called out after them, "Be careful." The wind from the sea was coming from the north and was blowing hard. The large fronds of the palm trees on the avenue swept up and down, and the dust flew in their faces as Este and Louis made their way.

"I am going to the British consulate and demand to see my father," said Este. "I am sure that's where my mother must be."

Louis wanted to touch her sleeve. He did not dare. She was not his.

"My English is not as good as yours," he said.

"I will talk," said Este. "They will listen to me. I am his daughter."

Louis was not so sure this was to her advantage. It was possible they could arrest her, too. Perhaps they had already taken Lydia Malina and put her behind bars to put pressure on her husband to confess. Confess to what? What could that man have done? He wanted to ask Este if her father had expressed any political opinions that might concern the English. He did not. He thought the question, which contained a seed of doubt about the virtue of her father, was impolite. Este paused, out of breath. A vendor standing behind a table on which he had coconut pieces spread out on a red striped cloth beckoned them over.

Este said, "I'm thirsty, let's buy one."

"No," said Louis. "We don't know who has touched them, where they have been, what they have been washed with. It's too dangerous."

"But the cholera is going," said Este. "That's why you're going back to Paris."

"Yes," said Louis, "but it doesn't go all of a sudden. It pulls back and back, but for a while it remains in these streets."

"All right," said Este, following him as he moved on.

When they arrived at the consulate, the guard at the door would not let them in. When Este explained that her father was inside somewhere and she must see him, the guard called over a second guard and they asked Louis to remove the lady immediately from the doorway. They raised their weapons. Louis and Este left, Este walking very slowly. She did not want the guards to think they had frightened her. They had.

Louis said to Este, "I will not go to France without you." Este said nothing. Louis said, "I came too late to talk to your father."

Este said, "I can't think about that now."

Why, what did this mean, that he was nothing to her, that this emergency made it impossible for her to care for him, that he no longer mattered to her? These thoughts gripped him and he grew silent, the kind of grim silence that makes its own sound.

"This is not between us," she said in a softer voice. "My father is my father." She seemed so fragile, so like an abandoned child, that tears came to his eyes, unmanly tears that he forced back instantly into his head. "Take me home," she said.

"Of course," he said. He wanted to tell her many things. As he looked down the street for an approaching carriage, he thought of one. "Do you know," he said, "that when you put a little flame in a bottle and seal it, the flame soon uses up the oxygen and without oxygen the flame burns out?"

"Is that true?" said Este.

"I'll show you," he said. "I promise."

Este smiled. She did want to see that. She did not touch him, but he saw her hand flutter at her side. This encouraged him.

INSIDE THE BACK rooms of the less public part of the consulate, Dr. Malina sat at a table and answered questions. Why did he want the English out of Egypt? What was his group, what were his reasons for aiding the enemies of the Crown? Why was he against the presence of the English in Egypt? Of what concern was it to Jews who governed in Cairo?

"None," he answered, "none at all." Why would they suspect him of wishing to harm the English, to sabotage the barracks of the British soldiers? He was not a man of politics. He was not a young, hotheaded nationalist. He was a member of a guest community, one that had lived in peace in Alexandria for centuries without causing trouble to any sovereign. He tried to reason with his captors. But they had evidence of his perfidy. They were certain they had caught a man who would do them harm. He hoped Lydia had done all that he had told her and more. As the morning turned into afternoon, he despaired.

THE TWO NEW friends, a Frenchman still a boy and the Englishman, went to the Museum of Greco-Roman Antiquities. There they learned about the excavations at the tombs of Hada and Khatby, and they saw how elegant the old things appeared mounted on pedestals in large rooms. They learned that there was an archaeological society that was respectable and set up by the Khedive for the public good. Eric and Marcus knew that there were always other paths, indirections, bribery, and parallel routes that would take them to the good fortune they knew waited for them in the near future.

Marcus and Eric walked through the bazaar. They found several stalls selling what they said were necklaces from Cleopatra's own jewelry chest. They found three long strands of green beads that had been found near the Pyramids by some Arab men returning to their villages from a pilgrimage. The merchant who sold Eric the Ganesh he had given to Este produced a bracelet that he claimed belonged to a slave girl who had served Ptolomy himself. Eric purchased everything.

Marcus spoke to a few of his donkey boy friends who told him that they knew someone who knew how to get the stones he was asking about. Marcus was led to a man who had bought some small heads from a wanderer who sold them from the sack he carried on his back. The man, who worked at the customs office, told Marcus where he could find the peddler. He lived by the river in a shack.

Eric and Marcus took a carriage out of town. They found the shack. They waited for the man to return. At nightfall, they saw him appearing down the path. He saw them and started to run. Were they robbers or murderers? Eric caught him. Marcus was able to explain in Arabic that they were customers, not thieves. When the man gave them a relieved grin, they saw that his teeth were black and his gums were red.

He went into his shack and reappeared with a stone head of an ancient Egyptian queen. Her long nose, her doelike eyes, her headdress, were all clearly chiseled. Chips of red and blue paint were still pasted here and there on the stone. "You think it's real?" Marcus asked Eric.

"I'm no expert," he said. "But this fellow didn't make it in his backyard, that's for certain."

"It's real," shouted Marcus, and so they bought it, after Marcus bargained and threatened to walk away. They also bought a small platter, a burial urn, and a dozen beads.

In the carriage on the way back to town, arrangements having been made to purchase more the following week, Eric said to Marcus, "We're good as gold. We'll open shop. No, not a shop, we'll sell from a fancy house, we'll be famous. We'll be asked to join the Circle Khedival. We'll walk into the Exchange like gentlemen. We'll be the richest men in Alexandria."

Marcus was less excited but still pleased. "It will work," he said.

Back in Alexandria, Marcus took a carriage to the apartment he shared with the French scientists, and from under his mattress he pulled a pouch that was fat and full. The two met back at the café at the wharf. Marcus had his few possessions in a bag. He would move in with Eric just for the time being, until he could afford a grand place of his own.

ONE MIGHT THINK that as each day brought fewer and fewer victims of cholera, the mood of the city would brighten. One would expect that lanterns in dark taverns would be relit, that children would be shouting in the streets, and that flower vendors and pastry sellers in the bazaar would be jubilant with a return to normalcy. But what the cholera left behind as it receded was grief. The numbers of weeping mothers, pale fathers, shaken widows were so enormous that the city itself seemed pale, quiet, stunned. It is true that those unaffected by the disease went about their business as usual, but at night when they returned to their homes they could hear weeping coming from the windows of this place or that, and they could see children's dark eyes peering listlessly from behind curtains. The city had lost many, and the loss hung in the air. It meant that as you walked in the public gardens you could catch the eye of a bereaved man, his face covered with stubble. It meant that when you sat at your favorite café, the lovely woman who wore a red sash over her robe and sold peanuts from a basket at the corner was gone and you looked for her in vain. It was a passing matter, this fog of grief that enveloped Alexandria. It would not last the month.

WHEN ESTE AND Louis reached the Malina home, the first thing they saw was a police carriage waiting outside. They saw two British soldiers standing idly at the threshold. One was smoking. The smell of his tobacco wafted in the air, mixing with some sweet, heavy odor from the horses whose tails were flicking at the flies that swarmed about their sweating bodies, undeterred.

"We should keep on walking," Louis said softly.

"No," said Este. "This is my house."

"I am coming with you, then," said Louis.

They approached the door. The soldiers, now alert, blocked their way. "No one is to enter here," one said in a dull voice.

"I live here," said Este.

"She lives here," said Louis.

One of the soldiers slipped inside while the other blocked their way. He came back within seconds with his superior. "Mademoiselle," the officer said, "I am deeply sorry for the disturbance here, but we found it necessary. You are free to go." He waved his hand across all of Alexandria and the lake and the rivers and the sea beyond. "Free like a bird," he added. He repeated himself in Italian, a language in which he felt more at home, and smiled as if he had offered her both a gift and a joke.

"I am not going away," said Este. "This is my home."

Louis said, "Let's go to the French consulate. They will settle the matter."

"The French," said Este, "are no longer the masters here." She stared at the officer. "I will go in. I will sit in the drawing room. You will know where I am. You will not have to worry about me." She held her head at an angle as she said these things.

The officer saw the shine in her eyes and her very fortunate face. "Mademoiselle," he said, "do not move about the house. Just sit in one room."

He put up his arm to block Louis from following her.

"Go," said Este. "I will wait for my mother. She will return soon. I will send word to you."

As she walked toward the stairs, Louis called out to her, "Come back to the laboratory with me." She did not turn around. "I'll find you wherever you are," he called out to her back.

The Arab maid, Layla, not the one who had changed Este's bed, drawn her bath, ironed her dresses for the last three years, but the one who helped cook in the kitchen, who cleaned the pots and the pans, stood in the drawing room with her battered suitcase in her hand. She looked at Este as if she had returned from the dead. Este put her hand on the girl's shoulder. "It's all right," she said.

The girl told her that the soldiers had ordered her to leave. "But go where, where, Mademoiselle?" she said in a tiny voice.

"Go to my aunt's," said Este. "She will find a place for you. Tell her what has happened. Go right away."

The girl put down her suitcase. "No," said Este, "take your suitcase."

"What can I do for you?" asked the girl. Este was going to say there was nothing, nothing to be done, but then she thought of something she wanted to do.

"The soldiers will let you go through the house. Go to my

room and get my Ganesh. My little elephant. It was on the dressing table, but perhaps it has fallen on the floor. Take it to the European Hospital on Boulevard Ismail Pasha, ask on the street and anyone will tell you where it is. When you get there, ask the way to the laboratory where the scientists are working on the cholera and give the elephant to the young Frenchman. Not the older one with a big mustache, not the other one who has many pounds on him, but the one named Louis. Give it to Louis from me. He will understand. Can you do this?"

The little Arab girl felt calmness return to her heart. There was something for her to do, to put right all that seemed wrong.

"And after you have done this, you must go to my aunt's. She will take care of you." Este wrote down on a piece of paper the address of her aunt. The girl took the paper, but held it upside down. Este then told her the address, made her repeat it three times. The Arab girl went into Este's room and, amid the disorder, began to search for the little elephant. It was not on the dressing table. It was not in the sheets that had been pulled from the bed. It was not under the pillow. But at last she found it, beside one of the shoes that had been swept from a shelf in the closet. She wrapped the elephant in a handkerchief that she found in the back of a drawer. She picked up Este's gold chain and some red beads and a few pairs of earrings and put the jewelry back in the pink box where it belonged, and then put the box in the drawer where it belonged. She would not rob the dead. She went to Este, who was sitting still in the drawing room, staring at nothing in particular, letting her mind drift to other times. She picked up her suitcase, said she would go with the elephant to the hospital as she had been asked, and went quickly out of the room. Este walked to the terrace and leaned over the railing until she could no longer see the girl. Would Louis understand that the Ganesh was a pledge, as good as a promise, or would he think her ridiculous to send him a child's toy? This elephant had traveled to her all the way across the oceans from India, and while she did not consider her Ganesh a god, she was fond of him just the same.

She should have insisted that the soldiers let Louis come into the house with her; she needed him now, and he was not here. Please, please, Mama, come back; silently she chanted the words over and over as if words had power, as if words could change the way things were, as if she were not alone in the house. What had happened? Had Jacob done something in Jerusalem? Had her father angered someone at the Committee of Public Safety? She could hardly sit still, rushing from the window to the chair to the table and back again. At last she reminded herself, I am not a child. She used all her strength and pushed away fear. Her father would find a solution. The misunderstanding would be cleared up. Her mother would return soon. And then, as she soothed herself, steadied herself, she thought of Louis, his arm extended to help her out of the carriage. His eyes, black and alert, looking at her as if he had known her all his life, as if an ocean had not separated them until just a few months ago. She thought of all the things he knew and would teach her. She saw herself in his laboratory in Paris, looking at the oven, the gas tubes, Monsieur Pasteur himself greeting her. She thought of him next to her in the train from Marseille, and then, despite all, she put her head on the pillow and stretched out on the divan. She considered her luck in meeting him. What if the cholera had broken out in Istanbul or Athens instead of Alexandria? Soon she was humming her favorite aria from *La Traviata* and feeling drowsy as well. But then she remembered her father, her mother, the empty house. When would her mother return? She became uneasy as she sat up straight in a chair, as if someone, something dangerous, were in the shadows. Where was her father?

❀

ROBERT KOCH WAS staring at his drawings. It was frustrating to have come so close and then to have to pack up and leave because the disease itself seemed to have departed. Dr. Koch sat down in his chair and rubbed his hands; sometimes they cramped in a painful spasm when he had been working too long. He looked through his papers. A diversion might help his fingers. He cleaned his glasses and then cleaned them again. He would have to go down to the Nordeutscher steamship company and book passage. He felt weary. He knew a good deal of traveling lay ahead. A man prefers his own home to all others, and in this Dr. Koch was no exception. He shuffled through his papers and found one that had slipped between two others and one unnoticed up until now. It contained an early record written by Gaspar Correa, under the title *Lendas da India.*

"... *a high mortality observed during the spring of the year 1503 in the army of the sovereign of Calicut was enhanced by the current small pox besides which there was another disease, sudden-like, which struck with pain in the belly so that a man did not last out eight hours' time and an outbreak in the spring of 1543 of a disease called moryxy by the local people, the fatality rate of which was so high that it was difficult to bury the dead. So grievous was the throe and so bad of a sort that the very worst of poison seemed to take effect as proved by vomiting with drought of water accompanying it as if the stomach were parched and cramps that fixed in the sinews of the joints and of the flat of the foot with pain so extreme that the sufferer seemed at point of death; the eyes dimmed to sense and the nails of the hands and feet black and arched.*"

❀

LAYLA STARTED OUT for the hospital with the handkerchief that held the little Ganesh in her apron pocket. She was holding her suitcase by its worn straps. It was an old, battered leather bag that had been given to her by her uncle who had traveled to Mecca one year and had no intention of ever leaving his bedroom in his sister's house again. She had taken the coins that Este had pressed into her hand, but would not have thought that she should use them to pay for a donkey to carry her there.

She was crossing rue Rosette when a donkey boy with a shirt that flapped over his torn shorts called to her. "Ride, ride," he said.

She shook her head and kept on walking, although the weight of the suitcase made her walk slowly and pause every now and then to regain her strength. The boy stood in front of her.

"Let me pass," she said to him.

"Don't be unkind," he said. "I'll take you for free."

"For free?" she said. She looked at him carefully. She had heard of girls being taken and sold to slavers, or sold to the brothels where they would be locked in rooms and given opium until they lost their minds. She said, "No, no, thanks, I can make it myself."

But the boy didn't move. "See," he said, "my donkey likes you. He wants to carry you through the city. My donkey is very wise and he knows a good girl when he sees one."

She tried to suppress the smile that came to her face, but only partially succeeded. The boy moved closer. She could smell him. The sweet, heavy smell from his sweat, the cod he had had for lunch, the leeks that covered it. She noticed he had good teeth. Her arms were tired. "All right," she said. "But go right to the European Hospital. I am on an important errand."

The boy helped her mount the donkey. He put her suitcase in a pack at the donkey's side and he walked along beside her. "There, isn't that better?" he said.

It *was* better. She was riding along, listening to the clop of the donkey's hooves and the sound of the boy talking to her about some dog he had lost and she heard the muezzin's call and she felt the heat of the day on her neck and she saw that her blouse was wet with perspiration and stained brown from the dust. That was all right, she felt that she was lucky and that her luck would hold.

Outside the back entrance to the hospital, the Arab girl dismounted from the donkey. The boy put his hands on her waist to help her down. There was no one on the narrow street. "One kiss," asked the donkey boy. "Just one, for the ride." He smiled at her.

"One kiss," she agreed.

He pushed her against the side of the building and took his kiss. She did not find it unpleasant, and held her face forward for a second kiss. The boy felt her breasts under her blouse. "Ah," he sighed, "we could have such fun together."

"No," said the girl. "I have to go."

"Yes," he said.

"Later, maybe," she said.

"Now," he insisted.

The donkey stood placidly by, waiting to be run again. Inside the hospital, someone was pouring water on the floors and the water was seeping out toward the door, around which a puddle had already gathered. The boy put his hands all over the girl's body and she twisted and turned, more in pleasure than in despair. He pulled at the strings of her apron and it fell to the ground. The handkerchief in her pocket fell into the mud. The loosely wrapped Ganesh followed.

"Look what you've done!" shouted the girl. How long had the Ganesh been floating in the slop by the door before she noticed it?

She picked it up, checking its small trunk, its tiny tusks, and its long tail. All were in place. She wrapped it again in the now-soiled handkerchief.

"Wait for me," she said to the donkey boy, and entered the hospital. She asked the woman with a bucket of water washing down the floors the way to the Frenchmen's laboratory. She pointed. Layla knocked on the door. She entered. "Louis, Louis?" she asked in a soft, shy voice.

"Me," said Louis, pointing to his chest.

She handed him the handkerchief and the drenched Ganesh that lay within it. "From my Mistress Este," she said.

The name Este was all he needed. He clasped the handkerchief tightly. He understood. It was a message.

"What has happened?" he asked.

The Arab girl shook her head. She spoke no French. She left, and Louis took the Ganesh out of the handkerchief and held it in his hand, cradled it in each palm. It meant more to him than the watch of his grandfather that had been given to him on his graduation from the École Normale.

"Let's see," said Nocard. Louis opened his hand.

"She sent you a toy?" said Emile.

"No," said Louis. "It's not a toy." He turned his back on his friends. He didn't want to talk about it. This was a private matter.

THE JEWISH COMMUNITY in Alexandria had existed long before Muhammad mounted his horse and rode into the clouds. It had arrived with the first boats from the Mediterranean ports, carrying bolts of cloth and barrels of iron ore to the continent of Africa, to the upper Nile, to the far edges of the empires of military men who pulled along behind their battles, traders and scribes, scholars, and holy men. The Jewish community in Alexandria was well aware of the exiles and burnings and disasters that had befallen their brethren elsewhere. Although they themselves had survived the centuries with only an occasional burning of their homes and businesses, they were always anxious to please whatever new ruler took the throne.

The chief rabbi had always believed that emergencies would arrive and help might be needed for members of his congregation. He had carefully won the respect of the Coptic archbishop at the cathedral in the rue de L'Église, who was enjoying studying the Talmud in the chief rabbi's study on Tuesday evenings. He had managed to persuade the vicar of the Latin Patriarchate of the Cathedral of St. Catherine to join him in a campaign for orphans of the Arab quarter. He had befriended a wealthy member of the Church of England whom he had met at the home of a congregant whose daughter had married an Englishman. The two men were both interested in Greek drama and had formed a group to read the plays in their original language. The Minister of Health had a son who had married a Jewish girl. She had converted, of course, and now attended the Armenian church, but her father-in-law would be willing to assist, or so the chief rabbi assumed.

LYDIA ACCOMPANIED THE chief rabbi on his rounds. She was left in the vestibule of the archbishop's residence to stand and wait. She was at last ushered into the room where the prelate sat on a purple cushion placed on a high wooden chair carved with flowers and berries. She curtsied before the archbishop. He said nothing to her but waved her aside. She was sent back out into the hallway. Then the chief rabbi hurried out, and they climbed back into the carriage and went on. In the home of a wealthy congregant she was sent to the kitchen for a cup of tea. In the residence of the Coptic priest a little boy offered her a sweet while she waited on the front steps. When they visited the German consulate, she was asked to speak about her husband's virtues as a doctor and a father. She spoke with simple sincerity. She told the assembled attachés that her husband responded to all who needed him and that he would be a good and loyal citizen wherever he lived. She told the men sitting in front of her that her cousin lived in Freiburg. She spoke of his innocence of the accusation. He had never conspired with his son to bring harm to the authorities in Alexandria. She wept as she spoke. The chief rabbi was fluent in German and translated as well as improved her words. She was sent back outside to wait in the carriage while the men talked and talked. At last the chief rabbi, looking pleased with himself, emerged from the building. He ordered the carriage back to the synagogue, where he told Lydia to wait on the steps. The sun was hot on her head. She felt dizzy. Meanwhile he went into his safe and withdrew the necessary funds.

The chief rabbi arrived at the British consulate with the five men at his side. They had formed an ad hoc committee for justice. As the British consulate understood, they represented a formidable strength, in numbers and influence in the Alexandrian community. What they wanted was not so very difficult to arrange. The city, so recently recovered from riot and war, was in need of peace. The British were most anxious not to upset vast numbers of the populace. They understood that Alexandria could be ruled only gently, with wiles rather than whips. They did not want to inflame the Jews. These Jews had friends across the city. But they could not set a precedent of toleration for spies. It was agreed that Dr. Malina and his wife and daughter were to be immediately deported to a destination of their own choosing outside the British

Empire, and that their son, under surveillance in Jerusalem, would be sent to them in one piece in due time. The rabbi would have preferred the charges to be dropped entirely and Dr. Abraham Malina, a beloved and respected man of medicine, restored to his work, but he was a realist. The arrangement he had negotiated was the best possible under the circumstances. It involved no public trials that would inevitably stir up feeling against the Jews who had lived among the populace for so many years. It involved no hangings, no executions, no newspaper reports. No word of treason in Alexandria would threaten Jewish communities in the Alsace. It was better this way.

14

D R. MALINA WAS being held in a cell in the British compound. He was chained to a chair. He could tell from the light that came from the small window far above his head that the hours were passing. He used the chamber pot and then placed it as far from his body as he could. There was a small chair in the room, but no bed, no blanket. He had been interviewed once already. He had denied the charges. He was not a spy, he was a doctor who practiced both at his home and at the European Hospital. He was held in high regard by his colleagues. He was a member of the Committee of Public Safety. He was, it was true, a Jew, a fact he did not deny, would never deny, but, he thought, irrelevant to the charges. This will be cleared up momentarily, he thought. This is a mistake that will be corrected. Certain of his innocence, he was certain that his freedom would be returned to him soon. He had only to be patient, to wait for the matter to be straightened out.

Despite his determined optimism, he understood that the reasonable world could disappear in an instant, and in the courts of the English who were the rulers here, an Egyptian man might be thrown on the dust heap as if he were worth no more than a chicken in the marketplace, his feathers plucked, his innards discarded, and an Egyptian Jew was in an even more precarious position. There were heavy footsteps in the hall. He heard the approach of a guard before he saw him, and for an instant he was afraid he would be shot or his throat cut right there. But the soldier simply opened the door, observed his prisoner, and shut it. As the day continued, he was brought some murky water, which he would not drink, and through the little window the heat came, and with it the flies and other insects attracted to the darker places. He allowed himself a few moments of profound sorrow. "Have pity on me," he called to the universe in a silent meditation that was perhaps a prayer and perhaps a little boy's wish. He rocked back and forth on his heels, overcome by a deep dread for the future of his family. What would become of his wife and daughter if he were no longer here to protect them? And then, out of exhaustion, he fell asleep on the hard chair.

THE PLANS WERE made in haste. They were facilitated by the authorities. The assistant rabbi himself went to the ship and booked the passage. The departure was set for the day after next. The lawyer Florent and the chief rabbi both were brought to the prison, where, in a small room with a scratched wooden desk, all was explained to Dr. Malina.

"My medical instruments?" he said.

"If you can pack them in two bags, you can take them," said the lawyer.

"I have done nothing against the British Crown," said the doctor. There were dark circles under his eyes. His beard was unkempt. His legs were weak. He needed water, his throat was parched. His bald spot seemed to have increased during the day of his incarceration.

"I know," sighed Florent.

"We don't doubt you," said the chief rabbi. "But so far the papers have not printed the story. These things, you know, they can bring trouble to the whole community. We need to keep the peace."

"At my expense," said Dr. Malina.

"Ah," sighed the rabbi.

"It is the only way to save you," said the lawyer. "And your son," he added.

"But my house, my money, my bond papers, my rugs, my chairs."

"It's a small price to pay for your life," said the lawyer. "Your wife has agreed. You will sail the day after tomorrow at dawn on the *Romulus*. You will dock in Trieste and travel by train to Freiburg. Your wife says you have relatives there."

Dr. Malina said nothing. They would begin again as paupers. He turned to the rabbi. "Is there no alternative?"

The rabbi shook his head.

"I do not know," he said, "if I have the strength."

"You do," said the rabbi. "For the sake of your wife and daughter."

Florent said, "I'm sure they need good doctors in Freiburg."

"Yes," said Dr. Malina, "they will welcome me with open arms." His tongue was bitter. His heart was bitter. His anger was great.

"You are still a young man," said the chief rabbi. "God will protect you."

The prisoner shrugged. The rabbi had no sense of irony. Dr. Malina understood that he had no choice. His future had been decided.

"You will stay here for two nights and then you will be escorted to the boat as soon as dawn breaks on the following morning," said the lawyer.

"In chains?" said Dr. Malina.

"They will remove the chains," said the chief rabbi, "I will see to that." Abraham Malina was returned to his cell to pass his last two nights in Alexandria, a city his family had lived in for over three hundred years, in solitude.

ESTE WAS SITTING in the drawing room as still as a rabbit on the path hearing a strange rustling from a nearby bush, when her mother rushed up the stairs. She embraced her daughter. "Pack," she said to her. "We are leaving the day after tomorrow. Everything must fit into two bags for each of us."

"Papa?" asked Este.

"Papa will meet us on the ship. We board the ship at dawn." Lydia was composed. There were no tears in her eyes.

"Hurry," she said, "we must take what we can." Lydia explained to Este that false charges had been brought against the family. They had no choice. "Be brave," she said to her daughter.

Este was not afraid. She believed that in all the confusion it would be possible for Louis to marry her, for her to live in Paris. She believed that in the midst of this calamity, providence had done her a favor. The soldiers guarding the drawing room moved back. It had been agreed the women could take what they needed. As Este rushed about her room, picking up those things that she loved the most, the red skirt, the yellow blouse, the necessities, and folding them as flat as possible into a bag, she considered how to tell Louis where to find her. There was so little time. Lydia opened the safe and lined her suitcases with bank statements as well as the funds that she had tucked under her chemises, saved for a special purpose, that would now be needed. She took her sewing kit and sewed the gold coins that Abraham had collected in a cigar box into the hem of her dress. She went in the kitchen and brought Este some of the soup that remained from the night before, that night when they had no idea, when everything seemed normal, as if it would continue forever, the sounds of the muezzin, the cries of the donkey boys, the midday heat, the smell of the sea when the dawn came.

Lydia moved about her house, the house she was about to leave behind forever, with determination, with speed. She packed a small drawing of her mother in a jade frame. She left the frame behind. She packed the necessities for Abraham, his favorite tie, his best shirt, the jacket with the ivory buttons. She packed Jacob's letters. She packed his commendation from school for excellent work in Greek. She would wear her pearls and her earrings, and she hid her gold bracelet in a handkerchief. "What will become of you in Freiburg?" she said, looking at her daughter.

"Don't worry, mother," said Este. "I will be fine, wherever we are."

"We will need coats in Freiburg," said Lydia. "Heavy wool coats with fur collars."

"I have always wanted to see snow," said Este.

"How lucky, then," said Lydia, "that we are going north."

"I can't wait to see Paris," said Este.

"Maybe if we are settled, we can take a trip to Paris in the spring," said Lydia.

"Sooner, I think," said Este. But Lydia was not paying attention.

Later, Lydia sat down on her bed. Exhaustion had come over her. "I need to say good-bye to my sister. She will tell my friends so they do not think we left without a thought of them," she said. She rushed to her table to find her stationery to write to her oldest friend. In her mind she made a list of those they would be leaving. The list was long. She couldn't find writing paper in the disorder of the room. It was still light outside. This day seemed endless and yet too short. "Este, maybe the soldiers will let you out. Go to the neighbors, tell them we are leaving. Tell them we have done no wrong. Go to my sister now, and tell her we sail the day after to-morrow and will go to Freiburg."

Este hugged her mother, who felt frail in her arms. She had dark circles under her eyes. She was not crying, but Este could feel that the tears would come soon.

She did not tell her mother that she had already sent the maid to her aunt's. She had to tell Louis where to find her. She went downstairs with her shawl on, ready to leave for the hospital. The two Egyptian policemen at the door stopped her. "Mademoiselle, you cannot go out," one said. The other put his hand on her arm in a way that was not polite, had in it a hint of contempt. His hand rubbed her arm in a way that alarmed her.

"Go back upstairs," said the first officer.

"This is my house," said Este. "You are my guests." This made the second soldier laugh, a not very pleasant laugh.

Este retreated back up the stairs. How was she going to tell Louis that they were going to board a ship and leave Alexandria so suddenly? Would he come to the house? Would he try to find her tonight or tomorrow while she was still there? Why were the soldiers holding her and her mother in their own house? What were they afraid might happen? What nonsense. As she returned to her mother in the drawing room, she stepped into her father's study. She picked several of his medical books and carried them to her bag. She unpacked her clothes and replaced them with his books. She made several trips up and down the stairs until she was satisfied that almost everything her father would want was in her bags. She sat down and opened a book. She stared at the drawings of the human body that were marked with Latin names.

As the dusk settled in, the lamps of the cafés were lit, and the tide was high. On the promenade you could hear the waves as they splashed across the jetty. Louis, who had waited impatiently to hear from Este, walked to the Malina house. The door was now shut. There was a dim light in the drawing room. The curtains were still down, casting a strange shadow across the window frame. A man's figure came to the terrace and then retreated. Louis knocked on the door. It was pulled open suddenly by a British soldier. Behind him stood two men from the Egyptian police force. "I am here to see Dr. Malina," Louis said.

The men did not open the door wider or invite him in. A British soldier appeared suddenly. He spoke to him in English. "Go away. You cannot enter."

Louis understood. "I need to see Madame Malina, important business from the French mission," he said in French.

The soldier shook his head. He didn't speak or want to speak this language. Between the men's shoulders, Louis saw that papers, pictures, and lamps remained in disarray on the floor.

"Whatever you are looking for," he said, "you will not find." The soldier looked blank. "I must insist you let me in. I will return with the French consul if you refuse me."

The Egyptian policeman translated for the soldier. "He wants to come in."

"Can't," came the reply.

"This is not possible," said Louis, who then shouted up the staircase, "Este, Este, come down."

She heard him and came to the top of the stairs. Another policeman pulled her roughly back into the drawing room. The door closed. Louis pounded on it again and again. At last the Egyptian soldier who spoke French opened the door. "Monsieur," he said, "you are not able to see anyone in this house. Go home before you, too, are arrested."

There was no possibility of telling Dr. Malina of his desire to marry his daughter if they wouldn't let him into the house. He went back to the laboratory and reported his failure to his friends. Roux suggested that they do indeed go immediately to the French consul. Edmond changed his shirt to a clean one he kept hanging in the back of the laboratory. "We are Pasteur's representatives," he said. "The ambassador will call for help. We'll force the door open. How dare they treat French citizens this way? They'll regret it."

Louis was silent. How could this be, and what was it that had happened? How could an innocent man be taken away, suddenly, in the middle of the day? He knew that Dr. Malina was innocent because Este was innocent, and he knew that as strongly as he knew anything in the world, the names of the known chemicals, the reactions of hydrogen to oxygen, the earth moving around the sun. As they stood in the street waiting for a cab, the smell of hashish floated by, hung for a moment, a heavy perfume in the air. Roux put his arm around Louis as if to steady his friend, who was not so much unsteady as stunned. This was a puzzle that he could not begin to unravel.

The French consul was dining out, the Frenchmen were informed. His wife was at home, but would not see visitors. Where was the consul dining? "I cannot say," said a servant.

"You must not say," said a man who suddenly appeared at the doorway and introduced himself as the consul's secretary. "Make an appointment," the man added in a less-than-friendly tone.

Roux explained that the three were the scientists with the French mission and needed to speak to the consul urgently.

"Nothing is urgent at this time of night," said the secretary. "A consul is not a doctor," he added.

Edmond pushed his way into the rotunda and sat down in a chair that was clearly too delicate for his large frame. "We are not leaving until you tell us where we can find the consul."

"Really?" said the secretary. "Who do you think you are?"

Just then the wife of the consul appeared in the hall. "I assume," she said to Nocard, "this visit has nothing to do with my cat. Let them come in." She waved the secretary away. "These are very important scientists," she said to his stiff and retreating back. The men followed her up the stairs and into the drawing room. Madame Cecile offered them coffee, but they refused. Nocard told her the entire reason for their visit. The Malinas were in trouble. The door to their house was closed by Egyptian police and British soldiers. Something terrible had happened, and it had to do with the British authorities.

"He's my doctor and my friend," said Madame Cecile. "How terrible."

Roux explained that his young colleague was about to ask Dr. Malina for his daughter's hand in marriage, but had not been permitted in the house.

Madame Cecile pointed out that perhaps under the circumstances Dr. Malina would not wish to consider such a proposal. "Young man," she said, "the timing does not seem right."

Her words, perfectly sensible as they were, made Louis miserable. "What can I do? What can I do?"

His obvious grief, his young face looking at her as if she held the key to his future, determined her next words. "I'll go to the house and find out myself what's going on. The consul is dining in an unknown place in the manner of men of this world, and we cannot disturb him this evening. But I will go with you and we'll see what is happening in that house."

The wife of the consul was not intimidated by the Egyptian police or the British soldier at the door of the Malina house. She demanded entrance, and the British officer was afraid both to let her in and not to let her in. In the end he admitted her. What harm, after all, could she do? The French scientists he kept waiting outside. Lydia Malina apologized for the chaos everywhere, and Este apologized for their personal disarray. In a tumble of words the situation was explained, or at least that part of it which Lydia and Este understood. Dr. Malina was being kept under tight supervision in the back of the British barracks. They were all to leave for Trieste the day after next. The first thing in the morning they would board the ship and the family would be reunited. The consul's wife said nothing about Louis waiting below. She had developed a professional sense of discretion. She said that she had heard of their difficulty from the three French scientists who had tried to visit them but were stopped. Este's eyes shone at these words, but she asked no questions. Perhaps, said the consul's wife, when my husband returns we can see if our country can be of service to your family. Lydia thanked her. Este got up and offered to go to the door with her. The policeman did not want to stop the young lady from going down the stairs in front of the consul's wife. Once out in the hall, Este said, "Could you send a message to Louis Thuillier?"

"I'll deliver your words in person," said the consul's wife.

"Tell him what has happened," said Este. "Tell him that I will expect him on the deck of the *Romulus,* the Italian Line, the morning after next. Tell him we are going to Freiburg."

"I'm sure, my dear," said the wife of the consul, "that he will come to the ship." The two women clasped hands and the consul's wife went out the door, which the policeman shut with a loud slam behind her. She explained everything to the Frenchmen.

"This makes no sense. They are crazy, these British," said Nocard.

"It's political," the consul's wife said. "In politics there is no room for reason."

When the consul did arrive at his own residence in the early hours of the morning, his wife was waiting for him in his bedroom. She told him the entire story. He was eager to lie down in his own bed. He had consumed many glasses of wine and smoked several pipes about whose contents he never inquired. He had enjoyed himself enormously, and his body was now ready for its rest. He had little interest in the tale she told.

"Nothing," he said, "nothing we can do about it. This is a matter for the British. They can do as they please. We can't help your scientists. We are not here to solve everyone's little difficulty."

"This is not a little difficulty," his wife said.

"We will find you another doctor, perhaps from the French community," he said. "These Jews are always traveling from one country to another. They can't seem to set down roots. Those scientists," he added, "what use have they been? They've brought no honor to France despite all the fine letters recommending them to

my good graces. I hear they're going to leave Alexandria soon."
With that he put on his nightshirt and rolled over in bed, his back
to his wife.

LOUIS KNEW THAT he would not be able to see Este the next day.
There was no point in trying. He would come to the Malina family
on the deck of the *Romulus* the following morning. He planned to
speak to Dr. Malina right there in the harbor, before the ship departed. This was not the best moment to convince the father of the
suitor's worthiness, the consul's wife was correct, but it would be
his last chance for a long while. He couldn't wait months. He
couldn't stand the uncertainty. He was sure that now that the doctor was beginning his own life again, he would want whatever security he, Louis Thuillier, assistant to Pasteur, could offer to his
daughter. His own passage was booked to Marseille. As soon as
the mission returned to France, he would take a train to Germany.
He would be there soon after she arrived. The French mission was
scheduled to leave in eight days. His disappointment over their inability to identify the cholera microbe saddened him, but he consoled himself that the trip that would not bring him honor had
instead brought him something of far more worth, the woman
with whom he would spend the rest of his days, in a life of complete joy.

In the laboratory, Edmond and Emile were looking at slides of
cow blood that they had collected from the slaughterhouse. They
were hoping to find something of importance for Pasteur's inves-
tigations in Paris on bovine plague. Emile was preoccupied now,
ready to go home to his family. Nocard was bored. Louis paced up
and down. He could talk only of his plans to go to Germany. He
demanded reassurance over and over again from his friends that

Dr. Malina would indeed accept him as a son-in-law. When Edmond said that the Malinas were Jews and that might give Dr. Malina pause, Louis insisted that all these distinctions between human beings would soon be viewed as mere superstitions and disappear in the light of human cooperation and understanding. Nocard did not believe this, but he didn't want to dampen his young colleague's hopes. Emile didn't believe it either. But it seemed the wrong time, at the edge of a young man's hopeful engagement, to insist on the perfidy of human society. All he said was "We were thrown out of Eden. I doubt if we're going back so soon." Louis ignored him.

They were accomplishing nothing in the laboratory and decided to leave the work and go for a swim in the ocean. The three went down to the sea, rented a cabana, changed into bathing attire, and went for a swim. Of the three, Louis was the strongest swimmer. The waves were not wild. The sun was strong. The men swam back and forth, exercising their limbs, giving their brains a chance to rest. Louis lost himself in the rhythmic rise and fall of his arms, the splash of his kick, the sounds of the birds above their heads. Back on the beach he pulled the long blue-and-white-striped towel he had rented around his shoulders and dried himself. The muscles in his arms baked in the sun. He was a young man who didn't think about standing and running and lifting, but moved easily, effortlessly, unself-consciously. He went for a walk along the shore. He walked too fast for Nocard, who turned back. He walked too far for Roux, who had enough after a quarter of a mile.

In the evening they were about to go out for dinner when Marcus appeared at the apartment door. They were not entirely delighted to see him. They waited for an explanation of his absence. "Come," he said to them. "I will take you for a ride about town in a carriage."

"You will pay for the carriage?" asked Emile, with a sarcasm that was rather unkind.

"Yes, I will," said Marcus. "I am in business now, the business of treasures, and I can afford a carriage." He told them all about his plans to buy and sell antiquities with Eric Fortman.

"An Englishman," snorted Nocard. "He'll probably cheat you."

"Not me, he won't," said Marcus.

The men climbed into the carriage. It sped off quickly down the rue Sultan, around the Râs el Tin. Marcus shouted in his loudest Arabic at a man who was crossing the street. He called in Greek to a man who was selling dates from a basket at his feet. He waved at some Arab girls walking along with their heads covered. They collapsed in giggles.

Louis was thinking about riding in a carriage with Este down the Champs Élysées. He imagined himself at her side. Nocard was leaning out of the carriage. *I may never return here*, he said to himself. It had been an adventure, after all, even if the journey had not ended in the hoped-for triumph. Marcus told the driver when to turn and where to go. He enjoyed giving directions. He enjoyed taking his former employers out for a spin around the city. He liked his own generosity. His mood was infectious. Before the end of the ride, all the occupants in the carriage felt a lifting of spirits, a hope for the future that was strong, even though it was based on nothing in particular.

"I prefer Alexandria to Paris," Marcus said. "Here a man is whatever he can make of himself. In Paris I am just the boy in Pasteur's lab, good for cleaning the glasses and feeding the animals. Here I am Apollo himself."

Roux smiled. "You have grown up these past months, but I'm not so sure you are Apollo."

"We'll see," said Marcus. "Soon I will be worth far more than the master himself."

Roux said, "Good for you."

"Where did you get the money to go into business?" asked Louis.

Marcus gave his former employer a wink. "Here and there," he said. "Odd jobs." He said nothing more.

"Here I stay," said Marcus as the carriage came to a final stop. "I am never going back to Paris. Tell the master adieu from me."

The three friends went out for dinner. Louis was in particularly good spirits. He kept the Ganesh in his pocket and caressed its head with his forefinger. He tapped his pipe with his hand. With his fingers he removed a spot of tobacco that had fallen on his lip. He ate a good dinner, but did not have the raw fruit that was presented to the table on a platter because they had all agreed to keep the precautions in place until they had returned to Paris.

At ten-thirty that night, as Lydia lay sleepless in her bed and Este was staring at the stars, saying silent good-byes to her childhood, Louis fell easily asleep in his bed. He knew he would wake with the first light. He would be at the dock before the Malinas arrived. But at three in the morning he woke up. He had a terrible pain in his stomach. He was cold and shivering. He was afraid, but the pain was greater than the fear and filled his mind with its presence. He made his way out of his room. He stumbled toward Emile's room. He opened the door and then said calmly, "Roux, I'm feeling really sick."

Emile woke up and saw Louis at the foot of his bed. Nocard woke up just as Louis collapsed on the floor, writhing in pain. His face was pale and sweaty and his hands were as cold as that of someone who had suffered a heart attack. His bowels had exploded and its contents were running down his legs.

Roux said to Nocard, "I think it's food poisoning."

They had all consumed the same meal, but it was possible that the portion that Louis had received had been spoiled. Emile and Nocard carried Louis back to his bed and put a blanket under his body to keep him warm.

Louis smiled at them. He seemed to feel a bit better. Roux prepared an opiate solution for him. Louis thanked him, drank it, and fell back to sleep. Emile fell asleep in Louis's bedroom on a chair.

At five in the morning, as the call to prayer floated over the city and the birds on the roof prepared to fly toward the lake, Louis woke up, and there was a terrible diarrhea over the blanket and the side of the bed. He was embarrassed and tried to hide the mess from Emile. He was white, and his face had taken on a skeletal look. This frightened Emile, who woke Nocard. The two of them stood beside his bed. Nocard rushed for a pan as Louis vomited up the entire meal of the previous evening. He then seemed to feel a little better. Emile gave him another opiate solution. He fell back asleep. Emile thought about calling for a doctor. Damn Marcus, if he'd been there he could have gone for help. Nocard offered to go, but Emile said, "Let's wait till morning. Perhaps he will be better in the morning."

Emile and Nocard did not name the thing they feared. They just stared at each other. Emile washed his hands again and again. Nocard heated water for them so they could boil the sheets and the blanket. At 7:00 a.m., Louis woke again. He was cold. He complained to Emile, "Please, please, let's make the room warm. My legs are so cold." He was shivering. "Please, Roux," he said, "help me, I'm so cold." He tried to stand up to go to the chamber pot, but he couldn't stand by himself. Nocard and Emile supported him. He had another episode of diarrhea. "I need to get to the quay, to the *Romulus,*" he said to Roux.

"Not now," said Roux soothingly. "Later, maybe. They will not leave the port until evening. They will have to wait for the tide."

Louis tried to stand up. He fell back. He did not have the strength. His legs were shaking.

At about the same time, Este stood for the last time in the doorway of her house. Her mother had already been helped into the carriage. The sun was barely visible, a pale pink in a gray sky. The sound of gulls welcomed the morning. The store owners were opening their curtains, setting out their wares on sidewalks. A child woke in his bed with an earache. A man turned his mistress over and took her again before rising to wash. Este looked at her street for the last time. She felt little sorrow and certainly no fear. She expected Louis to be at the boat, waiting for her. They would have a last conversation until they met again at Freiburg. She had written her cousin's address on a piece of paper she intended to give him so he could easily find her. As she entered the carriage, she felt her past slip away effortlessly, making space for her future. She held her mother's hand in the carriage. It was harder for the older woman to leave her coffee cups, her spoons, her drawers, her linens used for years and years, familiar, unremarked on, but hers. It would be difficult to leave the relatives and friends of a lifetime. Would she write to them? Would they care, or would she become a stranger, unimportant to those who she had once amused, dined, loved?

Lydia was worried. Would they in fact bring her husband to the boat, or were they lying to her? The authorities were never to be trusted. Would she see her son again? Anxiety over her future, despair at what was being left behind farther and farther with each turn of the carriage wheels, made her stiff. Her smile at Este was wooden, empty. Her eyes were wide and frightened.

They arrived at the quay. Their baggage was unloaded, and Arab boys carried it on board. They were helped up the ladder to the deck of the *Romulus,* where the Italian captain greeted them as if they were honored guests, not exiles who had been involved in criminal activity. The sun was higher in the sky. It warmed Este's shoulders and the back of her neck as she stood watching the dock for the arrival of her father and the man whose life she wished to join.

First she heard the wheels of the carriage and then she saw it. It stopped at the end of the quay. The carriage had come from the British consulate. Three soldiers alighted, pushing Abraham Malina in front of them. He had no baggage. His jacket seemed stained, he had lost the ascot he was wearing when he had been taken from his office. His beard was unkempt, his hair unwashed, his hands bound behind his back. As they approached the ship, the soldiers cut off the ropes that tied him and followed him up the plank. His wife rushed to his side. They embraced. Abraham Malina put his face into his wife's neck. He wanted to hide the tears that now came to his eyes. He smelled her familiar soap. He squeezed her arm.

"You do need to groom yourself," she said in a whisper. He nodded. She leaned against him as if he were a wall.

The captain said, "We sail in six hours. Welcome aboard. Exiles. Some of my best cargo have been exiles. Don't worry, we'll feed you well. The voyage will be easy if the weather holds."

"Thank you for your courtesy," said Dr. Malina. The two men shook hands. The soldiers handed the captain the funds for the passage of the Malina family, as had been agreed upon by the chief rabbi and the Malinas' lawyer. Seagulls settled on the rails and flew up and cawed whenever anyone approached. The cabin boy threw a piece of dirty bread into the air.

A nearby gull flapped open his wings, flew up a few feet, and, opening his beak to show a blood-orange gullet, gulped down the morsel. Then the gull screamed into the waves, as if he had won a victory in a war that no one else was fighting. His tail-feathers rippled in the slight wind. His eyes were without kindness or sorrow, just empty black stones on either side of his small-boned face. He settled back on the rail. Sailors carried barrels of supplies down into the hold. Some crawled along around the metal funnels, others were washing down the deck. Este felt water sopping her skirt. She paid no attention. She embraced her father. "Don't worry," she said to him, "this will be a fine adventure."

"Este," he said, "I'm sorry."

She looked down at the wharf. She would not move from her place on the deck of the boat even when invited to examine her quarters. She leaned far forward so that she could better see Louis as he approached the ship. She was certain he would appear in a moment, any moment.

In his small cabin, Abraham Malina took his wife in his arms. He thanked her for packing his medical bag. He thanked her for fixing his hair. He thanked her and apologized for the grief she suffered.

"It's not your fault," said Lydia. She kissed him on each eye. She kissed him on the back of his neck. She felt his arms. They were still strong arms. "This is the beginning of the German Malinas," she said.

"At least," he said to her, "our family will be safe in Freiburg, our great-grandchildren will live in that civilized country in comfort."

EMILE ROUX SENT an Arab child for the doctor. He sent another to the French consulate so that a French doctor could also be summoned. He send a third boy to the Italian doctor that he had befriended on the staff of the European Hospital. He sent a message to the director of the hospital. Within an hour, all the doctors had gathered at Louis's bedside. They consulted among themselves. They gave him a stronger dose of opiate, but he seemed to be failing. His breath was short, his eyes were sunken, he hardly moved. His legs cramped and gave him great pain, but he hardly had the strength to cry out. His face changed, the bones could be seen. He suddenly looked like a very old man. Feebly his arms kept thrashing about. The Italian doctor gave him an injection of ether and followed that with an injection of champagne. Neither seemed to help.

Nocard was frantic. "We could try salts," he said.

The Italian doctor said, "No, salts do not help."

They purchased three bottles of champagne and let it sit for a while on a block of ice. They gave him sips of the champagne, which seemed to calm him down.

The two Frenchmen started rubbing Louis's limbs. The rubbing would keep him warm, keep his blood flowing. They pulled his bed into the middle of the room so that one could kneel on each side of him, and they rubbed his arms and his legs and his torso constantly for over an hour and then they were too tired so they let the Arab boy who had served them at the café so many times take a turn. The Italian and French doctors also rubbed his fingers and his toes. Through this, all his bowels flowed out of his body, white flakes like small pellets of rice floated in the brown waters. His breathing was worse, and his fever did not go down. The rubbing kept him alive.

THE WOODEN GANGPLANK was pulled up. The pilot who would take them through the channel was on board. The skiff that would take him back to shore started on its way out of the harbor. The *Romulus* was ready to depart. Lydia and Abraham Malina stood on the deck. A little way out in the waters, three sloops bobbed in the waves. A British ironclad floated across the channel. For the last time they saw the place where the Nile had dropped its silt into the harbor thousands of years before. For the last time they saw the city where they had been born, where they had believed they would die. Este did not stop looking for Louis to appear, even as the call was given to raise the anchor, to let go the lines that were attached to the bollards at the quay's end. The captain was at the wheel, and the ship lurched backward as the Arabs on the dock pushed it out into the waters. The small boat that would pull it into deeper waters was attached by its own lines to the ship. The rowers waited, their backs rippling with muscles. The sun was now strong and the men were sweating in the heat. Este could not believe Louis had not come. Had he not received her message from the consul's wife? Had the girl not brought him the Ganesh? Had she misunderstood his intentions? Perhaps he would come to Freiburg and find her there, but perhaps not.

Now everything about her departure from Alexandria was different. Este had no future. She was still a girl and yet she had used herself up, poured her love on a man who had failed to arrive. There was a terrible vacancy inside her, where her former hopes had lived. Now suddenly she understood that she, too, was an exile, that the days ahead would be difficult, lonely, that her future was uncertain. She would have to be brave. She was prepared to be brave for the sake of her mother and for her father, who would not be able to bear her unhappiness as well as his own. But in the place in a young girl's mind where her deepest feelings reside, where the love she expects to receive sows a million blooms, there where all the colors of the universe had been painted, a wasteland now stretched out, a gray and dark landscape, with snatches of ruined memories lying about like so many buildings destroyed in a military action. There was anger, too. He had betrayed her. She would never again trust so easily, laugh so easily, love with such simplicity. Her heart had been infected by the world's treachery and would never again heal, or so she believed as the shores of Alexandria disappeared from sight, as the ship rocked in the waves, as the smoke belched out into the blue sky. She ached in every part of her body.

"Go away," she shouted at her mother when she knocked on the cabin door.

AROUND NOON, LOUIS'S condition seemed to improve. Roux reached down and felt a pulse in his arm. The French doctor checked, and he too found the pulse. The Italian doctor was not so sure. It might be a tremor, not a pulse. None of the men in the room left. Nocard went to the window to smoke a cigar. Emile Roux almost fell asleep in a chair but woke himself up. They wrapped Louis in two blankets and, one after another, continued to rub his legs. When Emile looked at his watch, he saw that it was two o'clock in the afternoon. His stomach rumbled from hunger. But now Louis had even more trouble breathing. The Italian doctor suggested that his heart might be failing, not allowing enough oxygen to enter his lungs. Louis was drawing air in and then immediately gasping for more. His lips were blue. His features grew even more gaunt. His nose was pronounced and his eye sockets seemed to swallow his eyes. But his face was still his face. He did not look like a cholera victim in every aspect. There was still some expression around his mouth, and he tried to smile encouragingly at Emile. He took his friend's hand and pressed it. He was not capable of speech because his breath would not tolerate it.

The Italian doctor had to leave to attend to his patients. The French doctor stayed until early evening, injecting Louis every hour and checking his pulse every half hour. He had not died. He had held on for a long time. This, the French doctor assured them, was a good sign that he might survive the disease. Nocard pressed him. "Is it a sign that he will survive, that he is likely to survive?" The doctor did not answer. All Louis's limbs trembled now. Nocard and Emile brought in all the blankets in their apartment and placed them on top of him. His face felt as cold as stone. Emile sent the Arab boy out for some food. They ate in Louis's room, reluctant to leave him. Emile drank a bottle of wine all by himself. Nocard left to make sure that the animals in the laboratory that were still there, those relevant to the bovine plague investigation, were fed and watered. "God damn Marcus," he said again. He came back to the apartment as soon as he could. There had been no change for the better or worse while he was gone. Louis did not sleep.

He knew the name of the disease that had reduced him so. If only they had found the microbe, he would have seen it, too. He wanted to fight back, to grab at the air and force it down into his reluctant lungs. He was weak. He knew he was weak. He did not want to die. He thought of Este on the ship expecting him to arrive, and he was ashamed that he had not come, or was there still time? He had lost track of the time. He would find her in Freiburg. He would go to Freiburg. He believed that he would force the illness to leave his body. He hurt, his legs hurt, his chest hurt, the cold was deep and terrible. At moments he thought about death. At other moments he refused to admit that death was waiting. He thought about confession and asking for a priest so that his mother would be comforted. He did not have the strength. It was too hard to get any words at all out of his mouth. Soon after, he didn't care about priests at all. For hours he drifted, sleep coming, dreams of yawning holes, shipwreck, his sister bleeding, his father screaming, devouring wolves broke into his mind and receded again and again. The nightmares did not stop. They interrupted his sleep over and over. Sometimes there was pain in his limbs. Sometimes he felt empty, as if his mind had gone away, leaving only his body to shiver under the blankets.

THE AFTERNOON TURNED into evening. The *Romulus* was out to sea. Lydia fought off seasickness. Her daughter stayed in her cabin. Abraham walked the deck observing the waves and the wake caused by the boat, comforted by the canopy of stars above.

The French doctor tried more opiates. The Italian doctor returned after midnight and injected more ether into Louis's now hard-to-find veins. The men dozed off in chairs from time to time. The only sound in the room was Louis's shallow and pained breathing as his lungs shrieked for more oxygen and his body again and again failed to deliver. As the sky once more eased to gray and the moon turned white and disappeared, Emile and Nocard were each by Louis's side. The death rattle began. As Alexandria was waking for the new day, Louis's breath stopped. From a certain point of view, this was merciful.

DAWN BROKE OVER the *Romulus*. Este had not been able to sleep. She had gone to the deck and leaned over the side, watching the waves lift and drop. She had never realized that the sky was so far above her and she so small a speck in the universe. Unmoored from the familiar, she saw herself with a seagull's eye, a mere morsel beneath. She was sailing on a ship on a black ocean that stretched out before and behind her, endless, the sky indifferent above. This was a perspective she vowed to hold in her mind for the rest of her life.

The word of Louis's death went out to the French consulate. The Italian doctor carried the report to the Italian community. Word was sent to the German consulate. Dr. Koch was immediately notified. He went directly to the apartment, where Roux and Nocard were making burial arrangements. There was a race, yes, between the French scientists and the German, but in the end this was a competition among colleagues. Above all national loyalties, these men were enlisted in the cause of human knowledge. They saw themselves as linked by knowledge, linked by passion, alike in the ways they spent their time, backs bent over the laboratory table. They knew the urgency of their work. In the end, they were more like each other than like the others who walked the earth in pursuit of other matters, waved flags of their countries, traded goods across oceans, talked about national virtues, waged wars against fellow humans. In the end, they were comrades. Dr. Koch, who was not a man who wasted emotion, was deeply affected by the death of the young scientist.

Messages began arriving, bringing consoling words and praise for Louis and his efforts on behalf of mankind. The German and Italian consulates offered their assistance to the remaining members of the mission. Marcus brought a box of strawberry cakes. The French consul sent his wife, who arrived at their quarters with tears in her eyes.

"Had someone sent word to the *Romulus* before it left port?" she asked. The men had not thought of it.

"The girl must be told," she said. "I'll have our consulate tell the family when the ship docks." She spoke of her husband's sorrow, the sorrow of all France. Nocard wanted to embrace her but held back. Emile sat down and wrote a telegram to Pasteur. He brought it to the telegraph office himself. He looked years older than he had just a day before. He had lost a friend, a colleague, to the very disease he was unsuccessfully pursuing. He was a defeated and grieving man.

At noon, a plain zinc coffin was brought to the apartment. An embalmer was called. He did his work. The coffin was closed. Within the hour, Dr. Koch arrived, bearing two funeral wreaths. Koch insisted on nailing the wreaths to the coffin himself. "These are modest," said Koch, "but made of laurel, awarded to the glorious ones." Dr. Koch picked up one corner of the coffin and, led by Roux and Nocard, there was a funeral procession down the rue Sultan through the Grand Square to the French cemetery. The coffin was followed by all of the members of the Committee of Public Safety except Dr. Malina. The street was filled with the diplomats and their assistants and their families from all the embassies. The doctors from the hospital walked behind the coffin, too. Many of the Alexandrians who had known of the mission joined the procession. The priest attached to the French consulate led the way. Bells were rung from the Catholic church.

Le Figaro sent a journalist who spoke to Roux, who was brusque in his grief and gave no information on the progress or lack of it the group had made in finding the cholera microbe. "Have you considered that there may be no microbe?" said the journalist.

Roux turned quickly away, without answering the question. People along the route leaned over their terraces to see the coffin. There was a respectful silence as the procession passed. The vendors stopped selling. The children stopped running. The donkeys were waiting by the side of the street, their long ears twitching, flies gathering about their moist eyes. The carriages pulled over and waited for the funeral to pass.

At four o'clock on the same day he died, Louis Thuillier was buried in the French cemetery. The coffin was placed in a shallow uncovered grave, because arrangements had been made to send the body back to France. The laws of Egypt required a year's wait for the export of a body. Emile Roux filled out the necessary papers. The French consul told Roux that the French colony would like to erect a monument in Alexandria dedicated to Louis Thuillier. This was his wife's idea, but he thought it a good one. It was important under the circumstances that France publicly respect their dead.

There had been no cases of cholera in Alexandria for the last twelve days. Louis Thuillier must have been the last to die in this epidemic. Roux wrote a long letter to Louis Pasteur describing Thuillier's death in exacting detail. He said in his letter, "Thuillier was the most cautious of all of us. He was most careful." The letter was carried by the next ship leaving for Italy and arrived in Paris only two weeks after the initial telegram. By the time it arrived, Nocard and Roux were themselves on their return journey.

IT WAS NOT a sign of soullessness on Este's part, but rather an inevitable assertion of the will to survive, when, just hours before they were to arrive in Trieste, she admitted to herself that her life was not entirely ruined. She was hungry for the first time in days. She pulled her hairbrush from her bag and brushed vigorously until her black curls renewed their shine. She was curious about Trieste, although they would remain there only six hours. She had brought in her bag a small German dictionary. She took it out and began to improve her German vocabulary. A person, she told herself sternly, cannot live in the past.

The *Romulus* finally docked, and as the Malinas waited for the Arab boys to bring down their bags, their entire worldly possessions, a French soldier came running toward them. He was out of breath when he reached their side. He had a message from the Alexandrian consul's wife for a Dr. Malina and family. Abraham Malina opened the folded paper. "My God," he said, "what bad news."

Lydia Malina was afraid the message was about her son. A wave of bile rose in her throat. She clasped her daughter's arm.

"Say it," she said to her husband. "Say it quickly."

"Our friend from the French mission, Louis Thuillier, died from the cholera the very day we sailed for Trieste."

Lydia breathed a deep sigh of relief. "How sad," she said, and she really was sorry for the young man and his family. "He had a mother and father at home, I believe. How awful for them."

Este had stepped away from her parents and turned her back on them. She was silent. She thought she might never find her tongue again.

"It's a setback for science," said her father, "to lose such a dedicated and talented young man."

Este turned back to her family. She nodded in agreement. She felt glad that she had not been betrayed. On the other hand, the news of his death ended any secret hopes of reconciliation, of rediscovery, of forgiveness, hopes she was not even aware she held. His death meant that they would never have what seemed to have been promised them, a love that would never die. But she understood that she was only a minor player in this tragedy and the loss was his, a life gone when it had just barely begun. Now she felt no anger, but only regret. She said nothing to her parents. There was no need. A few hours later they climbed aboard the train that would carry them north to Germany.

15

I N FRANCE, THE newspapers all reported the unexpected end to the French mission's attempt to identify the microbe. They praised Louis Thuillier as a scientist of courage and brilliance. A street was named for him in Amiens. His brother, who worked in the Ministry of Finance in Amiens, was given a promotion as a gift to the Thuillier family. Pasteur himself grieved deeply over the loss of his young scientist. A fog fell over him, leaving him staring into space in his armchair. But then he recovered and resumed his investigation of bovine plague and developed the vaccine that could save those who had been bitten by a rabid dog.

Dr. Koch left Alexandria within two weeks. He sailed on a ship for Hanover. From there he made his way to Berlin. His wife had barely time to sing to him after dinner his favorite lieder. He left several weeks later for India. There he found more examples from infected bodies and was able to confirm what he had suspected in his laboratory in Alexandria. He found the same microbe, whose shape he had first sketched out in Alexandria, in all cholera-infected tissue. He did not find it in tissue from any healthy body. He was able to outline its shape in blue dye. He was able to culture it in his beef broth and gelatine dish. He was able to rule out other causes. He was able to demonstrate that wherever he found the microbe, there cholera appeared. He was able to identify it for the Academy of Science in London and then in Paris, where he presented his evidence and his drawings the following March. It was *Vibrio comma,* the creature with the small tail that steered through waters, swimming long distances, surviving most happily in the human gut, where it spewed its toxins, draining the host of necessary fluids. What an artful creature it was, its tail propelling it through water to another host. A microbe that could surely be called a scourge now had a name and a shape. This was the first step toward rendering it harmless.

The Malinas arrived at Lydia's cousin's home in Freiburg. Several weeks later their son Jacob appeared. He'd sold his business to his partner. He had not felt as comfortable in the Holy Land as he had expected. He missed his family. He was ready to study medicine. He enrolled at the university. This pleased his father. Dr. Malina began to work at the Jewish Hospital, where he developed a fine reputation and soon had a private clinic very much like the one he had left in Alexandria. Este and Lydia mastered German. At a dinner given by an in-law of Lydia's cousin to welcome the strangers from abroad, Este met a young man who had trained in Doctor Koch's laboratory in Heidelberg. He himself was interested in the diseases of childhood. He, too, believed that everything would be discovered with the microscope. Este amazed him with her questions about his work. She was genuinely interested in his experiments and accepted eagerly his invitation to visit him in his laboratory.

Within a short time she made herself his assistant. She learned quickly. She had good, careful hands. She became a familiar figure in the back of the chemistry classroom at the university. She took notes in a black book that she carried with her everywhere. The Jewish community of Freiburg did not entirely approve of this unmarried woman spending so much time in the laboratory of an eligible man. There was some unpleasant talk. The young scientist, who knew, without knowing all the details, that fate had brought him a wonderful gift, proposed. The marriage pleased both families, and the wedding was held in the cousin's garden the following spring. Her name does not appear on her husband's scientific papers, but his career was distinguished and he traveled all over the continent and to London and Boston to deliver his papers to this scientific society and that faculty of medicine. He told everyone who would listen that the best ideas he ever had came from his wife. Without her patience and assistance he would have accomplished nothing. She smiled when he said that, in such a way that no one was sure whether this was true or simply a pleasantry between the spouses. She had three children who filled her life with all the usual anguish and joy that accompanies the project of raising the next generation. She never went back to Alexandria.

EPILOGUE

DOMAIN:	Bacteria
KINGDOM:	Eubacteria
PHYLUM:	Proteobacteria
CLASS:	Gamma Proteobacteria
ORDER:	Vibrionales
FAMILY:	Vibrionaceae
GENUS:	*Vibrio*
SPECIES:	*Vibrio cholerae* (or *Vibrio comma*)

SOON AFTER ROBERT KOCH discovered the cholera microbe on the heels of his discovery of the invisible cause of tuberculosis, all the civilized world believed in germs, and the night air was no longer thought of as suspect in the murder of men but was returned to its condition of mere air, air in the dark, cool and refreshing, air that circulated under the stars evening after evening.

Now we know these amoral specks are responsible for more human death than all the spears and arrows, all the bombs and explosives tossed tribe to tribe, nation to nation, from time immemorial to the present. This has been the way of the world since man dropped down from the trees, providing through his own body excellent food for the microbes that lived in the swamps and the grasses and the river waters.

Louis Thuillier was a fallen hero. He was not a king or a general, or a prime minister, nor a man of wealth. He found no new path to God. He was not a saint. He was a scientist working in the trenches, and he died there at age twenty-seven.

Author's Note and Acknowledgments

This book began with a sentence read many years ago in *The Microbe Hunters,* a book by Paul de Kruif published in 1926 and still in bookstores across America. In the chapter on Louis Pasteur, the author reports that an outbreak of cholera had occurred in Alexandria in 1883, and a French mission was sent to the city to find the responsible microbe. Pasteur's young assistant, Louis Thuillier, died of cholera on those foreign shores. I wanted to write a book about a hero who died because of his work on the frontiers of scientific discovery. My brother, a hematologist and a laboratory scientist, had recently died of AIDS and I hoped to honor him. I remembered the death of Louis Thuillier a century earlier.

The cholera epidemic in Alexandria is part of the historic record, as is the famous German microbiologist Dr. Robert Koch's appearance in Alexandria, which led to his ultimate discovery of the microbe. The mission sent by Louis Pasteur included members of his laboratory team, including Nocard, Roux, Thuillier, and Straus. I added Marcus and I deleted Straus for storytelling reasons. I invented the Malina family and the love story attached because that is what novelists do. I took some liberties with chronology and character because a novel is not a record of reality but a comment on it.

The description of Louis Thuillier's death was taken from a

letter to Pasteur from Emile Roux informing him of the tragedy. The instructions that Pasteur gave to his mission were taken from a letter from Pasteur. The descriptions of Alexandria came from a variety of sources, including a report from William Makepeace Thackeray on his journey to Egypt, E. M. Forster's *Alexandria—A History and a Guide,* and numerous accounts of Egyptian history and politics. Also useful were Lawrence Durrell's *The Alexandria Quartet* and the poems of C. P. Cavafy, as well as André Aciman's *Out of Egypt.* The scientific facts are based on research and source materials provided by the Pasteur Institute in Paris, as well as *Plagues and Peoples* by William H. McNeill, *Viruses, Plagues, and History* by Michael B. A. Oldstone, and *Man and Microbes: Disease and Plagues in History and Modern Times* by Arno Karlen. The emotional details rose from my brain, as they tend to do when telling a story.

Shaye Areheart has been enormously helpful in transforming this book from a wild beast into a presentable novel. I thank Sally Kim for her patience and friendship through the publishing process.

I want to thank my daughter, Katie, who read this book more than once, and her suggestions vastly improved the manuscript. I am grateful as always to my agent, Lisa Bankoff, who supports me even when I lose faith in my own project. I want to thank Jeffery Leininger, whose research I used and used. Also, Ina Caro for her support and friendship.

I hoped to express in this book my awe and admiration for those who spend their lives bending over microscopes measuring, repeating, imagining, watching. Without them we would be farther away from understanding, farther away from healing. Like most people, I owe my life to them, and my children's lives.

If any reader suspects that I would rather have been a scientist than a writer, I would immediately confess my preference for truth over fiction.

ABOUT THE AUTHOR

ANNE ROIPHE is the author of eight novels, including *Secrets of the City, Up the Sandbox, Lovingkindness,* and *The Pursuit of Happiness.* Her nonfiction books include National Book Award–nominee *Fruitful: A Real Mother in the Modern World; 1185 Park Avenue: A Memoir;* and *Marriage: A Fine Predicament.* For more than three decades, she has illuminated the complex realm of women's lives with her provocative insight.

About the Type

This book was set in Fournier MT, a typeface created by Monotype in 1924, based on type cut by Pierre Simon Fournier circa 1742 in Fournier's *Manual Typographie*.